The Dead Rock Stars

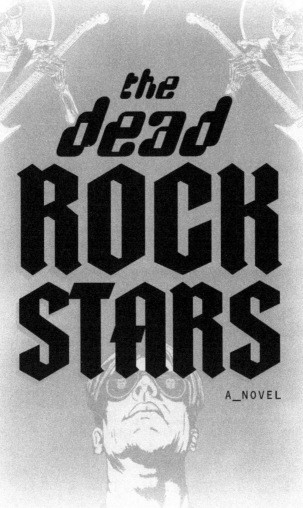

the dead ROCK STARS

A_NOVEL

JAY
WATSON

KYLE
WILTSHIRE

NEW YORK

LONDON • NASHVILLE • MELBOURNE • VANCOUVER

The Dead Rock Stars

A Novel

Published in New York, New York, by Morgan James Publishing. Morgan James is a trademark of Morgan James, LLC. www.MorganJamesPublishing.com

Proudly distributed by Publishers Group West®

Excerpt from *The Ballad of Reading Gaol* by Oscar Wilde is quoted from an 1897 work in the public domain.

A **FREE** ebook edition is available for you
or a friend with the purchase of this print book.

CLEARLY SIGN YOUR NAME ABOVE

Instructions to claim your free ebook edition:
1. Visit MorganJamesBOGO.com
2. Sign your name CLEARLY in the space above
3. Complete the form and submit a photo
   of this entire page
4. You or your friend can download the ebook
   to your preferred device

ISBN 9781636981642 paperback
ISBN 9781636981659 ebook
Library of Congress Control Number:
2023933291

Cover Design by:
Megan Phillips
meganphillipsdesign.com

Interior Design by:
Christopher Kirk
www.GFSstudio.com

Morgan James is a proud partner of Habitat for Humanity Peninsula
and Greater Williamsburg. Partners in building since 2006.

Get involved today! Visit: www.morgan-james-publishing.com/giving-back

To everyone we lost but still love…

chapter
ONE

August 31, 1999

He clenched a small, smooth rock in one hand and twirled a bronze poker chip in the other. Impatiently, he whined, "Come on, Buddy, it's almost midnight. Is this gonna happen? I swear, every time I let you borrow my guitar. . . . Remember Lubbock?"

His friend, an aging man in a black suit and skinny tie, replied, "Of course I do. It was 1955, the first time I opened for you." He strummed the borrowed guitar and wailed as if for the first time, "That'll be the day-ay-ay that I die."

Six people clapped as they passed the duo on the sidewalk.

"You rock . . . *for an old dude*," a passerby sneered.

"Nice glasses," jabbed another.

A few dollar bills were dropped into the open guitar case.

The first man, fit and lean and wearing sunglasses at night, leaned over and whispered, "If they only knew . . ."

Buddy Holly slapped his friend on the back, which was adorned with a cape covered in sequins. "You know they never will, E. This is Vegas, baby. Imposters everywhere. Speaking of which, how did your thing go? Better this time?"

"I got third place."

"What did they say? You sounded too much like him? Not fat enough? Too old?"

"You know me, Buddy. I was just happy to sing and play." He sniffed. "They did say my outfit wasn't authentic enough, though."

"Didn't you wear that one at the Hawaii show?"

"You know I did." Elvis Aaron Presley curled his lip and flashed one of his signature smiles.

The Las Vegas Strip was buzzing with the usual nightlife for a weekend. Standing atop a smattering of discarded paper flyers among a never-ending stream of humanity, the two men stood, waiting and watching.

Buddy returned the guitar to its case and slid a discreet earpiece into place. "Okay. Let's get into position and see if we can . . . *land this plane.*"

The sixty-something man in the sequined, time-capsule, nudie polyester jumpsuit lowered his mirrored sunglasses just enough to show the disapproval in his eyes.

"Too soon?" his partner asked.

The two men slipped into the stream of people and began making their way down the strip, looking not at all out of place. To everyone they passed, they were nothing more than aging impersonators. One had a salt-n-pepper mop of curls, horn-rimmed glasses, and a nicely pressed suit. The other was dressed like karate royalty and looking as though he could take care of business in a flash.

A few college-aged tourists rushed up to greet them, asking for a photo. One of them was waving a Fuji disposable camera.

Then one of the young men in the group began to sway as if he were standing up in a rowboat. He looked at Elvis and burped, "Long live the Ki—Oh no, I think I'm going to hur—"

Vomit rained down upon the white patent leather loafers worn by the King of Rock and Roll.

Elvis looked down and saw that the kid was wearing a T-shirt sporting the "love symbol" of The Artist Formerly Known as Prince. He laughed and sarcastically said, "Thank you. Thank you very much. I see you're partying like it's . . . well . . . *now.*" He and Buddy resumed walking.

A couple hundred feet ahead of them, a black Lincoln Town Car crept to a stop. A sweaty-looking man wearing a green crushed-velvet jumpsuit emerged from the back of the vehicle. He nervously scanned his surroundings then pulled an oversized duffle bag from the back seat.

"King, that's him," Buddy said as he tapped the side of his glasses, increasing their magnification by five times. "It's Langston."

They now picked up their pace, advancing on the target.

"Come in, HQ," Elvis said. "Facial recognition confirmed. We got our man."

A familiar voice rang in each man's ear. "You have the green light to pursue. Use extreme caution. We don't know how many of them there are."

Ahead of them, the sweaty man stumbled around the car, almost tripping over the bag he was carrying. He tried to smooth out the velvet but was too busy nervously glancing around to check for wrinkles. If the guy had five shoulders, he would have looked over every one of them. The man then headed south on the strip, and the town car pulled into traffic and quickly disappeared among a sea of black limousines and town cars.

"Vegas." Buddy shook his head and growled, "Someone *please* pick a different-color car."

As they came in view of the Las Vegas Hilton—formerly known as the International—a guy with a woman on each arm strutted across their path, stopped, and looked them both up and down.

"Who let these two out of the old folks' home to play dress-up? You should have let Elvis stay dead, bro. And who you supposed to be," he said to Buddy, "Honey I Aged the Rock Star?" He turned his head and shouted to no one in particular, "Somebody tell Rick Moranis that his dad is wandering the streets of Vegas!"

The young lady on the man's right asked, "Who's Rick Moranis?"

The three men stared each other down until the young man grew uncomfortable. Then he turned his escorts in another direction and went off to make fun of some zealous ticket holders who had painted their whole bodies blue just to "watch some mutes play drums." When he was almost out of earshot, the man shouted over his shoulder, "Geriatric Elvis is way worse than Fat Elvis!"

Buddy shrugged. "Maybe that's why you got third place."

For a man in his sixties, Elvis looked to be in peak condition.

Buddy could see his partner's knuckles whitening as Elvis clenched his fists. "Don't do it, King. Stick to the mission, or we're going to lose Langston."

At that moment, Langston turned into the Hilton. Buddy put a hand out and stopped Elvis as a bellhop swooped in and tried to wrest the duffle bag from Langston's grip.

"Can I take your bag, sir?"

3

"No!" Langston grunted. "Don't touch my stuff."

"So sorry, sir!" The bellhop quickly returned to his stand.

Buddy grinned. "Tracker is in place."

Elvis smoothed down his sideburns and said, "I've played the International almost a thousand times. Ain't nowhere this cat can go here without me knowing."

"Yes, eight hundred and thirty-seven consecutive shows to be exact, King," the voice from the earpiece chirped. "However, it is now called the Las Vegas Hilton."

"Thanks for nothing, Jan," Elvis responded.

As two of the most famous men of "their time" stepped into one of the largest hotels in the world, no one batted an eye.

Buddy handed the bellhop a crisp Ben Franklin as they passed his stand. "Thanks for the help, kid," he said with a wink.

"You sure about this, Buddy?"

"The intel is good, Elvis. Langston is meeting other high-level operatives in one of the suites on the twenty-eighth floor. They're all tied to the group I've been tracking. The Brotherhood." Holly checked the readout. "He's heading into the slots."

Elvis slapped him on the back. "Well, he can't get out of there. That place is a maze! You got this? I'm hungry. I'm going to Benihana," he said, motioning to the hotel restaurant. "You want me to get you some sushi to go?"

"Nothing fazes you, King. These are legit bad guys, and you're thinking sushi."

"Just another day on the job. Besides, I got you, Buddy!" Elvis strutted off.

Buddy shook his head and refocused on their prey. He inconspicuously followed the man in the green velvet tracksuit as he nervously weaved through tables, serving girls, gamblers, and slot machines. A few minutes later, the King of Rock and Roll appeared at Buddy's side, his shoulders slumping, his deep-V jumpsuit looking as dejected as he felt.

"They wouldn't let me in," he said. "I told them I was Elvis. I even wiggled my hips. Nothing."

Buddy didn't break concentration. "To them you're just a senior citizen weekend warrior trying to resurrect the King. Fake Elvis doesn't automatically get seats at Benihana, just like Fake Elvis doesn't get the girls. We've been over this, E."

"But you also said I have sex appeal."

"That's not what *sexagenarian* means, King."

Buddy looked past everything in front of him, fixated only on the navigational tracker on Langston's duffle bag. "He's clearly being careful not to be followed." Sud-

4

denly the signal stopped and started ascending. "He's going up. Elvis, how can the man trapped in the slot machine maze be going up?"

"No way, man. Only one way in and one way out," Elvis said, shaking his head. "Well, except for the service elevator, and that's reserved for royalty, celebrity, and . . . the King!"

Buddy handed him the guitar case, nodded, and took off toward the slots. "Elvis, you know what to do."

As Buddy Holly moved past the blackjack tables and roulette wheels, Elvis opened the case, pulled out the guitar, and in the middle of the room began belting out "Suspicious Minds." A crowd formed just outside the Benihana Village. Security was converging on Elvis and paid no attention to Buddy advancing towards the service elevator.

✯ ✯ ✯ ✯

It was just another Saturday night in Las Vegas. All indications were that no one saw anything unusual. Certainly no one seemed surprised to see the real Buddy Holly dashing through the casino or the real Elvis Presley giving an impromptu concert.

Buddy's voice crackled in Elvis's earpiece. "King, the tracker. It's stopped. Room 2834. I'm moving in to set up surveillance."

As security closed in on him, Elvis charmed the guards into letting him finish his mini-concert/distraction routine, ironically with "Heartbreak Hotel." As he strummed the final chord, he struck a pose and bowed quickly, sweat dripping from his face.

"He's still got it!" screeched an older woman to her girlfriends at the front of the crowd. They wanted to believe. Elvis wiped the sweat from his face and threw the hanky to the adoring gals. Then he grabbed the guitar case and headed for the public elevators. The older women fought for the hanky like it was 1968 again.

As the elevator doors closed, Elvis reached into the guitar case and pulled out a jar of Lover's Moon Pomade. He slicked his hair back with a comb and then smeared the security camera with the remnants.

"Elvis has left the building," he reported to headquarters.

"King . . . we have a problem," Janis said in his right ear. "I've lost communication with Buddy. He was in room 2834. Now, nothing."

Elvis reached inside his jumpsuit and pulled out a pair of earphones. Attached to his belt was an mp3 player, a state-of-the-art Personal Jukebox bedazzled in the same

5

ornamentation as his Aztec gold-encrusted belt, which also matched his cape. He put one earphone in his left ear, away from the comms, and pressed PLAY on the mp3 player. Twenty-eight floors gave him just enough time to get to the chorus. He rolled his neck, heard a few pops, then started to get loose.

"It's time to get *loco*," Elvis said aloud.

The elevator doors opened. Two men with earpieces and weapons holstered under their jackets were waiting. They looked at Elvis. Elvis looked at them and held a finger in the air, motioning for them to wait a moment. Then, right on cue, the King dropped into a karate stance and began belting out the chorus to Ricky Martin's "Livin' la Vida Loca." With a lightning-quick combination, Elvis had kicked one guy across the hall, and the other lay motionless with a snapped neck.

He strutted down the hallway, singing and thinking to himself, *Man, I love this song!*

He kicked the door to room 2834, and it flew open as if it had been blown off its hinges. Elvis looked down and saw a pool of blood and a pair of cracked horn-rimmed glasses. He grabbed the lamp off a table and used it to bash one oncoming attacker's head, then used the cord to strangle the next opponent.

Langston, the man in crushed green velvet, jumped behind the wet bar where Elvis spotted a black-and-white photograph of his face in younger years. Looking around, he realized he was standing in the Elvis Presley suite. This was not an accident. Someone knew who he was—who *they* were. And someone was sending a message.

This Brotherhood thing might be legit, he thought as he fought his way through the room.

Yet another foot soldier had chosen to no longer stand frozen with mouth agape while watching an old man dressed like Elvis Presley unleash fury in a blaze of sequins and sass while singing Ricky Martin. It was one thing to know something like this was coming but quite another to watch it live. He reached for his gun and unloaded a magazine in the direction of the King.

Elvis flung his cape over himself, and the lead fell to the floor after striking his bedazzled, bulletproof accessory. He pulled out the earphone and stared down the henchman. Before he could bring his righteous anger down upon the goon, he heard the familiar sound of a shotgun shell being racked. He dropped to the floor just as Langston pumped out a blast from a twelve-gauge shotgun. The buckshot meant for Elvis created a void in the torso of the man he'd been confronting.

Unscathed but smelling of gunpowder, the King lowered his shades, peered through the unfortunate henchmen, and saw a perfectly good velvet painting now ruined by the carnage. He sprang to his feet, leapt over the wet bar, and disarmed Langston.

"WHERE IS BUDDY?" the King raged.

Elvis felt the room vibrate as footsteps came pouring in from outside the suite. He reached under his cape, grabbed a flash grenade from his belt, and threw it toward the oncoming horde, blinding everyone in the room. Before they knew what was happening, Elvis had sprung back over the wet bar and worked the room over like a tornado. When he was finished, no one was left standing—with one exception. Langston, who had soiled himself, was pressed against the wall behind the wet bar.

"I thought you were just an old man," Langston stammered.

"You knew I was alive?" Elvis shouted. "How? Where is Holly?" He clenched a fist and began using it to repeat the questions. But Langston didn't say another word. He just pointed to the bedroom and then passed out.

Looking toward the bedroom door, Elvis noticed a trail of blood leading around the corner. He found Buddy Holly slumped over the side of an ottoman, beneath a picture of a heavy-set Elvis performing "Viva Las Vegas." The color had left the face of his friend.

"Buddy!" Elvis gasped. "What happened?"

Buddy acted as if he didn't hear the question. With a blood-smeared finger, he pointed past Elvis and then exhaled his final words: "I guess it's for real this time."

The King reached down and closed the eyes of one of his closest and oldest friends. On the wall was a bloody sketch of a symbol Elvis had never seen before.

He retrieved the guitar case from the hallway, pulled out a small digital 2.1-megapixel camera and took as many pictures as he could of the scene. He took several shots of the strange symbol Buddy had drawn with his own blood. The large duffle bag they had been tracking was nowhere to be found. Langston too had disappeared.

When he had finished, Elvis slumped down next to his partner's body. He lit a small, slim cigar and sang "Amazing Grace."

He then threw Buddy over his shoulder, grabbed the guitar case, and touched his ear. "I'm going for a clear exit. What can you tell me?"

"Elvis?"

His voice quivered. "We lost Buddy."

"I'm on it," the woman on the other end said, choking back tears. "Oh Buddy . . ."

A few moments passed, then the voice returned. "King, police and emergency have been dispatched to the hotel. If you're headed to the service elevator at the end of the hall, you're going to have to move fast. They're coming." Then Janis's voice softened. "Bring him home. Bring Buddy home to me, King."

"I will, Janis."

Before anyone arrived on the scene, Elvis rode the service elevator down and walked into the night with his best friend, his favorite guitar, and more questions than answers.

chapter

TWO

He looked at his pager for the fourth time in ten minutes. Nothing. Technically, she wasn't late, but he felt exposed seated alone at a table for two.

Cole Denton was handsome enough. He normally wore glasses but had decided to suffer through an evening of contact lenses to put his best foot forward. He was wearing his favorite plaid shirt that was a few years out of style, favorite jeans that were faded where his wallet and keys left an impression, and his favorite pair of Chuck Taylors.

As he shifted his weight from side to side, looking around uncomfortably, he saw her. She was wearing a purple dress as she had said in her email. Her hair was pulled back in a messy bun to reveal a graceful neck adorned by a simple necklace with a single black pearl. Cole had of course seen the photo she'd posted with her online profile, but lovely as the photo was, it failed to prepare him for her in-person presence.

He had done this many times before—sixty-four times, to be precise—but this felt different.

Cole stood up and froze in position, not sure whether to wave like a maniac or play it cool and pretend to barely notice her. What came out was an option he hadn't considered at all: a vertically raised hand with only the fingers making the wave motion. He was mortified as he realized that he appeared either to be trying to control a puppet or playing a piano suspended from the ceiling with its keys pointing toward the ground.

When she smiled and laughed, a wave of relief washed over him.

"Hi, Cole. I'm Savannah."

"Hi, Savannah. I'm . . ."

"Nervous?"

They both laughed at this.

He knew he shouldn't be so uncomfortable. After all, this was his plan. His software. His algorithm. His social experiment. When Cole created Connextion.com, he had set into motion something he hoped would change the world, one blind date at a time. So far it was working for thousands of people all over the country. Now if only he could make it work for him.

In fact, Cole Denton was a rising star in the tech world. At twenty-one years of age, he had already collected a few degrees and was currently weighing whether to seek job offers from major tech companies or to seek investors for his dating algorithm and strike out on his own. The internet was starting to come alive in ways that would radically change the way humanity communicated. But in this moment, Cole was more worried about coming off creepy than revolutionizing the way couples connected.

"Is this the first time you've used Connextion.com?" he asked with too much enthusiasm.

Savannah looked down, smirked, and then stared directly into his eyes.

Cole could not look away.

"Yes. It is. My friends joke about how much bad luck I have meeting guys. And they heard about this website that connects people, so . . . they made me sign up. They're all sitting over there." She pointed in the direction of the bar, where six women were no longer pretending to not be paying attention to everything that was going on.

Savannah giggled and blurted out, "They've been watching you for a half hour! They finally decided you weren't too creepy and let me come in to meet you."

"That's great!" Cole nervously laughed. "I think."

"I feel like I already know a few things about you. It doesn't really feel like a first date," she said. The two of them had been exchanging emails for a few days.

"I know, right? Thank you for coming to hang out. I was starting to get nervous you wouldn't show."

"Are you kidding? All my friends think I'm a pioneer! I can't let them down," Savannah joked. "It feels like there are scientists and security watching our every move." She looked over at the bar, smiled, and gave her friends a thumbs-up.

Cole looked over at her entourage and asked, "Is it going to be like this all night?"

She shrugged. "Probably."

By the time the appetizer was served, Cole and Savannah had forgotten there was anyone else in the restaurant. They had relaxed and moved on to more important topics, such as likes and dislikes.

Cole asked, "Favorite movie?"

"*Titanic.*"

"Really? *Shawshank* crushes *Titanic.*"

"*Shawshank* doesn't have Leo. Favorite comedy?"

Cole thought for a long time. "A tie between *Dumb and Dumber* and *Wayne's World.*"

"'Party time! Excellent!'" Savannah's messy bun bounced around as she laid down some air guitar.

"Swim . . . Swammy . . . Swanson . . . Oh, here it is. Savannah! I was way off!" Cole said, doing his best Lloyd Christmas.

Neither of them wanted to leave.

Savannah looked at her watch, then at her pager, then at her mobile phone. She had several missed calls and 4-1-1 texts.

"My girlfriends want to hear about this futuristic experiment."

"What are they asking?"

She rattled off a few questions in a squeaky, silly voice. "'Can you believe someone made this website?' 'Did he lie on his profile?' 'How did he get matched with you?'"

Cole shifted uncomfortably in his seat. "Well . . . about that. Remember when you asked me what I did for a living, and I said, 'boring computer stuff'? Well . . . this is what I do."

Both sat staring at each other, with Cole wondering what she was thinking and Savannah not sure what to think.

"So . . . you go on blind dates with computers?"

"Well, sort of. I went to college with a bunch of nerds, and none of us thought we had any hope of finding love. The website was a bit of a joke project at first. But the more I thought about it, the more this seemed to be a much easier way to meet someone I actually cared about."

"Okay-y-y," Savannah said. "How many women have you met through your 'project'?"

"Sixty-four," he answered enthusiastically, then immediately regretted answering so quickly. The mood had changed.

"Cole . . . I don't know what to say."

"It's okay. And I know it's weird," he said, searching for a plausible explanation as to why meeting sixty-four women online, one after another, would possibly be okay. "But don't you think at first everyone thought it was weird to have a telephone in their home? I bet they thought the radio was weird, too. My mom used to make me stand way far away from our microwave. Look, I'm not trying to cure hunger. I'm just trying to help people find each other with a tool no one has ever used before."

"Sixty-four times?"

There was a long silence. Cole imagined her reaching for a wet wipe to disinfect her brain from the thought of the many other dates he'd been on. He decided to help her out.

"Savannah, I've had a wonderful evening. I would love to see you again, but I understand if this is too strange for you. If it matters, the reason I had to go on so many dates was to figure out the significance of different points of connection—how to determine compatibility. I know it might sound lame, but it was for science."

Realizing how hollow that sounded, he added, "And until today I never met anyone I wanted to see again. You know, socially. I wanted to meet someone like you." Feeling like he'd blown it, he said, "I do think you're brave for trying it. And I hope it can help you meet someone great someday. Would you like me to call you a cab?"

At that moment, the waiter arrived to take their order for dinner. Savannah stared at Cole as she said to the waiter, "Excuse me, Flo. What is the soup du jour?"

The rest of the meal was like a dream. The food was great, the conversation was fun, and the grand social experiment was yielding exciting results.

When Cole asked for the check, the server leaned in and said quietly, "Chef Tony had date number three last night. He's like a new man. He said this one's on the house." Then he glanced at Savannah and back at Cole and grinned. "You guys seem like you're having fun. Shall I cancel your table for tomorrow night, Mr. Denton?"

★ ★ ★ ★

After dinner, they stepped out into the early autumn evening for a walk, in sight of the Massachusetts Institute of Technology. Savannah held on to Cole's arm, and he was fine with it. Cambridge was enjoying a string of unseasonably warm evenings, but everyone knew it wouldn't last. The leaves were already starting to fall.

"So, are you like Matt Damon in *Good Will Hunting*?" she asked.

"Absolutely not!" Cole laughed. "Everyone says everything is my fault."

"Seriously though, are you some kind of genius?"

"I wouldn't say that. I would say . . ." He was searching for the right way to say yes without sounding like a jerk. "A dreamer. I can kinda see where things are going before they get there."

"I bet your parents loaded your fridge full of A+ papers when you were growing up."

"Um . . . not exactly. No, my parents . . . um . . ."

Cole didn't want to talk about his parents on a first date.

Savannah let him off the hook. "Easy, tiger. I don't think I'm ready to meet the parents just yet."

"Good to know," he said with nervous laughter.

The night was going much better than Cole had anticipated. They had laughed and shared real things about themselves, although she had no idea he was planning on leaving MIT in a few months. Job offers, buyouts, even interviewers from the media were starting to chase him. He loved that Savannah didn't know about any of that stuff.

"I'm sorry, Cole, but I've got to go," she said, sounding sincerely disappointed that their night was drawing to a close. "I've got a big day tomorrow at work. We're dropping eggs off the roof in ninth-grade honors science."

"You're a freshman in high school?!?" he said, feigning shock.

"Thank you and *ew*, gross. Seriously though, I've got to get home and get ready for class."

"Yeah, I've got a big day tomorrow too. I've got some job interviews."

"Cool. Who with?"

"To be honest," he admitted, somewhat embarrassed, "I'm not really sure. My professor set them up." This seemed to satisfy her curiosity.

A half hour later, they were still walking, as though neither of them wanted it to be over. Somehow, they had found themselves holding hands. It felt natural.

"Savannah," Cole said. "You mentioned on your profile that you want to change the world. What did you mean by that?"

"I don't know. I guess I see my job as a calling. My students are special to me. I want them to learn and succeed. I suppose I'm trying to make the world better one student at a time."

Cole genuinely loved that answer, but before he could say anything, she asked, "So, Genius Boy, what are you trying to do, become the Chuck Woolery of the World Wide Web?"

"Well, I wouldn't Ask Jeeves about me." He smirked, trying to convey that this was a joke. But the smirk faded, and he said, "Seriously, don't Ask Jeeves about me."

A simple Internet Explorer search would have told her that Cole Denton was a rising star in the tech world. His little website and algorithm had put him on the map. The truth was, he was terrified that Connextion.com would be the only thing of significance he would do with his life. He too wanted to change the world. He wanted to make a real difference.

"Can I see you again?" Savannah asked.

He'd never been asked that question before. Cole wanted to shout "Woo-hoo!" and break into a victory dance, but he instead tried to play it cool. "I think I would like that." His smile gave him away.

She leaned in close and kissed him on the cheek. "I heard you cancel date number sixty-six with that server. Who's the genius now?"

Savannah walked off towards her apartment, and Cole stood alone on the sidewalk, unable to take his eyes off her. Then she quickly turned around, catching him off guard. She stuck her hand straight up in the air and waved with only her fingers, puppeteer-style.

Cole smirked and then very coolly half-waved, as if he were embarrassed by the whole scene.

As soon as she was out of sight, he collapsed on a park bench painted with an advertisement for CompuLive Online Chat. He tried to reconcile what had just happened to him. He had written a ground-breaking algorithm and, sixty-five dates later, made a connection. *Makes sense*, he thought. *Just as I'm probably about to leave this place, I think I've found the love of my life.*

chapter
THREE

I n Lubbock, Texas, a gentle rain fell on the quiet cemetery. The sun was starting to peek out from behind the gray clouds, but the mood was still somber for the assembled mourners. Elvis Presley stood over a gravestone marked *Charles Hardin Holley, September 7, 1936 – February 3, 1959.*

"Until today, this grave marked an empty casket," he said, his voice barely above a whisper. "Now it finally holds the remains of our dear brother Buddy. Every time we bury a member of our team, we fill an empty grave. We take a lie that everyone believes and finally make it true. The world thinks that Buddy died in a plane crash forty years ago, but we know the real story. Buddy helped save the world more times than anyone knows. He saved those who needed saving. He protected presidents, prime ministers, and kings. He sure saved this king."

Fighting back tears, Elvis said, "I'm going to miss you, man." Then he continued, his voice growing stronger. "Buddy Holly chose this life. He was a pioneer and an original. This goes without saying, but Buddy loved to play. We all owe a debt to his music, his friendship, and his legacy. He rescued each of us here from a path to self-destruction by recruiting us to make a difference in the world beyond music. Buddy helped us to heal. He died to save lives."

The assembled mourners replied in unison, "He died to save lives. *Debeo, redeo, schola.*"

"Anybody want to share any thoughts or memories about Buddy?" Elvis asked the gathered mourners. Many kind things were then said, and everyone shed tears. Then came Jimi Hendrix.

He was wearing a navy-blue suit, something he rarely wore. He paused as if to gather his thoughts and began rambling. "Yeah, one time Buddy and me was in Berlin, in like, '78. I was waiting on him outside some hotel in this awful VW Beetle. Anyway, we was trying to gather some intel on this Communist dude or something. I can't remember all the details. All of a sudden, Buddy comes running out, full sprint. Behind him is this guy waving an old German Luger. Like straight outta World War II, man. Buddy jumps in the car and starts yelling, 'Go man, go!' so I take off as fast as the stupid thing would go.

"I ask him, 'Was that the guy? Did he catch you?' He wipes the sweat off his forehead and just says, 'Nope.' And that's it. Silence, for like two minutes. Doesn't say nothing more, but he's kinda squirming, real shifty-like.

"I couldn't take it, so I ask him, 'Okay, then why was he pointing a gun at you?' And Buddy goes, 'You don't want to know.' And I say, 'Look, just tell me. It's all good, my man.' And Buddy goes, 'I'll tell ya, but you gotta promise you will never tell this to anyone else for as long as I live.' And I'm like, 'Yeah, of course.'

"So Buddy says, 'I'm standing there in the hall, trying to get into the room to set up the surveillance gear. But the key won't work. And then it hits me. I mean, hits me like a ton of bricks.' I say, 'What hit you?' And Buddy says, 'I had to go.' 'Like leave?' I say. 'No,' he says, 'I had to take a dump, man!'"

Everyone laughed. It was a welcome relief from the mournful affair the funeral had been to that point.

"Buddy keeps going and says, 'Since my key wasn't working, I put my shoulder into the door, and it opened right up, real easy. So I throw my gear down, turn the light on, and hurry into the bathroom. All of a sudden, I hear a commotion coming from outside the room. I pull up my britches and step out, and there is this old guy in his drawers, loading that Luger and screaming in German at me!'"

The mourners all laughed, harder this time.

"So I was like, 'Why was he in *your* room?'"

"Then Buddy goes, 'That's the thing, man. I was in *his* room!' Turns out his key didn't work because he was at the wrong door!" Jimi was crying now, he was laughing so hard. "And I kept my promise to Buddy that I'd never tell this story until now." Jimi smiled ear to ear. "Love you, Buddy!"

16

With that, he took his place with the other mourners.

"That was quite a story, Jimi," Elvis said with a smile. "It's good to laugh on days like this. Anybody else have a story they want to share? Any more sworn-to-secrecy tales?"

Kurt Cobain raised his hand and made his way to the grave marker. He was more serious. He was always more serious.

"I remember when I first joined the team," he said. "I was still pretty messed up, trying to get my head right. Missing my family. Buddy was always there for me. He would say, 'Man, the world thinks we're dead, but I've never felt more alive!' I know we all feel the same way. Alive. But this? This sucks. We're here to keep the world safe. It's what Buddy did. But a little part of me died with him . . ."

Cobain wrestled for the right words. "This . . . what we do . . . it's a good gig. But it's more than a job. This bond we share—it runs deep." He started to go back to his seat, then he paused. "Buddy always encouraged me. He picked me up at my lowest. And when I missed, you know, what we all left behind, he was a rock. That's pretty cool to me."

He then nodded, wiped away a tear, and returned to his place around the grave.

"Thanks, Kurt," Elvis said. "Anyone else?"

Jim Morrison raised his hand.

"Yes, that's right. Jim has a poem he wrote for Buddy. Janis is going to read it. Come on up here."

Janis Joplin and Jim Morrison walked to the grave.

"It's called 'Buddy,'" Janis said, clearing her throat and wiping her eyes. She began:

A cricket sings
too high for the ear to hear,
but the listeners feel
the burn of their hearts inside.
Upside down and
inside out,
the legs of the insect
Sing
a song of love
sung by a choir
a universe away
but so close they can feel it.

A word so strong:
Morning
Evening
Midnight
Dawn.
The light he gave
shone the way,
the cricket whose song was love.

Morrison solemnly nodded and returned to his seat, but Joplin remained, her hand on the gravestone. Everyone knew what she wanted to say, but she just couldn't bring herself to say it. Janis loved Buddy as deeply as two people could love each other. Elvis stood up and put his arm around her, and she crumbled into his embrace.

"This is why we have each other, ya know?" said Elvis. "Nobody knows what we do for this world. Nobody knows but us. We're all we have."

"Amen," said a man from behind the group.

Everyone turned around in pleasant surprise because they didn't realize he was there.

"I'm so glad you made it, John," Elvis said with real happiness in his voice.

John Lennon walked to the gravestone, knelt, and placed a hand on it. He too was wearing a suit. His was maroon with black treble clefs on the white lapel. His reddish hair was neatly trimmed and starting to go white at the temples. He hadn't shaved in days. He wore circular, wire-rimmed glasses with rose-colored lenses and white canvas shoes. No socks.

"I'm so sorry," he whispered, hugging the stone.

Then he stood up and took a deep breath. "Elvis is right, though. I think to meself, *Why?* How many times did he go into the field and come home safe? I dunno. Too many to count. I'm not too keen on looking back, youknowwhatImean? But what this man did for us all . . . can't be overstated. We are here today because of him . . . ahh, I'm a wreck right now."

Lennon was staring at the ground, unable to look at his friends. Then he took a deep breath, shook his head slowly, and made eye contact with everyone. His voice was now firm with resolve. "He wouldn't want us to quit now. We have to stay true to the cause."

Elvis came over and put an arm around him. Lennon gave him a nod.

"It's time to say goodbye to Buddy," Elvis said with a quiver in his voice. "I think we all know what we need to sing."

The group drew in close until they were shoulder to shoulder, encircling Buddy's grave. They all thrust one arm forward, palm up, revealing a stone in each hand. Then in unison and in harmony they all began singing "That'll Be the Day."

When they finished the song, the group dispersed. Those who needed solitude rode alone in separate cars. Those that needed companionship rode together. It was their way—spare no expense to process a death in the family.

Lennon pulled Elvis aside and said, "King, ride with me. We need to talk."

"Jerry," Elvis said. Jerry Garcia turned around. "You wanna drive my car?" he said as he tossed his keys. Garcia nodded and caught the airborne keys.

★ ★ ★ ★

"King," Lennon said, as he and Elvis climbed into his beat-up yellow 1980 Volvo 240, "these events Buddy was tracking are troubling. The assassinations he was monitoring, they're not random. Somehow, they are connected. He shared some of his notes with me before you left for Vegas. He hadn't put it all together, but it looks like he was starting to get close. This Langston guy, he's just a buffoon. But it goes much deeper and higher up than him."

"How could this happen, John?" Elvis said, burying his head in his hands. Lennon reached across and placed a hand on his friend's shoulder. They drove on quietly for a few minutes.

"I blame myself," Elvis confessed. "I wasn't locked in that night. I wasn't taking the threat seriously. I just tagged along with Buddy because he asked me to. And because . . . well, I still love going to Vegas."

"It's not your fault, King. Nobody knew how dangerous these guys were except for Buddy."

Elvis nodded, his resolve building with each bounce of his head. "That's why who we pick to replace Buddy is so important. The world is changing, man. There are threats out there we . . . honestly, we aren't equipped to tackle." He measured his next words with great care. "I've actually been thinking about going in another direction with this one."

"Whaddu mean? You thinking Bono? Or MJ? Maybe Springsteen or Vedder? Ohhh, no wait . . . how about Madonna?"

Elvis paused. "Remember when we brought in Pac and Chris? They were different—fresh guys with new ideas, new perspectives. I think it's time we do something like, but not *exactly* like, that."

"So, what are you saying? We need to get the kid with the curly hair from NSYNC?"

"No, man. I'm thinking something altogether different. Outside of music."

Lennon's face soured. "I don't like it, Elvis. We're musicians. The way we can navigate the world—the artistic perspective. The sensitivity. The mental dexterity to absorb all that we have to learn once we join the team. The angst. The inborn knowledge that something is wrong with the world and we need to make it right. That's what we bring to this team as artists."

"All that is true," Elvis said. "But do you think we're the only ones with those gifts or perspectives? Besides, the music industry is going belly up. The Napster is going to be the death of it. Pretty soon they'll be giving record deals to kids winning TV talent shows!"

"We had the same thing in our day, King. Back then it was called *The Ed Sullivan Show*, ya know?" Lennon chuckled.

Elvis continued his diatribe. "People don't care about talent anymore. They just want to see the little blonde girl shake her hips and prance around in a schoolgirl outfit. They don't care if the vocals are autotuned to death. It's changing, man. We need to change too."

"You do know they said the same thing about you, King?"

Elvis gave a wry smile then went on. "John, I'm talking about computers, man. That's the future. Kids are learning to program computers in elementary school. The internet, all that information right at their fingertips—it gives them an understanding and a worldview that's unlike anything we have on our team right now. It's 1999, and we need a computer rock star."

Now the duo of former superstars traveled in silence awhile. Elvis could sense Lennon's resistance to the idea. They pulled into a small private airport where the rest of the team had arrived moments before. There were two planes awaiting them. One for the team, and one for the King.

"Are you not going back to HQ with the others?" Lennon asked.

"No, I'm going to interview someone."

"You're really serious about this?"

"Yes, I am. We've got to meet the future, John. I think we need to change with the times. This isn't the first time, and it won't be the last."

The two men stared at each other a moment, an uneasy tension mounting between them. Finally, Lennon relented.

"I'm with you, Elvis. Always. I'm just not sold on the idea yet."

"I'm okay with that, John. I just can't have you going solo. We're a band here, no solo artists. Cool?"

"Cool," Lennon said with a nod.

Then the two men hugged. They didn't always see eye to eye, but they did love and respect one another.

"What's your next move on the Brotherhood?" Elvis asked Lennon.

"I need to get into Holly's study. He thought there was some sort of 'doomsday scenario' going down. I'm going to dig into his files and see what more I can find."

The rest of the team was boarding the plane—a massive C-130 troop transport the team affectionately called Hercules. It could carry all of them and their personal vehicles anywhere they wanted to go.

"Jimi, you ready?" Elvis asked.

"Ready as I'll ever be."

"Then let's fly."

Elvis said goodbye to the team. Then he and Jimi boarded the other plane and took off.

"Where are they going?" Jerry Garcia asked Lennon.

"They are going to try to replace Buddy. Elvis thinks he's found our future."

chapter

FOUR

ole awakened to chatter from his AM/FM radio alarm clock. Two deejays were battling over which was the more important album, Korn's *Issues* or *Willennium* by Will Smith.

"You've got to be kidding me." Cole laughed out loud as he rolled out of bed and rubbed his head, wondering if such a preposterous argument was an omen that meant he shouldn't bother leaving his room. He was not looking forward to this day as it was. He was to spend half the day interviewing with tech companies for a job that could change the course of his life. This type of thing always made Cole anxious and weirded him out.

Cole Denton's bedroom was not a sight to behold. He had a twin-size bed with Star Wars sheets, a desk, a modest chest of drawers, a few posters on the wall, and a 1:128 scale replica of the Starship *Enterprise* suspended from the ceiling by fishing line. Lying about were a pile of dirty clothes, empty coffee cups, and several plates of half-eaten food from recent and some not-so-recent coding sessions.

He scavenged the pile for just the right outfit, giving each item a sniff before tossing any scent-approved apparel on his desk chair. "There's dirty and then there's funky," Cole said aloud to no one, doing his best Sinbad voice. "Dirty you can wear again. Funky can walk itself to class!" He often fought off anxiety with humor.

He could already hear Taylor in the "family room," as he and his roommate called it. The room was just a tiny den furnished with a twenty-two-inch TV on a homemade stand and two ratty couches that faced each other so the roommates could lie down and watch TV together on their own couches. This setup was as unimpressive as Cole's bedroom, but these young men were all about function, not form. And they were very much bachelors to the core. A woman had never even been to the apartment since they moved in a few semesters earlier.

The aroma of coffee perked Cole up as he threw on his clothes. He slapped at his hair in a way that did little to nothing for it, slathered some Right Guard clear gel in the appropriate places, and went in search of the coffee.

Taylor Wainscott, his roommate, stood in the hall in his bathrobe, running a hand through his mop of blond-frosted-tip hair that had clumped to one side in the night. Taylor was listening to the stupid radio debate and waiting for Cole to emerge from his room. "The movie sucked, but that song is my jam!" Taylor wailed "Wild Wild West" as he handed Cole a cup of joe.

"You're killing me, Smalls. You too?"

"Hey man, you like what you like. Will Smith has got that 'it' factor. You know what I'm talking about?" Taylor looked Cole up and down, appraising his carefully curated outfit. "Also . . . *Real Genius?* Is that the look we're going for on our big day?"

Cole had put on a white short-sleeved T-shirt and khaki cargo shorts, with a red-and-black flannel button-up shirt tied around his waist.

Cole exhaled. "If today is going to be as weird as I think it is, I at least want to play the part of Val Kilmer."

"Yeah, how awful," Taylor sighed with mock sympathy. "Poor guy, to have the top tech companies on the planet fighting for your services and forcing you to take a huge salary. I know, I know," he said, throwing up his hands to cut off Cole's inevitable rebuttal. "We don't have to have that conversation again. I know you don't care about the money, but you know who says that? Rich people."

"Listen dude, you know where I'm at. I want to do something that matters."

"SIGNIFICANCE. I get it dude. Have a Coke and a smile! Why don't you try being rich, and if you don't like it, you can give all that cheddar to me!"

Cole dropped his head, shrugged, then laughed. "All right, man. Fair. Seems like you and Self are on the same page today."

"Low blow, Denton, low blow. It's just, not everyone can write algorithms like you. Your coding, it's a thing of beauty. Self gets it, but the professor is thinking about

23

your future right now, not your 'what ifs.'"

Dr. Clayton Self was Cole and Taylor's professor and career advisor. While he was a bright man, he was also pretty full of himself and the butt of more than a few jokes between the roommates. Self was one of those middle-aged guys who tried to fend off Father Time with youthful lingo and Grecian Formula hair coloring, often using both very unsuccessfully.

"Speaking of what-ifs," Taylor said, steering the conversation into calmer waters, "how did Number Sixty-Five go last night?"

Cole had been so wrapped up in dreading all the interviews Dr. Self had set up for him, he'd almost forgotten how great last night had been. "Can it be both completely embarrassing and epically awesome?" he asked, wincing.

"You did your wave again, didn't you?"

"I did. I can't help it! It's like it's hardcoded into my software. The arm goes straight—" Cole demonstrated the move. "And puppet wave every time."

Taylor erupted with laughter. "I would love to have seen that!"

"Well, you aren't alone apparently. Savannah had a half-dozen friends staked out in the restaurant, watching my every move."

"Whoa, Sixty-Five has a name! 'Savannah.' That sounds lovely."

"Honestly, she kind of messes things up in the best way."

"Go on."

Cole thought for a moment and then said, "I believe in my work, and I believe it can help people. I never doubted that. I knew my math could help others find love. I just never thought there could be someone for—"

"Okay, you are grossing me straight out. I think I liked the whole, 'working for the man' argument way better. Let's do that. Netscape, Apple, and CompuLive, huh? You going somewhere to be the next Woz, Real Genius?"

Cole snapped right back to thinking about his day of misery. "I've done my homework. You know me, man. I'm ready, I guess. But seriously, remind me why I need this again? Remind me why Self set all this up?"

"A few reasons. Number one, Self needs to pad his stats. If he gets you placed with a major tech firm, it makes the professor look better to the tenure board. Secondly, he only sees things so far. He probably thinks the internet is just a math machine and not the future the way you see it. Dude still uses a Commodore 64." They both knew that last part wasn't true, but they liked to make fun of Dr. Self.

"Taylor, you hear the voicemails," Cole said. "You know I could unload Connextion tomorrow and not have to get a job for . . . well, a while anyway. Why would I ever want to work for someone else?"

"Um, I don't know. Actual money? Security?"

"Yeah, but I want to help—"

"I'm going to stop you there. I get it. You and Sally Struthers want to feed the children. Love you, buddy, but here's the truth: Self just knows that sometimes your head is so far in the clouds, you're missing present needs that go a bit beyond spending your tuition stipend on a tiny *Enterprise* on a string."

Cole decided to ignore the shot at his most prized possession. "Cool. Got it. Thanks for sharing and caring." Weary of the microscope being trained on him, Cole asked, "What about you, Taylor? Who has Self set up for you?"

Taylor had known this question was coming. Like a child proudly showing off his new toys the day after Christmas, he opened his briefcase like Indiana Jones in front of the "top men" and pulled out a three-ring binder with color-coded tabs chock-full of brochures and printed pages. "I'm putting all my eggs in one basket," he said, displaying his masterpiece of research and information. "It's that energy giant down in Texas—Enron. They are doing some really exciting stuff. They want to be on the leading edge of tech for their industry, and they are interested in yours truly helping them transition into the twenty-first century." He dropped into a chair and leaned back with his arms behind his head like he was relaxing in a hammock. "I hope to work there long enough to retire. Texas, man! Warm weather. Football. Guns." He pointed at Cole with both index fingers and said, "Yeah, baby!" doing his best Austin Powers impression.

"Oh yeah? Wow. That sounds like . . . Texas." Cole started rattling off everything Texan he could think of. "Yippee-ki-yay! Cowboys! All my exes live in . . . you know. Anyway, that's great, man. Just that one company, huh? I guess this means I'll have to get me a ten-gallon hat and a belt buckle to come visit."

"Awesome, dude. That will go great with your cargo shorts."

Cole and Taylor both felt the significance of the moment. They had roomed together since they were freshmen. Taylor was there when Cole came up with the idea for his website and even framed the napkin he wrote the algorithm on that night at the school cafeteria. This day, too, felt important to both of them.

Taylor looked at Cole. "I'm not hugging you."

"Yep. Cool. Me neither. Going to my interviews. Love you, too."

"Okay, we're done here."

$$\star\ \star\ \star\ \star$$

Cole was late and he knew it. He jogged up the stairs and turned to the right to where study rooms had been converted into interview spaces. He checked his watch, which read 9:32 a.m. His first interview was scheduled for 9:30. He hurriedly scanned the doors until he found the one with a Netscape sign on it.

Bursting into the room, he breathlessly fibbed, "I'm so sorry I'm late. I usually live by the mantra 'Early is on time, on time is late, and late is toast.'"

"It's no problem," the Netscape representative said calmly. The man had graying temples and appeared to be in his late forties. He was seated behind a standard school desk, surrounded by a raft of computers and peripherals.

The man stood and stuck his hand out, and Cole shook it.

"My name is Nate, and I'm with Netscape. You come highly recommended by Dr. Self, though he said you live by anything *but* the mantra you mentioned when you came in. Have a seat."

Busted, Cole sat down and rocked his weight from side to side in the chair. Searching for the right words, he blurted, "Well, they say those that can't, teach! Huh? Huh?" reaching his hand out for a high five. Nate from Netscape gave him a whole lot of nothing.

Nate just eyed Cole, then asked, "Just how smart are you?"

"Um . . . uh . . ." Cole was caught off guard by the abrupt change in tone. "Well, I invented a website that connects people . . . like, romantically."

"Thanks, Mr. Denton. I can read that in *Wired*. Word in tech circles is that the site's growth appears to be exponential. Give me something more concrete. Tell me a story that illustrates the site's capability."

"Um, yeah. I met someone for dinner yesterday."

"Not quite what I meant, but okay."

"She's really cute . . ."

Nate from Netscape held up a hand. "I want to know, does the algorithm operate efficiently? How many successful matches have you made, exactly"?

"That's . . . proprietary," Cole said sheepishly.

"I understand. Can I see it?"

Starting to feel flush in his face, Cole waffled between confidence and embarrassment. He said, "It was a pretty extensive process to figure it out, but the algorithm is gold. Of course, it's not Netscape . . . yet. B-b-but this is the future. And I got a date! With a woman!"

"Congrats. I think," Nate from Netscape said dryly. "But that doesn't really speak to your intelligence. Possibly just your optimism." He steepled his fingertips in front of his chin. "It does show that you've worked hard on something. Hard work is good, but ants work hard, Mr. Denton. I'd hoped you might show me something more . . . impressive."

With some frustration, Cole thought, *This guy is Agent Smith from* The Matrix.

"Okay, how to quantify?" Cole said, almost to himself. Then he gave Nate from Netscape a mischievous grin. "How many dates have you been on lately, Nathaniel? Do you like the ladies? Do the ladies like you?"

"Excuse me?"

Cole's wheels were turning. "Are these computers hooked up to the internet?"

"Ye-e-e-s-s."

"Let's do something to boost your street cred. May I?" Cole asked, motioning to the keyboard in front of Nate. There was no stopping him now.

Nate didn't say a word, which Cole took as a green light to proceed. He turned the monitor toward himself so that the interviewer couldn't see it and started typing furiously. Nate watched Cole carefully, cocking his head to the side as if trying to figure out what he was doing.

This went on for a few minutes. Nate was starting to grow impatient when Cole turned the monitor back toward the interviewer and blurted out, "Man, 75k plus dental? Surely you can do better than that. You want a raise?"

"Excuse me? What are you talking about?"

"I hacked into the internal server at Netscape, and I'm now in your human resources department. Say the word, and I can give you a raise, undetected."

Cole knew this was illegal and inappropriate, but he couldn't help himself. And he couldn't wait to tell the sysops at IHOP about doing a real-time hack during an actual job interview.

"Maybe you could buy a vintage Chrysler LeBaron convertible with your raise. Ladies love a LeBaron!"

Nate from Netscape stood abruptly and howled. He ripped the cable out of the computer and shouted, "How did you do that?!?"

"The internet?"

Nate was furious, and Cole didn't know where to look. He just kept staring at the vein that was pulsing on the man's forehead.

"I've seen quite enough. You might have the skills, but you do not have . . ."—Nate was searching for the right word—". . . anything else we want at Netscape. Thank you for your time."

"That's it?" Cole asked, still seated.

"Yes," Nate from Netscape said matter-of-factly.

Cole looked at him for a moment, imagining being Neo and slicing through Nate like he was ones and zeroes.

As Cole left the room, he noticed a girl in formal business wear with huge shoulder pads seated in a chair outside the interview room. "Whatever you do," he said to her, "don't offer Nate a raise. Nice suit!"

★ ★ ★ ★

Cole stomped down the stairs, angered and frustrated by the interview, though it proved he was right to have dreaded the process. His next interview didn't start until 10:30 a.m., and it was only 9:57. He had some time to kill, and he needed to clear his head. Next up was Apple, and he didn't want to blow this one.

He wandered down a couple of flights until he found himself in the basement of the Stratton Center. Just as he was about to turn around and head back upstairs to the first floor, he spotted an older guy with killer sideburns sitting alone at a round table for two, sipping a cup of coffee. He was dressed in dingy, blue maintenance workers' coveralls. His name badge said "King." The man had headphones on and was listening to what appeared to be a bedazzled prototype of a Personal Jukebox mp3 player. Cole had seen a report on the Personal Jukebox from the Consumer Electronics Show, but it wasn't due in stores for months.

"Excuse me, sir," Cole said, waving to get the man's attention. "Where did you get that . . . coffee?" He didn't want to be rude.

The man motioned without looking up, pointing with his left hand to a door labeled "Break Room." Each finger on the hand, minus the thumb, was adorned with an elaborate ring.

"Thanks," Cole said, then went and poured himself a cup. On the way out the door, he tasted the coffee and made a sour face.

"Ugh," Cole winced. "This stuff is awful."

"Sorry, man," the maintenance guy said, taking off his headphones. "Never been much for making coffee, just drinking it."

"Oh, I didn't mean to insult your coffee-making abilities. I–I didn't know you made it."

"Aw, it's nothing. Don't sweat it, kid. Say, what are you doing here?"

"Interviews up on the second floor."

"All right, man. Way to go! Only the brainiacs are interviewing here today. Well, shoot, I guess there are only brainiacs at MIT. Hey, you like music?"

"I guess so."

"Who you like?"

"Uh, I have varied tastes," Cole said hesitantly. "Some days it's Beethoven or Counting Crows. Other days it's underground, industrial dance stuff. I dunno. I'm kinda all over the map."

"I dig it. I like oldies myself. And gospel. Oh, and that Ricky Martin! Can't get enough of him. Can you believe all the songs you can carry on this gadget? Take a seat, man."

Cole found himself sitting before he knew what he was doing. He was unsure why he was even talking with this guy. He really needed to prepare himself mentally for the next interview.

"What do you want to do with your life?" the maintenance man asked, taking a sip of his coffee.

Taken aback by the question, Cole answered slowly. "Well . . . I'm not sure. Something that matters. Something other than just making money. I guess that's what I'm here trying to figure out with these interviews."

"Now see, that's refreshing. Most folks, all they think about is making a buck. What makes you different?"

Cole had never really thought about where his desire to make a difference came from. He had this longing to matter as far back as he could remember. It's what drove him to learn computers. He was certain computers were his future. His way out. Out of Illinois. Out of his past. Out of all the things he never talked about with anyone. But why did money not feel like a big deal to him? He'd need to think about that a little more.

"That's a really good question," he said. "And I don't seem to know the answer right at this moment."

"I stumped Real Genius on Interview Day. Who's the man?!"

Cole choked on his coffee, wondering how this guy knew about Real Genius. Before he could ask, the maintenance guy continued.

"That's all right. You'll figure it out. I'll just tell you this: Don't settle. If you really care about doing something that matters, then do something about it. Nice talking to you. Maybe I'll see you around."

With that, the man with the killer sideburns stood up and left the room, strolling down the hall while singing the Rolling Stones' "Satisfaction." He was really good.

"Hey, man," Cole hollered down the hall at him. "You can really sing!"

"Thank you. Thank you very much," he said with flair.

✦ ✦ ✦ ✦

The conversation had done Cole good. His mind was clearer, calmer, and he felt ready for his next interview. He hustled upstairs, found the room marked "Apple," and rushed in.

This time he was a minute early, and the previous interview was still being conducted. The interviewer and the interviewee both turned and looked at him.

"Oh, I'm so sorry!" Cole said, backing out of the room.

"It's okay, Cole. We were just finishing up," the man from Apple said with a smile. "It was nice to meet you, and we'll be in touch," he said, shaking hands with the female student whose interview he was just finishing.

The young woman was wearing a nice gray pantsuit. As she walked out of the room, she gave Cole the stink eye for his untimely interruption.

"Sorry," he mouthed to her.

She responded with the universal hand gesture for "Apology not accepted."

"It's okay, Cole. I've been looking forward to this interview all morning," the man from Apple said, motioning for Cole to come in and sit down. "You are quite the big fish around here. I'm sure everyone wants you. My name is Jerome Crenshaw."

"Hi, Jerome Crenshaw. I'm Cole Denton," Cole said as they shook hands. "Uh, yeah, it's nice to be wanted," he said, trying to forget how horribly his first interview went and how weirdly this one had begun.

"Cole, I really like your website. It's a creative idea and seems really effective. At Apple, we believe the internet will become the medium people use for everything in the coming years, including dating."

30

"Yeah? Thanks, man—I mean, sir—I mean, Mr. Crenshaw."

"Call me Jerome."

"Um, okay, Mr. Jerome."

"It's okay Cole. Don't stress."

"Apparently, I'm better at forecasting future tech than I am at doing interviews."

"That's a valuable skill to have. Give me another idea you've thought up that's a step or two ahead of the curve."

"Um, okay." Cole paused for a second to consider this and noticed the man's personal digital assistant. "I see you still use the Newton."

Embarrassed, Jerome said, "Yeah, I just can't quit it. When Jobs came back, he canned the production of these, but I still love it. I only use it on the road. If he ever saw me with it, I'd probably get fired."

"Hey, I'm not judging," Cole said with a smile. "So . . . Jobs killed this because it was clunky and didn't sell, right?"

"Correct."

"Okay, imagine if it was also a phone. Something that combines the personal planner with cellular connectivity. And maybe throw in an mp3 player, while you're at it."

Jerome chuckled nervously. "Ha. Have you been reading our internal emails?"

Cole smirked. "Oh, and add a camera, of course."

"Of course. Why not make the battery last all day while you're at it, Cole?" Jerome said sarcastically.

"But why couldn't one device do all those things? The problem I see is definitely the hardware, but you'll figure that out. You've got great engineers. What you need is some more elegant coding."

Jerome moved to the edge of his seat. "What you got, Mr. Future Man?"

For the next few minutes, Cole Denton scribbled energetically on the back of one of the résumés another student had left with Jerome.

"Wait, that's . . ." Jerome glared. "How did you get that code? That's top secret stuff!"

"Jerome, the internet is like the best hide-and-seek player ever. Give me a few minutes, I can find anything. I just grabbed some old Newton code and added a few tweaks for battery efficiency and application swapping."

He continued filling up pages, and Jerome's eyes grew wider as Cole explained how it could all work with greater efficiency and optimizing RAM speed.

I'm really nailing this one, Cole thought as his confidence swelled.

"I could build this thing today," he said. "It would weigh five pounds and be super ugly. But not impossible. We could call it a 'smart phone.'"

"Whoa," Jerome said, as Cole brought his monologue to a close. "Why *couldn't* we do that?" he said more to himself. Then he looked up at Cole. "You have not disappointed, young man. Well, this has been great," he said, standing and hurriedly collecting his things. "Thanks for giving me such a great idea . . . uh . . . I mean, so much of your time."

"Wait, that's it?" Cole asked, incredulous.

"We'll be in touch," Jerome said and pushed his way past Cole on his way out the door. He turned toward the stairs and disappeared.

Cole realized what he had just done.

"Thief!" he yelled, kicking the interviewer's chair.

Cole collected himself and walked out of the room, trying to look confident and savvy and not like he'd just been fleeced for a billion-dollar idea.

The bejeweled maintenance guy with great sideburns was standing across the hall, leaning on a mop. He smiled sympathetically and said, "Tough break, kid. Well, you probably didn't want to work for them anyway."

"This day is not going the way I had envisioned it," Cole said.

"How did you see it going, son?"

"Like, with all these tech companies falling all over each other to offer me a fortune to work for them."

"Why did you think it would go that way?"

"I don't know. I really know computers, and my professor set up these interviews for me. He led me to believe that these were slam dunks, that all I had to do was pick my favorite."

"Maybe he was trying to teach you something."

"Like what?"

"I dunno. Maybe he felt you needed a dose of humility."

That stung a little, especially coming from a stranger.

"Or maybe," the maintenance guy said like a late-night informercial spokesman, "you still haven't found what you're looking for. You know, like the U2 song." He sang a couple of bars to make his point.

Impressed, Cole said, "Wow, Mr. . . ."

"King."

"Mr. King, you really can sing. Why haven't I ever seen you around campus?"

"I'm new," King said with a smile, his lip curling on the left side. "You have any more interviews today?"

"Just one more at 11:30 a.m. It's with CompuLive."

"Hm . . . not familiar with them."

"Really?"

"I'm not big on this stuff," Mr. King said with a wink. "Hope it goes well, man."

And with that, Mr. King twirled on his mop and danced down the hall like he was in a movie musical and everyone else were extras. He glided down the hall, singing more of the U2 song.

Cole chuckled. *This guy is something else*, he thought. Then he realized that, again after talking with Mr. King, he felt less angry. Less frustrated. Calm.

✯ ✯ ✯ ✯

Cole was early to his CompuLive interview. He was determined to get this one right. He wasn't sure he wanted to work for CompuLive, but he didn't want the morning to be a total waste. And on some level, he didn't want to disappoint Dr. Self.

He sat outside the interview room on a couch until the door opened and the interviewer asked him to come in. *So far, so good*, he thought. *I'm on time, and I didn't bust in on another interview.*

"Hi, I'm Sally Fields," said the woman from CompuLive. She was in her thirties, tall, wore smart-looking glasses, had beautiful blonde hair, and was quite attractive. Her being pretty made Cole a little nervous. And when he got nervous, he sometimes said stupid things like—

"Like the actress who played Forrest Gump's mom. *Mama*," he said doing a poor Gump impersonation. *Ugh! I just made a bad joke*, he scolded himself.

"No, I'm Sally Fields, plural," she said, laughing. "Mama," she said like Forrest Gump, "is played by Sally Field, singular."

Okay, maybe she liked my joke after all.

"Well, I'm Cole Denton, and it's grilly exciting to be heret."

Did I just say "grilly exciting to be heret"? What is wrong with me? Why am I so nervous? I don't even want this job. Or do I?

Now Cole was in his head, which often happened when he became anxious. He thought this was probably a major reason why he had been zero for sixty-four with the girls he met through his website. But then there was Savannah . . .

33

"It's nice to meet you, Cole. Relax. We're just talking here, trying to get to know each other. I like your whole vibe—the laid-back, chill thing. A stark contrast to . . . well, everyone else I've seen today."

"Okay, thanks," Cole said, suddenly feeling like he was on one of his failed dates. "I don't know why I'm so nervous. Maybe today just hasn't gone so well, and I'm hoping I don't blow thi—" Cole caught himself, but the cat was out of the bag. She now knew his other interviews hadn't gone well, and he was without leverage in the event she offered him a position.

"This isn't life or death," she said. "Just take a breath, and let's talk."

"Cool." Cole shifted his weight from side to side in the chair.

"Tell me about yourself."

"Well, I'm originally from Illinois. I've been to six *Star Trek* conventions. I graduated high school at fifteen, got my bachelor's at seventeen, and two master's degrees by twenty. I'm finishing up my doctorate at MIT, and I love computers. I've also avoided the Noid every time I ordered from Dominos."

"Wow, Doogie Howser! Congrats on the degrees and the pizza orders. How did you learn computers?"

"I guess when I was a kid, they always seemed to fascinate me. I remember the day our computer lab in elementary school got an Apple IIe, with that green screen and four-bit graphics. I spent hours on that thing every chance I got. By second grade, I was basically the tech guy for the school. When they upgraded to the Apple IIc, the principal let me have the old IIe. I probably took it apart and reassembled it twenty times over the years."

"When did you first learn how to effectively use the internet, Cole?"

"Well, it was at school again. I remember our middle school had Prodigy."

"Oh yes," she said. "I think we all cut our teeth on Prodigy."

"Yeah, I spent as much time as they would let me learning stuff online. I basically taught the computer science class when I got to high school."

Cole could feel himself calming down. Whenever he talked about computers, he felt at home, in his element. *Maybe CompuLive would be a place where I could fit in,* he thought. *Even thrive. And she likes my vibe.*

He really started to get excited as Sally Fields spoke about CompuLive's vision. This was a company that saw the future and had a plan to change with the times. And they needed people like Cole to help them move forward.

"If you were in our shoes, Cole, where would you lead us?"

Cole felt a slight twinge of déjà vu. He sighed and smiled. "I've got a lot of ideas, but . . . you know the expression about 'free milk and a cow,' right?"

"'Why buy the cow when you can get the milk for free?' Relax, Mr. Denton, I'm not here to steal anything today. And the Georgia Satellites, huh? Nice pull."

Relieved, Cole continued. "I'll just say this: I love what CompuLive does. You have software installed on every computer in the multiverse. Having access to every computer is access to every home, hospital, business . . ."

"Got it," she said, smiling.

"That's real power," Cole said, restarting his train of thought. "With that kind of access, the internet can truly influence the world. Way better than any newspaper or cable network. It's what's next."

Sally Fields sat back in her chair. "Cole, I can see a future for you at CompuLive. You would fit right in with our culture, and you have vision. You seem to be uniquely wired to navigate the twenty-first century."

Cole could feel his pulse rate rising. *Don't blow this, don't blow this, don't—*

"Awesome!" he exclaimed out loud. "So . . . what next?" He couldn't believe he was actually excited about one of these jobs.

"I'm prepared to offer you a job on our technology team right now. I am authorized to offer you an annual salary of $98,000 a year, plus benefits, upon your graduation."

This gave Cole a moment of pause. To his mind, the success of Connextion gave him real-world credentials more valid than a PhD. In fact, he was kind of over school. He didn't think the institution had much else to teach him.

"You really think I need to finish my doctorate for this job?" Cole asked.

"If you want to be able to reach the highest levels at CompuLive, yes."

"This is definitely something I'll need to think about," he said slowly.

"Read through this offer." Sally Fields handed Cole a manila folder with a quarter-inch stack of paper inside, held together with a large gem clip. "I have attached my business card, which has my cellular phone number on it. You have seventy-two hours to consider our offer, so I'll need an answer by 10:00 Monday morning."

"Okay, I will definitely give this a lot of thought."

"Cole." Sally Fields looked him straight in the eyes. "You could be a star at CompuLive. Make a good choice here."

"Thank you, I certainly will. You know, Mama always said, 'Life is like a box of chocolates . . .'"

"You never know what you're gonna get!" they said in unison, then laughing together.

"This was fun! Thanks, Cole. I look forward to hearing from you soon."

"You're welcome," he said, standing up and shaking her hand.

He had not seen this coming, especially after the day he'd had. He didn't expect to like what he heard from a company. But he also didn't expect to have to finish school. Didn't he have enough degrees already?

Cole walked out of Stratton and into the sunlight. Sitting on the step, seemingly waiting for him, was Mr. King.

"This is the third time I've bumped into you today," Cole said.

"Third time's a charm, Cole. I understand you just got a pretty sweet offer."

"Uh, yeah, from CompuLive. Wait . . . how did you know that?"

"I have the room bugged. A little earpiece lets me hear everything happening in there."

"Wait . . . what?"

"Just kidding, man. Good news travels fast."

"But I haven't told anyone yet."

"Forget about how I know what I know. You have a lot to think about, but I want to present you with one more option." He handed Cole a business card. "Come to the private hangars at Logan International Airport tonight at ten o'clock. Hangar four. I might have what you've been searching for."

This puzzled Cole immensely. How did this maintenance guy know so much, and what was this nighttime rendezvous all about?

"I know you want a life of significance, Cole," Mr. King said. "I'm prepared to offer you one. Just come to Logan tonight, and I'll fill in the blanks. Trust me. No strings attached," he added with a wink. Then he turned around and started walking away. It wasn't just a walk; it was more of a strut.

Cole looked at the business card Mr. King had handed him. It was blank, except for the initials DRS and a graphic of a cool-looking skull.

Then he heard Mr. King belt out, "Wild Wild West" just as Taylor had that morning.

This jolted Cole, and he stared in confusion as the maintenance man strolled off. There was definitely something strange about this old guy. But something inside told him tonight's meeting was one he should not miss.

chapter FIUE

John Lennon stood at the front door of the two-story San Francisco Victorian-style house. He raised his hand to rap on the door but held it in the air as if frozen. He didn't know what to say to Janis. He didn't know how to act. They didn't get a chance to talk after the funeral, so this would be his first opportunity to offer condolences to his friend and share her grief. He didn't know how he would feel inside the home that Janis and Buddy had shared for so many years.

He was lost in thought and didn't see Janis watching from the side window. So when she opened the door, he was taken by surprise. Lennon smiled, took off his black night porter hat, and offered a very exaggerated bow, as if humbling himself before royalty. Janis gave him a wan smile and then rushed to hug him.

He could tell she had been crying just moments earlier. This was not something he had ever seen her do. But Buddy was gone, and the atmosphere of the house was thick with his absence.

Janis poured tea, and they sat quietly together.

Finally, Lennon broke the silence. "Janis, I don't understand. YouknowwhatImean?" His words trailed off at the end of the sentence as if they both instinctively knew where he was heading with his thoughts.

Janis hung her head low and pushed out the words like they each weighed a ton. "He had found something . . . a clue he thought was connected to something big. I wasn't worried; he was with Elvis. How many times had they been in the field together? We know there are always risks, but, John . . . this seemed so routine."

"I am so sorry, love."

Janis looked away to hide her tears, and the two sat quietly in the sunlight of the bay window. As the day lingered, the minutes turned to hours and neither wanted to be anywhere else. Lennon had brought CDs of Emmylou Harris, Wilco, and Drive-By Truckers for her to listen to. Instead, Janis went to the turntable and put on *Aretha's Gold*.

"I need to visit his study, Jan."

Looking weary and not even asking the reason, Janis slowly nodded. "I think I'm going for a walk. I've got to get out of here before I fall apart. Just let yourself out when you're done. Take whatever you need."

John nodded with an understanding look.

As she opened the door to go out, she stopped and turned. Choking back tears, Janis said, "Find them, John. Get the bastards."

She didn't wait for a response. She hugged him once more and then stumbled out the door, heading anywhere but the place where she had known so much love for so many years. Now the house held only painful memories.

★ ★ ★ ★

Buddy's office was a shrine to information. The walls held an overflowing library covering every subject imaginable. When he was a musician, Buddy was always searching for a new sound; as a DRS agent, he was always searching for actionable intel. Over the past four decades, Buddy's curious nature and extensive knowledge base had been among the team's greatest assets.

Though it was never formally assigned to him, Buddy was also the team's de facto tech guy. Sure, the DRS had an R&D department staffed by talented inventors and machinists who produced the cutting-edge tech for their missions, but Buddy was the guy on the team who understood the science behind the stuff. Never one to stick with the tried-and-true, he was always on the lookout for the latest hardware being developed at tech companies and military contractors, eager to try something new. He was the one who acquired the early edition Personal Jukebox and gave it to Elvis for his birthday.

Beyond Buddy's knowledge and abilities as an agent, everyone in the DRS had also trusted his understanding and discernment. He was able to see connections where others saw only loose threads, and intricate schemes and strategies where others saw only random events. Amongst the books were mementos and spoils of war from a modern history he'd had a hand in reshaping.

His desk appeared simple. Clearly handmade, not for form or beauty but pure function. There were secret chambers tucked all over this piece of DIY mastery. On the desktop were three computer monitors positioned in a semicircle, along with a keyboard and ergonomic mouse faded and worn from extensive use. Behind the desk was a large painting of a pair of horn-rimmed glasses made up of psychedelic flower petals. Janis had painted it many years ago and surprised Buddy with it for Christmas.

Lennon didn't have to look hard. What he was seeking lay in the middle of his friend's desk. There were three green file folders tucked into a larger manila folder several inches thick.

Buddy Holly had scoured the internet, news outlets, and security agencies around the world for anything he could find on the group that called themselves the Brotherhood. What he had amassed painted a picture of a terrorist organization of some sort. One file held records of past attacks that didn't appear to be related at first or even second glance. Lennon wasn't sure why these events had caught Buddy's eye. In the next file, Buddy had worked out several theories of what this so-called brotherhood could be up to and why. One idea suggested global destabilization leading to some kind of unspecified apocalypse, although the ultimate benefit to the organization was unclear. Another surmised a financial technology theft of unprecedented proportions. There hadn't been a lot to go on, but Buddy had been in the process of building a convincing case. Lennon thought a few of the connections were a stretch, but all of it raised cause for serious concern.

The last folder held a rather thick FBI file on a man named Jason "Bull" Langston. Reading through it, Lennon couldn't believe the variety of crimes Langston had been involved in. Bank heists, high-level pyramid schemes, extortion. He'd even sold counterfeit baseball cards at one point. Langston was no altar boy, but he didn't exactly seem like the killing type either. There were no violent offenses on his record, but the fingerprints found onsite at the Las Vegas Hilton were a match for Langston.

Lennon fired up the triple-monitor array and began accessing government databases. He pulled up a mugshot of Langston that sent heat down the back of his neck. Now he had a face to go with the name of the man who murdered Buddy Holly.

Angry tears welled up in his eyes. Buddy had not only been a friend but also a mentor who taught Lennon everything he knew about field work. Even now, he could hear Buddy saying, "Empathize. Put yourself in his shoes." Lennon tried to calm his mind but could only think, *He has no idea of the fury he's unleashed.*

As he was considering the possible scenarios, a high-pitched ping drew his attention back to the screens, where an alert Buddy had engineered popped up from local law enforcement in the state of Tennessee. It was a warrant issued for Langston for unpaid parking violations.

"Crude, sloppy, and careless. Mr. Langston. You have been found. 'No need to waste the foolish tear, / Or heave the windy sigh: / The man had killed the thing he loved, / And so he had to die.'"

He scooped up all the paper files, a few floppy discs, and other data Buddy had collected and stowed them away in his woven hemp satchel. He noticed one of the desk's cabinet doors open slightly and stooped to close it. As he closed the door, he heard an unusual click. He opened the door again and found a hidden compartment had fallen from the top of the cabinet. He forced it open and pulled out another green folder, this one labeled "Tech."

Lennon opened the file and found page after page of notes on various items and individuals from the technology sector. These were inventions Buddy knew were coming and the people responsible for them. There were notes on lasers, cell phone technology, and microchips. Much of this stuff Lennon had little interest in, but he found the people fascinating. Mechanical engineers, guys obsessed with space exploration, cutting-edge programmers, and even antisocial nerds hacking into government websites.

He crammed this folder into his bag as well and gave the room one more look. He did a quick tap dance, blew a kiss to the air, and rushed out the door, heading straight for the hangar.

chapter
SIX

Cole drove around Cambridge for a couple of hours, thinking about Sally Fields, Mr. King, and the old man's insistence that he could offer him a life of significance. That and the fact that there was something strangely familiar about the guy . . .

When he returned to the apartment, he found Taylor working on his computer.

"Hey," Taylor said, as Cole tossed his keys on the kitchen table. "How did your interviews go?"

"Uh." He was struggling to find the right word. "Unexpected."

"Yeah, how so?"

"Well, I hacked the servers at Netscape and offered their rep a raise."

"Yeah, I heard about that one."

"How?" Cole howled. Everyone seemed to know an awful lot about his interviews without his telling a soul.

"Listen to the answering machine."

Cole saw the red light blinking on the machine. He hit PLAY, and a familiar voice crackled from the speaker.

"Hey, Love Shack! Self here. What on earth were you thinking?" This was said with a mixture of anger and astonishment that made Cole just a little bit proud. "I just talked with Nate Fielder from Netscape, and he told me about the stunt you pulled in your interview. I'm appalled and impressed all at once. Listen, I called his boss, who's an old college buddy of mine, and in spite of your best efforts to get arrested and alienate one of the biggest tech companies in the world, they're still going to offer you a position. You're welcome. You owe me lunch. Call me. I've got the details. Ciao!"

Cole hit the erase button with authority.

Taylor shrugged. "So . . . that's good news, right?"

"Maybe," Cole said, exhaling. He threw his hands in the air. "I don't know. I don't really see myself at Netscape. With people like that Nate character running things, I think they'll go the way of the dodo."

"Okay, what about the other two?"

"Let's see. The guy from Apple stole an idea I pitched him and is planning to pawn it off as his own."

"That sucks!"

"Yeah, it does. I wanted to punch that guy in his throat."

"Whoa. Surely the last one went well."

"It actually did," Cole said, smiling in spite of himself. "They offered me a job—98k a year to start. But they need an answer by Monday morning."

Taylor was dumbfounded. "Did you say 98k?"

"Yeah," Cole said, somewhat embarrassed.

Taylor stood up and applauded. "Congrats, my man! Drinks, dinner, and a movie are on you tonight. And I'm ordering appetizers—no ifs, ands, or buts."

"Yeah, I don't know," Cole said, scratching his head. "I'm not sure I'm going to accept the offer."

Taylor collapsed on his couch like he'd fainted. "What?!? Why not?"

"There might be something else out there for me." Cole reached his hand in his pocket and felt the DRS business card. "I need some time to think. Probably need to call Self, too."

"He's going to say you've lost your mind," Taylor said, shaking his head. Then he pointed at Cole like a mafia boss. "You're still buying tonight."

"Whatever," Cole said, making a *W* with his fingers, like in the movie *Clueless*, and then retreated to his room.

He settled in behind his computer, ready to do some research. Who was this Mr. King? And what was the DRS? For the next hour, Cole hacked into the MIT personnel files, the Massachusetts Registry of Motor Vehicles, and any trade unions involving maintenance workers in the greater New England area. He found no records or connection to his Mr. King in the region.

He then turned his attention to the name DRS and the skull symbol. Using every search engine he could think of, he found nothing. He then went to chat rooms and message boards where much of the deep, dark stuff on the internet was hiding. Cole was no stranger to the pirate boards, either. He was no Kevin Poulsen or Robert Tappan Morris, but he knew their work and had even built on it. On the boards, he was known affectionately as "10v35h4ck." His buddies at IHOP loved singing a few bars of the B-52's when he walked in the door and ordered those sweet silver dollar pancakes.

"Them Apples" was a local pirate board affectionately named for Matt Damon's famous line in *Good Will Hunting*. They all agreed that none of them looked like Matt Damon, which was the most unrealistic thing about the movie. And the math part was weak, too.

In fact, "10v35h4ck" had gained some notoriety at the Sysops at IHOP gatherings. His algorithm had managed to successfully score dates for a few guys who were starting to look like mole people from a lack of direct sunlight and nutrients. One of them *almost* had a girlfriend, which boosted Cole's 1337 status for sure. He rarely paid for a Rooty Tooty Fresh 'n Fruity anymore.

Cole had multiple phone lines running to his desk, each line labeled, though the cable running to his modem was doing the bulk of the work. MIT offered cable speeds his hometown of Troy, Illinois, couldn't, and it was a fantastic upgrade. He wanted to know where his data went and why, as it was crucial to his dating site. And truthfully, he was simply fascinated by IP addresses and the flow of data. Cole could see a time coming when online privacy would be a thing of the past.

He used the CompuLive chat service to IM some of the more accomplished SYSOPS he had met and showed them a digital copy of the logo. They had never seen the image before or heard of anything called DRS. For a man of Cole Denton's considerable abilities, to turn up nothing with a deep search online was astonishing. *I have no idea who or what these guys are*, he thought, and the realization intrigued him.

He logged off his computer and picked up the phone to return Dr. Self's call. As he dialed the number, he wondered if he should mention this DRS business. Then he heard Self's voice say, "Padawan! I know it's been around forever, but I still love caller ID. Knowing who's calling before you even pick up—fantastic!"

"Hey, Dr. Self. Listen, about Netscape . . ."

"No, no, don't mention it. That Nate is a real jerk. I talked to his boss. He apologized and said *he'd* take that raise you were offering."

Cole laughed nervously. "Yeah, about that . . . I don't think I want to work for Netscape."

"Whaaaa—? It's a great company! Come on, man, don't let one bad interview turn you off."

"It's not the interview," Cole replied, searching for the right words. "I don't think they have a bright future. And besides, I think there might be something better out there for me."

"Okay then, was it Apple or CompuLive that wowed you?"

Knowing Self wouldn't understand, Cole decided to take the path of least resistance. "CompuLive. They made me a really nice offer."

"Oh yeah? I bet they sent over that cute little Sally gal. Hard to say no to her, huh? Huh? Huh?"

"Yeah, she was really cool."

"Look, man," Self said, trying to get serious. "You are my finest student. No, you're not the most motivated, but your ability to synthesize information and analyze the data is second to none. The speed at which you write code and your preternatural understanding of the internet are the best I've ever seen. I just want to see you succeed. When you succeed, I succeed. Capisce?"

"Yeah, I get it. And I appreciate it, Dr. Self. I'm grateful for all you've done for me the last few years."

"Aw, don't mention it, Love Shack!"

Cole hated when he called him that. It was one of those things like when a guy can pick on his little brother but no one else had better. Only his hacker brothers were allowed to call him Love Shack.

"Thanks, Dr. Self," Cole said through clenched teeth.

"I know, I know. I just can't help myself. Anyways, let me know when you accept the CompuLive offer."

"Okay, will do. I have until Monday, so I'll probably email you when I make a decision."

"I'll pretend like I didn't hear that. You're taking that offer."

"See ya, Dr. Self."

Cole looked at his watch as he hung up the phone. It was 4:30 in the afternoon, and he was hungry. Then it dawned on him that he hadn't ingested any sustenance since that horrible cup of coffee Mr. King made.

The phone rang again, startling Cole. Taylor picked it up first and then bellowed from the living room, "Cole, it's yours!"

"Hello?" Cole answered.

"Hey, it's Savannah."

"Savannah?" Cole said, surprised.

"Didn't expect me to call, did you?"

"No, I did not." It was a pleasant surprise.

"Look, I'll cut to the chase. I had a great time meeting you, and I don't mean to be forward, but come on, you went on sixty-four dates before me. Doesn't seem like there were too many second dates. So I decided I'd do the hard part and make the move for you."

Cole's 0–64 record wasn't his proudest accomplishment, but many of the dates weren't really about making a connection. He was trying to gather data on what drew people together, which would help him streamline his algorithm. In some ways, he had to be unsuccessful in order for other guys like him to be successful. Or so that's what he told himself. No matter how he sliced it, not once had the girl he met called him afterward.

"Wow, I'm glad you called." Maybe Savannah would be a good person to talk with about his confusing day. "I'm starving. You want to get something to eat?"

"Um, it's a little early in the day, but sure. Where do you want to go? Piccadilly Cafeteria with all the other senior citizens?"

"Very funny!" Cole laughed. "Let's meet at 1369 in half an hour. Work for you?"

"Yeah, works great! See you there."

Cole was so excited he could hardly stand it. He dashed to the living room and grabbed his keys from the kitchen table.

"Where are you going?" Taylor asked, looking up from his computer.

"I got a date!"

"Hey, you owe me dinner and appetizers!"

"Not tonight, Kemosabe!" Cole called as he ran out the door and slammed it behind him.

He bounded down the stairs and out to his golden 1987 Honda Accord. He wiped the leaves and acorns from the windshield, jumped in the car, and started it up. The radio was playing Nirvana's "Come as You Are" at high volume. *That dude was too serious*, Cole thought, turning the sound down. *I need something happier.* He scanned the dial and landed on an oldies station where Roy Orbison was wailing "Pretty Woman." *Now that's more like it!*

★ ★ ★ ★

Cole found a place to park, fed the meter, and went in a full ten minutes early. To his surprise, Savannah was already there.

"Hey, you're early," Cole said, smiling ear to ear.

"Well, I thought I would make up for last time when I was a tad bit late," Savannah said with a chipper smile. "Besides, I was nearby and got a good parking spot. How was your day? Tell me about your interviews."

How much to say? Cole wondered. "Well, it was interesting. I had one bad interview, one maddening interview, one awesome interview, and one . . . let's just say it's an intriguing possibility."

"Okay, tell me about the awesome one first."

"It was with CompuLive."

"I use them every day! I've got chats with my students, my family back home, and the girls from the restaurant the other night."

"Well, they really want me. They like my website—"

"There's a lot to like."

This made Cole blush and lose his train of thought. "Anyway," he said, trying to regain his composure, "they want me to finish my degree, then come on board after graduation."

"That's cool. Where are they located?"

"California, I think," Cole said, realizing that he never asked where they would want him to move to.

"Oh, out west. Very beautiful."

"Yeah, I guess. But enough about my day. How about yours?" Cole said, trying to change the subject.

"I watched as ninth-graders threw eggs off the roof of our school. It was a massacre!" Savannah laughed. "Like an unborn-chicken horror movie. Yoke everywhere!"

Cole laughed too. It felt good. He felt at ease with her.

"How long have you been teaching?" he asked.

"Two years. I'm not as smart as you, but I did graduate college a year early."

"So, you're . . . what, twenty-three?"

"Yes, twenty-three and free!" she said, throwing her arms in the air like she was dancing in the rain.

This girl is amazing, Cole thought.

"You said one of your interviews was intriguing," Savannah said, snapping Cole out of his reverie.

"Yeah, it wasn't really an interview, but more of a chance encounter."

"So, what happened?"

"I kinda met someone by accident, and he made me an interesting offer," he replied, trying not to be evasive but remaining vague at the same time.

"Some people believe there's no such thing as coincidences. What do you think about that?"

"Um . . . I've always felt you make your own luck. Let me ask you," he said, trying to redirect the conversation, "how did you decide to be a teacher?"

"Well, I've always loved children, and I really do like science. I guess you put the two together and—boom—you have a natural-born educator."

"I wish I had your passion and direction," Cole said. "I mean, I'm passionate about technology and my website, but I feel like my future is an octopus—just tentacles feeling for opportunities all over the place. I don't have that singular focus that seems to drive you. A prime directive if you will."

Savannah smiled. "I wouldn't worry about that, Cole," she said sympathetically. "You're smart and you have vision. My dad always says," shifting into an exaggerated impersonation of a fatherly voice, 'Savannah, sometimes passion and employment don't collide for years, and it happens for different people at different times and in different ways.'" Then she looked into Cole's eyes and said, "I guess when something comes along that you really like and that makes you excited, you'll know it. It will fit and just click with who you are. Until then, just take a chance and do what feels right in the moment."

Cole couldn't tell if she was talking about his career options or if she was urging him to make a move on her. Either way, what she said made sense to him. Of all the options that were presented to him today, the only one that kept swimming about in his mind was Mr. King and his unique business card. Maybe it was the intrigue of the unknown or just the strangeness of it all, but he was drawn to it.

He decided: He was going to the meeting. He also decided that he liked the girl.

"Thanks," Cole said, reaching his hand across the table to grab hers.

"So, what are you going to do?" Savannah asked.

"I'm going to go for it."

And he leaned in and kissed her.

chapter

SEVEN

ole was still on cloud nine from the kiss a few hours later as he drove to Logan International Airport to meet Mr. King. The whole DRS thing was super weird, but he knew he wouldn't be able to let it go until he learned more. Savannah's pep talk about taking a chance was the best advice he'd heard so far.

When he pulled up to the gate for the private hangars, a security guard checked his ID, took down his license plate number, and asked if he was "packing heat." Cole laughed; the guard did not. Any jokes Cole considered making at the moment vanished quickly as he spotted a few more heavily armed guards taking notice of him.

"No, sir." Cole imagined a body cavity search, and his entire person clenched involuntarily.

After what seemed a stare-down eternity, he was permitted to proceed to hangar four. He could feel eyes, guns, and cameras trained on him, and a wave of anxiety about his decision to chase down this lead washed over him.

He had done everything he knew to do to find info about this company. But the more he searched, the more confused he got. The initials D.R.S. hadn't shown up anywhere on the net, although he did find a job listing for Director of Retail Services. He hoped it wasn't that. He was pretty sure it wasn't that.

He purposefully shifted his thoughts back to Savannah to calm himself down. He laughed thinking about a parking lot strewn with eggshells and yokes. It was all he could do not to turn around and head home to call her. Then he heard her voice say again, "Take a chance . . ."

He was slowly driving past taxiways and runways, looking for the right hangar, when he spied a faded number 4 on the side of one of the buildings. Two things made this hangar stand out from the rest: First, there was no outside lighting whatsoever, and second, the darkened structure seemed to suffer from decades of neglect, in stark contrast to the sharp, proud hangars around it where wealthy companies and private owners housed their sleek planes and jets.

Cole parked his car but didn't leave the Accord right away. He sat and thought and shook his head. *What am I doing? I could be accepting a great offer from CompuLive right now.* Then he laughed wryly and said aloud, "I guess I'll follow the strange man into the dark hangar. What's he going to do, sing me to death?"

He stepped out of the car and into the unknown.

There was only one door to hangar four. No sign. No lights. He turned the handle, not knowing what to expect. The door creaked open, complaining that it had not been used too often. Through the door was a dim hallway. Off to one side were a few rooms and nondescript offices that appeared to be filled with boxes and dust. At the end of the hall, light seeped out from under a closed door. Getting his bearings, Cole realized he had entered from the rear of the hangar. He opened the door into a cavernous room.

Hangar four was huge. Like empty Walmart huge. To his left, a spotlight shone on a small, black jet plane that looked like it had seen some action. Cole figured it probably seated no more than a handful of passengers. He could just barely make out a logo in a slightly lighter shade of black, almost like a shadow on the fuselage. The initials *D* on the left, *R* at the top, and *S* on the right, with a lightning bolt under them. Beneath the plane was a gleaming white floor that appeared to have just been scrubbed clean as though it had been disinfected for surgery.

In the middle of the hangar, another spotlight revealed a newer, larger plane, a magnificent private jet. Cole didn't know much about planes, but he knew this one could carry several people in style and was designed for substantial travel. Near the rudder was the same DRS logo, faint like a watermark on paper. Like someone was hiding in plain sight.

To the right, with seemingly acres of square feet around it, yet another spotlight shone down on two plush, yellow patent-leather easy chairs and a matching sofa. In the chair to the left sat Mr. King, but he didn't look like a janitor anymore. He was wearing a beautifully tailored, deep-black suit that fit him like a glove. His shirt was a slightly lighter shade of black with a dark gray collar. His cufflinks were gunmetal-gray lightning bolts. His black boots were square-toed and possibly lizard-skin. And there was something different about his hair. Mr. King had a comb in one hand and was running it through his hair over and over, teasing it to add a little height. He was also wearing a pair of aviator-style sunglasses despite the late hour. No, he didn't look like a janitor. He looked like he had stepped straight out of a movie.

He motioned to the empty chair and asked Cole Denton to have a seat.

Cole suddenly felt underdressed and completely unprepared for what would happen next. He could feel his nerves tightening, though Mr. King sat as cool as the breeze flowing through the open hangar bay.

"I'm glad you showed up."

"I wasn't sure about coming, to be honest, Mr. . . . . King?"

"You can still call me that, if you'd like."

"You know, 'Mr. King,' I might have spent a few hours trying to look you up today. There are no records of you at MIT, or the company that contracts out custodial work on campus. And here you are in a suit that probably costs more than a year's salary sweeping floors at a college."

Mr. King chuckled. "You should see my closet."

They were silent for the next few moments, each taking the measure of the other. Finally, Mr. King spoke.

"Cole, I know you don't know much about this job I'm offering."

"Job? Are you sure this isn't *Candid Camera*?"

Mr. King took off his glasses and looked him in the eyes, and Cole once again couldn't shake the feeling that he knew the face.

He had thought extensively about his earlier interaction with the janitor, but this felt different. The older man wasn't trying to impress, but he wasn't trying to put Cole at ease either. It almost felt like they were father and son, about to have a grown-up conversation about something neither of them really wanted to talk about.

"Are you about to tell me about the birds and bees, Mr. King? 'Cause I never had that talk with my dad," Cole said, trying to break the tension.

"Jim Denton didn't teach you much, did he?"

Cole flashed red. Uncomfortable. Embarrassed. Known. It was time for him to go on the offensive. "Yeah, yeah, you know about my family. Whatever. It's a sad story.

Pops liked the bottle, and he liked to hit Mom. It's about the worst country song you can imagine. Unlike DRS, anyone can find out about Cole Denton in a few clicks and a couple of phone calls."

Mr. King gave a comforting and empathetic look. "Family is important. It's part of the reason I am here tonight, with you. I'm asking you to join my family."

"Wait a second . . . this isn't one of those *Heaven's Gate*, chase-a-comet-while-wearing-a-jumpsuit kinds of family, is it? If I wanted that, I could have just worked for Apple."

"Not a cult. Just a family. A family that saves the world."

This rattled Cole. "Saves the world? Mr. King, what are you talking about?"

Mr. King reached into an ice chest next to his chair and grabbed two bottles of Black Cherry Shasta. "Would you like some Shasta?"

"How about Jack Daniels?" Cole was certain he might need some liquid courage for what he was about to hear.

"Sorry, Cole, none of that here. Some of our family has had a rough go with dependency issues. Hard living can take its toll."

"I'm sorry. I didn't know," Cole said, feeling like he should apologize one moment, then the next feeling miffed that he should be held responsible for offending someone whose "family" he knew nothing about.

Mr. King took a few swigs, sat back, and exhaled. "Where to begin? Cole, you're about to peek behind the curtain of a world you never knew existed. I promise, you will never see things the same again. Are you ready?"

There was a sincerity and seriousness to his tone that made Cole lean in and desperately want to know whatever it was that brought him out to an airfield in the middle of the night with two planes and a sharp-dressed man.

Cole nodded.

Mr. King began. "The DRS is a covert organization created to protect the world from all the things that could end it. No one knows we exist, let alone that any of us is still alive."

"So . . . let me guess. You chase the things that go bump in the night?"

"No. We *are* the things that go bump in the night. The things no one wants to believe. We are everywhere and nowhere. We have kept this country—this world—safe in one way or the other since 1865."

Cole couldn't move, couldn't think, as though he were watching an accident scene on the interstate. He just couldn't look away.

"Cole, you know your way around the internet like no one else. Did it bother you that you couldn't find anything about us? Almost like we had been scrubbed from the World Wide Web?"

Cole didn't answer. He just sat, waiting for more.

"I know you were born in Troy, Illinois, one year after I 'died.'" Mr. King used his fingers to make air quotes.

Cole was born in 1978. He was getting more uncomfortable by the moment.

"I know you grew up on your own, that your brains come from your father's side of the family, but your mom's side was the stable one. I know his drinking destroyed your family and brought tragedy upon you."

Cole tried to say something but could not. He stared at the ground now, unable to look Mr. King in the eye.

"I know you hate talking about the past and love the idea of the future. I know your algorithm is a thing of genius and that you put the work in to make sure it was solid gold. One for sixty-five, right?"

At this point, Cole was just numb.

Mr. King continued. "Your ideas about the future have caught the attention of some high-level thinkers in the tech world. You are an up-and-coming rock star, kid."

Before Cole could begin to contemplate what was about to be offered, an alarming thought came to mind. He remembered the year, the hair, and the voice.

He blurted, "Who are you, really?"

"I was born in Tupelo, grew up in Memphis, and people really do call me the King."

"NO."

"Yes."

"No-no-no-no-no-no. No no, no no no. Impossible. You're—"

"Elvis Aaron Presley."

Cole felt faint. He squinted. He looked at the outfit. He looked at his hair. He tried to imagine what Elvis Presley would look like if he were still alive after twenty-plus years. As he tried to process the possibility, a tall and thin African American man with a salt-and-pepper baby afro wearing a sleek Adidas jumpsuit strolled into the hangar.

"Hey, Jimi!"

"King."

Jimi Hendrix strutted over to the twin-engine jet and leaned against a wing. He was fifty-six years old, but he still had it. He patted the plane like it was his dog. "Izabella is ready to fly when you are, King. Tell me, has the kid said yes yet?"

"We haven't got to the asking yet, Jimi. Nice jumpsuit."

"Thanks, man. At my age, comfort rules the day."

Cole looked at the jumpsuit and then back at Mr. King.

Elvis said, "The jumpsuit was Jimi's choice. I swear, we're not a cult."

"Wait a second. Is that supposed to be Jimi Hendrix?"

"It's not supposed to be. It is."

"You hiding Kurt Cobain somewhere? What about Biggie and Tupac?"

Elvis laughed and looked at Jimi. "If I hear Kurt talk about how talented he thinks that Foo Fighter is one more time . . ."

"You have got to be kidding me." Cole went pale and felt lucky he was sitting down. His head was spinning.

"Cole. There is more to this than you can ever imagine. We are the DRS—the Dead Rock Stars. We protect the world as we see need. We report to no government. We have died to save lives."

"Why? Where did this come from? Whose idea was this? How do you fund it? How do people not know? Why are you talking to *me*?"

"All great questions. I can answer some of them tonight. The rest will have to wait."

"Let's start with why and how," Cole said frantically, his head still spinning.

"The why shouldn't be a surprise. There is wrong in the world. Sometimes governments can't see it soon enough to stop it. Sometimes, politics get in the way of protecting the innocent. This was something our founder knew. On occasion, legend is more powerful than reality. A legacy creates freedom to operate outside the boundaries of governments and politics. Someone reached out to us and recruited us, just like you're being recruited now. A few of us needed a shot at redemption, a chance to really make a difference beyond mere fame. Our untimely 'deaths' made us legends, and legend made for substantial income and the freedom to live apart from who we were on stage. The DRS gave us a fresh start. It sounds crazy, but it's true."

"Who recruited *you*?"

"Buddy Holly."

"Wait, he's—" Then Cole remembered who he was talking to.

"Holly was a game changer. Prior to him, this group was mainly made up of former politicians."

Cole shook his head, trying to make sense of what he was hearing. "How did this all begin?"

"The organization was originally formed by Abraham Lincoln. He found a Latin phrase that described what he hoped to accomplish: *Debeo Redeo Schola.* DRS. Roughly translated, it means "Morally bound to return as elite soldiers." Lincoln saw a world that was constantly at war with itself, and he knew something drastic needed to be done. His first attempt to address this need was to create the Secret Service; Abe did love his secrets. But something more was needed. He finally decided he could be of better use to the government and the United States if he were dead rather than alive. His death would galvanize the country, bring the people back together after the war. The assassination of a president created legend, mystery. Meanwhile, as one who knew the secrets of the world, and knew what was needed, he could operate more freely from the shadows. So he faked his death in 1865 and started the DRS."

Cole swooned in his chair, as Elvis continued to unspool the story.

"Working behind the scenes, the DRS helped to safeguard liberty through a second industrial revolution and two world wars. But the 1950s created a new era of uncertainty. The nuclear age was upon us, and new cultural influences were changing the world as we knew it. Music, radio, record players, and television were becoming commonplace in homes around the world. The DRS noticed the shift and began recruiting people from the world of entertainment to step out of the spotlight and serve mankind in much greater ways.

"They saw the future. Soon it would be rock stars, not presidents, who held sway over the hearts of the people. That kind of celebrity and fame could bring about influence and funding far exceeding anything the death of a politician had done. Buddy Holly was one of the first. Honestly, he saved me. The truth is, many of us had abuse and addiction in our lives. We had lost who we were. We were changing the world with our music, but the lifestyle was killing us at the same time. Trying to be larger than life meant our lives grew out of control. I had drifted so far away from who I was that I was gone years before I died. Dying on the toilet was my idea, by the way. The King on his throne—funny and poetic at the same time."

Elvis seemed almost wistful as he described the secret society, he was recruiting Cole to join.

"In the eighties, I became the leader of the DRS, and we began calling ourselves the Dead Rock Stars. The DRS had given many of us a second chance at life. Man, some of us *had* to die. We had to give up that life to get clean. We all loved singing and performing, and for the most part, none of us have stopped. We just don't do it for the glory or a paycheck now; we do it for our souls. We're a family now. A family more secret than any black ops force. These men and women have fought and bled and worked hard—some died for real—to help keep the world safe for everyone else. We are constantly training and developing skills and tools that allow us to serve the world in this way."

Cole rocked backwards in his yellow chair. "So . . . you want *me* to be a dead rock star?"

"Yes."

"But I'm not a rock star, I'm not dead, and I don't get why any of this has anything to do with me. I'm just a computer geek." Suddenly, he had a thought—maybe a perfect solution. "Hey, I know! What if I just sort of serve as a consultant for you guys? Like your IT Geek Support Squad? Then I can, you know . . . stay alive."

Elvis smiled. "Man, you sound like Jim Morrison right now. I wish it were possible, but I'm afraid it's all or nothing. We have to die to protect the ones we love. Our enemies are vast and well informed. If they knew who we were, or who you were, your entire world would be at risk. Dying disconnects us from our lives to protect the people we love the most. I know it's not fair. But if you care about Savannah, this is the best thing you can do to keep her safe."

"How do you know about—"

"We know."

Cole felt nauseated. He never thought when his opportunity came to help the world, it would mean having to leave it.

"Okay, so why me?"

"In the same way there was a shift in the fifties, I'm watching one now. It's arrived much sooner than I expected. The world is changing, and the future is now. Some real George Jetson stuff. I've been watching you. We've been watching a lot of young talent. Everyone hates the Sean Parker kid, Gates is all brains and no physical ability, and Steve Jobs wears black turtlenecks. Do I need to say more about them?"

"You want a rock star . . . from the *tech world*?"

"Something is coming, Cole. And we aren't prepared. Modern warfare is becoming less about fists and bullets and bombs. It's all about ones and zeros. Cole, I'm sixty-four years young. The Big Man upstairs has been good to me—better than I deserve. I love computers, and I love what they can do, but I don't understand how they do it. We need someone on our team who is a technology expert. Buddy Holly was a good man. My best friend. He had done his best to move us into the twenty-first century, but he's gone now."

"What do you mean, 'he's gone now'?"

56

"I mean, he died for real this time. Someone killed him. I am trying to understand who and why. There's someone coming for us. I think they know about the DRS. They're already a few steps ahead of us, and that puts the whole world at risk. We need someone to help us stop this new threat. Cole, you've been searching your whole life for significance. Website dating is a great way to help lonely people. But I think you're more than that. I think you're able to see the future before most people, and I believe you can help us."

Cole thought about the many times he had said and heard the phrase, "I'm speechless." He finally knew what it felt like. After a long silence, he stammered, "What am I supposed to say to all this?"

"Cole, I am asking you to die. I'm asking you to give up your life, your future, and the possible millions—shoot, maybe even billions—you could make being a love connection guru or being at the forefront of the next Microsoft or Apple. I'm asking you to give up Savannah in order to protect her. I'm also giving you a chance to make a very real difference in the world. To save it."

Elvis leaned back in his seat. "Tell you what: I'll give you thirty-six hours to imagine your future with us. If you choose to accept it, meet me back here, and this jet will take you to a new life. Of course, if you choose to stay, we'll have to wipe your brain."

"What?"

Elvis laughed. "Relax, Cole. I'm a funny guy."

I don't think he was joking about the brain wipe, Cole thought. He tried to get to his feet, and finally managed to stand upright.

"Mr. . . . King. It was nice to meet you. How can I know anything you just told me was real?"

"Thirty-six hours, Mr. Denton. I'll be watching and waiting."

Cole stumbled to his car outside the hangar, attempting to process all that he had just learned. He wondered what it would be like to be a secret agent. He wondered if he really had what it took to save the world. He never once thought about Compu-Live. He did, however, think a lot about Savannah. His mind flashed to what their future could look like. What their children might be like.

Then he had the most uncomfortable thought since meeting a couple of living dead men: *What if Elvis is right? What if there is no world left for us to have a future?*

chapter

EIGHT

On a Friday night Cole knew exactly where to find Dr. Self. He needed to talk this decision over with someone, and Self was the closest thing he had to a father. Dr. Self was a decent teacher, but turning to him as a father figure said much about how Cole was lacking in the family department. Cole walked into the Toad, Self's favorite dive bar, and found him exactly where he had expected: seated at the bar and nursing a Sam Adams.

On stage, a local band was trying—loudly and gratingly—to combine traditional Irish music with heavy metal. Cole reached for his left ear, thankful to find that his eardrum hadn't burst.

As if catching his scent, Self turned, spotted Cole, and shouted a slurred, "Padawan!"

Cole waved and walked over. "Can we go somewhere and talk?" he yelled over the band.

"Yeah, sure!" Self was wearing sunglasses indoors, though it was nearly midnight. He wore a neatly trimmed salt-and pepper-goatee and a spot-on Clooney Caesar haircut colored to match the beard. He wore light-gray jogging pants and a sweat-stained, oversized Everlast T-shirt, white with purple three-quarter-length sleeves. Cole rightly guessed that Self had come straight to the Toad from his kickboxing workout.

Self stood up unsteadily and motioned for Cole to follow him. They went down a back hallway to a door marked "Office." Inside was an overstuffed file cabinet, a desk, two chairs, a mini fridge, a Tyra Banks wall calendar, and a window with a neon PBR sign.

"Take a load off," Self said, clearing a stack of *Sports Illustrated* and *Maxim* magazines from the chair he was offering Cole. "What's up?"

Cole sat down, trying to give off as much "This is serious" vibe as he could muster. "I need some advice. I've been made an offer."

"Other than CompuLive? Did Apple come to their senses?"

"No." Cole was searching for the words to explain what he had been offered, without going into detail. "Unfortunately, it's proprietary, and I can't tell you who it's with. But it's big. Bigger than I could have ever imagined."

"Ohhh…" Self nodded, feigning like he knew what was really going on. "Give me more!" Self pantomimed pulling on a rope to drag Cole closer.

"Well, it's like a government job, but not." Cole immediately regretted making this comparison because all Self would hear was the word "government."

"No, no, no, no!" Self belched, wagging a finger at Cole. The good doctor wasn't a fan of the government. Not quite a believer in black helicopter conspiracy theories, but not far off. "No pupil of mine is working for the government. Is it the CIA? It's the CIA, right? They want you to weaponize computer viruses and stuff, am I right?"

"No, Dr. Self, it's not the CIA. I swear," Cole said, trying very hard to be reassuring. "I really need your help here. Other than your bias against the government, why shouldn't I take this job? It's the chance of a lifetime."

"The government will screw you up. It'll chew you up and spit you out. Don't take this job, son." Self was trying very hard to be paternal. He rambled for the next hour while nearly wiping out the contents of the mini fridge. He chased down several rabbit trails, but always managed to return to his warning that Cole run from anything that remotely seemed like working for the government.

Cole now knew he wouldn't receive any useful advice from Dr. Self. He listened patiently, pushing back on a few points, but ultimately sought to shift the conversation toward an exit. "All good points, Dr. Self, which I will give serious consideration to," he said, standing up to leave.

"Sit down, Love Shack, I'm not done," Self said. And he continued his anti-government rant.

Cole's eyelids started growing heavy, and his head began nodding until suddenly he jolted upright. He had fallen asleep, but Self hadn't noticed. While Cole was snoozing, Self had moved on from his diatribe against the government and was neck-deep into baring his soul about his many regrets in life.

"…it's what happens when you never hear your father say 'I love you,' you know, man?"

"Yeah, yeah, totally," Cole said, trying to wake up. "Listen, man, it's really late. I've had a long day, so I need to run."

"Yeah, okay. Well, thanks for listening, kid."

"Sure, anytime, Dr. Self." Cole said.

Suddenly, Dr. Self moved in for a very uncomfortable and lingering hug. Cole sensed that he was crying. *I guess he's a weepy drunk*, Cole thought.

"Okay, okay," Cole said, trying to wrestle himself free from the hug. "You need me to call you a cab?"

"No, I'm fine. Sully will take me home."

Of course Self knows a guy named Sully. "Okay, be careful, Dr. Self. Thanks for everything."

"Yeah, okay, get outta here man."

And Cole left. He hadn't really got what he was looking for, and it reminded him that he wished he had a real family he could lean on. The words of Elvis echoed in his head, "We're a family. . . ."

A family would be nice.

Back at his apartment, he found Taylor asleep on his couch. *Friday Night Videos* was playing on the TV. Weezer's "Buddy Holly" video was showing. Cole watched for a minute, long enough to see the Fonz dance the Kazotsky Kick, then he retired to his room without disturbing his roommate. His bed was calling.

✯ ✯ ✯ ✯

At 9:34 a.m., Cole walked into the kitchen and found that Taylor had already made a pot of coffee and was seated at the kitchen table in front of his laptop.

"Morning, night owl," Taylor said.

"Morning," Cole responded, pouring a cup of black coffee.

"Based on the 'aroma' coming off your clothes, you've either been to the Toad or taken up smoking. How *is* the good professor? Wait . . . you didn't take Savannah to meet Dr. Self, did you?" Taylor asked.

"What? No!" Cole laughed. He didn't want to talk about Savannah. He wanted to jump right to the thing that had kept him up all night.

"Listen, I need to run something by you."

Taylor could see the seriousness in Cole's expression. "What's up?"

"I got an . . . unexpected offer."

"She ask you to marry her?"

"No!" Cole exclaimed. "An unexpected *job* offer. Before you ask, I can't tell you the details. Just generalities."

"Cool. No details. This will be fun making things up in my head. Okay, go."

"It's big. Bigger than I ever dreamed. But there are drawbacks. . . ."

"Forget the drawbacks!" Taylor said excitedly. "If you're about to get paid, then take the paycheck and run with it. Don't look back in anger, my friend!"

"Very funny." Just then, it occurred to Cole that he hadn't asked about how much he would be paid. "It's a job that would be really significant. Like world-changing significance."

"Dude, go change the world. That's awesome. I'm happy for you. But for reals, you're getting your cheddar, right? Gonna get paaaaaaaid!"

"Look, I get it. But mo' money, mo' problems."

Taylor shrugged, knowing this circular argument would only circle round again. He asked a few more questions that Cole really couldn't answer but wanted to very much.

Finally, Taylor looked Cole in the eye and said, "Listen, man, without knowing a whole bunch, I do know you've always wanted to make a difference. If this allows you to be you and still do that, I don't see how you can say no."

Cole grabbed his friend and gave him a hug.

"Bro, that's long enough. You smell like a literal toad."

Cole headed to the shower, knowing he had one more hurdle to clear.

★ ★ ★ ★

"Hi, Cole! I'm so glad you called. I've been wondering how your mystery meeting went." Savannah sounded excited to hear from him.

"Yeah . . . about that . . . I need to talk to you. It's, uh, really important."

"Oh. Okay. Is everything all right?"

"I got offered the job."

"Cole, that's wonderful."

"Yeah, but it comes with a catch. If I take this job, I will have to go away."

"Like, Silicon Valley?"

"No, I mean . . . I don't know how to explain it. I would have to pretty much walk away from everything. My entire life."

"Why? What kind of job makes you have to leave everything?"

"I . . . I–I can't really explain it. It's, well . . . it's like the CIA . . . but it's not the CIA."

"So, what are you saying?"

"You told me to follow my dreams. You told me to go for it. I need your help figuring out what to do."

"Wait. Let me get this straight. You want me to help you decide if you should take a job you can't explain? A job that would mean walking away from everything you know?"

"Yeah, that's pretty much it."

"That's a lot to ask, Cole."

"I know."

"Would you have to walk away from me? From us?"

Cole couldn't bring himself to say the words. He was silent for a long time.

Then he said it.

"Yeah."

"How am I supposed to respond? You're putting me in an impossible spot. If I say go for it, I lose you. If I say stay, you don't get to chase your dream. Why would you even ask me this?" The anger in Savannah's voice was growing.

"I . . . I don't have anyone else to ask."

"Why don't you ask your algorithm? It seems to be able to answer every other question for you. Did it match you up with this job?!"

That stung.

"Don't hang up, Savannah. Please don't hang up!" Cole begged.

Silence.

"Savannah? Are you still there?"

"Yes."

"I'm sorry to put you in this position. I never meant to hurt you. I'm . . . I'm sorry that . . . that I made you cry. I never wanted to hurt you."

"Wait . . . Cole, that's a song."

"It is?"

"You're an idiot," she said, laughing softly.

"I know."

They sat in silence for a long moment. Then Savannah spoke.

"What are you going to do?"

"Savannah, I don't want to lose you. But believe it or not . . . this is gonna sound weird . . . but if I don't take this job, I still might lose you—and a whole lot more. I know it's confusing and vague and all kinds of crazy. . . ."

"Well, I hardly know you . . . but I believe you. You just have really bad timing."

"I know. I'm sorry."

"Don't be sorry. I'm just glad we met."

"Me too."

"How will I know what decision you make?"

"Um, well . . . if you don't hear from me in the next twenty-four hours . . . I took it."

"Okay. Should we get together one more time before you decide?"

"I don't know if I could handle that. I think seeing you would make my decision for me. I want to be as clear-minded as I can be."

"Okay. I wish you could tell me everything about this."

"Me too, Savannah. Me too. I . . . I need to go."

"Okay. I don't know what to say to end this."

"Me neither."

Neither wanted to hang up, so they sat in more awkward silence.

Then Savannah said, "How about 'See you later'?"

"I wish I could say that."

"Me too. How about 'So long'?" She didn't want to say the word *goodbye*.

"Okay. So long, Savannah."

"So long, Cole."

★ ★ ★ ★

His eyes were filled with tears as he drove. His CD of John Lennon's *Imagine* was playing on repeat. He stopped at a used bookstore and bought a copy of the Bible. He then drove to the Madonna Queen of the Universe shrine overlooking East Boston and Logan International. He had never been here before. Cole wasn't necessarily religious, and he definitely wasn't Catholic, but he felt like maybe he should reach out to a higher power for help with this decision.

Staring up at the statue of Mary, he prayed, "God . . . it's me. Cole Denton. I know I haven't talked to you much—ever—but I need some help. What should I do?

I want to make a difference. I think you probably put that . . . that longing in me. To help. To find significance. Is this how I do it? Is this how I make a difference in the world, by walking away from everything and everyone?"

He paused. He thought about it from every angle he could think of. Then the words of Elvis came back to him: "We have to die to protect the ones we love."

In front of the shrine to Mary was a statue of Jesus, standing before the cross with His arms raised as if to say, "Come to me." Cole thumbed through the Bible he had purchased. It was a well-worn Bible. The inside cover said that it used to belong to a person named Mary Smith. The pages were yellowed with age and possibly water damage. Then he spotted a passage that was underlined. It read:

Greater love hath no man than this, that a man lay down his life for his friends.

Cole looked up at the statue of Jesus. He stood in front of the cross for a long time. Pondering. Praying.

As the sun began to set, he watched the planes landing and taking off from the airport. He didn't know if he had the courage to do what he needed to do. He walked back to his car and started it up. He switched the radio to the oldies station. Paul McCartney was singing "Let It Be," the Beatles' final single before he announced he was leaving the band. There had been much debate about whether Paul was singing about his own late mother, Mary, or the mother of Christ comforting him with words of wisdom.

Either way, Cole knew his answer.

As hard as it was going to be, all signs pointed to one thing.

To truly live, he would have to die.

chapter

NINE

"**H**olly was not supposed to die. You were just supposed to incapacitate him," the voice on the other end of the line yelled. The voice was distorted, but its tone was unmistakable. "And after everything we've done for you. . . ."

"I don't know what happened, Boss!" Langston pleaded. "I guess my guys were just a little too amped up. But Elvis . . ."

"Yes. Elvis. He mopped the floor with your team, and you crapped your pants."

"You don't know what he can do. You've never seen him up close. He fights like something out of *Mortal Kombat*."

"Oh, I know what he can do. Nevertheless, I want him dealt with. Do you understand? Dealt with!"

"Yes, s-sir," Langston sputtered. "It–it won't happen again. I'll get it right this time."

"You'd better. You will be receiving further instructions soon. Do not fail us again."

The line clicked, and a dial tone droned in Langston's ear. He hung up the phone and took a deep breath.

Jason "Bull" Langston had started out as a petty criminal. He and his high school buddies got their kicks shoplifting and committing burglaries in their small hometown of Dyer, Tennessee. Working their way up to robbing rural banks and committing mail fraud, they were racking up a rap sheet that was equal parts sizable and pathetic. After one heist gone wrong, they found themselves in police custody.

While sitting in lockup, Langston got a call. "It's your attorney," the cop had said. Langston was understandably puzzled. Not only did he not have a lawyer, but who in their right mind would take him on as a client?

The voice on the line was electronically distorted. "Today is your lucky day, Jason."

"Who is this?" Langston asked.

"Your salvation," the voice answered. "We will pay bail for you and your accomplices and get the FBI off your trail. Then you will come work for us. How does that suit you?"

"The FBI is on our trail?"

"You've been robbing banks. Yes, the FBI is on to you."

"Well, you just tell me what to do, and we'll do it," Langston said, shaken by the FBI revelation.

"We will come and get you out. Just comply and play it cool."

A few hours later, a smartly dressed blonde woman they had never seen before showed up and paid their bail, then took them to a small private airport. They all boarded the plane and were gone.

For the next two years, Langston and his crew were given room and board in a barracks situated in what might otherwise be described as a summer camp from a 1980s horror movie. The facility was home to a few dozen other underachieving criminals with similar backgrounds, many of whom came and went. Here, for the first time in their lives, Langston and his buddies found purpose and meaning. They now belonged to something that was bigger than themselves. They trained to use computers, handle explosives, and wield various types of weaponry. On top of that, they learned the right way to do things that came natural to them—sowing chaos and destruction.

This was the way of the Brotherhood: find low-level hoodlums, social outcasts at the end of their rope. Indoctrinate them. Train them. Give them a place to belong. Then own them for the rest of their lives.

Two years later, Langston and his men were sent back into the world as Brotherhood operatives. They regularly met in public settings with strangers who would hand them their instructions on floppy disks. At first their assignments involved simple tasks like retrieving packages from airport lockers and dropping them off in what seemed like random, insignificant locations. Eventually, the jobs increased in scope and responsibility, what Langston and his friends called Robin Hood missions. Sometimes these tasks involved coordinating with others to smuggle people and equipment from Mexico and Cuba across the border to the U.S. These kinds of assignments gave Langston the thrill he got from his previous life of petty crime, but now he had a purpose.

After a dozen successful missions, he was given charge of a team. He led excursions to Mexico and the Caribbean, flying small planes into private airports, completing one or more simple tasks, then flying out again in secret. Often these missions seemed rather innocuous, such as delivering food to poverty-stricken regions or smuggling out people identified as political prisoners. But Langston didn't ask questions; he just did what he was told. He would then log in to a CompuLive message board called Equal=Equal to get further instructions.

After six months of running these missions for the Brotherhood, Langston started getting calls from the person with the distorted voice, the one he called Boss. Langston didn't know this person's name or anything else, but he liked to think this was the one in charge of everything. It was at this stage that his assignments started getting . . . weird. He would be tasked with transferring duffel bags or cardboard boxes full of files from one hotel to another. He would be sent to observe and report on things like Elvis impersonator contests and karaoke nights. Langston had no idea *why* he was doing the things he was doing, but he wanted to believe that they were contributing to a greater cause. So he did them dutifully, if sometimes sloppily.

Finally, the Boss dropped the bombshell on him. He received an email that read:

Go to Vegas. A duffel bag will be awaiting you in your rental car. Take it to the Elvis Presley Suite at the Las Vegas Hilton. There you will be met by the singers Buddy Holly and Elvis Presley. They are the real thing, not imposters. Both men are extremely dangerous. They will try to stop you. Whatever you do, do not engage Presley. Just incapacitate Holly. This is the most important task you have ever performed for the Brotherhood. Follow these orders to the letter. Go in peace, my brother.

Langston couldn't believe what he was reading. He responded to the email, saying, "You saved my life. You know I will do anything for the cause, but this is the weirdest thing you've ever given me to do. How does this help change the world?"

The reply came back: "More than you will ever know. These men are against everything we stand for."

Since bungling the mission in Vegas, Langston and his men had been doing nothing but collecting parking tickets, listening to Cypress Hill, and playing video games. Then the call came.

"There was a man who had close ties to Presley. He died recently. Surveil his home in Madison, Tennessee, and collect all the data you can on his estate. Account numbers, tax records, anything you can find."

There was a brief pause, then one more piece of information.

"Our enemies may find out about what you are doing. If someone confronts you, do not hesitate to take drastic action. You will not be spared by them. Tell them nothing. It is better for you to die than to reveal anything you know about the Brotherhood. Go in peace."

Langston had no idea what to do with this information. It didn't make any sense, but he was a committed believer. The Brotherhood was everything to him, and he would do as he was told—even if it meant his life.

chapter
TEN

As instructed, Cole returned to hangar four thirty-six hours later.

Elvis was there waiting for him. The King grinned.

"I'm guessing since you came back your answer is yes?"

"Mr. King . . ."

"Come on man, you know who I am. Just call me Elvis. Or King or E. Anything but Mr. King. You were saying?"

"Um, yeah, Mister . . . er, E . . . I mean, King. I'm in. I think this is the life I've always wanted."

"Good," Elvis said warmly. "Let's rock and roll!"

"Yessir!" Cole said, saluting.

Elvis looked up in the cockpit of the plane and saw Jimi laughing. Elvis chuckled. "You don't salute, man. This isn't the military."

Cole boarded while trying not to pass out. "Welcome aboard Izabella. It's Jimi's pride and joy."

Just then, it occurred to him. "Uh, Elvis. I don't have any clothes. Or anything else, for that matter. And what about my car?"

Elvis threw him a full duffle bag with Cole's name embroidered on it. "We got you covered," he said with a wink and a smile.

Cole didn't know where he was going or what came next, but he was very excited. A little sad but mostly excited. Elvis motioned to one of the seats, and Cole sat down. Elvis went to the cockpit and sat down next to Jimi. The plane taxied out to the runway, and they were cleared for takeoff. Within minutes they were in the air.

Cole's head was spinning. *What did I just do?* This was simultaneously the most exciting and scariest thing he'd ever done. He watched out the window as Boston disappeared below. The city had been his home for seven years, and everyone in the world he cared for was there.

Elvis finally came back and sat down next to Cole. "I know this is going to be hard to understand at first, so you're just going to have to trust me at every turn. Got it?"

"Yeah, I'm cool." Cole nodded. His shaky voice sounded anything but cool.

"We're going to have to stage your death. How does a plane crash sound to you?"

"O-kay?"

"We also need to make a pit stop," Elvis said with a smirk. "We have to kiss the ring."

Elvis abruptly stood up and returned to the copilot's seat. He put the headset on and began saying pilot-y things. Cole was dizzy from processing everything, so he didn't really pay any mind to what Elvis was saying.

"Ground control, this is the King, you read me down there?"

"Go, King," crackled a voice on the radio.

"I'm coming down, and I have the package. We need to visit the Prez. Can you be there to pick us up?"

"Sure thing."

"Thank you. Thank you very much," Elvis said with exaggerated gusto. "They don't call him Kurt for nothing," Elvis said, smirking at Jimi. "Buckle in, kid," he yelled back to Cole. "We're going down!"

The words "going down" snapped Cole back into reality.

"I thought you said we would *stage* my death. We're not crashing for real, are we?"

Elvis heartily laughed, but Cole noticed he didn't answer the question. Cole fastened his seatbelt and pulled it as tightly as he could, as Jimi tipped the nose of the plane downward into a steep nosedive. The altimeter spun furiously as the plane rapidly descended. Cole gripped the armrests so tightly he thought he might tear them off. He looked out the window and saw trees below approaching at a speed he was decidedly uncomfortable with.

"Is this how it always happens?" Cole hollered at Elvis, hoping for any sign that this was not really happening.

"Nah, man! We haven't done a plane crash since the seventies!"

"Huh? Why . . . what?"

"Just take it easy, man. We got this under control."

Cole thought he might throw up any second. *I'm going to die in a plane crash, he thought. Nothing this guy told me was true. He's an imposter.*

Then the trees parted, and Cole saw a landing strip emerge.

Jimi gently rocked the yoke back and leveled the plane into a normal descent.

Elvis turned to look at Cole and started laughing hysterically. "I'm sorry, man," he cackled. "I just had to. You're white as a ghost!"

"I nearly tossed my cookies all over your nice plane," Cole said with much relief.

"Glad you didn't," Jimi said, breaking his silence.

"You should've seen Cobain when we did the same thing to him," Elvis said, still laughing. "I think he almost got religion!"

Cole's heart rate slowed to near normal as Jimi skillfully touched the plane down as though it were a feather. A car was waiting for them on the remote airstrip. It was a blue 1970 Mustang Mach 1 with a black racing stripe down the side. A slender man in his early thirties, with shoulder-length blonde hair hanging in his eyes, was leaning against the car and smoking a cigarette. He wore faded jeans and a plain white T-shirt. He had a rope necklace and a guitar pick in his left hand.

"Cole Denton, meet Kurt Cobain," Elvis said.

"Hey," Cobain said coolly, extending his right hand.

In his excitement and confusion, Cole raised up his right hand and did his awkward fingers-only wave. When he realized Cobain was offering to shake hands, he brought his hand down to shake just as Cobain brought his hand up for what appeared to be a high five. Cole met his hand halfway up and they ended up in a strange, midair handshake that looked more like they were arm wrestling. The awkwardness of the moment brought to mind his first date with Savannah just a few days earlier, and he felt a deep, sudden pang of sadness.

"Yeah, okay." Cobain turned his back on Cole and said to Elvis, "This is him, huh?"

"Yes. He's agreed to take Buddy's place."

"Okay," Cobain replied coldly, clearly unconvinced. Then looking at Cole, he asked, "Can you play?"

"What, music? I played trumpet in high school. I can do the 'Ring of Fire' intro. I bet Johnny Cash will love that!"

"He's not dead!" Cobain said with undisguised disdain.

71

"Sorry," Cole said, withering with embarrassment.

"Cool it, Kurt!" The tone of the King's voice let Cobain know it was time to back off. "I need to take him to see the president."

"I get to meet Clinton?" Cole asked excitedly, snapping out of his embarrassment. "He knows about you guys and all this stuff you do?"

"You'll see," Elvis said with a smile.

"Get in," Jimi said, taking the Mustang keys from Cobain.

Elvis got in the front seat on the passenger side, and Cole and Cobain slid into the back. He tried to lean forward to hear what Elvis and Jimi were talking about over the roar of the V-8 engine. Cobain just stared at him in disbelief.

"What kinda tunes y'all want to listen to?" Jimi asked. He reached over Elvis and opened the glove box. Several 8-track tapes came tumbling out.

"Eight-tracks!" Cole exclaimed, with genuine excitement. "We used to listen to these in my mom's Pinto!"

"Pinto?" Jimi said with disgust. Cole would later learn that Jimi Hendrix was the best wheelman the Dead Rock Stars had, and he had no use for inferior automobiles.

"Let's listen to this," Elvis said, handing Jimi the Rolling Stones' *Sticky Fingers*. "Track four."

Jimi inserted the cartridge in the tape player and punched up track four. "Can't You Hear Me Knocking" came blaring out of a state-of-the-art sound system that clearly was not part of the original equipment. A tingle ran up Cole's spine as Keith Richards's opening riff played to the evident approval of Jimi Hendrix, Kurt Cobain, and Elvis Presley. It was like a scene out of a movie.

This is my life now, Cole thought.

The Mustang pulled out of the private airport and jumped on Highway 29 towards Silver Spring, Maryland. They were just out for a drive. No disguises. No cover. Fully exposed to the world. This caused Cole to wonder aloud, "How do you guys just drive around and not get noticed? You're not even trying to hide who you are."

"We're dead," Elvis said with a shrug. "You ever check out at a grocery store and see those tabloids with the headline, 'Woman Spots Elvis at Shopping Mall'?"

"Yeah, all the time."

"At least half of the time they're telling the truth." Elvis laughed. "But the world believes beyond a shadow of a doubt that we're dead, so nobody bats an eye when someone sees us in public. Our death certificates and coroner's notes are a matter of public record."

"Amazing." Cole shook his head in awe.

"Even the editors at the *National Enquirer* don't even believe we're alive. The stories just help them sell papers."

This made sense to Cole. People pretty much believe what they're told. When the world *knows* that a famous person is dead, the suggestion that he or she is really alive is considered preposterous. Dead is dead. Cole chuckled at the absurd genius of it all.

As they continued down the highway, they passed a police officer standing on the side of the road with a radar gun. Cole glanced at the speedometer and saw that Jimi was indeed speeding. Cole looked behind and saw that the cop had jumped on his motorcycle, threw on his lights, and was chasing after them.

Jimi calmly glanced in his rearview mirror, carefully pulled over to the shoulder of the road, then casually rolled down his window. Cole started sweating as the police officer pulled in behind them and started making his way toward the Mustang.

"What are we going to do?" Cole whispered loudly, trying to contain his panic.

"Relax," Elvis said with way more confidence than Cole was comfortable with.

"Relax? How can I relax? The freaking T-1000 is right behind us!"

"Afternoon, gentlemen," the officer said, peering into the car. "License and registration, please."

Jimi pulled out his wallet and handed the license over. Elvis opened the glove box, and the same 8-tracks came tumbling out. He fished out the registration and passed it to Jimi, who passed both items to the police officer.

Cole thought everyone in the car was acting entirely too calm. *This is how the whole operation gets busted—and on my first day on the job!*

The police officer examined Jimi's ID then leaned into the window.

"Mr. Klinefelter, do you have any idea how fast you were going?"

"Yes, sir," Jimi said. "I was hitting right about sixty-six."

"You do realize this is a fifty-five zone?"

"I'm sorry, officer," Jimi said, cool as a cucumber. "I thought it was a sixty-five. My bad."

The officer glanced around at everyone in the car. He stared at Cole the longest.

"You guys . . . what are you? Where are you trying to go? I recognize everyone but you," he said, pointing at Cole.

"Roadie," Elvis said with a smile. The officer chuckled and handed Jimi the license and registration.

"Look, I dig the outfits and the whole look you guys have going. I guess you're some kind of cross-generational impersonators' group or something. Just slow down, okay? You know, I do a mean Elvis impersonation, myself." The cop then started flailing his hips and singing "Teddy Bear"—kind of—like Elvis.

"You go, man!" Jimi encouraged him.

The officer stopped and laughed, "Takes me back. I loved all those guys. Darn shame what happened to this guy" he said, pointing a thumb at Kurt. "Could have been one of the all-time greats if he had his head on straight."

Kurt let out an audible groan.

"Anyway, you guys slow it down and be careful out there. Otherwise, I'll have to check you into the Heartbreak Hotel, huh?"

"You know it, man! We don't want to be doing the Jailhouse Rock!" Elvis said with more energy than necessary.

The officer gave out a hearty laugh, strolled back to his motorcycle, and went on his way.

Cole finally started breathing again. "I thought we were toast," he said. "How did we get out of that?"

"We're rock stars, baby" Jimi smirked. "The rules don't apply to us. Never have!"

Cole looked puzzled.

Elvis said, "We have all this covered, man. We have aliases and fake social security numbers. We have completely new identities for anything we need to do publicly. My street name is John Greedack."

"Mine is Howard Klinefelter," Jimi added.

It was becoming apparent that the rabbit hole Cole had entered was deeper than he knew. As Cole's heartbeat resumed its normal pace, Jimi pulled the car back on the road, and they continued their journey.

"What's your alias, Kurt?" Cole asked. Cobain just glared straight ahead, his face like stone.

"We'll get you all hooked up with that stuff soon," Elvis assured Cole. "Oh, and by the way, you're not dead yet. So if you run into anyone you know while we're out, it's okay to talk to them. You aren't scheduled to die for of couple of days yet."

When Elvis put it that way, the reality of it all began to set in for Cole in a different way. Maybe he should've said a few goodbyes. So many new questions popped into his mind, but before he could put them into words, the Mustang had reached its destination. Jimi had stopped in what looked to be a normal suburban neighborhood.

"I thought we were going to see the president," Cole asked.

"We are," Elvis replied.

Jimi pulled the car into a driveway and pressed the button on a device clipped to the visor. The garage door of what seemed like a very modest suburban home opened. Inside, there were shelves lined with half-used paint cans. A riding lawnmower, missing a wheel, sat in the corner. A fluorescent Bud Lite sign hung over a stolen 45-miles-per-hour street sign. Once the car was fully in the garage, Jimi again hit the button, and the garage door closed behind them. He did not turn off the car, however, which Cole felt was strange. Once the garage door was completely down, Elvis reached into his pocket and pulled out a green rabbit's foot keychain. He pressed the rabbit's foot, a large motor thrummed to life with the whirring of gears, and the Mustang began slowly descending to a subterranean level beneath the house. Once the elevator came to a stop, Jimi drove the car off the ramp and into a dark tunnel gaping before them. He turned his headlights on to reveal they were traveling through a narrow earthen passageway. It was shocking to Cole how tight the fit was, but his companions didn't bat an eye.

Jimi weaved skillfully through the tunnel, making a few turns along the way. Eventually the earthen walls gave way to concrete, and soon they emerged in a large, well-lit, military-style bunker. One other car was parked there, a 1961 Lincoln Continental. Jimi pulled up next to it, and the four men climbed from the vehicle.

"Stay here," Elvis said to Cole. "I'll come get you when he's ready." He then walked up a short flight of stairs and disappeared through another door.

Cole wasn't looking forward to more small talk with Kurt Cobain after the initial frosty reception he'd received. After several minutes, Jimi Hendrix broke the silence. "A trumpet player, huh?"

"Yeah, but I haven't played in years."

The silence hung awkwardly.

"Do you guys know how long this place has been here?" Cole asked.

"I don't know for sure, but it's at least since the 1870s," Jimi said nonchalantly. "Lincoln had it built. It's been retrofitted several times over the years."

"It's just so hard to believe. So much of the American history I learned in school is untrue," Cole said in wonder.

"You don't know the half of it," Jimi replied, shaking his head.

Just then, Elvis reappeared at the top of the stairs. "Cole, you can come up now."

"Wish me luck," Cole said to Jimi and Kurt. They nodded at him in return. He trudged up the stairs, feeling nervous but excited. He'd never met a president before. Until Friday, he'd never met a rock star either. Now he'd met three of the most famous of all time. *I guess I'd better get used to this*, he thought as he climbed the stairs.

75

"Don't be nervous, kid," Elvis said. "The Prez is excited to meet you."

Cole followed Elvis through the door and into what looked like a hospital waiting room. Two men were waiting there for them.

"Cole, this is Richie Valens," Elvis said. "He's been with us for a long time. For the last five years or so he's been off the road and living here working with the president. This here is Hank Williams. He was the guinea pig—the first musician to join this team way back in 1953. He retired a few years ago, too."

"Wow, it's an honor to meet you both!" Cole said. He vaguely knew who these men were, but he didn't know much about them. He knew that Valens was reportedly killed in the same "plane crash" as Buddy Holly and the Big Bopper because of the story behind the song "American Pie." Richie later told Cole that he and Buddy always joked that it was really the day they "came alive." He would confess he missed being in the field but had found great fulfillment in his current assignment. He also didn't miss getting shot at since retiring.

Hank Williams was nearly eighty years old. The Dead Rock Stars had helped many an older performer seemingly discover the fountain of youth, but after he'd spent more than forty years with the team, Elvis had convinced him to hang up his spurs. Hank would later tell Cole he had been "dead" for so long that he was able to fully reintegrate into society and live under his alias without notice. "We live hard, die young, then work long enough for everyone to forget us." Hank Williams carried an air of sadness about him. This was part of the bargain Cole had not considered: What happens when you get too old to serve?

Cole would later learn that, as the first musician to join the team, Hank wasn't allowed to do much until Buddy, Richie, and the Bopper came on board. The powers that be at the time had to be convinced that musicians could carry their weight. "The Four Horsemen," as they sometimes called themselves, were the pioneers of the new model in which the team would be primarily rock stars. Elvis's bringing Cole on board represented the first real shift in the makeup of the team in decades.

"So, you ain't a musician," Hank said, looking Cole up and down.

"No, sir. I am not."

"I don't care," Hank said with a wink. Then he leaned in closely and said, "I was the first of my kind, too. Go get 'em, son."

Cole would never forget these words of encouragement.

"Come on in here and meet the Prez," Elvis said.

"It was very nice to meet you both," Cole said to the two legends standing before him. Then he followed Elvis through metal double doors and into a posh hospital room. The carpet was a rich maroon and decorated with a golden crest woven into the center of the floor with the phrase *Debeo Redeo Schola* on it. The king-size bed was adorned with cream-colored silk sheets. A man in his early eighties was sitting up in the bed with the sheets turned down across his lap. He was wearing red silk pajamas and had a monogrammed golden silk handkerchief in his left breast pocket. The monogram read "JFK."

Of all the things Cole had seen the last few days, this was the hardest to believe. John F. Kennedy was alive and in league with this secret society of Dead Rock Stars. Cole felt weak in the knees, and he felt his ears starting to get hot. Stars swarmed his vision, and the blood drained from his head.

Thump! Cole went down like a sack of potatoes.

The next thing he knew, he was seated in the bed with President Kennedy, sheets neatly folded across his lap, too, and an ice pack on his head.

"You took a tumble there, son," Kennedy said to him.

"What happened?"

"You passed out," Elvis replied. The King was seated in a plush chair adorned with polished brass buttons. It looked more like a throne than a chair. He was shining up a Colt .45 automatic pistol.

Cole didn't remember anything other than his ears growing hot.

"Don't worry about it," Kennedy reassured him. "When Buddy brought Jim Morrison to see me for the first time, he thought he was having an acid flashback. He honestly thought I was a ghost."

"That was a long time ago," Elvis retorted.

"Yes, it was," Kennedy acknowledged.

"Cole," Elvis said, "meet John F. Kennedy, thirty-fifth president of the United State of America."

"It's an honor to meet you, Mr. President," Cole said, his head still swimming. "Are you in charge of this thing?"

"No, Cole, I have entrusted Elvis to run the day-to-day operations of the team."

"But," Elvis butted in, "the president has resources and friends in places his office does not afford me. His value can't be overstated, and he's a trusted voice."

"Now, Cole, let's get down to business," Kennedy said. "Elvis tells me that you are not a rock star at all but, rather, a technology expert."

"Yes, sir, that's correct."

"He also tells me that some members of the team are none too thrilled with your addition."

"I don't know about that," Cole replied. "I guess Kurt wasn't too happy to meet me. Jimi seemed okay."

"Don't worry about it, Mr. President," Elvis said, cocking his gun and securing it in the holster at his side. "I'll get the rest of the gang on board. They'll come around."

"I remember a few years ago when we butted heads about Ronald Reagan. You remember that, Elvis?"

"Of course." He turned his gaze to Cole. "In 1981, the Prez here wanted to bring politicians back to the team. I was opposed. I had just recruited John Lennon, and the timing felt wrong."

"Remember when Reagan was shot?" the president asked Cole.

"I remember learning about it," Cole said. "I was only three years old when it happened."

Elvis and Kennedy looked at each other and laughed. "You *are* a young buck, son," Kennedy said, patting Cole over the covers where his knee was.

"Anyway, the Prez here thought Reagan should join the team and could take us to a new level. I felt the team still needed to be rock stars. But when some nut job tried to kill him, we took advantage of the opportunity and brought him to this compound for two days. He nearly accepted the President Kennedy's offer, but ultimately, he turned us down and went back to the White House. We did have to wipe his brain, though."

Maybe he was serious about the brain wipe thing, Cole thought.

"He was perfect, Elvis," Kennedy said, picking up the nearly two decades old argument. "Both a politician *and* an entertainer. Would have been a perfect fit."

"I gave in to the Prez," Elvis admitted, looking at Kennedy, "but in the end Reagan didn't want to join the team. If he had, he probably would have been the one to recruit you and not me.

"Anyway, enough about the past. Let's talk about you, Mr. Denton. Why did you say yes to Elvis's offer?"

"I guess because what he described is something I've wanted for a long time," Cole said thoughtfully. "Elvis described this group as a family—one that changes the world. That's all I've ever wanted: to do something meaningful and find a place to belong."

"Well, you couldn't have picked a better spot," Kennedy said. "This *is* a family. When's his first sit-down with Jerry?"

"Soon," Elvis replied.

"Jerry?" Cole asked.

"I'll tell you about it later," Elvis said. "First, we need to clue you into what's happening. You up for it?"

"I'm ready. Yes, I can do it," Cole said, trying to sound confident.

"I hope so," Kennedy said. "You can start by putting some thought to what John Lennon's out there trying to figure out. Earlier this year, Ibrahim Baré Maïnassara, president of the African nation of Niger, was assassinated. This started a domino effect in the region, with several neighboring nations now plunged into disorder. Around the same time, an ocean away, Jaime Hurtado, a promising candidate for the presidency of Ecuador, was assassinated as well, causing turmoil throughout South America. Both of these assassinations remain unsolved."

"I haven't heard anything about this," Cole admitted.

"Most Americans haven't," Kennedy said. "They're all too busy worrying about Y2K. Through my sources at the CIA, I have been able to acquire profiles on several potential suspects. But we know it wasn't an individual. Buddy Holly had discovered it was a terrorist group calling themselves the Brotherhood. He was unable to locate the organization's headquarters, but he did manage to collect a good deal of data.

"On top of that, three months ago, a leading cardinal in the Catholic Church, Giovanni Esposito, the man many thought would become the next pope, was killed outside Vatican City in a car bombing. We suspect the Brotherhood is responsible for his death as well. Now there's a great upheaval in the church with many men jockeying for position to succeed the pope."

"That's why I'm a Pentecostal," Elvis chimed in. "Nobody has to answer to no Pope in my church."

"Mr. Presley," Kennedy said, shooting Elvis a look. "I'm eighty-two, and I have all my marbles, sir. I remember all seven times we've argued about this. Let's get back to the point. Cole, we received intel that members of this Brotherhood were convening in Las Vegas last week, supposedly to plot another assassination. Following through on that lead led to Buddy's death. That's why you're here, Cole. To help us solve this mystery."

"Most disturbing of all," Elvis said solemnly, "they knew we were coming in Vegas. They knew who we were."

Cole pondered all that the president and the King had said. "Well, it seems that each of these assassinations were timed to create upheaval, and on three different continents. I mean, I just got here, but it seems like whoever is behind this is trying to shake things up on a worldwide scale."

"Buddy surmised the same thing," Elvis said. "We need to figure out who the next target is and what the link is between the previous three. And we need to find out how they know about the DRS. A good start might be figuring out what this means." Elvis handed Cole a picture of the symbol Buddy drew on the wall with his own blood. "This is our first clue."

★ ★ ★ ★

Elvis and Cole descended the stairs back to where the car was parked. Somehow, Jimi, Hank, Richie, and Cobain had found guitars, chords, amps, and mics and were wailing away on the Rolling Stones' "It's Only Rock and Roll," taking turns soloing and singing. Elvis ran down the stairs, grabbed a mic, and started singing along.

The impromptu supergroup finished off the song as Cole leaned up against the Mustang, relishing his front-row seat at a concert no one in their wildest dreams could ever imagine happening. When all was said and done, Richie Valens and Hank Williams took off in the Continental with a wave and a honk of the horn. Elvis Presley, Jimi Hendrix, Kurt Cobain, and Cole Denton followed close behind in the Mustang. When the tunnel forked, the Continental went right and disappeared into the darkness. The Mustang went left and returned to the garage from whence it came.

"Where to now, King?" Jimi asked as he backed down the driveway into the suburban neighborhood.

"We need to take Mr. Denton here to see the Founder," Elvis replied.

"A'ight," Jimi affirmed. He drove the car into Washington DC and made his way to the Lincoln Memorial. The men got out of the car and walked up the steps until they stood before the giant statue. Cobain didn't come as close as the others, stopping short and lighting a cigarette. Cole looked back at him, but Elvis pushed him closer to Lincoln.

"This is our founder. Don't pass out again, Cole," Elvis said, looking serious.

"What?" Jimi asked.

"Aw, dang it man, I shouldn't have brought it up," the King said, his scowl giving way to a sheepish grin as Jimi laughed hysterically.

"Thanks," Cole said, not sure how much he could push back or if, as the neophyte, he just had to take the constant harassment from the veteran members of the

80

team. He decided to take his chances. "At least I didn't try to argue religion with the president."

"Aw, tell me he didn't," Jimi said.

"He wanted to," Cole said, digging in.

Elvis gave Cole a look. Not one that said, *Watch it*, but one that said, *I'll allow it—this time.*

Jimi pushed Cole's shoulder and laughed. "You all right, kid. Nobody gives it back to the King so soon. You got guts."

Elvis put an arm around Cole and said, "I think you're going to be just fine." Then he bowed his head and started humming "The Battle Hymn of the Republic." Cobain, Jimi, and Cole stood silently and let the King do his thing. When Elvis was done, he looked up at Lincoln and said, "We died to save lives."

Cobain and Jimi repeated, "We died to save lives."

chapter

ELEVEN

ole had lost track of how long they had been flying and had no clue where they were. He rubbed his eyes from the co-pilot' chair, yawned, and asked Jimi Hendrix, "Are we in Omaha? Somewhere in middle America?" He wondered if Jimi even knew who the Counting Crows were.

Jimi didn't skip a beat. "You know that dude has fake dreads, right? Trying to be something he's not."

Cole hoped his jaw hadn't actually hit the floor.

Jimi noticed, then belted out a verse from "Mr. Jones."

"I can't believe you know the Counting Crows!" Cole said.

"I might be *dead*, kid, but I got ears."

Cole didn't know whether to laugh, apologize, or ask more of the thousands of questions he had. He looked around at the scenery and tried to absorb the moment. He was on the DRS jet and flying over the middle of nowhere with a *deceased*, world-famous rock star at the controls. It was like a strange dream that's so close to reality but unable to come fully into focus.

"So, where did the King and Teen Spirit run off to?"

"Yeah, Kurt is going to *love* that. Keep it up. Seems to be going well with you two already."

"You noticed? Why do I get the feeling this isn't going to be like joining the Super Friends or the A-Team? I loved the Faceman. Always wanted to be Face, but I feel more like Howling Mad Murdock right now. 'TRA-A-ASH BAGS! TRA-A-ASH BAGS! I want 'em!'"

Jimi just looked at him, shook his head, and went back to flying. He didn't say it out loud, but Cole could tell he pitied this fool. It was clear Cole had no idea what he'd signed up for.

Jimi said, "Elvis and Kurt had some things to handle. They took another way home. Until you have completed training, people on the team are going to come and go, and you will be none the wiser. The DRS is everywhere, all the time, saving the world, man."

As Izabella began its descent, Cole made out a perfectly manicured runway in the middle of a field that was hedged in by forest on both sides. It looked like a six-thou-sand-foot-long putting green. Small trees with blinking lights among the branches came into focus on either side of the runway.

Instead of landing immediately, Jimi radioed in, "I'm going to give the new kid a look at the compound." He banked Izabella to the right, and Cole spotted a group of buildings that almost resembled a town. The whole area appeared to be surrounded by dense, outrageously erratic-looking forest filled with the worst kinds of invasive vegetation. He thought it might be bamboo intermingled with kudzu, ivy, and giant thorn bushes. Cole decided he was looking at the compound's security walls.

To the east, he saw multiple greenhouses, gardens, and irrigation systems. There were also windmills, water tanks, solar panels, and what appeared to be grain silos. He could also make out an animal farm. Chickens, cattle, pigs, and several ponds he thought might be growing trout. More than a commune, this was an engineering feat. It appeared to have the appropriate amount of space, order, and accoutrements befit-ting a world-class farm-to-table experience.

Cole then spotted a gated community that had to be the most eclectic neigh-borhood he had ever seen. There were log cabins, modern architecture, brick homes, stucco houses, and some new construction that looked like an apartment building. As they drew closer, he could see that each home was five to ten acres away from its neighbors. In the middle of this odd community was a two-story, columned mansion made of white brick. *Could that be Graceland?* Cole wondered.

Off to the west, another few miles away, he noticed a humongous radio tower jut-ting into the sky. The tower stood in the midst of several large buildings that could be hangars or warehouses. He imagined warehouses full of ammunition, hairspray, and gold records. Perhaps one was a laboratory where someone was cooking up next-level, super-secret spy tech. He chuckled to himself and then asked, "Hey Jimi, is that where they keep the 'sharks with frickin' laser beams attached to their heads'?"

Jimi tried not to laugh but couldn't help himself.

As the plane continued circling, Cole saw an area south of the gated homes with a much softer landscape. Here there were waterfalls, exotic plants, and an almost Hawaiian feel. In the center of this secret garden was a giant dome reflecting the rays of the sun in every direction. Cole stared in awe.

Jimi leaned in and whispered, "This is HQ. It sits on almost a million acres of land. Before you ask, the answer is yes. Collectively, the DRS has more wealth than almost every second- and third-world country on Earth combined. We can travel secretly and privately anywhere in the world. We can develop almost anything we need right here. All you have to do is pick up the phone and ask for it."

"Wow" was all Cole could come up with.

"I know it's a lot to take in. Buckle up, we are about to land. I know your questions have questions. Just write them down. Garcia will answer them."

Izabella landed smoothly as if the runway were made of glass. Jimi glided down the greenway and let the plane slow to a roll before turning toward the hangar. "On behalf of your crew, I'd like to welcome you to the Netherworld."

"Nether . . . world?"

Jimi smirked. "You didn't think rock stars went to heaven, did you?"

Cole was bewildered. This felt like equal parts theme park, Hollywood backlot, and space colony. He half-wondered as the door opened, if he clicked his heels three times, would he wake up in Kansas. Maybe he *was* in Kansas. It sure didn't feel like Boston, Illinois, or anywhere else he had ever been.

Jimi knowingly grinned. "Cole, it's okay man. It's okay not to know what to think. I've been here nearly thirty years, and even I don't know what to do with it. The Netherworld used to be frontier land. Abe's men 'acquisitioned' it in the late 1800s. Here, the secrets have secrets."

They were pulling into the hangar when Cole couldn't help himself any longer. "I know you said Garcia would answer my questions but . . . wait . . . *Jerry* Garcia?" The questions flooded his brain, and out they came.

"Where is this place?"

"Is Freddie Mercury alive?"

84

"What do you *do* every day?"

"Why did they recruit you?"

"Where did you learn to fly?"

"Do I get a gun?"

"How *big* is Biggie?"

"Does Biggie like hugs?"

"Do you guys do a lot of partying?"

"Who built this place?"

"Do I get a mansion?"

"Are there girls here?"

"What is your favorite guitar?"

"Favorite headband?"

"Do you like Slash?"

"Just how awesome *is* Elvis?"

"Do we get matching outfits?"

"Do I get a code name?"

"When is my first mission?"

"Is Jerry more grateful now that he's fake-dead?"

"What happened to Buddy Holly?"

"Do we get our own cell phones?"

"Do you *have* cell coverage out here?"

"Where are we again?"

Cole sighed like a balloon pushing out its last remnant of air. He slumped over in his seat and held his head in his hands.

"I'll answer one of those," Jimi replied.

Cole looked puzzled, trying to remember all the questions he had just asked.

Jimi sighed. "Being a rock star isn't exactly easy, man. Some cats just dig making music. Some dig people staring at them—attention, fame. Success has a way of stealing your soul like an evil temptress. Next thing you know, you got no privacy. The fans know more about you than you know about yourself. We chased after success, and when we got it, it was like water running through our fingers. No matter how tight we held onto it, it just kept slipping away. See . . . we all have demons. Cole Denton, you have demons. You'll see.

"I will tell you that I hated who I became. I lost myself. I was some version of Jimi Hendrix that I thought people wanted to see. Cole, I wasn't so sure about you

85

at first, but I like you. You don't know this yet, but we're about to become brothers. And as your brother, I'm going to shed some light on something about me you haven't even thought to ask, and it's going to help you with everyone here. I died a long time ago. Fame killed me. Today, I'm in recovery. There are no drinks or drugs in this place. There is nothing to numb the loneliness or pain. Everyone is recovering from something, man. Everyone deals with some kind of pain or hurt. There's no hide-and-seek from your pain here. It's the Netherworld. We're all dead. Might as well face your demons, your past, whatever monsters might be in your closet or under your bed. We have died to save lives. *Debeo redeo schola.* 'Morally bound to return as elite soldiers.' That means we can't hold anything back or let anything hold us back. We can't be numb; we have to feel, have to hurt. We have to heal. No cats here, Mainframe Coletrane. We have to be lions."

Cole didn't speak for a few moments. He didn't know what to say. He looked at Jimi then nodded. Jimi nodded back. Then Cole stood up and asked, "Seriously though, what about Biggie? He's a hugger, isn't he?"

Jimi laughed, put his hand on Cole's shoulder, and pushed him back down in his seat. He sighed again and said, "Hey man, you know, a lot of stuff is about to go down. Elvis Presley is like, you know, outrageously persuasive. Almost impossible to disagree with. He has a gift for getting his way. Always has. Especially when he starts calling everyone 'family.'"

Cole flinched. "Jimi, didn't we just have this talk?"

"There's more, and I just want to be real with you. It's possible that you really don't belong here. I don't mean to be, you know, like condescending or rude, but . . . you're not like us."

There was a long silence. Cole nodded and took a deep breath. "I know. I don't believe in any way that I am like you guys. I've never had groupies, never had to register at a hotel under a fake name. I've never been to Vegas or California or even out of the country. Unless . . . I'm out of the country right now? Anyways, I don't think I've had an addiction. I've *seen* addiction. Up close. I hate it. I don't trust addicts. And I don't relate to you. *You* are Jimi Hendrix. You ruled the world . . ."

Cole took another breath before continuing. He had anticipated having this conversation with members of the team; he just didn't realize it would happen before he even stepped off the plane.

"But here's the thing, Jimi. I can see the future. Elvis wasn't wrong to seek out a guy like me. Technology is going to rule the world in the coming years. The future is paved with ones and zeros that are going to create jobs that no one has never even thought of before. Computers are going to get smaller, more mobile, more prevalent, and pervasive, and we are going to depend on technology in ways you can't even imagine. If I had chosen that life, stayed on that path, I could have been like you in my own way. I probably would have had groupies—really nerdy groupies but groupies nonetheless. I could have traveled the world and collected my own personal poisons. But I don't want that. I don't care about money, and I don't care about fame. I want to make the world a better place. I want to make a difference. If that takes *dying* and leaving behind everything I've ever known . . . then so be it."

Jimi didn't respond immediately. He leaned back in the pilot's chair, looked Cole up and down, furrowed his brow, and studied Cole's face. Then he nodded his head slightly, squinted his eyes, and said, "Cool. Welcome to the DRS."

As they exited the plane, Jimi carried a small bag. Cole had the giant duffle bag that Elvis had provided. Cole hoped it contained everything he would need. Then a thought hit him. "Do you guys ever go to the store? You know, like Walgreens or something?"

"We have people for that."

"People?"

"The Netherworld has a bit more going on than you'd expect. There are always people who need a place to go or somewhere to hide. We've protected world leaders and refugees under threat of genocide. And more often than not, even though this is not something you are going to have to worry about, most of them never knew who we were in the real world."

"So, you guys have people who work for you?"

"I wouldn't say that. I'd say we've got a small community who works *with* us. They only know as much as they need to know. There are levels of security and secrecy. Some of them . . . are just happy not to be raising their family in the middle of a war-torn country."

"How is all of this . . . allowed?"

"Allowed?"

"I mean, you guys basically have a country inside a country. What about Visas? Passports? You know, government stuff."

"You met JFK?"

"Yes."

"And you're asking me about 'government stuff'?"

87

"Fair enough."

Jimi led Cole to a 1968 Chevrolet Corvette, opened the door, cranked the engine, and motioned for Cole to join him. Cole did a perfectly awful job trying to carefully stow his bag in the back of the Corvette. Finally, he sat down, wrapped his body around the duffle, and bearhugged it all the way to their destination.

Cole looked behind him as best he could as they sped away from the runway. "Jimi, there were like six cars to choose from. There was an SUV, a pickup, an insanely painted Porsche, even a crummy VW beetle. Why did you pick this to cram me into?"

"I wanted you to look ridiculous," he said with a smile.

"Thanks."

"You're welcome, lil bro."

It felt like Jimi was driving at least a hundred miles an hour, but Cole couldn't really see the speedometer around his bag. He did manage to spot a few people walking about as they sped down the street. Nobody he saw appeared to have been famous. In fact, this didn't look much different from an ordinary suburban community, other than being completely closed off from the rest of the world. Cole laughed at the absurdity of it all. He guessed it was completely normal to the people he saw. As they drove past playgrounds and manicured flower beds, he wondered if any of this was ever going to feel normal to him.

"Is Biggie going to hate me?"

"Call him 'Chrissy-pooh.' Everyone else does."

The putting-green runway was at one end of the Netherworld, and even though Jimi was driving fast, it felt like it was taking a while to get where they were going. There had been a lot to see at first, then nothing. Then warehouses. Then a gated community that they blew right past. Then some sort of Zen garden where Cole imagined various rock stars zoning out and seeking higher planes of existence.

"Seriously, Jimi, you have to at least answer one more question for me before we get to wherever it is we are going."

"All right man, one more."

Cole hesitated and then asked, "Am I supposed to train to be—how did you say it—an elite soldier? Elvis told me this wasn't military. I mean, I know computers, and I've watched a lot of professional wrestling. I went through a James Bond phase, I guess. But dude, you fly planes."

"Your training has already begun. You just didn't know it."

"What is that supposed to mean?"

"Exactly." Jimi looked at him with knowing eyes, then laughed. "Since the King came to lead DRS, each agent has had to be fully capable. You know, Elvis did most of his own stunts in the old movies. He still studies karate, and he loves a good fight. You are going to learn to fight like a ninja. You are going to learn to think differently. You are going to learn to drive it like you stole it. You are going to be educated in philosophy and strategy. Eventually, you'll even learn some different languages. Trust me when I say, you will be trained. You'll train till you bleed."

As they continued their drive, Cole's obstructed view caused his mind to drift, and he began to daydream. He imagined himself inside the Matrix, only instead of Laurence Fishburne training Keanu Reeves, he imagined Jerry Garcia floating in the air and striking the Karate Kid's crane pose.

Then Jimi slammed on the brakes, and the car drifted sideways to a hard stop.

"We're home."

"In . . . Omaha?"

"Something like that."

Cole thought, *Is this where they ask me to take the blue pill or the red pill?* He pushed his bag out of the corvette and wished someone had given him some Dramamine. As he stumbled out of the car, he suddenly felt sick, lost, and bewildered. Strangely enough, he found comfort in seeing a former dead man strolling his way.

"Elvis!"

"Cole Denton. Meet the DRS. Well, some of them. Y'all this is Cole. Circle up."

As the King slowly walked toward him, Cole realized he was followed by a small group of people. One by one they stepped forward and created a circle around Cole. As Elvis and Jimi moved into place, they were joined by Janis Joplin, Jim Morrison, Tupac Shakur, and Christopher "Biggie Smalls" Wallace. They all held out a hand, a small rock in each of their palms. They looked like a bunch of teenagers who had just been told to clean their rooms by their dad. No one was smiling. Yet Cole couldn't stop smiling. He tried to stop but couldn't. He wondered for a moment if this was a dream. But if this was a dream, he didn't want to wake up.

Elvis nodded, and the group joined hands around Cole and said in unison, "We died to save lives."

Cole noticed that Jim Morrison had said nothing. Instead, as soon as the ritual was over, he simply shook his head and walked away.

Janis just stared right through him.

Tupac and Chris smirked.

89

Cole could physically feel tension in the air.

He leaned over and said to Elvis, "I see dead people."

But no one laughed.

✦ ✦ ✦ ✦

Cole stared up at the giant warehouse-like building. It was called the McKinley Building. There were dozens just like it all over the Netherworld, but for some reason Elvis had brought him to this one.

Then the front doors swung open and out walked a jolly man with wild gray hair and bare feet. He was wearing baggy cargo shorts and a blue Hawaiian shirt with pink flowers on it.

"Cole, this is Jerry Garcia," Elvis said. Cole extended his right hand—happy he didn't do his awkward puppet wave—but Jerry brought Cole in for the real thing and gave him a giant bear hug.

"Hey, man, great to meet you!" Jerry said, holding the embrace an extra beat before letting go. Cole noticed he smelled like lavender.

Elvis said, "Jerry serves as our counselor, our sounding board, our guru—whatever you want to call him. You can tell him anything. That's his job. That's why he's here."

"Great," Cole said cheerfully, knowing he had no intention of using Jerry Garcia's services. He wasn't one to open up about his feelings, especially to people he didn't really know.

"So is that everyone?" Cole asked. "Have I met the whole team?"

"No," Elvis said flatly.

"Where's Cobain?"

"He's busy."

"Doing what?"

"Nunya. As in, 'None ya biz-nazz!'" Elvis said, laughing. "Look man, this team has a lot going on, and some elements are need-to-know. And right now, you don't need to know."

They followed Jerry into the warehouse, which to Cole's surprise looked like an office building inside. Their pace was brisk, but Cole tried to make out a few details. He saw cubicles, offices with windows, break rooms, and a few conference rooms. There were some people milling about, but he couldn't really make out who they were and what they were doing.

90

Jerry led them into an elevator and pressed 7, the second floor from the top. Some of the floor buttons were labeled. Floor 2, for example, was labeled "R&D."

The elevator doors opened on the seventh floor, and Cole stepped into a room that could have been a time capsule from the 1960s. The carpet was tie-dyed, strands of beads hung from all the doorways, and the walls were draped with outlandish fabrics in the brightest of colors. Jerry led them to a room that looked like the interior of the genie's bottle in the TV show *I Dream of Jeannie*. Jerry crossed his legs as he sat down on a cushion in the middle of the floor and motioned for Cole to do the same.

Elvis remained standing and asked, "Everybody good here?"

"Sure, King, we got it," Jerry replied with a warm smile.

"Cole, I mean it," Elvis said. "Talk to this man."

"Got it." Cole said, trying to hide his annoyance. After all, he wasn't some kind of reclamation project like most of the "deceased" rock stars he'd just met. He had no interest in therapy or analysis. And he certainly didn't need to be "resurrected" like the others. But Elvis had made it clear that this was a mandatory element of his training, so Cole figured he'd just jump through this hoop and get it over with.

"Now," Jerry said, "I'm about to open up your mind. You ready for this?"

"Um . . . okay."

"Tell me about your last dream."

Three hours later, they emerged from their session. As he was led out of the psychedelic digs and back into the sunlight, Cole noticed that Jerry was carrying a small, smooth stone and was turning it over and over in his hand while they spoke.

"What's that?" Cole asked.

"All in due time, Mr. Denton. All in due time."

"So this counseling . . . the talking-about-our-feelings stuff. We done with that?"

"Far from it, Mr. Denton," Garcia said matter-of-factly.

"Right," Cole said. "Um . . . why?"

"We've only just begun," Jerry said with a wink. "If you are going to reach your full potential as a member of this team—this 'band' if you will—you have to open up. It'll come with time. When you're a little further along in your training, we'll revisit all this. Until then . . . good luck!"

chapter
TWELVE

John Lennon thought it was unseasonably warm for an autumn night in middle Tennessee.

He was one of the more skilled and accomplished members of the DRS. He had excelled at just about every aspect of spy craft. He could fight; he was equally deadly with or without weapons. He could pilot almost any type of vehicle. More importantly, he had mastered the art of blending in. Lennon never hid but was rarely noticed, ironic considering his previous life as one of the most famous people on the planet. Elvis joked that this was the beauty of being an average-looking middle-aged white man rather than a teen heartthrob. He could also make his Liverpool accent completely disappear when the need arose.

Lennon's greatest asset, though, may have been his patience, which he had honed through many years of meditating. He had been commissioned for hundreds of missions during his years of service with the DRS, and Lennon always got his man. This trip would be no different.

The reason for Lennon's success was simple and obvious to those who paid attention: His belief in his purpose was unwavering. He had a deep-seated sense of justice that required him to work outside the establishment. He had never trusted politicians or government systems. Even before his "death," he had longed desperately for a world at peace. A world that made sense. A world where everyone got a fair shake. It was this longing that drew the attention of the DRS to begin with. John Lennon was a man whose heart cried out for the world to be made right.

Through all of his training and his many missions, he had seen the worst humanity had to offer. Yet he had kept his sense of humor. He was quick to crack a joke, often of the slightly off-color variety, but his current mission wasn't a laughing matter. This was personal. Buddy Holly was dead, and someone would have to pay for it.

Lennon sat in a parked car a few mailboxes down from the house where the man responsible for Buddy's death was living. The man's name was Jason "Bull" Langston, but the house was leased to a Jason Langstone. *This guy even mucked up his alias!* Lennon's blood boiled at the thought of this idiot getting the best of one of his closest friends.

He had been watching the house for days, never parking in the same spot twice, observing everything around him. He knew that the neighbors across the street from Langston checked their mail at the same time every day. He knew that the boy next door to Langston was using binoculars to peep at a teen girl across the street, and that the girl knew he was peeping. Lennon knew the walking schedule of each of the neighborhood pets and which trees they favored for doing their business. He knew the timer settings for every sprinkler on the street and how often the nosy old lady four doors down from Langston looked out her window. He knew everything and everyone coming and going in the Westchester neighborhood of Madison, Tennessee.

The two-story ranch that served as the "Langstone" residence was located in the middle of the most suburban neighborhood Lennon had ever seen. Yet the house's bushes and shrubbery were unkempt and the lawn overgrown, calling unnecessary attention to the occupants, as nothing about the house matched the other homes on the block in terms of cleanliness or care.

The day before, he had noticed their trash piled up and overflowing by the back alley. It was possible that Langston had not expected to be in the house very long and therefore hadn't bothered to pay for weekly collection service. Lennon joked to himself that this was "sloppy" tradecraft, typical of the man's carelessness. So he acquired a nondescript sanitation worker's uniform and collected the offending refuse. Ostensibly, this was done as a service to the Westchester community, and so no one thought to question his presence or his actions. That evening, he sorted through the garbage, itemizing and tagging receipts, drawings, even printed emails detailing future Brotherhood plans. All that was left now was to take out the garbage living inside the house.

Now it was 3 a.m., and Lennon knew exactly where Langston and his compatriots were at that moment. There were four of them in the house. Potter and Patterson had the night shift and were in the living room, playing video games. The one they called O'Bee was asleep in the rear second-story bedroom. Langston was asleep in the master bedroom, also on the second floor, in the front.

All the second-story windows were open because Langston insisted, claiming the breeze helped him sleep despite the humid Tennessee air. With great ease and lightness of foot, Lennon scaled the wall and slipped into the bedroom where O'Bee was supposed to be sleeping, but the bed was empty. The sound of a flushing toilet came from the bathroom in the hall.

"One can plan for everything except a full bladder," Lennon said aloud as the man who had just relieved himself reentered the room.

O'Bee was startled but then lunged at the intruder while wearing nothing but boxer shorts and a stained "wife beater" tank top. Lennon caught a blow intended for his face and twisted the man's arm around his back. He then quickly and quietly drew a knife and dispatched O'Bee. "One down, three to go," he whispered to no one.

Langston was sleeping in the master bedroom at the end of the hall only a few feet from where the former Beatle currently stood. Lennon wanted to save him for last, so he turned his attention to the men downstairs. He knew that, at this hour, they were likely playing Tecmo Super Bowl, an arcade-style video game that simulated American football. Potter would be sitting in his pleather beanbag chair and Patterson in an overstuffed grass-green La-Z-Boy recliner, both just a few feet from the television screen.

As Lennon crept down the 1950s staircase, the third step from the top let out an unexpected groan that drew the attention of his prey. He heard Potter call out, "O'Bee? That you? You sleepwalking again? You better not whizz on the carpet, or Bull is gonna kill you."

Potter appeared at the bottom of the stairs. He was a tall, well-built man wearing a mesh football jersey and cut-off shorts. He clearly didn't recognize Lennon, but when he saw that the intruder wasn't O'Bee, Potter immediately charged up the stairs. Lennon calmly pulled his silenced pistol and fired three shots into the heart of his assailant, all while gracefully descending the steps.

Patterson vaulted out of his recliner when he saw Potter fall back lifelessly onto the landing, followed quickly by the man who killed him. The only weapon Patterson could muster was the video game controller in his hand, and he attempted to throw it at Lennon. But the controller was still plugged into the gaming system, which came crashing to the ground as Patterson yanked it violently from its shelf on the entertainment console.

Patterson backed up as Lennon sprang over the recliner between them. Patterson wildly threw a roundhouse punch that Lennon easily ducked while at the same time grabbing the controller that had just been thrown at him. As he came up out of his crouch, Lennon neatly stepped behind his opponent and quickly wrapped the cord three times around his throat and began choking him with it. In his fight for survival, Patterson kicked over a lamp and knocked down a sizable pyramid of empty beer cans stacked in a nearby windowsill. As Patterson breathed his last, Lennon could hear a door open at the top of the stairs.

Langston yelled through a yawn as he started down the steps, "I'm going to murder you jackwagons! You *know* I have a sleep disorder!"

The man whose dead friends had called him Bull was wearing an orange #27 football jersey and boxers. Lennon could see that it took him a moment to register the carnage in the rented living room. "Sleep disorder? Is that what you have?" Lennon replied. "Well, I'm about to give you a breathing disorder."

Langston bolted back up the steps and sprinted down the hall. Lennon dashed up the stairs in pursuit, reaching the top just as Langston ducked into the bathroom, slamming the door and locking it behind him. Through the door, Lennon could hear the panicked man inside scrabbling about as if looking for something. Then there was silence.

Lennon kicked the door in and saw that the bathroom window was open and the screen knocked out. Not new to the game of chase, he didn't bother looking out the window but instead pulled open the shower curtain. Langston was standing in the tub and holding the porcelain toilet tank cover with two hands, ready to pulverize his attacker. Lennon threw up his arms but could only manage a partial block. The blow was enough to stun him, allowing Langston to jump out of the tub and dive through the second-story window onto a lower level of the gabled roof.

Lennon shook the cobwebs from his brain and moved to the side of the window; he was alert enough not to expose himself to enemy fire. Langston had dropped from the roof and onto the driveway, where, curiously, he now stood while talking on a cellular phone: "I've been compromised. My team is dead. The dead Beatle is here, and he's trying to kill me. I know what I have to do. Nothing will be left to chance. Go in peace, my brother." Lennon heard him then go into the garage through a side door.

Lennon swiftly moved back down the hallway to the window through which he had initially entered and climbed out onto the lower roof. He stealthily traversed the edge until he was above the two-car garage, then dropped down into the front yard. The garage door was partially open, and Lennon could hear something rocking back and forth from within. He could picture Langston sitting there, shotgun in hand, ready to blast him should he emerge from inside the house. Lennon quietly but quickly rolled under the partially opened garage door and sprang to his feet, hoping to surprise his quarry. Instead, he found Langston hanging from his own belt from the rafters above, a chair kicked over beneath him. The man was not yet dead but was losing consciousness while gurgling something about his brothers.

Lennon rushed over, grabbed the chair, and propped it back under Langston's feet. The man was too exhausted and oxygen-deprived to put up a fight as Lennon held him up just enough to allow some air in. Langston looked at Lennon, recognized his situation, then passed out.

"Mr. Langston," Lennon said to the man who was responsible for the death of Buddy Holly, "welcome to the nightmare."

★ ★ ★ ★

"Mmmaaaugh."

"Good morning, Jason. I hoped you'd come around soon. Would you like some tea?"

Jason "Bull" Langston woozily opened his eyes. His body felt all kinds of wrong. The belt was still tight around his neck, and he could feel the friction burns from what he had thought would be his last moments on earth. He was now seated in the chair he had used to hang himself and was tied up with a long strand of old Christmas lights wrapped tightly around him. He was bound at the wrists with a length of rope. His feet were bare and soaking in a ten-gallon metal basin filled with water. Nearby was a car battery Lennon had apparently taken from the vehicle parked in the other bay of the two-car garage. Jumper cables were clamped to the car battery at one end, with the other clamps on the other end lying on the floor and waiting for the circuit to be completed. Limb shears sat on a folding card table nearby. There was no mistaking this do-it-yourself torture special. Langston realized what was about to happen.

"Oh, no. No no no no no no."

"And to think, less than an hour ago you were worried about a sleep disorder."

"Aren't you supposed to be all about love? Nonviolence? 'Give peace a chance,' am I right?"

"You killed my friend."

Langston had already prepared himself for death. What he hadn't counted on was pain.

"Mr. Langston, I'll make this simple. If you tell me everything you know, I'll let you . . . rest. YouknowwhatImean?"

Langston drooped his head and moaned, then began struggling with all his might to loosen his restraints. After a few moments, he recognized the futility of his efforts. He slumped over and gave in, body, soul, and mind.

"Man, I don't really know anything," he said. "That's how it works. One group. One task. One target. Then we disappear. After Vegas, the four of us were told to wait in this dump. We were told to collect information. Bank routing numbers of some fat old military guy who died a few years back. I don't know anything more, I swear. After we got the info they wanted, they provided us explosives to torch the place to cover our tracks. We were just waiting for orders."

"Who is 'they'?"

"I think you know our name."

"Who did you call outside?"

"I—I don't know his name. I just call him Boss. I've never really seen him up close. It's always dark, and he sometimes wears a mask. His voice sounds like that science guy in the wheelchair—Hawkins or something. He mostly sends emails or calls me on a phone. He tells me what to do, and I do it. I don't ask questions. Check my phone. It's the last number I dialed. Just hit redial, and he'll pick up . . ."

★ ★ ★ ★

Lennon flinched. He had heard enough.

With a flick of his wrist he produced a blade from behind his back. With a slice, the Christmas lights dropped to the floor. He then yanked Langston out of the seated position, stood him on the chair, and in little more than a second had him hanging once again from the rafters. However, he left the chair in place and then raised Langston just enough so he could stand on his tiptoes.

In silent rage, Lennon pulled a second blade from behind his back and proceeded to loose his fury upon Langston, a blade in each hand, stabbing him in the midsection repeatedly and so rapidly that the strikes outpaced the body's ability to respond to its wounding. Once his rage was spent, Lennon stepped back.

Then the blood came.

As life ebbed from the body, he could see the misery and fear in Langston's eyes. Lennon pulled the pistol from the small of his back and fired three shots into Langston's heart.

Then, for the first time, Lennon wept for Buddy Holly. He sat on the floor in the lotus position, placed his head in his hands, and mourned. After a few minutes, he straightened his posture and tried to re-center his mind. A short time later, he stood without effort. He then took the phone from Langston's pocket, flipped it open, and hit redial.

A distorted voice answered. "Yes?"

Lennon did not respond.

"Langston, is that you?"

He remained quiet.

"Bull, are you there?"

He cleared his throat and said "Bull is tied up at the moment. Anything I can help you with?"

The connection ended abruptly.

Lennon searched the back seat of the car in the garage and found the duffle Elvis and Buddy had been tracking in Vegas. The duffle contained documents, drawings, and enough materials to construct a few explosives. He stowed the duffle in his car, pulled the car into the drive, and then went inside to clean himself up.

The sun was a few minutes from rising when he started his car and popped a disc into the CD player. He searched until he found the right exit music, lowered the windows, and then peeled out of the drive. Rage Against the Machine's "Bulls on Parade" blared out of the speakers for all the Westchester community to hear. Just as he turned the corner out of the neighborhood, Langston's house exploded with such intensity that the concussive force blew out the windows of the house next door where the Peeping Tom boy lived.

★ ★ ★ ★

"You'll find my report exhaustive."

Elvis Presley combed through the piles of documents and evidence that Lennon had gathered from Buddy Holly's office and the safe house in Tennessee.

"So the bag Buddy and I were tracking was just low-level schematics and some small explosives?

"It appears so, King."

Elvis furrowed his brow with concern. Then he looked back at Lennon. "John, did you have to kill them?"

Lennon thought for a moment and responded, "No."

Elvis furrowed his brow again but nodded in understanding. Buddy had been beloved by his colleagues, and some measure of vengeance was not inappropriate.

"Elvis, I also have some troubling news."

"More?"

"Did you notice where they were holed up?"

"Nashville."

"Not just Nashville. It was Madison."

Some of the color drained from the King's face. "NO."

"Yes. The 'military' man the Brotherhood was surveilling was the estate of Colonel Tom Parker. I believe they were there trying to collect data points to find a money trail leading back to you. Not your estate. Not Graceland. But *you*. I suppose they thought if anyone could lead them your way, it would be your lifelong manager—the man who controlled your life."

"Parker died two years ago, John. There is no way this gets back to me. He had no idea I'm still alive."

"Parker was a pack rat. He kept everything. I think the Brotherhood was looking to collect something, anything, that might draw you out into the open."

Elvis, head in hands, could not look up. The very thing the DRS had thrived on since the beginning—their anonymity—was now directly in the crosshairs.

"What's your next step, John?" he asked.

"I was able to get the phone number of Langston's handler. I'll track him down next."

"Good. When?"

"Soon."

"Find out everything you can. It's time to get our new boy up to speed. I believe he can help us here."

"Do whatever you need to, because I'm telling you, Elvis, I think the Brotherhood not only knows how the DRS operates, I think they're out to destroy us. Maybe not by direct assault, but with money. Bank accounts. Financial transaction trails. Exposure. I don't know how they know, but I think Buddy was right: They know. And I think *you* are the target."

chapter
THIRTEEN

lvis circled Cole, examining him up and down from all sides. The room they were in was empty save two chairs and a mirror on the wall. Cole sat in one of the chairs. Elvis rubbed his chin, then said, "We're going to have to create a new protocol for you, Cole. Usually when someone joins the team, they're famous. When the press reports that person has died, most everybody believes it. You, my friend, are not famous. That means if someone who knows you were to see you walking down the street, they would think it's you. When someone on the street sees me, they think I'm either an Elvis impersonator or a wack job."

"Okay, so what does that mean?" Cole asked.

"It means we're going to have to change your look. You can't hide in plain sight like the rest of us."

Janis Joplin walked in the room, carrying a duffle bag and pair of scissors. Apart from being nearly thirty years older, Janis's appearance hadn't changed at all since her "death" in 1970. Her untamed brown hair with streaks of gray was restrained casually by a purple bandana. She wore rose-colored glasses, dark-blue bell-bottom jeans, and a pink-and-orange flower print shirt. Her wrists jangled with a dozen bracelets, and rings adorned most of her fingers. Around her neck she wore a beaded necklace with a pewter cricket as its centerpiece charm.

Cole smirked. "Isn't it a little cliché for a girl on the team to be the hairdresser and stylist, King?"

Without hesitation, Janis slapped the taste out of Cole's mouth.

"What was that for?" he asked, his face smarting from the blow.

"First of all," Janis said, "I am not a hairdresser or a stylist. I am a Dead Rock Star, and I do whatever this team needs to get the job done. It just so happens that I can cut hair. Secondly, to some of us you're not exactly a welcome addition, Cole Denton. So just keep your mouth shut and let me cut your hair."

"Yes ma'am," Cole said, as Janis turned his head to face the mirror.

Elvis watched as this scene unfolded. He knew that Janis was still mourning Buddy and was taking it out on Cole. But he also knew he needed her to accept him. Her opinion carried a lot of weight with the team. Elvis sat down in the other chair, where Cole could see him in the mirror. He pulled out a comb and began combing his chemically enhanced jet-black hair.

"You know, Janis, Cole didn't ask to join this team. He's here because I asked him. He has freely chosen to die and join us."

"Yeah, well, you know what they say about freedom," Janis spat.

"I know," Elvis said soothingly, "but Cole had a *lot* to lose. He walked away from a certain fortune. He walked away from a girl. He left everything, just like us. And he just wants to help."

Janis didn't say anything but began aggressively combing and cutting Cole's hair. His sandy blond locks fell to the floor, and Elvis watched as she skillfully crafted a new hairstyle for their new recruit.

She then started putting chemicals in his hair. Elvis knew from experience the burning sensation Cole must be feeling, as though his scalp were on fire. No doubt he wanted to shout, but the young man neither flinched nor said a word.

Then Janis began rummaging through her duffle bag, pulling out clothes and various accessories. She would hold a shirt up in front of Cole and decide if it was right for the look she was crafting for him. This fashion matchmaking went on for the next several minutes, during which Cole's remaining hair had turned black.

"You're going to have to grow a beard," she said to Cole. "You can grow a beard, right? And we'll have to laser that ridiculous tribal tattoo on your arm."

"Aw, man. Goodbye, Spring Break '95!" Cole lamented.

Janis went back to clipping and shaping his new hairstyle.

The room was very quiet.

Elvis broke the silence. "Cole, tell Janis what you're working on."

"Uh, I've been studying that funky symbol Buddy drew. I can't make heads or tails of its meaning, but there's something familiar about the shape."

"Talk to Tupac," Janis said tersely. "He's our linguist, you know."

"No, I didn't know that. I'll see what he thinks."

Janis was clearly not interested in talking shop with Cole, and she wouldn't yet be impressed with his skill set. So the King took another tack. "Cole, why don't you tell Janis a little more about yourself? Maybe tell her about growing up in Illinois."

This made Cole flinch. Elvis knew he would have rather endure a root canal without Novocain than talk about his childhood. Especially to a stranger who hadn't warmed to him and was holding scissors in her hand.

"What do you want me to say, King? That I was a weirdo? That I enjoyed the company of a keyboard and mouse more than people? That I didn't have many friends because I was always two or three grades ahead of kids my age?"

"Yeah. Go on."

"Okay. Um . . . I fell in love with computers when I was six or seven. I learned everything I could about them. I learned how to program them and write code. I spent all my time on the internet when it came out, so I stayed in the house a lot. I got chubby. I liked Cheetos."

Janis chuckled under her breath a little. Her tension seemed to ease a bit as Cole described his childhood. Elvis gave Cole a hand gesture to keep going. Janis was too preoccupied with her task to see the little game Elvis was playing.

"My, uh . . . mom, uh . . ." Cole was wrestling with how to say it without coming right out and saying it. "You know those women who show up at the emergency room because they 'fell down the stairs'?" he said making air quotes. "Yeah, that was my mom." He shifted his weight in his chair from side to side, as though physically uncomfortable. "My dad . . . he was probably a genius, but he also didn't like his liver very much. I dunno, I guess he was under a lot of pressure."

Elvis knew it pained him to speak the next words.

"One night, when I was fourteen, Dad got really hammered. I don't know exactly what happened; I wasn't there. I was with my aunt and uncle. They're not really my aunt and uncle; I just called them that. Anyway, Dad somehow, uh . . . started a fire. Our house . . . the whole place burned down. Mom and Dad were both killed. I literally lost everything in one day."

Janis had stopped cutting. Cole stared at the floor. The room was eerily quiet.

Cole tried to lighten the moment. "Sorry to, uh—I don't know, how would a rock star say it? Sorry to 'harsh everyone's mellow.'" The bad joke hung in the air like a rain cloud.

Then Elvis thought he heard Janis sniffle a little. In the King's mind, this was progress. He wanted her and the others to trust Cole, but he knew it wouldn't happen without Cole being real and open with them about who he was.

"I was a weirdo, too," Janis offered slowly. "I loved music. People thought I was strange. I was pudgy, too. And I had acne."

"Oh *man*, did I have acne!" Cole said, rolling his eyes.

Elvis stood up and smiled at Cole in the mirror. This relationship was now heading in the right direction.

★ ★ ★ ★

Cole's head still stung a little from the chemicals Janis had used to dye his hair. His eyes were dry, too, due to the contacts he now wore to change his eye color. And his face itched from not having shaved for a few days. The outward transformation of Cole Denton was in full swing. No one had mentioned a spray tan yet, but he suspected it was coming.

Jerry Garcia was taking him to Jim Morrison's house to continue his training for the day. "Cole, do you like L. L. Cool J?"

"He's okay, why?"

"Because Mama said knock you out! And when I say Mama, I mean Jim Morrison. He's about to knock you out."

"Oh great," Cole moaned.

Jerry led him to the room the DRS affectionately called the Dojo. Morrison was already there, awaiting their arrival. Jerry brought Cole to the middle of the room and stepped aside.

Morrison began walking circles around Cole.

On the way over, Jerry had given Cole some background on Morrison. Since the mid-1970s, the Dojo was where Morrison had taught all the Dead Rock Stars to fight. When Buddy Holly recruited Morrison in 1971, he didn't know just how adept Jim would become at hand-to-hand combat. While always ready for a scrap in his old life, he was not focused, and he had no formal training. Something about being "dead" liberated the inner warrior that had been locked away in Morrison his whole life. He began training and took to disciplined fighting styles like a duck to water. He became swift, strong, and smart in battle. Today, no one would want to meet a middle-aged Jim Morrison in a dark alley.

The floor of the Dojo was covered in stretched canvas. There Morrison had painted a gigantic Gila monster perched on a cactus. On the bamboo-lined walls were hung three posters. The first was the famous shot of Bruce Lee from *Enter the Dragon* with bloody scratches on his chest, a poster that decorated the room of every teenage boy in the 1970s and '80s. The second poster showed Pearl Jam's Eddie Vedder leaning against bassist and bandmate Jeff Ament as they performed onstage, an image that hung on the wall of every guy's dorm room in the nineties. The third was the movie poster for the 1987 film *The Lost Boys*. Cole figured Morrison must have loved that movie. People are strange.

In one corner was a built-in cabinet that housed an elaborate 1970s-era stereo system and record player. There were twenty-four-inch speakers in each corner of the Dojo from which emanated sounds of thunderstorms and nature. Jerry had told Cole that the others had long tried to convince Morrison to upgrade to CDs, or at least cassette tapes, but he remained loyal to vinyl.

Morrison was barefoot and wore only faded blue jeans with holes in the knees. He was lean and muscular. His graying hair was still long but pulled back into a ponytail. His blue eyes were clear and focused. Jim Morrison was the very picture of health, mentally and physically. According to Jerry, he hadn't taken a drink since the day he "died," and he hadn't spoken a word since 1993. No one in the DRS really understood the vow of silence thing.

"Jim doesn't speak, so I will serve as his mouthpiece," Garcia said to Cole, as Morrison continued to circle him. "He always asks his trainees three questions: One, have you had any training?"

"Not really," Cole said, "unless you count a few weeks of karate lessons back in 1984 as training? Everyone my age had to take lessons after seeing *Karate Kid*." Cole then struck the Crane Kick pose. Swiftly and with great force, Morrison chopped Cole's plant leg at the shin, dropping him to the floor.

"Heeeeey, man!" Cole shouted.

Jerry dropped to his knees and grabbed Cole by the face, looking him square in the eyes. "Never, and I mean *never*, do that again. You understand?"

"Yeah," Cole said, rubbing his shin.

"He hates that movie," Jerry said. "He thinks the Crane Kick was an illegal move."

Morrison motioned for him to stand back up. He then brought his hands together, as if praying, and bowed toward Cole.

"This is how he apologizes," Jerry explained. "It's also how he says, 'Thank you,' so I'm not really sure which he means right now," he said with a raspy laugh. Morrison smirked as well.

"Okay, question two," Jerry said, regaining his train of thought. "Have you ever been in a fight?"

"Not really, unless you count Tony Scardino in the fourth grade," Cole said, lying. He'd taken many a beating during his childhood. Morrison lunged again to strike Cole, but this time he avoided the blow.

Morrison nodded in approval.

"Oh, very good," Garcia said. "Jim likes it when his students are fast learners. Okay, last question." Jerry paused. Simultaneously Morrison stopped circling and positioned himself directly behind Cole.

Cole stopped rubbing his leg, stood straight up, and tried to face his teacher.

"No, man, you have to face forward," Jerry said apologetically, turning Cole back around. "Here it is, last question: Do you absolutely believe in our cause?"

Cole paused. The computer in his brain ran through all the possible scenarios of what would happen based on how he answered. They all seemed to lead to Morrison attacking him in some fashion, so he braced himself as he answered.

"Yes. I've left everything for this. Why would I do that if I didn't believe?"

Cole waited for a blow from behind, but it never came.

After a moment, he turned around to find Morrison gone. Jerry was gone too. Suddenly the lights went off, and the sounds of nature from the speakers intensified. Then the room was cast in a strange purple light. As Cole's eyes adjusted, he could start to make out words on the bamboo wall in front of him. He realized the purple was coming from a black light and the words were written with a black light pen.

He would later learn that Morrison called these his Ten Commandments:

You will do 500 push-ups a day.
You will do 500 sit-ups a day.
You will do 500 bodyweight squats a day.
You will run 5 miles a day.
You will train with me 5 days a week for 2 hours a day.
You will drink one ounce of water for every pound you weigh, every day.

You will eat the food I tell you to eat.
You will meditate every day.
You will make music every day.
You will commit, heart, mind, and soul to the cause.

No sooner had Cole finished reading than the lights came back on, and Jerry was standing next to him.

"When am I going to have any time to do anything else?" Cole whined.

"Dead men have a lot of time on their hands. Happy death day—tomorrow!" Garcia said with a laugh.

"Wha—?"

"To the world, Cole Denton dies tomorrow. Congratulations."

chapter
FOURTEEN

The Muslim call to prayer echoed throughout the city of Barukh. For the next five minutes, much of the city's routine—shopping, deliveries, and business transactions—ground to a halt. Everything except for prayer. The non-Muslims, which were few, continued on their way while respectfully dodging those who had stopped in their tracks to face east and pray.

Arham Ali Syed spent these five minutes praying in an air-conditioned mosque. A leading cleric in the Arab Republic of Ammon who was likely to be elected the newly formed country's first prime minister, he was visiting his hometown to politick and network. He wouldn't have to work hard to make a good impression because he was beloved in Barukh, but it never hurt for cameras to capture the adoration of the masses. And there were cameras. This being Ammon's first election, the world's press was captivated by the story of the birth of a democratic nation in the Middle East.

As prayer time drew to a close, Syed rose from his knees and prepared to exit the mosque. Handlers swooped in to make sure his appearance was just right for the Western cameras waiting to take his picture on this historic day. Judging by the buzz coming from outside the building, a crowd had gathered and was clamoring to catch a glimpse of him and maybe even touch the hem of his garment.

"It is time," Syed said.

Twelve men clad in dark suits, sunglasses, and earpieces nodded and formed a tight wedge-shaped perimeter around him. Their job was to keep Syed safe yet allow the masses to draw close enough to feel as though they'd been in the presence of greatness.

The doors swung open, and the oppressive desert sun shone through, drenching the twelve men in dark suits in sweat almost immediately. Syed wore a white robe appropriate for the ninety-degree day, but he registered the heat all the same. As he exited the building, the crowds began pushing toward him. He waved and smiled affectionately as he walked a few feet to the steps of the mosque and stopped. This was the perfect vantage point for the assembled press to capture the moment.

The wedge of protection morphed as Syed's security detail shifted into a rectangular box formation—better for maintaining perimeter integrity—and the crowd, like water, rushed to fill every conceivable space around them. Cameras snapped frame after frame as hands reached past the bodyguards to touch the man they hoped would lead their country.

Not far away, dozens of TV reporters were on camera, sending reports on the scene back to their countries. An American reporter from a major cable news network was reporting live, saying, "It's an historic day in the Arab Republic of Ammon. Arham Ali Syed, once a humble cleric, is now on the threshold of history as the popular choice to become the nation's first elected prime minister. It's a festive scene here in the city of Baruch as thousands have gathered to express their love and support. Syed has just emerged from the mosque after prayer, and it looks like he is going to address the crowd. Let's see if we can hear what he has to say."

A small portable sound system had been set up at the foot of the steps. Syed took the mic and said, "As-salāmu 'alaykum, my friends! Thank you for coming today. In the West there is a writer who said, 'You cannot go home again.' That might be true in America, but not here. Not today, my friends. You honor me with your presence and warmth. I am grateful for you. I am so glad to be home."

The crowd roared its approval.

Syed continued, "I dreamed long ago that we would one day become a nation of our own, free to live and govern our people as we see fit under the eyes of Allah. Today we are on the brink of that dream becoming a reality. Today I am asking you to join me as we lead our country into a new century of peace, freedom, and prosperity!"

Suddenly, from the other side of the city, an explosion erupted, shaking the area with the force of a mild earthquake. Many near the steps of the mosque did not hear the explosion or feel the tremor due to the swell of humanity. A clamor arose at the back of the crowd, and Syed registered that something was wrong but didn't know exactly what was happening. As word spread and the commotion grew, Syed addressed the crowd again, "Peace, friends! Everyone stay calm." The twelve bodyguards all touched their earpieces in unison as communication began flooding in from Syed's security detail in other parts of the city.

"What's going on?"

"What happened?"

"Is Syed injured?"

Then a voice pierced through the confusion. "Get him to a car, now! There's been a bombing!"

Immediately, the twelve formed a tight diamond around Syed and began pushing forward throw the crowd. Syed was confused but maintained an outwardly calm demeanor; he didn't yet know what had happened, but he trusted these men to protect him with their lives.

As news of a bombing spread through the streets like a wave, panic took over and chaos set in as people began running in all directions. A black BMW sedan aggressively made its way through the crowd and got as close to the steps of the mosque as it could. Its driver was wearing a gas mask. The leader of the security detail got in the passenger seat; two others piled into the back seat with Syed in the middle, shielding him with their arms. The driver handed Syed a gas mask just as another explosion was heard a few blocks away. They could now see flames and smoke rising above nearby buildings.

"What is happening?" Syed asked as he attempted to put on the gas mask.

"There are bombs going off in the city," one of the bodyguards said as he helped Syed with his gas mask. "We must get you to safety."

"Why the mask?"

"We have to protect you," the bodyguard replied as he adjusted the straps.

"What about you? You have no masks," Syed observed, concerned for his men.

"We'll be fine."

A few feet away, the American reporter was still broadcasting live: "Chaos has broken out in Barukh. There have been at least two bombings in the city where Arham Ali Syed was greeting crowds after midday prayers. Security has escorted him to a vehicle, and the driver is now trying to make a way through the panicked masses. Wait . . . shots are being fired . . ."

The remaining bodyguards were trying to clear a path for the car to get away by firing automatic weapons into the air. This only made the panic worse. The driver laid on the horn of the BMW and did everything but run over potential voters.

"Go!" the lead bodyguard yelled from the passenger seat. "We have to get Syed away from here. They'll move out of the way!"

With one long blast of the horn the driver pushed the car forward. Sure enough, the crowd began to part as the car started accelerating and grazing people along the road. A pathway cleared, and the driver accelerated through it. The two bodyguards in the back seat turned to look behind them. They could see another explosion go off not far from where they had just been.

A voice crackled in the earpieces of the bodyguards in the vehicle.

"Is Syed safe?"

"Yes," the lead bodyguard reported. "We are taking him to the safe house now."

Then he turned and saw the driver reach beneath the seat, pull out a canister, and remove the pin. Gas started spewing out of the canister, and immediately the bodyguards began coughing and choking and quickly passed out.

The driver looked back at Syed, and for the first time, Syed could see that the driver had white skin and blonde hair escaping from beneath the gas mask. The driver pulled the car to the side of the road.

"Who are you?" Syed asked.

"We are the Brotherhood," the driver answered and pointed a pistol at Syed. "I want you to imagine a world where people would not attempt to bomb a peaceful man who is just trying to help his people. That is our goal: To create a world where everybody lives as one."

"But I want the same thing!" Syed cried. "Why do this, friend?"

"Because today you become a martyr. Today your death helps the greater cause. Go in peace, my brother!" The driver then pulled the gas mask off Syed's face and laid it in the front seat. Syed began coughing and choking before slumping over, unconscious like the others.

The driver got out of the car, pulled one of the men from the back seat, and put him in the driver's seat. Once the scene was staged, the driver took the two gas masks and walked away from the vehicle. A few hundred feet from the car, the Brotherhood agent pulled out a device and pressed the red button on it.

The car exploded in a brilliant display of fire and smoke.

The next day, front-page headlines in America were mainly about the coming new year and how to prepare for Y2K. Elsewhere in the papers, some ran brief wire reports of Syed's assassination. Experts believed that his security detail had turned and assassinated him. There was no mention of the Brotherhood.

chapter

FIFTEEN

avannah Hulette's first few classes had been fairly normal. She gave two pop quizzes in preparation for the end of the quarter. She caught a boy cheating off the quiet girl in the second row who was too afraid to turn him in. A pair of lovebirds were passing notes in class, but probably because of her own circumstances, she let them off with a warning and a wink.

Between operating the scantron, ordering her dissection specimens for next quarter, and lining up parent-teacher conferences, Savannah barely had time to breathe, let alone eat. She grabbed a bag of Bugles and a Honey Bun from the vending machine and used her lunch time to grade papers. Savannah had learned to stay away from the Cheetos after the day neon orange dust appeared on her hip where she had wiped her hands before class. The ninth-grade boys had giggled all day about that one.

A voice blared over the speaker in her classroom, "Ms. Hulette, you have a phone call."

Savannah smiled politely at her fifth-period students, who were still settling in before the start of class. She said, "I'll be back in a moment. Take this time to study for the quiz you'll take when I return. Also, Tiffany, please turn on the TV for Channel One, which should be on in two minutes." With that, she went to the teachers' lounge for a bit of privacy.

The red light was blinking on the phone. She picked up the handset, pressed the button for line one, and as professionally as possible said, "Hello, this is Ms. Hulette. How can I help you?"

"Savannah, have you heard? Are you okay? What are you going to do?" Savannah recognized her sister Amy's voice.

"What are you talking about? Are Mom and Dad okay?"

"It's about Cole. You didn't see it this morning in the newspaper?"

"Amy, you know I've been swamped with midterms. Besides, he started that job a few days ago. He's gone, and he told me I'd never see him again. What are you talking about? What happened?"

"They found his car burned down to the frame. He's dead."

Savannah found she could no longer form words with her mouth.

"Savannah, are you there? I'm so sorry. Do you want me to come get you?"

"No," she said abruptly and hung up.

She rushed out of the teachers' lounge but stopped just outside the door. To her left, the hallway led back to her classroom. To her right, the hallway led to the teachers' parking lot. With a determined scowl, she retrieved her jacket, keys, and purse, her quarter-inch heels clicking on glossy tiles down a hall decorated for the Halloween dance at the end of the month. She slammed the crash bar on the exit door and was blasted with daylight.

She needed to know what happened to Cole, she needed to read it for herself, and she needed a place to be alone. And she needed it all now.

By the time Savannah reached the Toyota Celica her grandparents had given her when she graduated from college, tears were welling up in her eyes. While she buckled up and started the car, she said aloud, "He had no one else. Who would come to his funeral?" She wiped away a tear trying to escape down her cheek, put the car in reverse, and took off without telling a soul where she was going.

★ ★ ★ ★

". . . Denton had a bright future. Deemed an up-and-comer in the field of computer technology, he was being courted by several high-tech giants in Silicon Valley. *Wired* magazine recently profiled Denton as the founder of Connextion.com, a matchmaking site that has grown exponentially simply through word of mouth in the online community. . . ."

Headline News had been running the same report every thirty minutes. Savannah watched each time, hoping for more information about the accident.

She had also logged onto CompuLive and its news aggregator. There she found a headline that read, "The Chuck Woolery of Dating Websites Dies in Horrific Car Crash." She clicked the link and read and re-read the details:

> *The twenty-one-year-old internet entrepreneur and MIT Ph.D. student was pronounced dead following the single-car accident on Interstate 70, between St. Louis and Kansas City, MO. There were no eyewitnesses to the crash, but Denton's car is believed to have careened off a bridge and exploded on an embankment of the Missouri River. There is no word as to whether anyone was with him at the time. Investigators have not yet determined the cause of the accident, though an individual close to the investigation, speaking on condition of anonymity, suggested that mechanical failure, excessive speed, or drugs may be involved—possibly all three. An autopsy is not expected to reveal much, as the body was burned beyond recognition. Thousands of Connextion.com members have expressed their sorrow and condolences on the website's message boards.*

After several hours of searching the internet, asking Jeeves, and calling law enforcement officials across the state of Missouri, Savannah finally reached the coroner's office in Columbia. She had been transferred to three different people and was starting to lose patience when someone picked up.

"This is Steven."

"Um, yes, Mr. . . . Steven, my name is Savannah Hulette."

"Well, hello, Savannah. I have to admit, I don't usually find myself talking to someone who sounds as lovely as you. I spend a lot of time around people who don't talk back, if you know what I mean."

Steven chuckled at his own joke, but Savannah did not respond.

"I'm sorry, Ms. Hulette, what can I do for you?" he said, trying to reestablish some semblance of decorum.

"I'm calling about Cole Denton."

"Oh. I'm so sorry, who are you again? Is this a reporter? Because I can't comment pending results of the autopsy."

"No. I'm his . . ." Savannah had thought about what to say the entire time she had been on hold, but now she was struggling to speak these words into existence. "I was his girlfriend."

"I'm supposed to say I'm sorry for your loss," Steven muttered.

"Thanks."

There was more awkward silence.

"About me hitting on you . . ."

"Let's forget that happened."

"Man, that would be awesome, I can't have another one of these on my recor—

. . . I'm going to stop talking now."

"Steven, do you think you could help me?"

"Um, yeah, I kinda owe you."

"What happened to him? What can you tell me?"

"I really can't tell you much."

"Why not?"

"Well, there isn't much to tell." Before he could filter what he needed to say appropriately, he blurted out, "I mean, I've never seen anything like it. It almost makes me believe in spontaneous combustion. This guy was crispy!"

Silence.

"I'm sorry, Ms. Hulette. I mean, your boyfriend was cris—. I don't think I'm helping. I really shouldn't talk to people."

Savannah held her tongue, knowing this man was likely the only one who could possibly tell her more than what was being reported in the media. "Steven, it's okay. I teach science; I can handle this. If you could explain, how did you identify the body as Cole?"

"We have his dental records, and a portion of a tattoo was preserved by the non-flammable seatbelt."

Cole had never shown her his tattoo. This made her insides ache; there was so much she didn't know. She started to cry enough that Steven could hear her.

"I don't know what else I can tell you. Again, I'm sorry for your loss."

"Thanks, Steven."

Savannah hung up the phone and fell into a heap on the floor.

★ ★ ★ ★

She stood outside the door of the local address she had found for Cole. She had never been to his place. They hadn't gotten that far before he took this mysterious job and was snatched away from her. As she stood there, frozen by pain and loss, the door flew open. Taylor was carrying three open trash bags full of what appeared to be Eggo boxes and Hot Pocket cartons. He never looked up until he almost plowed into Savannah.

"Whoa, my bad! Sorry."

"Are you Taylor?" she asked

Taylor stared at her for a moment and couldn't help but notice a shadow of sadness over her face. "Yeah, I'm Taylor. Are you . . ."

"Savannah. Yes. I found this address for Cole. I know we didn't know each other, but I–I just can't let it go."

"Me too! I haven't left my apartment in three days."

She looked down. He didn't know where to look.

"Hey, you wanna come inside?"

"Thanks. Can I see his room?"

"Um, yeah. There's not much left, but he did pack up in kind of a hurry. You're welcome to go through what's left. I'm going to take these bags down to the dumpster. His room is on the right. I'll give you some time."

Savannah nodded and then slowly entered the apartment. It was exactly what she expected. Nothing on the walls. All the furniture looked like they had gotten it off the side of the road. There were three televisions right next to each other, with three different video gaming systems perched on old milk crates. There was a poster on the wall of a dark, ominous sky with the words, "The truth is out there."

She took a breath and walked back to his room, where she found a single bed and a bunch of pinholes in the wall. Dust on the hardwood floors revealed the outlines of a desk and a few other things she couldn't identify.

Savannah sat down on the bed and thought. She thought about all the conversations they had, their first date, the kiss, and the last time she talked to him on the phone. Her mind raced as she replayed every talk, every touch, even how he smelled.

She kicked her shoes off and laid on her back. She wanted to imagine what had been going through his head—what he had planned and where he was going. It was clear he had been home and was on his way out west, but to do what? Why the secrecy? There were so many things she'd never know. As she stared up at the ceiling, she noticed a piece of fishing line that had been snipped on one end hanging from the popcorn-textured drywall.

She wept.

After enough time had passed that she felt like her puffy eyes wouldn't betray her, she opened the bedroom door and looked around for Taylor. After realizing she had been alone in the apartment, she went to the door to leave. She found Taylor leaning against the outside wall, waiting.

"Thank you, Taylor."

"You are welcome. I'm going to miss him, too."

"It's like he left us twice."

"I know what you mean. The first time, I knew he was going to change the world. This time, I just feel empty."

"Taylor, did you know where he was going?"

"Nope. We're dudes. We never talked about important stuff."

Taylor made a move towards Savannah. She hesitated but then realized what he was doing and decided to let it happen. Taylor and Savannah hugged like two people at a funeral home. It was a hug for comfort, a hug for support. It was two humans who had lost someone and didn't have words to express how they felt.

"I was mad at him for leaving us. But I was happy for him at the same time," Taylor said eventually.

"Me too. I feel like I had known him for years, even though it was only a few days."

"He really liked you."

Savannah's knees buckled, and she braced herself against the wall.

"What are we supposed to do now?" she asked.

★ ★ ★ ★

The following week was fall break. Savannah turned down every phone call and deleted messages from her girlfriends. They and her sister were really the only ones who knew about her relationship with Cole. She hadn't talked to her parents about him yet, and honestly, wasn't sure anyone would understand how she felt, other than Taylor. She was lying on her couch, in her robe, and hadn't showered for a few days when the doorbell rang. She ignored it, but it rang again. The lights and TV were on, and she didn't know what to do. Finally, her vanity lost the battle, and she answered the door looking like a homeless person.

"Who is it?" she bellowed through the door without opening it.

"United Parcel Service, or UPS to the layman."

"I didn't order anything, sir. I'm not expecting a package."

"I'm just UPS, ma'am. I deliver. Package label says it's from Taylor Wainscott."

"Leave it by the front door. Thank you."

She counted to thirty and then opened the door. It was a big box. It would fit through the door and was easy enough for her to carry, but it wasn't a small package.

After closing the door, she plopped the box on her dining room table and went for her scissors in the craft drawer. She made quick work of the wrapping and bubble wrap to find a smaller box that looked like it had been opened and then re-taped. There was a letter taped to the top of it:

Dear Savannah,

I told him not to do this. To be honest, I didn't know he'd even followed through with it. When I opened it, I knew he wanted you to have it. Cole loved this TV show. This was like the one that hung above his bed, but he wanted to order you a "special" one. I tried to tell him that women don't like things like this, but you know how Cole was. Once he got an idea, it was hard for him to shake. I don't know what you'll do with it now, but I just wanted you to know—he obviously cared a lot about you.
Live Long and Prosper,
Taylor

★ ★ ★ ★

The superintendent of her apartment complex wasn't sure about the request but could tell Savannah had been going through something. She got home after school one day and found a note attached to her front door: "I hung the thing you asked for. Ran the electricity too. This is the weirdest thing I've ever seen a woman hang above her bed."

Savannah dropped her things on the floor and ran into the bedroom. She closed the curtains and turned off the lights. Then she stood on her bed and clicked the small button on the model. An array of lights shot out of the top of the saucer section of the *USS Enterprise.* On her ceiling was the galaxy. Her father used to watch *Star Trek* on TV and had dragged her to a few movies at a theater. She liked the one with the whales in San Francisco, and that was enough for her.

But this was different. She had something that Cole had made just for her. She studied every part of it. It looked like an exact replica but was all geeked out. The thrusters glowed, and the ship hummed when she pushed the right buttons. The supervisor had wired it through the place formerly occupied by her ceiling fan, so she'd never have to worry about replacing batteries.

There was one thing she found odd about this handmade, customized replica. She picked up on it only after renting a few DVDs of the show from Blockbuster. In the

TV series, the alpha-numeric registration of the *Enterprise* was NCC-1701. The one that flew above her bed had a completely different designation:

DRS-1865.

Savannah lay on her bed, closed her eyes, and hoped to dream about Cole.

chapter

SIXTEEN

ole walked up to the ivy-covered house and knocked on the front door. No answer. He knocked again. Still nothing. Then he listened. He faintly heard music coming from somewhere, so he wandered around the house to the back yard. That's where he found Tupac Shakur.

Tupac was lounging beside a resort-like pool, shirtless, barefoot, and wearing black boardshorts and dark-rimmed sunglasses. Hans Zimmer's score for the movie *The Thin Red Line* was enveloping the pool from hidden speakers. Tupac seemed to be engrossed in a book.

It was a lovely fall day, cool but not cold. Portable heaters dotted the landscape like giant silver mushrooms to ensure the ambient temperature was shirtless-level comfortable.

"Anybody home?" Cole called when he was within earshot.

"Cole Denton," Tupac said, looking up from his book. "Welcome to the crib."

"Thanks, man. This place has quite the vibe. Love the space heaters. Makes it feel perfect back here."

"You can take the man outta the West Coast, but you can't take the West Coast outta the man. Gotta be a perfect seventy-two degrees, just like it was in L.A."

"The music?"

"One of the greatest geniuses out there right now. Hans Zimmer."

"Hmm, okay. Never heard of him."

"Film scores. Soundtracks. Genius."

Film scores, huh? Cole thought. *I need to lock that away.*

"What are you reading?"

"*The Lexus and the Olive Tree.*"

"What's it about?"

"Globalization."

"Cool." Then he just stood there, staring at Tupac.

"So, you need something, man?"

"Oh, yeah. I still get a little overwhelmed by this whole deal."

Tupac chuckled. "I feel ya. Whatchu need from me, though?" He wasn't being rude, but he clearly didn't want to have a full-on hang session with the new kid, either.

"Janis told me I should talk to you about this," Cole said, handing Tupac the picture of the symbol Buddy drew on the wall in his own blood the night he died. "She told me you were the resident linguist and that I should pick your brain about it."

"Yeah, okay, let's have a look." Tupac took the picture and examined it. It was fitting, in Cole's estimation, that Tupac was the DRS linguist. The way he could string together layers of ideas into a seamless lyric indicated an artist who had a deep, intuitive grasp of linguistic complexity.

Tupac stared at the picture for quite some time, while Cole just stood there nervously.

Finally, Tupac said, "It's not any language that I know of. At first glance, somebody might think it was an Asian language, but nah, it ain't. I'd say this is not a language but a symbol."

"You don't think it could be something ancient like Sanskrit or an Egyptian hieroglyph, do you?"

"I said it wasn't a language," Tupac said, somewhat annoyed.

Cole picked up on the annoyance and carefully asked, "How would you go about determining what it means?"

Tupac again studied it for a long time. Almost uncomfortably long. The CD had switched from Hans Zimmer to Tupac himself. Cole knew Tupac's music but wasn't familiar with the song that was playing.

"This is you, right?"

"Yeah, I'm droppin' a new record in a month or so. Don't interrupt my flow again. You came here asking for my help," he said to Cole sternly.

Cole pulled an imaginary zipper across his lips and put his hands in the air. Then it hit him, and he couldn't help but talk again.

"Dude, you're supposed to be dead. How can you release new music?"

Tupac now glared at Denton. He shook his head and continued to study the symbol. The minutes ticked away. Cole was starting to wonder if this was some sort of joke when Tupac broke the silence.

"Break it down. See if there is meaning within the meaning."

"Um . . . thanks?" Cole said, somewhat confused at this vague advice. "Any chance I can get an advance copy of that record?"

"No," Tupac replied flatly.

"Okay, then. Thanks for the help." Cole pivoted to exit.

"It's in you, Cole Denton. You just gotta dig," Tupac said as Cole was walking away. "If you are gonna be everything King brought you here to be, you gotta work for it."

"Will do," Cole said and quickened the pace of his exit.

★ ★ ★ ★

Cole went back to his apartment. Much to his amazement his apartment truly *was* his apartment. Everything looked just like his old place, right down to the 1/128 replica of the Starship *Enterprise* hanging in the corner. Taylor wasn't there, however. And outside his front door was the biggest, weirdest neighborhood of all time and not his old apartment complex in Cambridge. He dubbed this place the "Nu-partment." Ultimately, he wasn't sure how he felt about living in this replica, but for now it would do. He also couldn't believe it had been built so fast; it had been waiting for him when he arrived in the Netherworld.

He had already worked out for the day but was so engrossed in the symbol that he didn't think about how sore his body was. He kept rolling around in his mind what Tupac said, "Break it down." So he broke it down. What did he see?

It kind of looked like an hourglass. Could it mean that time was running out? He turned it on its side, upside down, and every which way. Nothing jumped out at him.

Cole had drawn the symbol on so many pieces of paper and had made so many photocopies of the original that he couldn't walk anywhere in his apartment without stepping on a copy of Buddy's symbol. He took a few of the copies and cut out different shapes he saw within the symbol—a triangle, a half circle, greater-than and less-than signs, and something that sort of looked like an *X*. He then deconstructed the symbol, forming different shapes and pieces, rearranging the components to make something else that might be meaningful.

He tried to imagine it as a 3-D object and folded it into a circle. He tried to fit the pieces to build another object. He put multiple copies of the image on top of each other to see if it made a secret word or blueprint, like in the movie *Contact*.

Could the symbol have meant something specific to Buddy? Cole thought. He looked Buddy up online and read everything he could find about him. He learned he was from Texas, that he was married, and that he "died" when he was only twenty-two. He read lyrics from his songs. He read liner notes from the Crickets albums. He didn't find anything that was helpful for interpreting the symbol, but he learned a lot about the man he was tasked with replacing. He was moved by the sacrifice of such a young man, leaving behind a family to save the world. While Cole had sacrificed a lot to join the DRS, Buddy had given more, ultimately giving his life. Still, none of this helped Cole to discern what the symbol meant.

He dropped to the floor and started doing push-ups. He wasn't very good at push-ups. In fact, he hated push-ups, but he knew he needed to get stronger. As he raised up then lowered his body, he stared at the image. Then, like a picture hidden in a novelty 3-D book, something jumped out at him. He stopped doing push-ups and grabbed a copy of the symbol. He stared and stared. *Could it be that simple?* He traced his finger along the picture and spelled out what he thought he was looking at.

"It's a *2*!" he cried out loud. "There's a *2* right there!" He could clearly make out a distinct numeral two. But what did *2* mean? Cole wasn't sure, but he felt good about deciphering part of the puzzle. It wasn't the whole thing, but it was a start.

Elvis had not mandated that Cole spend all his time on this, and he knew he had to train rigorously, but getting to this point felt like an accomplishment. It was something he could build on.

Learning how to talk with dead people, though? That was a skill he knew needed more refinement.

chapter

SEVENTEEN

John Lennon was on his way to the Big Easy. That's where he expected to find the owner of the distorted voice he heard on Langston's phone the night he eliminated Bull and his team in Tennessee. He was able to trace the number on Langston's phone to an apartment in New Orleans.

After landing, Lennon procured a vehicle from long-term parking and drove to an area of town called the Garden District, where the apartment was located. He parked the car and began his usual surveillance routine, watching and waiting. Patiently. Carefully. Invisibly. He observed only one person, a middle-aged woman, who came and went from the second-story apartment. This woman spent every waking hour in the apartment, except for thirty minutes starting precisely at noon when she went to lunch. The window was small, but thirty minutes would give Lennon time to enter the apartment and sweep the premises for information on the Brotherhood and its operations.

The day he chose to infiltrate the apartment, he parked a block away and watched. The apartment building backed up to an alley that was empty, save for a dumpster and a few rodents. As the woman descended the steps for her lunch break, Lennon stepped out of his car and began walking down the block toward the building. He scooted around back, where he carefully climbed the drainpipe to the second story, making his entry through a bedroom window that faced the alley. He didn't even chip the paint on the frame as he slid his knife in to undo the latch. Once inside, he found the apartment to be completely empty aside from a chest of drawers, a modest closet of clothes, a hide-a-bed couch, a desk, a TV, a few books and magazines, dozens of telephone lines, and an old-fashioned switchboard.

He was able to discern from studying the switchboard that there were connections to phone lines all over the world converging in this tiny apartment. The middle-aged woman who occupied the space acted as an operator, plugging in phone lines from one port to another. Each line was labeled with a number but was run through a box designed to mask the location and identification of the operative on the other end of the line. Lennon scanned the switchboard until he found the number that Langston had called and traced its source to an address in Cleveland, Ohio.

On the desk where the operator sat was a notebook. Inside the notebook he found a list of numbers and addresses—a directory of every phone number used by the Brotherhood.

Lennon put in a call to headquarters.

Janis had been expecting to hear from him. "Yes, John."

"I've found what I believe to be the Brotherhood's phone hive."

"That's a good find, John," Janis said, sounding giddy as a schoolgirl. "Plant a bug so we can track what they're doing."

He reached into his satchel to grab a bugging package but then hesitated. "I think I'm going to burn it to the ground."

"Do you really think that's best?" Janis sounded confused by the suggestion. Then she said assertively, "We need to gather all the intel we can on these guys."

"Don't worry. I've found another location. This is not the endgame. If we cut off their communications, we disrupt the flow of information. How will they operate if they can't talk to each other, youknowwhatImean?"

"I'm not sure . . ."

"Don't you want to destroy these guys, Jan? This is how we do it. We know they're planning something big, and soon. This is no time to play the long game. We strike now and strike hard!" He hung up.

Lennon went to the tiny kitchen and found a natural gas line behind the oven. He picked up the kitchen phone and mustered up a thick but convincing New Orleans accent. He then called the nearest fire station. "Yeah, I live in the Garden Apartments up on Magazine Street. I keep smellin' some, like, gas or somethin.' Ya think y'all can come an' check it out fa me?"

"Sure," the fire operator said. "Which apartment are you in, sir?"

"Yeah, I live in unit 136. Second floor."

"A'ight. We'll be there in a minute or two."

"Thanks. Say hi to ya mamma and them."

Lennon hung up the phone and then broke the input valve on the natural gas line. A hissing sound and the tell-tale odor of rotten eggs let him know that gas was now filling the kitchen.

He spent the next few minutes scouring the apartment for any other clues but found nothing. He then went to the apartment's only bathroom, lit a candle, and shut the door. He tucked the notebook under his arm, went back to the window he came in, and scanned side to side to ensure no one would witness his exit. That's when he heard the sirens. He skillfully shinnied down the drainpipe with grace and ease.

He dropped to the ground, emerged from behind the building, and began strolling toward his car as if out for a casual afternoon walk. He was whistling "When the Saints Go Marching In" when, thirty seconds later, the second-story apartment exploded behind him. The natural gas had found its way under the bathroom door to the lit candle.

The whole apartment was incinerated in a matter of seconds, not that there had been much inside to burn. The phone lines quickly melted into an unrecognizable slag of rubber and wires. The fire trucks pulled up just as the flames began to lick the sky from the roof and windows. The firefighters leapt into action, soaking the building down and putting out the flames in mere minutes. But the damage to the Brother-hood call center was irreversible.

★ ★ ★ ★

Lennon drove off just as the woman who manned the phones returned from her lunch break. Her eyes went wide when she saw the commotion outside the apartment building. She immediately turned and walked in the other direction. She found the nearest pay phone and dialed a number. An answering machine received the call. Trying to control her panic, the woman said, "The call center has been hit. I am compromised. Go in peace, my brothers."

★ ★ ★ ★

John Lennon's next stop was Cleveland, where he set out to explore the downtown address indicated as the true location of Langston's contact. What he found there appeared to be a massive, deserted warehouse. He made a lap around the building, watching for security cameras, taking careful notes, and looking for an easy entry and finding none. He did discover a transformer feeding power to the building; it was way too much electricity for an abandoned warehouse. No doubt this place was secured to the hilt; access by traditional means was not an option. So he made his way to the roof where he found a tight ventilation shaft. With satchel in tow, Lennon shimmied into the metal casing and began descending into the interior of the building.

He quietly maneuvered his way to a ceiling vent that afforded him an excellent view of happenings in the warehouse below. Lennon observed at least two dozen men coming and going, many participating in various training exercises. Some were engaged in hand-to-hand fighting. Some were target practicing with pistols. Others were alternately constructing and disarming small explosives. As adept as he was as an agent, Lennon was not about to take on this many Brotherhood goons by himself. Given the building's location in Cleveland's downtown warehouse district, he ruled out the use of explosives, as the resulting conflagration could take out an entire city block in no time flat. Discovering a Brotherhood training facility was victory enough for one day. Lennon removed a Hi8 video camera from his satchel and started documenting the scene while quietly narrating.

"I'm in what appears to be a Brotherhood training facility in Cleveland. Hullo, Cleveland!" He made himself smile with the Spinal Tap reference. "I count at least twenty henchmen, but there are rooms I cannot see from my vantage point." He panned the camera around the room. "Here are six sparring in pairs. Oh, good jab! Here are four goons on a pistol range. Good shot, green!" A man in a green shirt had just pumped three straight shots to the heart of a target in rapid succession. "That had to be twenty-five feet out. Well done!" Lennon then turned the camera and pointed it at himself. "I'm going to sign off now, but I think this footage will be useful. Ciao! I am the walrus."

Just as he was about to stow the camera, he noticed a new person in the corner, talking to a group of trainees and issuing orders. This individual had a slender but athletic build and, as far as Lennon could make out, was about 5'9" or so. He couldn't hear voices, but he noted the new person had shoulder-length dishwater-blond hair and appeared to be a leader of some sort. One after another, each trainee walked up to this individual, had a very brief conversation, then returned to his task.

Lennon turned the camera back on and started shooting, zooming in as close as possible. "New person I just discovered. A blond chap who seems to be in charge. Giving orders and telling people what to do. Can't see anything but blond hair and a view from behind." He waited and waited, but the person never turned around. "I'm going to maintain position and observe for now. I'll film more again if necessary. I am the egg man."

He remained in place until nightfall but saw nothing more of note. As the light coming through the windows dimmed and the warehouse darkened, training began to break up for the day. Lennon stowed the camera and other gear in his satchel and made his way back through the ventilation shaft to the roof. The brisk evening air of late autumn on the lake hit his lungs, and he exhaled a long sigh of success.

As he made his way back to the airport, he called Elvis at the Netherworld.

"King, I found a training center."

"That's excellent, John! Should we infiltrate it?"

"No, it's heavily guarded, and it's in downtown Cleveland. I don't know how we get in without being seen or causing civilian casualties if there's a shootout. I think it's enough to know this place is here and come back to gather intel if need be."

"I concur. Good work, John. Are you planning on coming home soon? We need you for another op. And I'd love for you to spend some time with Cole."

"I'll be home soon." John paused a moment. "King . . ."

"Yeah."

"You ever think there will come a day when we're done with all this and we can have some semblance of a normal life?"

"That's not what we signed up for, friend. You know that."

"I know," John said wistfully. "But a man can dream, youknowwhatImean?"

Cole stood beside the gated entrance to the DRS neighborhood housing complex, waiting. Today, he was going to get his first behind-the-wheel driving lesson. He had spent time in a simulator, but this would be his first live roadwork. His muscles ached from his woeful attempts to abide by Jim Morrison's Ten Commandments, and he was looking forward to driving lessons, if only because it meant he could sit down for a while. Also, it meant spending time with Jimi Hendrix. To this point, the team's response to him had oscillated from indifferent to cold to downright hostile, but Jimi had given him a mostly warm welcome.

The 1968 Corvette convertible he rode in when he first arrived at the Netherworld screamed down the street, top down, and pulled up beside him.

"What's up, Jimi?" Cole called.

"You want to drive?" Jimi asked with a gleam in his eyes.

"Yeah, you bet!"

"Get in!"

Cole jogged to the driver's side of the car, but when he went to grab the door handle, Jimi abruptly lunged the car forward a few feet.

"Whatchu thinking, man?" Jimi scolded, looking back at Cole. "You're not driving *this* car."

"Oh," Cole said, chagrined. Moments later, as they got underway, he tried to laugh it off. "I remember when Wayne used to do that to Kevin on *The Wonder Years*. If I had a little brother, there's no question I would have pulled that trick on him. So, Jimi, where are we going?"

Jimi didn't answer. He just smirked at Cole and jammed the pedal to the floor.

Cole shifted in his seat, searching for a conversation starter. "Have you always been a great driver?"

"Nah, man!" Jimi laughed. "I was as blind as a bat, cat. King arranged for me to get this new surgery on my eyes, though, and it's like I can see colors I didn't know existed before! When I joined the team, Hank taught me to drive. He was our wheelman before me."

Cole appreciated being able to experience the drive this time without the massive duffle bag in his lap. He could take in the scenery better this way. He noticed things he hadn't seen before like a movie theater, currently showing *Star Wars I: The Phantom Menace*, according to the marquee out front. Cole remembered standing in line with Taylor for six hours to get great seats for that movie. That was only a few months ago, but it felt like a lifetime.

"Does the number two mean anything to you?" Cole asked.

Jimi just snickered.

"I don't mean like that. Get your mind out of the gutter, Hendrix!"

"Nah, for real," Jimi said, stroking his chin. "For musicians, two is a difficult thing. One is often easy. You stumble on some magic and write one good song or have one good album or even get one good riff. Sometimes, finding that second one is tough. They call it the sophomore slump. Lotta one-hit wonders out there."

Cole paused to consider if this idea had any correlation to his discovery of a *2* in the symbol. All the people he'd met on the team had had successful careers, gaining massive followings with hit after hit under their belts. Not Rolling Stones long, but enough to become legends. Not a one-hit wonder among them. Cole reckoned this probably wasn't what the *2* meant.

Jimi pulled into the humongous plane hangar they called "The Amelia" and parked the car alongside Izabella, the jet in which they had arrived at the Netherworld.

"Let's go," Jimi said, jumping out of the car and moving toward the plane.

"Are we flying somewhere?" Cole asked.

"Yeah. To your driving lesson."

They boarded the plane, and Cole sat down in the co-pilot's seat. Once they were in the air, Cole asked, "Who taught you to fly?"

"You wouldn't believe me if I told you," Jimi said, shaking his head and laughing.

"At this point, if you told me Superman taught you to fly, I'd believe it."

"Amelia Earhart."

"Wow!" Cole exclaimed. "It was right there in front of me, and I missed it! The name of the hangar! When was this? How old was she? Was she on the team?"

"Woah, young player! Pump the breaks! One at a time. I joined the team in 1970. Amelia was seventy-three at the time. She was spunky, man. A bundle of energy. And funny, too. She was our pilot until she was seventy-five. She started teaching me to fly almost immediately after I joined the team. Amelia was a great teacher."

"What happened to her?"

"She died in '87," Hendrix said wistfully. "She was ninety. Can you believe that? She passed in her sleep in that compound where you met the Prez. Lot of DRS agents have died there over the years. Peaceful way to go."

"What happens when someone dies?" Cole asked.

"They say you see a bright light, then you see your dead relatives . . ."

"I mean when a Dead Rock Star dies." Cole didn't know if Jimi was being serious or just pulling his chain. Regardless, he enjoyed having a pleasant interchange with someone on the team and laughing together.

"We put them in their real grave," Jimi said sadly. "Like King always says when we bury someone, 'We take a lie the world believes and make it true.'"

"That's deep," Cole said thoughtfully.

"Yeah, it is."

"So where did you bury Amelia Earhart? The world thinks she vanished over the Pacific."

"The Prez pulled some strings, and we buried her in DC, at Arlington National. A fitting place for a hero. Under a fake name, though."

They flew in solemn silence for the next few minutes. Cole stared out the window at the landscape below. He still had no idea where he was. He started wondering what people were saying about his "death." What did Savannah think? Was she heartbroken? Was she shocked? Would she move on quickly?

Dwelling too much on your loved ones is a dangerous line of thought, he remembered Jerry saying. He knew this was true, but he just couldn't help it at the moment. At some point, during his mental drift, Cole dozed off.

Minutes—maybe hours later for all he knew—he woke to the sound of Jimi snapping his fingers in Cole's face.

"Hey, kid. Wake up."

Cole shuddered, trying to rouse himself. They were on the ground in a small airport hangar.

As if reading his mind, Jimi said, "I know you're curious where we are. Don't worry about that for now. We'll clue you in eventually. For today, just focus on what we're here to do, and that's learn to drive like a Rock Star, got it?"

"Yeah, sure, okay," Cole said, still groggy from his nap.

There was a car waiting for them, a modest, red 1995 Toyota Camry that Jimi wasn't thrilled about. But it would suffice for their needs. They were in a small town, but one with all the modern accoutrements—a shopping mall, restaurants, a Blockbuster Video, and movie theaters. As they drove through town, Cole drifted into a daydream state. He'd been working so hard he hadn't had much time just to zone out.

"Hey, we're here," Jimi said.

"Here" was not what Cole expected. Jimi had pulled into the parking lot of a place called Kart Kountry. It was a Putt-Putt Fun Center, complete with three miniature golf courses, batting cages, a video arcade, and more.

"Why are we at a mini-golf place?"

"You have to crawl before you can walk, Grasshopper," Jimi said, motioning to the center's go-kart track.

"Wait. Go-karts?!?" Cole howled.

Jimi just laughed.

"All right, fine!" Cole said with disappointment.

Jimi paid the fee for unlimited racing for both of them, an exorbitant $24.99 per person for a full day of driving. The attendant put green paper bracelets around their wrists. She looked at Jimi a little funny. He just smiled back at her, recognizing that not many fifty-six-year-old men came here to drive go-karts once, much less all day.

"You told me you can almost see the future," Jimi said to Cole, "like you know where things are going before they get there. If this is true, that's the best skill you can have as a driver. When you're behind the wheel, you have to anticipate what the other drivers are going to do, then do what you need to do, at great speed and without killing yourself or anyone else in the process."

The kids in line paid them no mind as they waited, but the few parents among them couldn't take their eyes off the older man with the graying afro. Eventually, Jimi and Cole worked their way to the front. Twenty-five raggedy old go-karts were queued in two rows. Jimi pointed at the last kart, a green one with the number 27, indicating that he wanted Cole to take that one. Jimi climbed into the kart next to him, number 56. For both men, their knees poked up around the steering wheel of the tiny vehicles.

Jimi gave Cole some quick instructions. "I want you to drive your way to the front of the line. Anticipate where these kids are going and pass them. You've got to pass me, too, and you have to do it in three laps."

A teenage boy, barely older than the kids who had excitedly piled into the go-karts, walked down the line, checking the drivers' seatbelts.

"Hey," the boy croaked, stopping in front of Hendrix, "You look just like—"

"Morgan Freeman," Jimi said smiling. "I know, I get it all the time."

The boy had a puzzled look on his face but said nothing more. He walked back to the front of the line, stepped up onto a small box and began shouting out the rules. Maybe two kids were listening. Then he grabbed a green flag and frantically started waving it while screaming, "Go-o-o-o-o!"

As if on cue, the overhead speakers at the track began blaring Jimi's own song, "Fire."

"Now *this* is a racing song," Jimi hollered as he stomped on the accelerator.

The go-karts began filing out of the chute. Somehow, before they even got to the track, Jimi had passed two preoccupied preteens who were more focused on each other than on racing. Cole tried to accelerate, but his kart had very little go. He worked his way onto the track and began driving toward the mass of preteen humanity in front of him. A couple of karts had already spun out, and Cole passed them with ease. He glanced up ahead and spotted Jimi gliding through the traffic, darting around kids like he was the Little Old Lady from Pasadena.

Cole grew more and more frustrated with his own kart, lunging his body weight forward trying to make the kart go faster. After the first lap he was still mired near the back of the pack, while Jimi had nearly made his way to the front.

A crash happened a few karts ahead of Cole. He saw it happen and managed to avoid the spun-out kids, putting him now near the middle of the pack. He looked ahead again and saw Jimi out in front of everyone, waving like he'd just won the Indy 500. *How did he do that?* Cole wondered as he completed his second lap.

He then saw the teenage boy "in charge" was squirting oil onto the track around the sharpest turns. Before he could react, Cole hit one of the oil slicks and spun out himself. Jimi passed him, yelling, "Move over, Rover!" Several other preteens passed him as well, laughing at the twenty-one-year-old guy with more degrees than a thermometer.

Cole finally got his kart facing the right direction and proceeded to complete his last lap, finishing dead last. Jimi had been done for a while and was waiting for Cole as he pulled up.

"You had a better kart!" Cole complained.

"Fine," Jimi replied. "Next time you get my kart—number *56*, I think it was—and I'll take yours here. Number *27*, huh? That's ironic."

"Why?"

"I'm fifty-six now, and I died when I was twenty-seven. God is mysterious," he said, waving his fingers in front of Cole's face as though he were casting a spell.

The two men got back in line with a new group of hormonal preteens. Some of them were mired in an argument as to which boy band was better, the Backstreet Boys or NSYNC.

"Kids used to have arguments like that about me," Jimi said nostalgically. "'Who's the better guitarist, Jimi Hendrix or Jimmy Page?'" he said nasally, shaking his head

"Well, who was a better wheelman for the DRS," Cole asked, "Jimi or Hank?"

Jimi laughed. "Ole Hank never met a truck he couldn't drive. That man loved his trucks. But I could drive circles around him in a car." Jimi said this with a gleam in his eye.

"Help me, Obi Wan Kenobi, you're my only hope," Cole said, begging for a clue as to how Jimi drove so well in their first race.

"Nope. Today, I'm just seeing what you've got. We'll get to the lessons later."

As they climbed into their respective karts, the same kid came around to check their seatbelts, then gave the same spiel that no one listened to again.

This time, "Free Ride" by the Edgar Winter Group started blaring from the speakers as the kid waved the green flag.

Jimi again jumped out to a scorching start, zooming past kids left and right. Cole again felt like his kart struggled to accelerate. This time, however, he knew to look out for oil slicks. He also learned to not just watch the kart in front of him but the one two karts ahead. Ultimately, he did better, avoiding wrecks and passing kids who were just dillydallying around, but he still finished the race in the middle of the pack. Jimi again was waiting for Cole at the finish line.

"So the cars are equal," Cole admitted. "I still don't know how you drive so fast."

"It ain't about the speed, baby, it's about the smarts," Jimi said with a smile. "I saw some smarts outta you that time around. Let's keep working."

For the next few hours, they raced, got back in line, and raced again. Wash, rinse, and repeat. Cole got better, but Jimi always won.

133

The sun was setting as Jimi said, "Okay, last race of the day."

"Then I challenge you," Cole said confidently. "I start up front, you start in the last kart, and I bet I win."

"You're on," Jimi said with a smile, offering his hand to shake on it. Cole aggressively shook his hand.

Foghat's "Slow Ride" kicked in over the speakers, and Cole took off, thinking it would be easier this time, not having to worry about where Jimi was and just drive his own race. For the first lap, he didn't do anything but hit the turns smoothly while maintaining his position. While making a turn he saw that Jimi had passed a few kids but was driving with a concerned look on his face. *I got him*, Cole thought.

The second lap came and went without any issues. He passed several kids who had wrecked, stalled, or spun out and once spotted Jimi three or four turns behind him. As Cole began his third and final lap, he was feeling confident, certain he would coast to victory.

Suddenly, he felt someone tap his bumper from behind. He looked back and realized it was Jimi. *How did he catch up?* Jimi gave him a wide smile. This threw Cole off just enough for him to take a turn too wide, and Jimi eased his kart into the gap alongside. Now Cole was in trouble. With the two karts traveling at essentially the same speed, it was just a matter of who could take the turns tighter and keep the other from gaining an advantage.

With two turns remaining, a kart Cole had passed twice already spun out right in front of them. Jimi eased off the accelerator just slightly, and Cole nosed ahead by a few feet as he angled to avoid the spun-out kart and dive into the final turn. Jimi then stomped on the gas and nudged Cole just as they passed the stalled kart. This spun Cole out completely, and Jimi flew by with a wave.

"Take it easy, baby!" he yelled as he crossed the finish line.

"Mister," the teenage Kart Kountry employee said in awe as Jimi parked his vehicle. "I ain't never seen anyone drive the way you do."

"I didn't spend all those years driving Miss Daisy for nothing," Jimi said with a wink. The kid didn't understand the joke.

Cole pulled alongside him, flustered. "How did you do that?"

Jimi smiled. "In due time, kid."

★ ★ ★ ★

The next day found Cole sitting handcuffed and blindfolded in the back of what seemed to be a van rumbling down what felt like a dirt road. They had been driving for what seemed like an hour, but he couldn't really tell. Early that morning, about sunrise, he had been abducted from his bed, wrapped in a sleeping bag, and tossed into the van. He didn't know who grabbed him or where they were now headed, but he assumed this was some sort of DRS initiation. He wondered why it hadn't happened before now. Even so, he had a bad feeling about whatever was coming next.

The van crept to a stop, so he was pretty certain his captor wasn't Jimi Hendrix. The rear doors opened, and someone grabbed him by the arm and dragged him out of the vehicle. Cole was wearing nothing but a white T-shirt and a pair of Mickey Mouse boxer shorts. The air was uncomfortably cool, given what he was wearing. The blindfold was yanked from his face, and the rush of midmorning sunlight blinded him. Then a voice spoke, and his heart sank. It was Kurt Cobain.

"You ever fire a gun before?" Cobain asked.

"Yeah. My granddad taught me to shoot."

"You any good?"

"I'm okay. I'd rather be a little warmer, though."

Cobain got in Cole's face, his jaw clenched. With controlled rage he said through his teeth, "When you have to shoot, it's not always going to be perfect conditions. But you still have to make the shot."

Cole's eyes were starting to adjust, and he could see that they were standing on a flat area atop a small hill, with knee-length grass all around them. Cobain uncuffed him then shoved a rifle into his chest and pointed at a target fifty feet away. Cole recognized the rifle as a Winchester 70 bolt-action sporting rifle. He chambered a round, took aim, and fired. He hit the target but not the bullseye.

"Not bad," Cobain conceded. "Keep firing until you hit the bullseye."

Three shots later, Cole scored a bullseye.

"Okay. Now move back," Cobain said, "until I say stop."

Cole started inching backwards.

"No, no, no! Big steps!"

Cole startled and began taking bigger steps.

"Okay, stop."

He stopped, now about seventy-five feet from the target.

"Shoot," Cobain ordered.

Cole raised the rifle to aim, but his hands and arms were shivering from the cold.

"I—I can't, Kurt," Cole said. "I won't hit it."

Kurt moved on him quickly, his eyes steely blue and jaw clenched like a sprung bear trap. Cobain grabbed the gun from Cole, swept his blonde hair from his eyes, and took aim. He fired and hit the bullseye, dead center. Then he shoved the gun back into Cole's gut. Cobain stared through him. "Now shoot."

Cole withered inside a bit but had been expecting much worse. The adrenaline of fear released and rushed over him like a warm blanket. A resolve swelled from within. He raised the gun and fired. Not quite a bullseye but close.

"Again," Cobain said.

Cole fired round after round until he hit the bullseye from this distance. Then Cobain made him back up and do the same from farther and farther distances. The farther away he moved, the more rounds it took him to hit the target. The adrenaline spike wore off, and Cole got cold again.

Cobain said little, speaking in clipped sentences instructing him what to do next, giving Cole a pointer or two along the way. This went on for an hour or so. Finally, Cobain said, "Stop. Let's go."

Cole found his blindfold and began to put it back on himself.

"You don't need that anymore," Cobain said. "Just get in the van. The passenger seat."

Cole was very appreciative of this. Kurt climbed into the driver's seat and started the van. The air from the heater blew cold at first but quickly turned warm. Cole was very, very appreciative of this.

Cobain turned to Cole and said, "Listen, I don't like you. I don't know why King picked you. But I'm going to teach you to shoot. Are we clear?"

"Yeah. Okay." Cole shivered, though not from the cold.

Then Cobain turned on the CD player. R.E.M.'s "Begin the Begin" was playing. Cole gave his instructor a curious look.

"What?" Cobain asked.

"I just wouldn't have taken you for an R.E.M. guy, that's all."

"I love R.E.M.," Cobain said without enthusiasm.

They drove back to headquarters in silence, save for Michael Stipe's voice.

Cole's mind raced, wondering why Kurt Cobain seemed to harbor so much animosity toward him.

★ ★ ★ ★

"What are your assessments so far?"

Elvis, Jimi, Jerry, Janis, Cobain, and Morrison sat around a conference room table in the Wilkes-Booth Room. The table was made of dark, rich mahogany and shaped like the head of a bald eagle. This had been Lincoln's table. On the walls of the conference room were American flags of every known configuration mounted in glass display cases. One, a burned and battered flag that had survived the Battle of Gettysburg, was said to have been among Lincoln's most treasured possessions. Elvis was standing next to it, studying the Gettysburg flag while also checking his hair in the reflection from the glass.

"Jimi," Elvis said, still looking at the flag, "how's our boy doing?"

"He's a fast learner," Jimi said. "A little cocky, though."

"Can he drive?"

"He's learning, King."

"Keep training him. Get him in the air soon, too. Jim?" Elvis asked, looking at Morrison. "Can he fight?"

"Uh . . ." Jerry Garcia hesitated, searching Morrison's eyes to determine what to say. "Not yet."

Morrison nodded in agreement.

"Does he have potential?"

"Too soon to tell," Jerry answered, while Morrison just looked straight ahead. "Elvis, he's trying. He's not hitting his marks on the Commandments yet, but he is improving," Jerry said sympathetically. He liked everyone and had no issues with Cole. He knew that Morrison felt differently, but he always needed a while to warm up to new agents.

"Kurt?" Elvis said, indicating Cobain.

"He's okay."

"Elaborate, please."

"He's shot a gun before. He wasn't terrible. That's all."

"Good. Janis, how do you feel after spending some time with him?"

Janis didn't immediately answer. She chewed her bottom lip and then said, "He ain't no Buddy Holly. But no one could be."

It wasn't the ringing endorsement Elvis had hoped for. He thought that Cole opening up to Janis about his past would warm her to him a bit more.

Then Janis spoke again, "He ain't no rock star either . . . but I think he's got some soul, man. And that's a good thing."

Still looking at his reflection in the glass, Elvis curled his upper lip in a slight smile.

137

chapter

NINETEEN

ole was creeped out. Every time he woke up in the morning, just for a moment he thought he was in his old apartment in Cambridge. Then he remembered he was in the Netherworld, wherever that was, in his nu-partment. He had thought he could get used to it, but so far it was a no-go. He resolved to talk to Elvis about getting new digs; surely on this massive compound there was another place he could live.

Even before he was out of bed, Cole's thoughts turned again to the symbol that dogged his waking moments. The night before, he had noticed three *V* shapes within the symbol, two right side up, next to each other, and one on the right on its side, open wide in an obtuse angle. *What could V stand for? Victory. Second victory? There are three Vs—maybe it's something about World War III?* He turned this idea over and over in his mind, but it didn't ring true.

Cole had to let it go for now. It was time to work out.

He was now attacking his workouts with increased vigor. He knew he needed to get stronger, faster, and smarter if he was ever going to be anything more than the team's annoying IT guy. He was now up to 400 sit-ups but could still do no more than 250 push-ups. Push-ups, he thought, were hard for a guy who spent most of his time sitting at a computer. The squats were grueling, but his lower body was progressing ahead of his upper body so far, and he was able to do all 500 squats called for in Jim Morrison's commandments. Cole was a decent runner, but most mornings he had to walk the last mile or so of his five-mile run. Still, running was a great time to think. He knew he had been recruited for his mind, so he had learned to enjoy running most among the exercises in his required regimen.

His training sessions with Morrison were also going better, or so he thought. He now spent only *most* of his time being tossed about the Dojo instead of the *whole* time. Best of all, his body was starting to adapt and adjust to all this physical conditioning. He was still sore most days, but it wasn't a crippling soreness like in the beginning. He even liked how he was starting to look in the mirror. This morning, he had wished Savannah could see him like this, but he put that thought out of his mind very quickly. He did miss that tattoo, though.

He was also making progress with his music. The trumpet hadn't come back as naturally as he'd hoped, so Cole had begun to fiddle with another form of music-making more up his alley, though he didn't know how the rest of the team would feel about it. Tonight, he would find out.

This was a big day for Cole. After the evidence Lennon uncovered in Tennessee indicating that the Brotherhood knew about Elvis and the DRS, the King decided it was time for Cole to introduce some of his technological advances to the team. Cole suggested a presentation about how these advances would benefit everyone. The DRS had gadgets aplenty, some really cool tech even, but they were just tools the agents had learned to use over the years. Almost to a person, the team had not yet embraced the internet. They had also failed to adopt some of the basic advances that were becoming commonplace in the rest of the world. For example, the team's understanding of cell phones seemed to be limited to making and taking mobile calls. Buddy Holly had been ahead of the curve, but now he was gone.

Elvis had agreed to the presentation, knowing it was time for Cole to show what he could bring to the team.

For two weeks, as Cole prepared his presentation, he felt like he was in school again. He welcomed this feeling as something familiar amid the whole lotta weird that now daily defined his existence. Tonight, however, instead of a bunch of fellow nerds, his audience would be some of the most famous and talented people who ever lived.

★ ★ ★ ★

139

After changing into his running clothes and stretching, Cole hit the pavement for his daily run. He could see his breath with every exhale in the frosty morning air. In less than two months winter would officially arrive. Cole had no idea how cold it would get here, but he wasn't looking forward to it.

Cole spotted Chris running about a quarter mile ahead, so he increased his pace to catch up with him. To this point, Cole had had little interaction with Chris Wallace, formally known as the Notorious B.I.G., a.k.a. Biggie Smalls. It was rare he crossed paths with DRS agents outside of meetings or training. Cole thought this might be an opportunity to get to know a team member he hadn't spent much time with and maybe even fanboy out a bit.

"Hey, Chris," Cole said, catching up to the now-medium-sized one-time hip-hop star.

"Whazzup, Cole?"

"Not much, man, not much. Hey, listen, I just have to ask you, since other than me you're the youngest guy in the group: What's your take on all this?" Cole said, motioning to the surrounding wonderland they now called home.

"All dis? Man, it's wack. Like, straight . . . just unbelievable, you know what I'm sayin'?"

"Yeah, for sure, for sure," Cole said, unintentionally matching the rapper's vocal cadence and rhythm.

"But don't trip. It's for real, but dis ain't where it's at. Yeah, we live here. But what we do, it's much greater. We do what we gotta do to protect the world, straight up."

"Sure, yeah, for sure, for sure."

"Relax, Cole," Chris said with a laugh. "You ain't gotta front. Just be yo' self. Do whatchu do. You'll be a'ight."

"Thanks, man," Cole said sincerely. "Can I ask you something else?"

"Fo' sure."

"Why did you do it? Why did you leave everything behind and join the team?"

Chris didn't immediately reply. After a thoughtful moment, he said, "Before I broke out in the game, I was broke. Like dead broke. Then I got paid. Money wasn't nothin' no more, know what I'm sayin'?"

"Yeah. Well . . . no. I've never been, you know, a money guy, but I understand what you mean."

"I *was* a money guy. I wanted it all. I wanted to be off the street, doin' my thang in the game and gettin' paid. Then I got it all, and it still wasn't enough, know what I'm sayin'? I had whateva I wanted—cars, girls, houses, whateva. It was dope for a minute, then it hit me, dog. I was still empty inside. I couldn't fill that emptiness fo' nuthin,' no matter what I tried."

Cole listened as they jogged. It was cool to hear Chris be real with him.

"When E came to me and laid it all out, at first I was like, 'Nah.' But then when he broke it down and got real, talking about his demons and how this group—this family—helped fill his emptiness, I really had to give it some serious consideration, know what I'm sayin'?"

"Did you know Pac was in before you joined?"

"Nah, but E said I wouldn't be alone. He said there was someone else from the game in the fam."

"Didn't you and Pac have like a feud or something back in the day?"

"Yeah, we had a beef. But before all that, we was tight. It was all that stuff I was just talkin' about, the emptiness and whatnot, got us both . . . it turned us into some-thing . . . someone that wasn't true to who we really was."

The two men jogged on for a few more minutes in silence.

Then Chris said, "You gotta understand, we all came here running from some-thing. I don't mean like we afraid, or chicken, know what I'm sayin'? I mean, we was all gettin' chased by something. Some of us done got caught by it too. And this family was the only way out. E would tell you that's where he was. Cole, the question you gotta answer for yo' self is this: What was you runnin' from?"

Cole stopped dead in his tracks, but Chris kept running. He had thought a lot about the things that *pulled* him toward making the decision to join the DRS—being part of a family, meaningful work, a life of significance, keeping the world and those he left behind safe. But he had not once considered what was *pushing* him to make this move. What was he running from? What was chasing him? Unlike the rest of the DRS, it wasn't substance abuse or the trappings of fame, but he knew something was chasing him. And he knew he was going to have to give this more thought.

He came out of his reverie and saw that he had stopped running in front of Jim Morrison's house. Morrison was in the front yard, doing something that looked like Tai Chi. Despite the cold, he was shirtless and barefoot, wearing only denim cutoffs, what Cole had heard called "jorts."

Cole caught his eye and gave a slight wave. Morrison just shook his head. Cole didn't know what that meant. Was he saying, "Don't come over here; I'm busy"? Or was he expressing disapproval that Cole had stopped running before completing his five miles? Or was he giving his opinion of Cole's very existence? Cole didn't know. Regardless, there wasn't any warmth in it, so he started walking back to his replica apartment.

It was a lonely moment. In his brief experience with the DRS, the highs were high, the lows were low, and one often followed immediately after the other. Like passing out after meeting President Kennedy.

★ ★ ★ ★

Cole still locked his apartment door, even though there was no reason to. He threw his keys on the kitchen table and half expected to see Taylor behind his laptop working on some project for school. Instead, Elvis came around the corner from the kitchen with a cup of coffee.

"Whoa, King, you scared me!"

"Sorry about that, man."

"What are you doing here?"

"I wanted to talk to you about your presentation tonight. I have a key to everything around here, so I came in and helped myself to some coffee. How is your prep going?"

"Fine . . . I think. Why do you ask?"

"No reason. I just thought maybe you'd want to talk about it beforehand."

"No, I think I'm good."

"*Are* you good, Cole?"

Cole knew he didn't just mean the presentation.

"Um . . . yeah."

"If you weren't good, you would tell me, right?"

"Yeah, yeah, sure, sure," Cole replied, overcompensating for his previous hesitance.

"Alllll right, then," Elvis said, making his way to the door. He paused at the exit, as though waiting for Cole to say more.

On cue, Cole blurted, "I hate this apartment! It just creeps me out. Is there any other place I could live?"

"Sure," Elvis said with a reassuring smile.

"Not with Jim. Anyone but him!"

Elvis gave a hearty laugh. "I wouldn't put anyone with Jim. That vow of silence thing is just weird, man."

"Yeah, what's up with that?"

"I'm not sure, but I think that FBI thing that went down in Waco a few years ago did something to him. Ever since then, he hasn't said a word. Come on, grab your gear. I'll take you someplace to bunk."

Cole gathered up the few belongings he wanted to take with him, and the King of Rock and Roll led him to his own place at the center of the neighborhood—Graceland II.

"You're going to let me live with *you*, King?"

"In the guest house, until we figure something else out. We all need our own space, but I want you to be comfortable until we get you situated."

"Thanks!"

Elvis led him to the guest house and showed him around. Cole threw his stuff down on a futon bed in the living room. This place was perfect.

As he made his way to the door, Elvis said, "Now aren't you glad you told me what was going on?"

"Yeah, I am."

Elvis placed a hand on Cole's shoulder. "This is part of what it means to be a family, Cole. You tell each other things. You open up. We are rock stars, not mind readers."

Cole knew he was right. It just wasn't in his nature to be an open book with others. Maybe that was some of what Chris was talking about. He decided to ask Elvis something that had been bothering him from the beginning.

"King, why don't they like me?"

"Why don't you ask them?" Elvis suggested. "Conflict is important. The road to peace is paved with resolved conflict."

"That's deep. Who said that? Confucius? Aristotle? Jesus?"

"Nah, man," Elvis said with a laugh. "I got it from a fortune cookie! Hey, come to dinner tonight at my place. We're having meatloaf, with a little bit of bacon on top."

"Sounds delicious," Cole said, somewhat sarcastically.

"It is. See ya at six sharp," Elvis said in earnest.

★ ★ ★ ★

Cole set up his computer and got back to work on his presentation. The symbol would have to wait for now.

He repeated to himself the mantra that had guided his preparation: "If I were a rock star frozen in time, what would I need to hear to convince me to embrace modern technology?" For the next several hours he tweaked and honed his presentation to the point where it felt ready for the team.

He glanced at his watch and saw it was nearly 6:00. He hadn't stopped to shower, eat, or even visit the bathroom since he first sat down to work. This happened whenever he was consumed by a project.

He sprang up and jumped in the shower, where he made sure to hit the usual trouble spots to ward off unwanted odoriferous emanations. He pulled a clean set of clothes out of his duffle bag, threw on his coat, combed his hair hurriedly, and ran over to Graceland II.

As he approached the mansion, Cole didn't know if he needed to ring the doorbell at the front door or find a back door and just walk in. He decided to ring the doorbell, but no one answered. After another ring failed to bring someone to the door, he walked around the house to see if there was another way in. He found a back door and knocked. Nothing. *Well, if we're a family, I guess I should just walk right in.*

Cole opened the door and was met by the joyful sound of music. Cole followed the sound to the replica Jungle Room. There, standing in a circle with Elvis were Janis Joplin, Jim Morrison, and Kurt Cobain. Cole's heart sank a little. These were the three team members who had been coldest to him since his arrival.

Elvis and Cobain were playing guitars, Morrison had a maraca, and Janis was working a tambourine like it owed her money. They were singing the Oasis song "Wonderwall." No one seemed to notice that Cole had walked in, so he slid to one side and just took in the music. He couldn't help himself but tap his foot to the beat.

"Well, look what the cat dragged in," Elvis said merrily as the song ended. The other three were putting their instruments up and didn't acknowledge Cole's quiet entrance.

"I didn't think you spoke, Jim," Cole said.

"He doesn't speak, but he still sings," Elvis said with a shrug. "Anybody hungry?"

"I'm famished," Janis said. Cobain and Morrison just nodded.

They made their way to the kitchen. Graceland II had the same layout as Elvis's home in Memphis, but the kitchen was outfitted with all the modern conveniences. A woman and a young girl were in the kitchen cooking as they entered.

"Cole, this is Consuela and her daughter Gabriela," Elvis said. "Consuela, Gabriela, este es el Señor Cole."

"Hola, Señor Cole," mother and daughter said in unison.

"Hola," Cole responded politely.

"Gracias por esta hermosa comida," Elvis said.

"De nada, Señor King," the ladies said again in unison.

"Hola, Señor Kurt," Gabriela said bashfully, looking up at Cobain.

Much to Cole's surprise, Cobain lit up with a huge smile, got down on his knees, and embraced the little girl in a warm hug.

"Where did they come from, King?" Cole asked under his breath.

"Venezuela, Señor Cole," Elvis said with a smile. "Kurt and I met Consuela and little Gabby earlier this year when we were in South America, trying to stabilize a political upheaval in Ecuador."

"When you bring people here, how do you explain . . ." Cole paused, searching for the right word, "all of this, to them?"

"People in desperate need of help don't care about who we were in our old lives. Shoot, most of them don't even *know* who we were. That's good for the ol' ego," Elvis said with a wink and a smile. "They don't care where this place is or how it got here. They don't even care that we're in America. They just needed help, and we helped them. Simple as that."

"Do they stay here forever?"

"Some do. Some go home once conditions there have improved. But they go home with a trade or a craft that they learned here. They go back as community leaders and contributors to their society. We got a regular 'We are the World' thing happening here. It's beautiful, man!"

"This place never ceases to amaze me," Cole said.

"Well thank you. Thank you very much. But enough yapping. I'm starving, and this meal that Consuela and Gabby made looks amazing. These plates aren't going to serve themselves, people!"

They all made their own plates and then found a seat at the table in the adjacent dining room. Before sitting down, each DRS member pulled out something different and placed it on the table. For Elvis, it was a bronze poker chip. For Cobain, it was a guitar pick. Morrison set down a pen dipped in silver that Cole had not noticed was behind his ear. Jan took off an earring, a black pearl, and put it on the table. They then joined hands, and Elvis recited the Serenity Prayer. Cole just stood there, not knowing exactly what to do. When he finished, most said, "Amen," in unison and sat down. "Amen," Cole said a half beat behind everyone else. Morrison didn't say anything but remained solemn the whole time.

Everyone began digging into their meatloaf.

"This is delicious, King," Janis said. Morrison nodded in agreement.

"I'm so glad you're enjoying it. It's one of my favorite dishes,' Elvis said. Then abruptly changing the subject, he said, "Now, you know that tonight at eleven, Cole is going to be giving a presentation about how modern technology can help us. I went by his place earlier today to check on him, and he asked me a very poignant question. Cole, why don't you ask these folks here the same question you asked me?"

Every corpuscle in Cole's body seemed to rush to his head as a wave of panic and fear came over him. "Wha—what do you mean?"

"You know," King said pleasantly. "You asked why the team doesn't like you."

Cole was horrified. He didn't know whether to run out of the house, puke, or take a swing at Elvis. They all felt like bad ideas. So he just sat there in silence, trying to choke down his meatloaf.

Kurt Cobain broke the silence. "You don't play."

Jim Morrison nodded in agreement.

While mortified that Elvis had tossed this hand grenade into their quiet dinner, Cole had enough fight in him to bite back when backed into a corner. "He didn't bring me here to play music with you guys!" he screamed, pointing at Elvis. "If he wanted Eddie Vedder, he would have asked him. He got me instead."

Cobain made a sour face. Morrison shot Cobain a look. Everyone knew that Morrison loved Pearl Jam. Janis stayed out of the fray.

"It's not just that you don't play," Cobain added. "You haven't done anything. You're a nobody."

This cut deep to Cole's core. "I'm not a nobody," Cole said through his teeth, rage starting to build within him.

"Oh, I'm sorry. You made a website. Well done," Cobain said sarcastically. "I might feel differently if you had your own company, or were a CEO or something, but you're just a kid. I don't know what you have to offer us."

Cole looked around the table for someone to come to his defense. Elvis looked like he wanted to say something but held back. Janis just chewed her lip and stared at her food. Morrison stared into space, probably thinking about an episode of *Kung Fu*.

Cole pushed away from the table and stood up. "I'm sorry if I'm not a musician," he said angrily. "I'm sorry if I'm not as accomplished as you guys *were*. You're all has-beens. Me? I'm the future! I *do* have skills that I know are going to do this team a lot of good. And tonight I'm going to prove it," he said, pointing at Cobain. "Excuse me, I have a presentation to finish." Then he exited the room and the house, slamming every door he walked through.

★ ★ ★ ★

"Well, that went well," Janis said. "I like his spunk, though."

Morrison begrudgingly nodded in agreement.

Cobain stared a hole through the table in front of him.

Elvis sat back, took a breath, and continued to chew his food. He wanted to say something to defend Cole, but he decided to let it ride in the moment. He had wagered a lot on Cole Denton, like putting everything you've got on red. The roulette wheel was slowing down, but the ball was still bouncing. He hoped that Cole's presentation tonight would turn the tide with the team and prove he was a winner.

chapter

TWENTY

ole gathered all the equipment he needed and loaded it onto one of the ubiqui-
tous Netherworld golf carts. He then headed for the J. P. Richardson Building,
affectionately known as "The Bop." It was named for the Big Bopper, who had
died in the service of the DRS many years earlier. For all intents and purposes, the Bop
was a school building filled with classrooms of all sizes and shapes.

The room where Cole was to present was a theater-style classroom with tiered stadium seating that could accommodate about thirty people. The team often used it for
mission briefings. The facility had a stage and was tricked out with professional lighting and state-of-the-art audio-visual capabilities that Cole was counting on to make an
impact. For this audience, this had to be more than a presentation; it had to be a show.

For the next hour he did a run-through, making sure everything was synched up
and ready to roll. Now it was time to change clothes and do the thing. As he changed
behind the curtain, he could hear people beginning to gather in the room and take
their seats. Cole pulled a remote control from his pocket and tapped a button. The
Doors' song "Riders on the Storm" began playing, filling the room with the sounds of
rain and the chimes of a keyboard.

Precisely at 11:00 p.m., Cole hit another button on the remote, and the lights
went down, save for a single spotlight focused on the stage and illuminating a desk

with a computer and monitor on it. The music continued to play and swell. The sounds of thunder echoed as the song neared its end. Cole tapped another button, and a video began playing on a large screen. An upbeat synth soundtrack began playing, and photos of the assembled rock stars in their younger years began to flash on the screen.

From backstage, Cole spoke through a Countryman microphone headset. "All of you are icons. Legends. Innovators. Dead. And yet still alive. You changed the world. Then you saved the world. Now it's time to go to the next level. You are morally bound to become innovators again . . ."

The synth music hit a crescendo, and Cole walked out from behind the curtain. He was wearing blue jeans, gray New Balance shoes, and a black turtleneck. Tupac and Chris howled with delight as he walked out; they seemed to be the only ones young enough to get the Steve Jobs reference.

"Thank you, guys," Cole said sheepishly. His first joke had fallen flat. He should have known better. Even Cobain was too old for this cultural callback.

Cole hesitated, took a breath, and went for it. "What is the most important aspect of running missions for the DRS?"

The room was silent for a moment, but then the team began throwing out ideas.

"Saving lives."

"Protecting the innocent."

"Strategy."

"Shooting stuff."

"Exotic locations."

"The chicks."

Cole felt the audience slipping from his grasp.

He raised his hands and said, "Security."

No one flinched. Elvis rocked back and folded his arms.

"You all have signed on to save the world. Yet it is evident, since I am here, you don't always have the ability to save each other."

Cole was cut off by Kurt Cobain. "Kid, we know what we are doing. We know what's on the ground. We know what the mission is. We know our infil and exfil. We know our weapons and our transportation, and we trust each other. How do you expect to come in here and—"

Cole interrupted him. "Your backdoor is wide open."

After a few obvious jokes, someone had to restrain Cobain.

Cole fussed with his turtleneck, which he now regretted wearing. "What I am saying is, your cyber security is nonexistent. Your IP address is essentially public. You have no router, no firewalls, no security."

Cole felt the room collectively turn from confidence to concern. "You are exposed. The world is changing, and you must adapt and prepare. You need security from both physical threats and the world of ones and zeros. I want you all to know that I believe Elvis is a visionary. He took a risk by bringing me on to the team . . . and I'm not going to let him down. You need to hear me say that. You know what else? I'm not going to let *you* down."

Many heads in the audience nodded with this sentiment. Elvis stood in the rear, leaning against a wall.

"So far tonight, everything you have seen—except for me and my poor choice of outfit—I've controlled with this remote control. How did I do that, you might ask? With the magic of something called Wi-Fi. Wireless networking. Elvis has agreed to begin the process of installing this technology all over the Netherworld."

For the next few minutes Cole expounded on how Wi-Fi and increased online capacity would change the way they lived in their strange corner of the world. Then he also showed how this tech could help them in the field.

"This is how exposed you are and others can be." He sat down at the desk and began hacking into government websites and revealed data that would have taken months of intel to uncover in the past. All of this was projected onto the big screen in real time. He carefully built a case for how the internet would be the key to safer, more efficient missions and cleaner strategies for elite intelligence gathering.

"Tonight, when you get back to wherever you call home, you'll find a laptop computer there waiting for you. They're top of the line, the fastest processors available. I built them myself, and I've installed all of the software you'll need. There will be a password on a sticky note on top of your machine and step-by-step instructions on how to personalize your computer and change your password."

He waited for applause or affirmation. He got silence.

"These new computers are also Y2K-compliant. It's not a complicated process, but when the ball drops in Times Square, rest assured your laptop won't explode. Also, I've upgraded your CompuLive chat feature.

Pac slyly grinned, "The end of the world. Apocalypse, baby."

Cole said, "I'm not sure what message boards you read, Lesane, but Y2K is nothing more than a simple oversight by computer coders. Moving on."

He then transitioned his talk towards cell phone technology. Cole asked Jerry Garcia to join him on the stage.

"Jerry, I want you to take this phone and stand at the edge of the light. I am going to go over to the other end of the light."

Jerry did as instructed. Suddenly his hand started vibrating.

"Hey, man, what's going on?" Jerry asked.

"I just sent you a text message. Read the display on your phone."

Jerry put on his glasses and squinted at the phone. "Music has . . . infinite space. You can go as far into music . . . as you can fill millions of lifetimes," he read with a smile. "That's cool, man. Did I say that?" Everyone chuckled.

"The *Rolling Stone* interview in '72."

"Far out!"

"Thanks, Jerry, you can sit down now." Cole again addressed the whole room. "There's nothing fancy about a text message. It's just something that few of you have ever really used. However, I foresee us creating our own cellular network, accessible all over the world, but one that only *we* can use. This will take an incredible effort, satellites, networking, and fiber, but from what I'm told our pockets are pretty deep."

Laughter circulated around the room. Cole continued to expand on how creating their own DRS cellular network could help them with logistical coordination while enhancing their ability to secretly communicate with one another. Cole could feel the room was with him now. The spotlight made it difficult to see individual faces, but he felt like he could sense their approval. He was ready to reveal the *pièce de résistance*.

"I know that some of you have struggled with my inclusion on the team because I'm not a musician." Cole hit a button on the remote, and more synth music began. Cole then walked off stage and came right back pushing a cart with a laptop computer on it. He disconnected a few cords from the desktop computer and plugged them into the laptop.

"I also know that one of Jim's Ten Commandments is to make music every day. It's not been easy, but I've done that. Every song you've heard since this presentation began, I made using this." Cole picked up his laptop. "Using a program called Neon, I can create synth music using my laptop computer. I don't know notes and chords like you all, but I have ears and I know what sounds good. So, using my laptop, I made this . . ." Cole hit another button on the remote, and a light show started, accompanied by more upbeat synth music. Then he hesitantly brought up the house lights. To his great relief, most of the Dead Rock Stars were on their feet clapping along to the music he'd created. Of his dinner companions from earlier in the evening, Janis looked like she was having a good time. Kurt Cobain still sat with his arms folded. Jim Morrison was standing, not clapping but not scowling either.

Suddenly, Cole realized that Tupac and Chris had joined him on stage. They were waving their arms and hyping the crowd. Jimi had somehow found a guitar and was plugging into the sound system behind the curtain. He started playing along to the music Cole had created. Then Tupac grabbed a mic and started freestyling with the music.

> Steppin' up into the twenty-first century
> Cole Denton reppin' modern technology
> Teachin' us how to keep the world free
> Gonna be a new day for you and me!

Then he handed Chris the mic, and he picked up the rap.

> It's poppin,' beat droppin'
> Playa' change the world
> Keep tha hits hoppin'
> Tupac, Biggie, Jimi, and Cole
> Comin' atcha with the dead legends of rock and roll
> Showin' us how to change, fittin' in like a glove
> Cole Denton's tech showin' the world some love!

Cole locked eyes with Elvis in the back of the room. The King of Rock and Roll gave him a wink and nod. Then, as the music came to a close, Elvis approached the stage and motioned for everyone to settle down and listen. Chris handed him the mic, and he, Jimi, and Tupac returned to their seats.

"Wow, thank you, Cole," Elvis said. "I think Cole has made a very strong case for why we need to change with the times. But I'm going to do him one better. As some of you may know, there is an enemy out there right now the likes of which we've never encountered."

Everyone in the room stirred in their seats.

"They are called the Brotherhood. Most of you are hearing about this for the first time. Buddy was hard on their trail, and they killed him in Vegas. Now John has taken the lead and picked up where Buddy left off."

At the mention of John Lennon's name, Cole's heart leapt. He had not yet met the former Beatle but was excited for their introduction. He scanned the room to see if he was there. Sure enough, in the back row of the room, there he was—seated alone, arms behind his head, reclined, barefoot, and clad in something that looked like pajamas. Cole wanted to wave but restrained himself.

Elvis continued. "What Cole can do to help us find Buddy's killers cannot be overstated. His tech, his vision, is the key to hunting this group and defeating them. If you've been slow to warm up to Cole, that's fine. No one wanted to replace Buddy. But you better get on board with what Cole can do to help us move into the future, because the future is here. Now."

He nodded to Cole, then said, "This is going to be hard to see, but you all need to see it." Cole clicked his remote to project a new slide on the screen. It was a picture of an exploded car with four charred bodies inside. Elvis nodded again, and Cole clicked to the next slide. This one was a close-up of the body in the middle of the back seat. Pinned to his chest was a piece of paper with the same mysterious symbol that Buddy had drawn on the hotel wall before he died. "Cole is trying to decipher this symbol. He's got a start, but he's not there yet."

Elvis went on. "These images are from an attack that happened last week. This was Arham Ali Syed, a peaceful man hoping to become the first prime minister of his country. He was assassinated by the Brotherhood. Kennedy sent me these pictures from his contacts in the CIA. But I'm telling you, this symbol was meant as a message for us. A shot across our bow. This is a declaration of war against the Dead Rock Stars.

"First, they killed Buddy in Vegas. The same team was assigned to sniff around Colonel Tom's place. John found them . . . and he dealt with them," Elvis said hesitantly. "Buddy knew this symbol and drew it on the wall before he died. They know who we are. I don't know how, but they know, and they're coming after us. They're coming after me."

Cole stood to the side of the stage, listening as Elvis spoke. His heart rate had finally returned to normal, but his mind was still in overdrive. As he listened to the King unravel what the Brotherhood had done, something hit him like a lightning bolt.

He started processing, getting lost in thought. *The Dead Rock Stars is the most secret of secret organizations in the world. There is no trace of them to be found on the internet or anywhere else. They are ghosts. There's only one way for anyone to know about us . . .*

Cole scanned the audience. Who could it be? Who would have betrayed the DRS? He'd spent the most time with Jimi, who'd been almost like a big brother to him from the start. Janis had not taken to him at first, but he had learned it was largely because he was replacing Buddy. She had even started to show signs of thawing toward him in recent days. Cole had yet to meet John Lennon, but he was at the forefront of hunting down this group. Jim Morrison had been antagonistic toward him from the beginning, but from what Elvis said, he was antagonistic toward everyone at first.

Then he noticed Kurt Cobain, who sat with arms folded, totally checked out. He had been hostile toward Cole from the moment he arrived. As these thoughts raced through his mind, panic set in. If Cobain—or anyone on the team—was in league with the Brotherhood, then every word Elvis said was saying was feeding information to the enemy.

Cole took a deep breath, then walked over to Elvis as he continued briefing the team on the Brotherhood. Cole put his arm around the King and smiled a broad smile. Elvis stopped talking and looked at Cole.

"Uh . . . hey, Cole," Elvis stammered, surprised by the interruption. "What's going on?"

"Look, man, I think they get it. They understand that these guys are bad and we have to catch them. We will, King. We will. Just give me time, and I'll figure it out."

"I dig your confidence, man," Elvis said, a fire starting to burn in his eyes, "but you do not interrupt me when I'm talking."

"I'm sorry, man," Cole said, regretting ever acting on this idea. "I was just reading the room, and they looked bored. You know, kinda checked out. Right, Kurt?"

Cobain slowly looked up and glared at Cole. "No, actually. I was listening to every word."

"Could have fooled me," Cole said, glaring back and mustering up all his courage. "You've just been sitting there with your arms folded, scowling the whole time."

"That's just how I am," Kurt shouted. "It's how I process. You don't know me at all! Why would you single me out?"

Elvis jumped in. "Okay, that's enough. It's late, and we've got work to do. Maybe on some level you're right, Cole. They get it. I don't have to elaborate further at this time . . ." As Elvis said this, he turned away from the microphone, and his voice trailed off to where only Cole could hear him. "But there's a right way and a wrong way to do things around here, and brother, that was the wrong way."

"I'm sorry, King," Cole whispered back with real remorse. "I really am."

"It's cool," Elvis replied softly. "Just don't let it happen again." Then Elvis turned back to the mic. "Let's call it a night. Tomorrow, we put our collective minds and energies toward figuring out who the Brotherhood is and how we're gonna stop them. Cool?"

"Cool," the room replied, and team members began filing out. Cobain stopped at the top of the stairs and stared back at Cole, shaking his head, before departing.

Once the room was empty, Elvis turned his attention to Cole. "What were you thinking?"

"Elvis, I'm so sorry. I meant no disrespect, but I need to tell you something. I think—I can't believe I'm going to say this—I think we have a mole in the DRS. I think the threat is coming from within."

Elvis dropped his head. Cole didn't know if it was in frustration, anger, sadness, or weariness. The King kept this pose for a beat, then started rubbing his head, messing up his hair in the process.

"Are you okay?" Cole asked slowly.

"This is my worst nightmare," Elvis said mournfully. "Why do you think the threat is coming from the inside?"

"Think about it, King. The DRS is the best-kept secret in the history of the world. Who else knows about us but us?"

Elvis stroked his chin and looked into the distance. "Let's say for a moment you're right, Cole. Who do you think it is?"

"Isn't it obvious? It's got to be Kurt. You saw how he acted when I called him out."

Elvis laughed. "Kurt Cobain is many things, but he's not a traitor. What would be his motivation? Why would he do this?"

"I don't know?" Cole admitted. "I know he's been no friend to me since I got here. Maybe he's afraid I'll sniff him out."

"If this threat is from within, I don't believe it's Kurt." Elvis hesitated. "Then again, I wouldn't believe it could be any of us." He paused again. "Listen, I don't want you breathing a word of this to anyone until we have something more solid to stand on. *Do not go accusing Kurt or anyone,*" he said sternly. "Is that understood?"

"Yeah, absolutely."

"Keep digging but keep whatever you find to yourself. Report to me and me alone."

"Will do."

"Thanks, kid. You did a good job tonight. I think you won them over with that song-and-dance routine."

"But I didn't dance, King."

"Yeah, but it would have been a lot cooler if you did!" Elvis said with a wink.

chapter

TWENTY-ONE

ole fought sleep that night, unable to turn his mind off. Was he right about his hunch that the threat was from within? Who was the traitor? Why would any of them turn? Was the symbol the key to figuring everything out? He tossed and turned on the couch in Elvis's guest house until the wee hours of morning. Eventually, sleep won, conquering his restless mind and sending Cole into the deepest slumber he'd known since joining the DRS.

When he awoke, it was late in the afternoon. He'd slept for nearly fourteen hours. There was a note resting on his chest that read:

Come to the giant radio tower as soon as you wake up. — E

Cole made himself a cup of coffee, threw on a coat, jumped into a golf cart, and made his way to the radio tower rising above all this madness. The tower was at least 500 feet tall, and yet there was so much to see in the Netherworld that Cole had hardly even noticed it, much less given it any thought. Like the Dead Rock Stars, the radio tower was hiding in plain sight.

Like many large structures, the tower appeared closer than it was. What Cole thought was going to be about a ten-minute ride by golf cart turned out to be closer to thirty. Along the way he passed a couple of landmarks he'd not visited yet, including a fishing pond and an outdoor shooting range. Both were as quiet as a mouse.

When he finally arrived at the tower, Cole drove the perimeter of the tower, looking for a point of entry. Elvis's note had said to come to the tower, but it didn't say where to go or what to do once he got there. He got out of the golf cart and stood there, waiting. No one came to meet him. There were no signs or messages to provide him with further instructions. After ten minutes of kicking rocks under the tower, he decided this must have been some strange test. With a shrug, he jumped in the golf cart and was about to head back when something caught his eye. In the space under the tower were two inconspicuous, vertical metallic bars sticking just a few inches out of the ground.

As Cole approached, he realized the bars were, in fact, handrails at the top of steps that led down to a door. Feeling a bit foolish for having missed this previously, he went down the steps and through the door. It took a good thirty seconds for his eyes to adjust from the afternoon sunlight to the dimly lit interior, but once they did, he saw a single set of elevator doors several yards in front of him.

Cole approached the elevator and hit the only button to be found. Nothing happened. He waited and waited. Nothing. Just when he'd almost decided again to leave, the doors opened. He stepped into the elevator and saw that, again, there was only one button. The button was marked with a *B*. Cole pressed it, and the elevator started to rapidly descend. After several seconds, the elevator stopped, and the doors slowly opened. He heard a buzz of commotion outside the doors.

Not knowing what he might be walking into, Cole cautiously eased out. The doors shut behind him, nearly clipping his coat. Immediately, he felt a presence closing in on him. He turned to his left and saw Jim Morrison lunging for him. Cole blocked his thrust and assumed a fighting stance. Morrison again lunged, turned Cole around, grabbed him around the waist, and flung him to the ground with a belly-to-back suplex. Cole landed on his back with a thud, knocking the wind out of him.

This kind of sneak attack happened to him most every day he trained with Morrison, so he was prepared and countered by twisting and wrapping his legs around Morrison's waist. Cole then grabbed him in a bearhug-like grip and flipped him over, trying to smother him with all his admittedly meager weight. Morrison tossed him aside like a rag doll, then sprang to his feet. Cole did the same.

Morrison straightened, brought his palms together, and bowed toward him. Cole, out of breath and still in an attack stance, relaxed and did the same. Then, for the first time, the teacher gave his student the slightest of smiles and clapped him on the back. This gesture hurt worse than the suplex Cole just experienced, but he received it for what it was—acknowledgement of a test passed.

"Glad you found us," Elvis said, walking over to shake Cole's hand.

"Yeah, some signage would be nice . . ."

"You've never been to this place, have you?" Elvis asked, ignoring Cole's comment. "Ever wondered why we have a 500-foot radio tower?"

"Well, to be honest, it was just a giant radio tower," Cole said, starting to recover his breath. "Of all the things I've seen these past few weeks, this is about the least interesting."

"This is probably the most secret place in the world," Elvis replied, "and you call it uninteresting! Welcome Backstage! You usually need a pass to get backstage."

"Or to be a beautiful blonde," someone said. It was Janis, who walked past them wearing a headset.

Cole finally realized where they were. There were a dozen consoles with computer screens, set in a circle, constantly spitting out data and printing readouts. Most of the Dead Rock Stars he had met so far were here, each seated behind a console and focused on his or her own monitor.

"Ohhhh," he said, "this is comms, huh?"

"Exactly, the DRS communications center," Elvis said. "Let's get to work, Cole."

The King walked him inside the circle of rock stars doing their thing. They were clearly in the middle of some sort of operation. Elvis whispered in Cole's ear, "Jim was just checking your credentials. Can't get backstage without credentials."

Cole laughed and then asked, "So what's going on here?"

"Two of our team are in the Arab Republic of Ammon, digging into the assassination I talked about at the Bop last night."

The mention of the previous evening triggered a fresh rush of panic, and Cole had to fight the urge to remind Elvis that a traitor could very well be in this room.

Janis, who was running comms, sat down at the center of the circle in a chair like Captain Kirk's from the Enterprise. A flatscreen monitor in front of her constantly fed her updates from the rest of the team, each of whom was monitoring a different component of the operation.

Elvis explained to Cole that the team was processing real-time data beamed to the Netherworld from one or more satellites in orbit. There was a large overhead screen at the front of the room where, with the press of a button, Janis could view all the team's monitors at once.

Cole noticed there seemed to be very little video surveillance.

He followed Elvis to the back of the room, where the King donned his own head-set. Elvis whispered to him, "We have two of our best field agents at the hospital where the bodies are being held. They're there to gather information about the bombing."

"Cass, Karen," Janis said, "you're cleared to head to the morgue and inspect the bodies."

"Cass and Karen?" Cole said. "I don't think I've met them."

"Cass Elliot and Karen Carpenter," Elvis said. "They haven't been in since you joined. They've been in the field, chasing down intel. This is only one of several high-level assassinations in recent weeks."

"Just how many of you are there?" Cole asked.

"More than you know, kid," the King replied with a gleam in his eye.

"How does Janis know the coast is clear?"

"Old-school spy craft, my man. Chris is listening in through bugs the gals have planted throughout the hospital. He's monitoring what people are saying and where they're going. Pac is on the phone with security, keeping them tied up so that they won't notice Cass and Karen snooping around. Jimi is updating their position on a map and as they make their way through the hospital. John is translating the doctors' notes from files the ladies managed to lift from a nurses' station. Kurt is remotely manning a sniper rifle that's trained on the entrance to the building."

"So that's John Lennon," Cole said, trying to hide his excitement.

"Yes. He just got back, and he has more info he needs to give you about the Brotherhood—stuff that will help you get to the bottom of what they're up to."

"Great. But let's backtrack just a sec. No one here *really has eyes* inside this hospi-tal?" Cole asked incredulously.

"No," Elvis replied. "Except for Jerry, who's monitoring the entrance, but the satellite image is pretty grainy. So, I guess not—no one has eyes on the inside."

Cole stepped over to an empty console and made himself at home. He didn't immediately pick up on the uneasiness his seat selection brought to the room. This was Buddy's chair, and no one had sat in it since he died.

"Sure," Elvis said for the benefit of the others.

Cole logged on to the internet and began furiously typing and asking questions aloud. "What city are they in? What hospital? Can I talk to Cass?"

Elvis spoke into his headset. "Mama, our new kid needs to chat with you."

Cole dispensed with pleasantries and instructed Cass to go to the security station monitoring the hospital's CCTV feeds.

"Nice to meet you, too," she replied.

Cole started giving orders. He had her doing things he knew she didn't understand or had ever tried before. He was aware of the team looking at him, confused as to what he and Cass were doing. Again, he started rapidly pecking at his keyboard. Abruptly, he stopped typing and looked up. "Janis, throw my monitor to the big screen."

She punched the button linked to Cole's station, which on her console was still labeled "Buddy." Then a black-and-white view of a long hospital corridor appeared on the overhead screen, revealing doctors and nurses coming and going about their business.

"How . . . did you . . . do that?" Janis asked, in astonishment.

"I walked Cass through a simple procedure to hack into the hospital's closed circuit video monitors. Guys, I was doing this stuff in high school," Cole said with a smirk. "Welcome to the twenty-first century."

"What do we do now?" Jerry asked, confused.

"Just keep doing your jobs," Janis said. "Cole, find the camera showing our agents. Cass, Karen, head to the elevator and get to the morgue."

Cole shuffled through the hall cams until he found two women dressed in scrubs and wearing armbands showing the insignia of a generic relief organization.

Cole stared at the two agents through the feed, confused. "Hey, King. Which one's which?"

Elvis laughed. "That goes to show how far these two ladies have come. Karen's armband is on her left arm. Cass is wearing hers on the right. Other than that, they look much the same, don't they? Hasn't always been like that. Everybody has their stuff."

"Cass, look up," Janis said. The woman on the right of the screen looked up and spotted the camera. "We now have eyes on you and Karen."

"The new kid?" Cass asked.

"Yeah," Janis replied, impressed. "Cole, can you give Jimi access to where these cameras are in the hospital?"

"Yes," Cole said and tapped a few keys. "I just sent him an instant message with a list of cameras, which should correspond to the floor plan he's looking at on his monitor."

"Instant message?" Janis asked.

"Yeah, I used the CompuLive message feature built into the software to send a link to Jimi."

"What language is he speaking?" Cobain asked a bit rudely, without looking up from his console.

"I don't know, and don't care so long as it helps us get the job done," Janis said. "Okay, Jimi, tell Cole which camera to switch to so we can track Cass and Karen as they make their way through the hospital."

"Okay, go to camera eight," Jimi said, working from the camera list he'd just received.

As Cass and Karen stepped off the elevator and out of sight, camera eight picked them up as they walked down the hall toward the morgue.

"Morgue cam is number eleven," Jimi said, just as the agents entered.

Karen asked, "Where is the body?"

"The chart says slab five," Lennon answered.

Karen opened the fifth slab in the morgue and found the body of Syed, covered in a plastic bag. She unzipped the bag and began inspecting the corpse.

Lennon consulted his translation of the doctor's notes. "According to his chart, gas was found in the bodies of all four men in the car, but less gas was found in Syed's system than in the others. The doctor also noted that there were marks, or impressions, on his face that none of the others had."

"What does that mean?" Elvis asked.

"It means he must have had a gas mask on at some point prior to the explosion," Karen answered.

"Take a look at this." Cole had pulled up an online news article about the assassination. "This says Syed was 'whisked away in a black Mercedes-Benz, accompanied by three of his bodyguards.'"

"Okay," Elvis said, "so one of the bodyguards must have taken him out in a suicide bombing."

"No," Cole said. "Look at this." He then played them footage from one of the American news cameras he found on another site. The footage was taken outside the mosque and distinctly showed Syed and three bodyguards getting in the already-running car. "There was a driver. That makes five," Cole said.

"Can you find some footage that gives us a better look at this driver?" Elvis said, approaching the big screen.

Cole quickly explored several different search engines to find video taken from other angles. "With all the media there to cover the event, it's not only possible, it's likely," he said. "But finding it could be difficult."

He searched through various websites from media outlets that covered the bombing, but he kept coming up with the same footage.

Lennon then spoke up. "Here, I found a snippet of video taken from the opposite direction."

Janis threw Lennon's console onto the big screen. The driver of the car was clearly visible, but all they really saw was a person in a gas mask.

Elvis asked, "Do we have any notes from the crime scene?"

"Yes," Lennon replied. "We have the full police report."

"Where is the body of the man they think was the driver?"

Lennon looked back at the doctor's notes, then instructed Cass to open slab seven. She opened the drawer, revealing another corpse shrouded in plastic. Lennon said, "This is the guy they found in the driver's seat, and he had the same amount of gas in him as the others. More than Syed."

"So, the driver gave his mask to Syed?" Elvis guessed. "Is that what you're getting at?"

"This wasn't the driver," Lennon said. "Look at the corpse of the man found in the driver's seat. He was quite large, ya know? Maybe six-four and eighteen stone. Now, look at our footage of the driver. He couldn't be more than five-nine or five-ten."

"And he has blond hair," Cole added. "Look." He paused the video of the opposite-angle footage. At one point the head of the driver turned, and a few locks of blond hair could be seen from behind the gas mask.

Janis said, "I wouldn't think there'd be many blonds working security in the Middle East."

Elvis said, "So somebody picked up Syed and his men, drove him away from the chaos, then stopped and gassed them, knocking them out. He then staged the scene by putting this bigger guy in the driver's seat, blew up the car, and walked away, taking one or more gas masks with him. Is that what we're saying?"

"I think that's what happened, King," Lennon replied.

"I agree," Cole said. *A Beatle just agreed with me!* he thought.

This discussion had drawn the team's focus away from the video feed.

Janis glanced up at the big screen and saw two masked individuals entering the morgue and carrying automatic rifles. "Cass! Karen! Look out!" she shouted.

The agents flipped a metal table over and dropped down behind it as bullets began ricocheting off the tabletop. Cass pulled a pistol from a holster in the small of her back. "Cover me," she shouted.

Karen had pulled a pistol from an ankle holster and started firing blindly over the desk in the direction of the two shooters. As the attackers backed out of the room to take cover, Cass rolled out from behind the table, took aim at a fire extinguisher mounted on the wall, and fired. A brilliant cloud of carbon dioxide burst forth, obscuring the camera and the team's view of the unfolding events.

"Quick," Jimi shouted, "switch to camera thirteen."

Cole switched the feed just in time to see the two masked attackers escape down the hallway and into a stairwell.

"Are there cameras in that stairway?" Janis asked.

"No," Jimi responded. "Only in the hallways, elevators, and lobbies."

"Where does that stairway lead?"

"Looks like a parking garage," he said, studying the floorplan on his screen.

"Jerry, re-task the satellite to see if we can get a look at whoever comes out of that parking garage," Janis said, barking out orders. "Cass, Karen, are you okay?"

"We're fine," Karen responded.

"Get to that garage and see if you can find them."

"On it."

"Now we're blind again," Janis said as she exhaled.

"Security has been notified," Tupac said, "and they're on their way."

"Girls," Janis said, "your cover is blown. Security is on the way. Look alive."

"I've re-tasked the sat," Jerry said. "But look, there's no way of knowing who they could be or what they're driving. There's a steady flow of traffic in and out of that garage."

Just then Karen reported, "We've lost them."

"Get out of there and get safe," Elvis said. "We've got the information we need for now. Go to the safe house and await instructions."

"You got it."

"Well done, team." Elvis beamed at the room. "Let's close up shop and call it a day."

The team began packing up and powering down their stations. Adrenaline coursed through Cole's system. It was his first op, and he'd played a significant role. John Lennon gingerly approached Cole like he was going to ask for his autograph.

"You did well, son," he said, patting Cole on the shoulder. "I know we've not met yet, but I have to say, I was most impressed with what you did back there."

"Thanks . . ." Cole was starstruck.

"Ride with me, Cole," Lennon said, motioning to the elevator. Cole followed him in, and they began their ascent, leaving the rest of the team to clean up after the op. "You know, I wasn't too keen on you joining this team to begin with. I've been skeptical, youknowwhatImean?"

"I kinda get it. I'm sorry." Cole had met with every kind of reception from cold shoulders to outright hostility. He'd had cross words with a few team members. But this was the first time someone had been nice about not wanting him there. It was a new experience and somewhat disorienting.

"No need to apologize, man," Lennon said with a laugh. "I don't know, call me a purist, but I thought King should get a rock star, not a kid who knows how to play video games." He then looked Cole in the eyes and said, "I was wrong."

"That . . . that means a lot."

"You know what else?" Lennon said, as the elevator reached its destination. "You and me, we've got more in common than just about everyone else on the team."

"How do you figure?"

"We both lost our mums when we were teens."

Cole was taken aback.

"I mean . . . I think that makes us special . . . unique in this group. I still miss me mum. What about you?"

Cole couldn't choke out an answer.

Lennon didn't pause long but changed the subject as they walked outside. "Which brings me to my Brotherhood intel. The information I found through Langston in Tennessee led me to his handler, which took me to a training site in Cleveland. I think he's the blond bloke who drove the car and killed Syed in Ammon."

"How do you know?" Cole asked, his mind blown by this revelation.

"The person I saw running things at the training facility has the same height and build. Slender, athletic, and about five-nine or so. Shorter than Elvis but more like . . .'"

Just then, Kurt Cobain emerged from the bunker.

This was another piece of the puzzle—one more brick in the wall in Cole's case against Cobain. His brain was buzzing, and chills ran down his spine. Then he chuckled and mumbled, "I'm not like them, but I sure can pretend . . ."

"Come again?" Lennon said, looking curious.

"Never mind." Cole laughed to himself. *I've got to be more careful,* he thought. *These people are smart.*

"This is really good info, John. More helpful than you know."

"It's me job," Lennon said cheerily. "I think it's about time we get you in the field. I'll talk to Elvis and see if we can't set you up for your first field assignment."

"Are you sure I'm ready for that?" Cole asked, flattered.

"No one is ever ready, lad. But when it's your time, it's your time. And your time is soon."

chapter

TWENTY-TWO

ole ran his hand along the side of the plane to calm his nerves.

"You ready for this?" Jimi asked.

"No, but what choice do I have?"

"All right then, let's do it," Jimi said, grinning.

As they took off into the afternoon sun, Cole was in the co-pilot seat and nervously shifting his weight from side to side.

"Today, I give you only two instructions. Stay alive and don't crash the plane."

"Very encouraging," Cole moaned.

"So," Jimi said, "your driving is progressing very well. I'll have you in a *real* car any day now."

"Good, I'm tired of go-karts and golf carts. I want to drive something with muscle!"

"In time, Grasshopper. In time. How's the rest of your training going?"

"Uh . . . well . . . I think," Cole said. "Jim kicks my butt every day, but every now and then I get a shot in. Pretty sure Kurt hates me, but my shooting is getting better. He's graduated me to handguns."

"Kurt's an onion—he's got layers, man. He teach you the two-to-the-chest, one-to-the-head routine yet?"

"Yes. He got that from *Heat,* didn't he? De Niro-style?"

"Probably. What do you think of your time with Jerry?"

"It's fun sitting down with him. Best part of my day. He's a trip, man."

"Hmm . . . okay."

"Why do you say it like that? He's been nothing but cool to me."

"You'll see," Jimi said with a coy smile.

Cole grew more at ease as they talked about his training.

Jimi continued to fire questions at him. "Your presentation was amazing—how did you learn to make music that way?" "How fast you running your five miles?" "Are you hitting your target numbers on the push-ups?' "What do you think of the weird diet Jim's got you on?" "Does the face still itch from the new beard?"

As Cole rambled on in answer to his questions, Jimi started to nod off.

"Is this it?" Cole asked, noticing Jimi's heavy eyelids.

"I think s . . ." Jimi was out like a light, gently snoring, head pressed up against the side window.

Cole grabbed the yoke and started flying. So far, he had spent twenty hours in a plane with Jimi, and he knew this little drill was coming. But nothing could prepare him for the moment when Jimi Hendrix intentionally gave himself a sedative and fell asleep at the wheel, leaving Cole to fly the plane and, if necessary, land it by himself. He had no idea how long Jimi would be passed out. He would rather not land the plane if he didn't have to. That was always the trickiest part for him.

He checked the fuel. It was low.

"Hey, Hendrix!" he called, but Jimi didn't budge. Cole laughed nervously. "When I land this plane, I'm going to watch *Ace Ventura* on LaserDisc. You wanna join me? Oh, cool! You bring the popcorn!"

Cole scanned the instruments and took a deep breath. "Okay, okay, Denton, you can do this. Air speed indicator? Indicating. Radar? Radaring. Altimeter? Altimeter-ing. All right. So far, so good." Soon he began to relax and just fly the plane.

Jimi had not given him a destination. His only instructions were to stay alive and don't crash the plane, in that order. With nothing else to do but fly, his mind wandered back to the traitor he was certain was in their midst.

He turned the facts over and over in his mind, and at every turn, he came back to Kurt Cobain. In Cole's experience, the simplest explanation usually was the best one. Not only had Cobain been hostile to his presence from the first, but he was the same height and build as the blond assassin from Ammon. According to Lennon, the assassin might be the same person he saw running the training facility in Cleveland.

166

But what would be Cobain's motivation for turning against the DRS? He had left behind a wife and child. Cole wondered if he might be ready to blow this whole thing up and go home. He had more money now than he ever had alive; he could easily take his family and disappear forever. Especially with the skills he had developed as a Dead Rock Star.

He remembered how Cobain had taken to the little girl who helped prepare their meal at Graceland II. His daughter might have been about that age by now.

Cole wished Jerry were with him so he could ask about this train of thought. Of course he couldn't just flat out ask if Jerry though Kurt Cobain could turn traitor. He knew he would have to be circumspect in his inquiry.

His thoughts turned back to the symbol. He had hit a roadblock with it. Nothing new had come to him since discovering the *2* and the three *V*s, if indeed that's what they were. Taken as a whole, the symbol didn't look like anything he'd ever seen. Using a new screen name—10v35h4ck was dead, after all—he had scoured the hacker message boards and asked if anyone knew anything about it. Using a new handle didn't help, as 133t hacker types didn't trust newbies.

Assuming a connection with Cobain, Cole had even read the lyrics and liner notes from every Nirvana album, but nothing seemed even remotely close. He wondered if maybe the symbol was a dead end.

Then he thought back to the Brotherhood activities JFK had enumerated, particularly the assassinations of political and religious leaders on multiple continents. Chaos and destabilization of the establishment seemed to be the motivation, but to what purpose? Why tear at the fabric of societies by eliminating their leaders and chipping away at their core beliefs? Could it be that destruction of the DRS was the organization's ultimate objective? Or could these events be a means of distracting the team? A way of occupying their time and focus to keep them from seeing—and stopping—a far more cataclysmic endgame.

Then he remembered Buddy's hunch that there was a doomsday scenario in play. Suddenly, it all crystallized, and Cole could see it as clearly as if he had designed the symbol himself.

Those weren't *V*s; they were pieces of another letter altogether. The number two he'd discovered confirmed this thought and served as the bridge between the other pieces.

He knew what the symbol meant. Now all he had to figure out was how Kurt Cobain was involved.

Cole wanted to land the plane immediately.

He got his wish.

Suddenly, the plane started making all kinds of concerning noises. Startled, Cole snapped back into the moment and read his instruments. Sure enough, the fuel was nearly out. He had no idea how far he'd flown, but he knew he had to get this bird on the ground. He looked over at Jimi, who was sleeping like a baby.

Cole shouted, "Stay alive and don't crash the plane, Denton!"

He refocused and turned the plane around. He set the coordinates to return to their point of departure, to the Netherworld. He calculated that he might just have enough fuel to get home but with no room for error or waste.

He thought about shaking Jimi and trying to wake him up but then reconsidered. *This is the exercise*, he thought. *I can do this. I have to do this.*

After a few more minutes of flying, the terrain began to look more familiar. He thought he could see the strange, invasive trees that bordered the Netherworld on the horizon, and he knew he was getting close.

He called in for permission to land. "Tower, this is Coletrane. I've got a sleeping rock star here, and I'm requesting permission to land."

"Permission granted," came the voice of Elvis Presley. "I take it things have gone well up there?"

"To this point, I've followed the only instructions Jimi gave me. I'm still alive, and I haven't crashed the plane."

"Let's keep it that way, hoss."

"You got it. Oh, and I think I figured out that assignment you gave me."

"You just land that bird, and we'll talk about that later."

The engines of the plane started to labor and sputter.

"Uh, King, we may have a problem up here. My engines are starting to falter. I'm almost completely out of gas."

"What would you do if this was a live op and you found yourself in this situation?"

"First, I would try not to freak out, and then I would attempt to land the plane."

"Then do that. Now. Practice like you play, son."

Cole took a deep breath and continued his descent, monitoring his gauges and instruments. All at once, the console started making all sorts of new racket. His fuel gauge went from blinking to a constant red, accompanied by a shrill noise, meaning he was now completely out of gas. The engine lights came on, too, offering a glowing reminder that the craft he was now piloting was little more than an expensive hang glider. Off in the distance, though, he could see the lights of home. The beautifully manicured, putting-green-like runway of the Netherworld was illuminated in all its glory. He was in range.

Cole glided the plane closer and closer to the ground. He was attempting to level the plane out when Elvis screamed from the tower, "Landing gear, Cole!"

"Whoops!" Cole hit the switch to release the wheels. He had to adjust his altitude to give the wheels the few seconds they needed to lock into place. This cost him precious runway space, but he had no fuel to pull out and make another run at it. It was going to be close.

He tried again to level the plane out to land, but his right rear wheel hit the ground first and made the plane take a huge hop back into the sky. Just then, Jimi let out a loud snore.

"Land the plane, Love Shack!" Cole yelled at himself.

The runway was running out. He tried one more time to ease the plane to the ground. This time, both wheels hit simultaneously. Cole abruptly dropped the nose to the ground, the front wheel coming down with a bang. The flaps caught the wind, and the plane began to slow but not quickly enough. There were only a few hundred feet of runway left before ending in a steep ditch. Cole turned the yoke hard to the left and locked up the brakes, and the plane skidded to a stop at a ninety-degree angle to the runway.

Cole breathed a huge sigh of relief.

"You made it, Grasshopper," Jimi said, looking at Cole with one eye open and smiling like a Cheshire cat.

"Hey! Wait a second! Were you awake the whole time?"

"You think I'm an idiot? Of course I was awake! You think I'd trust Izabella to a flier as inexperienced as you?"

"I could have sworn you were out like a light. I think I even saw drool coming out of your mouth."

"It's all part of the magic," Jimi said, waving his fingers in Cole's face. "Congratulations, you are now a first-degree DRS pilot. What time are you starting the movie?"

Cole felt a swell of pride in his chest. He not only passed his flying test, but he also thought he'd solved the mystery of the symbol. It was a key that might unlock the plans of the Brotherhood.

★ ★ ★ ★

"King, I figured out the symbol."

"What is it?" Elvis asked with great enthusiasm.

Cole grabbed a notebook from his backpack. He began to sketch it out. "It's not one symbol but three overlaid, one on top of each other."

"Well, what does it mean?"

"Y2K!" Cole said triumphantly. "Kurt Cobain is planning something huge on New Year's Day!"

Again, Elvis' whole demeanor darkened. "You can't go accusing Kurt of this!"

"I've got proof," Cole snapped back. "John found a Brotherhood cell. He told me all about it. He figured out that the driver in the Syed assassination is also the guy who gave Langston his orders. He's got blond hair and the same height and build as Cobain."

Elvis calmed down a bit but looked dubious. "This isn't much to go on, Cole. Could be mere coincidence. You need more."

"I don't need more proof, King! This is what I do. I figure things out, with or without all of the information."

"Well, enlighten me then, kid. What's his motive to blow up the world?"

"Maybe he wants out. You know, I've seen everything he looks at on his computer. I know what and who he searches for. He's unstable. Always has been. You can't explain crazy. Maybe he's stopped believing in what we do, and he wants to go back to his family, and the only way to do that is to tear everything apart. Elvis, you know I see things. This is what I see. Someone is trying to distract us, to pull us apart while upending the world."

Elvis laughed out loud.

"What's so funny?"

"Listen, kid. Kurt loves his family very deeply. But he knows that the best way to keep them safe is to serve on this team. He also knows that there's no going back to them. When he made the choice to join us, he knew what it meant. But he also knew it was the only way he would ever heal. He died to save lives."

Cole gave Elvis the stink eye of doubt.

"You don't have to believe me at the moment," the King said. "But when the time is right, you'll see and believe, Cole. Just because he doesn't like you doesn't mean he's a traitor. But let's say you're right. You're going to have to come up with more evidence than you've got to convince me."

"I'll find it. I promise you. And . . . King . . . I hope you're right about Kurt. But the truth is, I'm rarely wrong."

chapter
TWENTY-THREE

"**E**inhorn is Finkle, Finkle is Einhorn . . ."

Cole Denton had been wearing down a pattern in the carpet, pacing back and forth, trying to connect all the dots to prove what he thought he knew.

"Finkle and Einhorn, Einhorn and Finkle."

He had left the safe confines of the guest house at Graceland II and gone back to the "nu-partment" that was custom made just for him. Yes, the place creeped him out, but he needed space to think, and the tech he'd already had built into the apartment would help. The familiar screech of his modem brought the World Wide Web to his fingertips.

Cole had been scouring the internet for any kind of clue that might help him make his case. He'd even been to a fan page dedicated to guys who *kind of* looked like Kurt Cobain.

A chime from his computer screen notified him of an email from GuruGarcia. The subject line read, "Time for Training." The text of the email was brief:

```
1pm. McKinley Building. 8th floor, room 27.
Dress comfortably. Shoes optional.
```

More training? It was all he could do to keep up with Morrison's conditioning program. Meanwhile, daily lessons in weaponry, fighting, driving, and flying were ongoing. Whereas most dead people had plenty of time on their hands, Cole couldn't imagine adding anything else to his plate.

✷ ✷ ✷ ✷

As Cole was about to push the "Up" button on the elevator, the doors gave way to a man who appeared both more Grateful and slightly less Dead than had been reported in 1995.

"Mr. Denton, lovely to see you this fine afternoon."

"Dude, at what point is any of this going to feel . . . normal?"

Jerry Garcia pondered this for a moment, then quizzically observed, "It's been four years, Cole. I'll let you know when I arrive." His eyes always looked as if he were in on the joke before the joke was ever conceived.

Cole joined him in the elevator. Jerry was wearing black on black on black, calling attention to his ever-whitening hair. He was smirking, waiting for Cole to push the button for the eighth floor.

"You look like it's Christmas morning, Jer-Bear. What gives?"

"This is always my favorite part of training."

Cole had a feeling this was going to be way harder than getting tossed around by Jim Morrison. He ran his fingers across a few of the welts and bruises that had become commonplace on his body. Less than two months ago, his biggest callus was on his thumb from a marathon weekend of playing Tomb Raider.

The eighth floor of the warehouse was open-air with exposed ductwork and hanging light fixtures. A couple hundred feet in both directions were multiple groupings of chairs and couches set around a large rug, each setting situated far enough from the others so that conversations could not be overheard. Oversized windows allowed light to flood the room with warmth. On one side of the room, a gifted artist had painted a message on the wall, writ large. Amongst flourishes of abstract art, these words were written: *Somebody has to do something, and it seems incredibly pathetic that it has to be us.*

As Cole was taking in the scene, he realized the entire floor was vacated except for one group milling around in a corner nook. Above them hung a sign that read, "Room 27." He wondered if this was going to be espionage training or some type of interpersonal communication course. *Jerry would be great at that,* he thought.

Cole felt that the two of them had deeply connected through their conversations. Jerry was nothing like he'd expected. Not just creative, but deeply intelligent and soulful. Last week, they had talked about postmodernism, computer engineering, and the Simpsons all in the same conversation. And yet, if there was in fact a mole in the DRS, Cole didn't know if he could fully trust Jerry. Or anyone else, for that matter. Could he even trust Elvis?

Seltzer water and light snacks had been set out on a table. Cole mingled with the small crowd and acknowledged several DRS team members, but there were other people he didn't recognize at all. *Where do these people come from?* he wondered.

And then there was a person he didn't know yet somehow seemed familiar. It was this person who held up his hands and spoke to the room. "All right, everybody, find a seat. Jerry asked me to lead this meeting, so I guess that makes me your *motivational speaker!* Hey, Jerry, you remember that time you played 'Casey Jones' for us at Thirty Rock? Man, that was awesome!"

Cole's jaw dropped. He looked at Jerry, hoping for confirmation that he was seeing who he thought he was seeing. Jerry shook him off and motioned for him to sit down. As everyone settled into a chair or a spot on the carpet, Cole snuck into an oversized chair with giant arms and an ottoman that acted as a kind of barrier between himself and the others. The meeting leader stood up, this time looking centered and serious. He then began reciting, as everyone else chimed in:

God, grant me the serenity to accept the things I cannot change,
Courage to change the things I can,
And wisdom to know the difference.

"Wait, what?" Cole said before he could close his mouth. He couldn't move. He didn't want to breathe. He looked around for help but realized that Jerry had ducked into the back row

"A few ground rules," the leader said. "First, this meeting is voluntary and confidential. Second, everyone must speak, and it can only be about recovery. Third, cross talk is allowed; when someone shares, if you have something helpful, speak up. Finally, is it anyone's first time to join us for a meeting?"

Cole was dumbfounded as he found himself in the world's most clandestine recovery meeting. As his mind was reeling, he realized that everyone in the circle of trust was now staring directly at him. Cole, usually gifted at defusing a tense moment with situational comedy, couldn't come up with anything. He broke into a sweat.

"Ummm . . . Hi, my name is Cole, and I'm a Dead Rock Star. Nice to be here with you people. Um, and by 'you people,' I mean . . ."

No one laughed.

Cole was embarrassed and angry and unsure why. When no one came to his rescue by easing the tension, he ducked his head and swiftly headed for the elevator a couple hundred feet away. It was the longest walk of shame he'd ever experienced. Before the elevator doors could close, Jerry stepped in and pressed the button for the seventh floor.

As soon as the doors were completely closed, Cole screamed, "What kind of 'training' was *that*?!?"

"Cole, why did you react that way?"

"What was I supposed to do, sing 'Kumbaya' and say the Lord's Prayer?"

"What would be so wrong with that?"

Cole screamed, "What do you want from me? To say that my dad was a lousy drunk who ruined my life? That I'm just like these people who had the world given to them on a silver platter but snorted and drank it all away? Well, I'm *not* like them. I am not like *you*. I'm not addicted to *anything*. And honestly, how am I supposed to trust them anyway? They're going to burn this place down eventually, just like they did with their real lives!"

Garcia said nothing.

The doors opened, and they were back on the set of *I Dream of Jeannie*. Jerry motioned for Cole to come and sit, and he did so without hesitation. Neither of them said anything for a long time.

"What was that supposed to do for me?" Cole finally asked.

"What do you think it should do?"

"Freak me out and make me run away from a truly gifted Chippendale dancer who never got his big break."

Jerry chuckled and leaned back, not saying anything.

"I mean, I guess I figured there had to be some element of counseling and therapy for a crowd like this, and I know we've had our moments already, Jerry. In many ways you've helped keep me sane throughout this experience. But how am I supposed to trust the others?"

"Why wouldn't you? You've trusted them to teach you combat and other life-saving skills, haven't you? Why would you want to go into battle with people yet choose not to understand them on their deepest, most vulnerable level?"

Cole felt he had accepted some insane things already as part of this new reality. But Jerry pushing him to be totally vulnerable wasn't something he was prepared for, especially when Cole was convinced there was a mole in the group. As for his past, he had long ago accepted that tragic things happen to people all the time. And although he couldn't deny that tragedy had shaped his own life, he also knew he had never truly dealt with this fact on an emotional level. But trusting a bunch of addicts like his father felt like an impossible expectation.

Cole pleaded with Jerry for the next few minutes. He yelled. He laughed. He joked. He even threw a pillow with an embroidered peace sign at Jerry, which really tickled the rock legend. Ultimately, Cole realized that he wasn't going to let him out of this. "I guess I can't hack or joke my way out of this one, huh?"

"No amount of keyboard calisthenics, sarcastic sniping, or backdoor coding is going to allow you to bypass this training, Cole. I'm sorry. It's necessary to get you where you need to be as a member of this team."

★ ★ ★ ★

Each person stood and spoke their truth. And with every testimony, Cole felt the weight lessen. Each person who shared was so open, raw, and real, it felt almost embarrassing to witness. Cole wondered if anyone cared that he was in the room and hearing these intimate details. There were stories of pain, loss, shame, and grief. But there were also clear signs of health, peace, and contentment. The session honestly made him feel, like Elvis, that there was no way someone could betray this group of people. Yet Cole noticed that Kurt Cobain was noticeably absent from the gathering.

Janis Joplin was now sharing. "It's been a few weeks since he died, but I keep expecting him to walk through the door. Everything else has moved back to normal. At least, as normal as this place can be. I've promised myself some things, and I promised him too. But I'm scared of relapsing. It's been twelve years since I did. Buddy helped me. And I know you are all my family, but I feel so alone."

Cole watched as love was poured out on Janis. One after the other, people in the room offered encouragement, grace, understanding, and some tough love. After most everyone had their moment to share, he once again felt all eyes were trained on him.

"Hello, my name is Cole," he began, "and my father was an alcoholic."

★ ★ ★ ★

There were no clocks on Jerry's walls. Cole had no clue how long they had been talking one-on-one, debriefing after his first group meeting. To be in a place where someone could share everything and not be judged had been revelatory to Cole. He had learned he wasn't the only who always felt like someone was seeing right through their shame and the facade they had built to protect themselves.

Jerry leaned in and said, "Sometimes you need to hear from a roomful of sick people to get healthy. I think as you give this more time, you will experience the miracle of recovery."

The elevator dinged. Jerry's next appointment had arrived. Cole looked over at the elevator and found Kurt Cobain staring a hole right through him.

Cole was visibly uneasy.

Jerry said, "Mr. Denton, I'd like to remind you of something. The DRS is a family. Fully committed to the cause. I have personally invested in everyone here, just like they've invested in me. I am no different. I have been understood and loved. I believe in helping the world. 'Somebody has to do something, and it seems incredibly pathetic that it has to be us.' I was credited with saying that in 1988. Then I found it painted on the walls of this place before I ever arrived. These gifted men and women were protecting the world long before you or I knew any of this existed. We are a part of something they deeply believe in. They've sacrificed everything. It might be hard to imagine, but they are all willing to give even more than that."

"Even Lithium over there?"

"Especially Mr. Cobain."

Cole hesitated and then said, "Jerry, I hate to ask this, but I have to know. Are there ever relapses on the team? You know, like active-duty people in the field who hold my life in their hands?"

"How do you feel about your father? Have you forgiven him?"

"Why would you ask that?"

"Do you think you'll forgive him one time and that will be that?"

"I don't even—"

"Cole. We are human. Each of us is an imperfect creature with a capacity for love or hate. I think you'll find that *we* want love to win."

"Are you about to tell me that love is all I need?"

"I'm trying to tell you that the DRS is a family, and that family believes in this cause. We all know we must do it right and well and together. That means, no matter how many relapses, we'll be there for each other. It also means that part of my job is to determine who is healthy for operations and who isn't. I am focused on the emotional health of each DRS agent, including yourself. So, yes, we sometimes relapse."

"You will be the one to clear me for operational duty?"

"I do the same for everyone."

"How am I doing so far?"

"I'll see you tomorrow. Same time. Same place."

✮ ✮ ✮ ✮

Time seemed to move more slowly over the next week or so. Cole wasn't only sore from working out; at the end of each day, he found himself emotionally exhausted as well. He slept *very* well. Every day, he unpacked a bit more of his soul and self to Guru Garcia. Or at least the parts he felt he could trust him with. He still didn't know which of his teammates might be out to destroy the team and the world. But the fact was, Cole had built firewalls in his mind and heart that no one was getting through.

Still, each day he found the group sessions to be as cathartic and helpful as he'd let them be. The people in this group freely shared stories. They laughed, cried, and yelled quite often. It was raw and real.

But Jerry could see that Cole was holding back.

"Why won't you fully commit to this?"

"I *am*," Cole said defensively.

"No. No, you're not. I can tell. You'll let us into your heart—but only so far and not all the way."

Cole knew that Elvis didn't want him to say anything to anyone about a possible mole in the organization, but he wondered if he could ask Jerry for his thoughts in a roundabout way. He remembered trying to tell Savannah about the DRS without revealing too—

Savannah. There she was again. He tried not to think about Savannah. Besides, that was one area he wasn't letting anyone in yet.

Still, he needed to try to see if he could pry something out of Jerry. Then an idea hit him.

"Okay, Jerry, let me put it this way. You know how sometimes in a band you write a hit song, and everybody loves you? You got the world by the tail, and everyone is getting along. Right?"

"Well, we didn't have many 'hits' per se, but I know what you mean."

"Okay, good. Stay with me now. You're riding high, then suddenly hard times come along. The songs aren't hits anymore, the record label drops you, and then—*boom*—the band breaks up for . . . you know . . . whatever reason."

A look of understanding came across Jerry's face, and he smiled a warm smile. "So, you're worried you might get kicked out?"

"Um . . . yeah, sort of. Has anyone ever been kicked out of the DRS? You know, like, maybe they did something wrong or like, heaven forbid, they abused their position or power?"

Jerry laughed a hearty laugh. "No, man. No one ever gets kicked out. Reassigned? Yes. All the time. That's why there's people in the group you haven't met yet. But we've never kicked someone out."

"In all the years the organization's existed, no one has ever . . . you know . . . gone bad?"

"What does that have to do with you opening up to the group?"

"I mean, if I share my deepest darkest secrets with someone, and they . . . I don't know . . . go off the deep end, I don't want that coming back to haunt me."

"I don't think your deepest darkest secrets are *that* deep or dark," Jerry said with a laugh.

"You don't even know me," Cole said indignantly, forgetting for a moment why he had started the conversation down this path.

"You think that's true?" Jerry said. "My friend, I know you are scared to death of failure, so you don't take many chances. I know you're simultaneously supremely confident in some areas of life and deeply insecure in others. I know you have felt that much of your life has been a waste and that you long to make a difference in the world. I know you crave connection with others but don't know how to get there. I know you loved your dad deeply, and what he did to you and your family is the deepest hurt you've ever known. I don't blame you, man; it would hurt me, too. But look, I'm not your father. Elvis is not your father. Jimi's not your father. We aren't going to hurt you like that. We might make mistakes, but we are never going to do you like that. Do you understand?"

Cole fought back tears. Everything inside of him wanted to believe this. He could get ninety-nine percent of the way there, but he couldn't cross the finish line. He went quiet for a long time. Then he whispered in a cracking voice, "How do you know?"

"Honestly, I don't," Jerry said with a hearty laugh. "But I do know that once I gave up and let everybody in, everything came together for me. And I think that if you'll do the same, it will all come together for you, too."

178

chapter

TWENTY-FOUR

Savannah stared into her cup of coffee. Her sister, Amy, stared back at her blankly from across the table.

"So, what are you saying, Savannah?"

"I don't know! I'm just saying it's weird. He told me if he took the job he'd be going away, and he couldn't tell me anything about it. Next thing I know, he's dead. Now they're saying his website has been sold. Actually, not even his website—just his algorithm. I bet they change the name to something lame like LoveConnection.com or WeHarmony or something stupid like that."

"You think someone killed him for his dating website?" Amy asked with disgust.

"No! I'm just saying it doesn't add up. Every way I try to slice it, I keep coming back to one thing: What kind of job is so secret that you can't tell anyone about it? And if there *is* such a job, what better way to make sure that no one knows you're doing it than for the world to think you're dead."

"Well, I don't know what to tell you," Amy said, standing up in exasperation and collecting her things. She stomped to the door, then turned around and mustered as much sympathy as she could. "Savannah . . . I love you. And I think you need to do whatever you have to do to get over him. You only dated a short time, and he's been gone longer than that. It's time to let go and move on."

Savannah broke into sobs. She knew Amy was right. But she just couldn't shake the feeling that there was something off about Cole's death. Amy grabbed her little sister and enveloped her in a big-sister embrace. Savannah melted into her arms, and they stayed that way for several minutes.

"Ames, I just need closure."

The rest of the morning and into the afternoon, they remained in Savannah's apartment and talked. They sat on the living room floor and listened to TLC's "Unpretty" on repeat. They braided each other's hair and pretended they were eleven and thirteen again. They told and retold stories from their past and laughed. After several hours of this, it was time for Amy to go home to her husband and baby.

"Are you going to be okay?" she asked.

"Yeah." Savannah sighed and smiled. "This was just what I needed. I just needed my big sister. Thank you so much."

After Amy left, Savannah went back to her bedroom to lie down. When she saw the replica of the Starship *Enterprise*, she nearly yanked it from the ceiling. Then from her desktop computer came the familiar words: "You've got mail."

She sat down at the computer and opened her email. There was one new message from an unfamiliar address, AlUNedney80@compulive.com. "Must be junk mail," she said to no one, but the subject line intrigued her: "Ur not wrong."

Against her better judgment she opened the email. It read:

```
Savannah,
You're right about Cole's death. It is
fishy.
Reply if you want to know more.
Sincerely,
Al Nedney
```

All the progress she had made moving on from Cole that afternoon went right down the drain. Who was this person? How did he know she had questions about Cole's death? How did he get her email address? The whole thing was unsettling, but her curiosity overwhelmed her.

She decided to reply. She wrote:

```
Al,
Who are you? What do you know about Cole's
death?
Savannah
```

She hit send and immediately regretted it. "Why did I do that?" she said out loud and banged her keyboard with her fists. She started fishing around the settings on her email account to see if there was a way to delete an email after it was sent. She wasn't super-familiar with the software, but it felt like that would be a useful feature.

Then, once again, her computer chirped, "You've got mail," startling her.

It was Al Nedney again.

```
Meet me at 1369, the place you and Cole
had your second date.
Be there today at 4:30 pm.
```

Warning bells were going off in her mind. It was one thing to correspond via email with a stranger; it was quite another to meet him at a restaurant. And how did he know that was where she and Cole had their second date? But then she thought, *If he wanted to do something bad to me, he wouldn't ask to meet in a coffee shop where there are people. He'd ask me to meet him in some sort of deserted location.*

Savannah waffled as to whether she should do this.

Then she had an idea. *Don't go alone.*

She picked up the phone and dialed a number. It rang and rang.

She was about to hang up when she heard a sleepy voice say, "Hello?"

"Taylor," she said. "This is Savannah, Cole's old girlfriend. I'm sorry, did I wake you up?"

"Uh, yeah, I was just catching some Zs. I'm really glad you called, though. In fact, I was thinking about calling *you.*"

"Oh yeah? Why?"

"Well, I'm not sure how to say this, but I've been thinking a lot about Cole's death, and it's just not sitting well with me."

"SHUT UP!" Savannah shouted, doing her best Elaine Benes impersonation. "I've been thinking the same thing."

Surprised, Taylor continued. "I've even talked it over with Cole's old professor Dr. Self, and he agrees that something's just not right about it."

"Taylor, I got an email today from someone I don't know. It said—"

"'You're not wrong.' I got one too! And so did Dr. Self!"

"Was it from Al Nedney?"

"Yes!"

"Did he ask you to meet him at 1369 at 4:30?"

"No," Taylor said. "But I think we should all meet him and get to the bottom of this. I'll call Dr. Self and call you right back."

Savannah hung up the phone. Her head was spinning. What was happening? Why did she reply to that email? Moments later, the phone rang, startling her again.

She picked it up and said, "Taylor, is that you?"

"Yes, and I have Dr. Self."

"So, you're Love Shack's girlfriend," Self said.

"Love Shack?" Savannah said.

"Never mind," Self said. "Let's get down to brass tacks. Some creep-o emailed you and said Cole's death is fishy, and he wants to meet you at a coffee shop?"

"Yes, that's right."

"Well, the gentleman invited you for coffee. By all means, you must go. He didn't insist that you come alone, did he?"

"No. Okay, then let's do this! Meet me there at 4:30."

Taylor said, "We'll be there."

Savannah nervously paced her apartment until it was time to leave, then drove to the coffee shop. Taylor and Dr. Self were waiting outside in the fading afternoon light. After a brief introduction, they went in together.

As they walked in the door, the girl working the check-in station asked, "Are you Savannah?"

"Yes, I am."

"You have a phone call," the girl said and handed Savannah the phone.

Savannah took the phone and put it to her ear. "Hello?"

"Savannah, this is Nedney." The voice was distorted like the TV news did when interviewing an anonymous informant. "I didn't know you'd be bringing friends. This complicates things slightly. It's okay, though. We'll make accommodations. Please get in the car that is waiting outside." And the caller hung up.

"Who was that?" Self asked.

"It was Nedney. He wants us to get in that car," she said, pointing to a black sedan that had just pulled up to the curb.

Self said hesitantly, "No . . . I don't think so . . ."

Savannah, however, bolted out the door. Taylor was right behind her. Dr. Self shook his head and reluctantly followed.

Savannah walked up to the car, and the passenger window rolled down. She froze when she saw the driver. She took two steps back, bumping into Taylor.

"Get in the car," said the driver.

Savannah turned around and looked at Taylor and Dr. Self. They, too, had seen who was driving the car, and the color left their faces. Just then, two men in black suits came from inside the restaurant and pushed them toward the backseat door.

The driver said, "We don't want to hurt you, but we do need your cooperation. So please, get in the car."

All three got into the black sedan, and it sped off into the twilight.

chapter

TWENTY-FIVE

The calendar turned to December, and Cole knew time was running out. If he was right about the Brotherhood and Y2K, he didn't have a minute to spare. By contrast, his few short months with the DRS had felt like a lifetime. All the training, the new skills acquired, and the things he'd learned meant that Cole Denton was no longer who or what he once was.

A few weeks earlier, after wondering time and again how his nu-partment had been built so quickly, Cole decided to try something. Jimi once told him that if he needed something all he had to do was pick up a phone and ask for it. So he tried it.

"Yeah, I need a state-of-the-art TV. Best that money can buy." The next morning a forty-two-inch Panasonic plasma TV showed up on his doorstep. So he picked up the phone and asked for a whole host of things, including a couple of new computers, a DVD player, an ICEE machine, and a Vintage Kenner Prototype Rocket-Firing Boba Fett action figure. The following day it was all there except for Boba Fett, which took a week to arrive. As he held the action figure in his hand, he said, "I didn't even know if this was real." That's when an idea was born.

Cole decided to fully utilize the funding and abilities the DRS had to offer. First, he scoured the Netherworld and picked the most obscure spot he could find. *This is where it will go.* He placed another order and provided the location of where to drop everything off. The next day all the items he ordered were there. Then he picked up the phone again and asked for construction workers to come to the spot and build what he was envisioning. They, too, showed up the next day.

After that, an endless stream of delivery trucks arrived to drop off supplies, and no one asked any questions. Construction workers labored around the clock to assemble what Cole thought of as the perfect "lair." In between workouts and training Cole would stop by and check on the crew's progress, and every time he shook his head in awe at the speed it was all coming together.

More than a few times since his arrival at the Netherworld someone had mentioned to him the organization's extensive wealth and financial connections. This being a rabbit hole he had only begun to explore, Cole decided to dig down and see just how deep it really was. What he discovered astounded him. The DRS's holding included stocks and bonds that were issued long before Charles Dow began tracking stocks in 1884. In fact, the Dead Rock Stars owned a portion of almost every major company in existence! Cole found the organization's massive wealth and far-reaching influence rather troubling, but that was a worry for another time. His immediate concern was the threat posed by the Brotherhood.

Cole's brand-new center of operations afforded him the privacy he needed to investigate free of oversight or interference (especially from a certain agent with shoulder-length blond hair and expertise with firearms). The lair functioned on its own digital grid so that his activities stayed off the radar of everyone, friend or foe.

Once construction was complete, he decided it was time to reveal to the agents he trusted most what he had been building and where his investigation had led him. Cole sent email invitations to Elvis Presley, Jimi Hendrix, John Lennon, and Janis Joplin. His reasoning went something like this: Elvis wouldn't have recruited him in the first place if he were the one plotting what Cole thought was about to go down. Had he wanted to, Jimi could have taken him out at any point during their time together without raising too much suspicion. He didn't know Lennon well, but the former Beatle had done the most to expose the Brotherhood since Buddy's death and could therefore be trusted. As for Janis, she loved Buddy Holly; Cole simply couldn't believe she would have colluded with his murderers.

He had thought about inviting Jerry Garcia, but the mere fact that Jerry pushed him so hard to be transparent gave Cole just enough pause to leave him off the guest list. Other members of the team he didn't yet know well enough to trust.

Cole's email read:

Team, I think I've figured some things
out. Meet me at the coordinates below at
4:00 pm. Tell no one."

★ ★ ★ ★

"Thanks for coming, guys. We need to get inside to be on the safe side."

"Cool," Elvis said. "Do we finally get to visit your lair? Can't wait to see what you've done with the place!"

Cole looked at him with a mixture of surprise and frustration. With all the precautions he'd taken, no one should have known this place existed, let alone the fact that he called it his lair.

Lennon smirked, and Janis leaned in and whispered to Cole, "Can't get anything past the King."

"Good to know. Well, at least he can't bypass my retinal scanner."

Janis gave him a deadpan look. "All he needs is your eye for that. Not the rest of you."

Elvis chuckled. "Don't worry, Cole, I like you. I wouldn't pluck anything out. Not yet anyway."

Cole leaned into the retinal scanner while simultaneously placing his right hand on a separate biometric device. The sealed door popped open, and Cole led them inside. He was pleased to note that at least Jimi looked half surprised that this place existed.

By design, the lair was basically a room inside a room with multiple levels of security. Inside the room, a single rocker gaming chair offered the only place to sit. Scattered around the room were several whiteboards on wheels, most of which were filled with photos and sticky notes that were covered in scribbling even Tupac wouldn't have been able to decipher. Next to the chair was a portable desk with three video monitors and a pair of computing towers. A VGA cable connected one of the towers to a projector that shone a light on a whiteboard that was barely wiped clean.

"Sorry, folks, no flashy presentation today," Cole said.

"What have you got for us, Cole?" Elvis asked.

"Something, but not all of it. I believe I've got enough for us to take action. I have a mission for the team."

Joplin folded her arms and flatly responded, "Spill it kid."

Cole couldn't yet prove with a hundred percent certainty the identity of the mole, or even that a mole existed, and thus decided to leave this part out.

"Albert U. Nedney."

"All right. A name," Lennon said with hopeful anticipation behind his gold wire-rimmed glasses. "We can work with a name. Who is he, and how did you come about locating Mr. Nedney?"

Cole said, "First of all, you should know that I've been collecting and compiling everything I could find on every member of the Dead Rock Stars, at least the ones I know about. I'm sorry if any of you feel like your privacy has been compromised. I believe you'll see the results are worth it."

Janis looked skeptical. "What are you saying?"

"Clearly, the Brotherhood has some sort of special interest in the King, and I don't mean they're fans of his music. First, Buddy was killed in the Elvis Presley Suite at the Las Vegas Hilton, and then Langston was found spying on Colonel Tom Parker's estate. Why would they make a show of telling us they know Elvis is alive and running a super-secret agency designed to stop threats like the one they pose? I can think of only one reason: to destabilize us.

"Think about it this way. Political assassinations like those carried out in Niger, Ecuador, and Ammon are a destabilization technique meant to sow chaos and confusion. Buddy Holly looked at these events and saw a pattern taking shape. He recognized that these were not random acts of violence but were part of a systematic conspiracy to undermine stability both regionally and on a global scale. During his investigation, Buddy uncovered the existence of the Brotherhood, found the symbol, and figured out that it was all leading to something big—very big. He was piecing everything together before he got too close and was killed for it."

Cole understood that by raising the specter of Buddy's death, he was reopening emotional wounds that had only recently begun to heal. He noticed that his guests were growing visibly uncomfortable, but it couldn't be helped.

"Stay with me, okay? The ones and zeros add up," he said. "Based on the evidence that destabilizing the DRS is one of the Brotherhood's primary goals, I set about adding security to the Netherworld. Not more guns or cameras, but cybersecurity—that is, protecting our systems from digital attacks. I began by building firewalls and adding routing. I also created specific IP addresses for every agent. Everything you have looked at on the laptops I gave you, I have seen. Now, don't get weird about it. I'm not judging anyone; I'm only looking for data."

Elvis said, "Just don't tell anyone where I found my peanut butter and banana sandwich recipe. That's between me and Netscape."

Lennon looked restless. "Where's all of this going, Cole?"

"Two things. Number one: Data doesn't lie. Number two: Someone has been using Buddy Holly's network."

Janis spoke up. "We've been looking at Buddy's files to track down the people who murdered him. John helped. Elvis knew. Tell us something we don't know."

Cole said, "It's more than that. I think someone outside the DRS has been tunneling into our network through Buddy's address. I think we're being silk-roped."

"Silk-roped?" Jimi asked.

"It's a hacker term for introducing a hostile virus or Trojan horse program to someone's computer. You know the story of the Greeks and the Trojan horse, right? Well, I believe the Brotherhood has used a silk rope to gain access to our systems, thereby opening a backdoor we didn't know existed. That's how they knew what Buddy and Elvis were doing in Vegas, and it's how they knew Karen and Cass were at the hospital in Ammon. How else would they know exactly where and when to attack them?"

The room was silent. Even Elvis looked stunned.

"Now, this is where things really get interesting. I've also been looking into the financial holdings of the Dead Rock Stars. As most of you probably know, we have significant stakes in oil, steel, plastics, precious metals, and America's number one food export, soybeans. Through various holding companies, we're major investors in Microsoft, Exxon, G.E., Walmart, Apple . . . in fact, we own a piece of almost every important company in America, with one notable exception: CompuLive. I couldn't find one single share of CompuLive among DRS holdings.

"At first, I thought it was because you guys didn't care about a chat service. But come on, this is one of the fastest-growing companies in the universe. Pretty much every new computer today comes preloaded with CompuLive. Ninety percent of the world's people have a CompuLive email address, including most corporate leaders and government officials. CompuLive also happens to be installed on every laptop owned by the DRS."

The four agents not named Cole Denton looked at each other, puzzled, failing to see a connection between Albert U. Nedney, Buddy's death, silk ropes, and the organization's portfolio.

Jimi spoke up. "So what? We don't own a piece of NASCAR either. There's lots of things the DRS doesn't invest in. I know; I spend a lot of time with our investment group and the R&D team."

"Fair enough," Cole replied. "But hear me out. As Elvis has already told you, I finally cracked the symbol that Buddy left for us to find. You all know it's a reference to

Y2K. I don't mean the Y2K everybody's worried about, the so-called millennium bug that the media keeps saying will fry the world's computers at midnight on January 1, 2000, sending us all back to the stone age. That problem got solved a long time ago—an easy fix, really. And yet we know that Buddy feared a doomsday scenario was somehow in the works. Then, when I deciphered the symbol, it hit me: What if Y2K is real?"

Janis protested. "But you just said—"

"What I mean is, what if someone has found a way to intentionally cause the end of the world as we know it? What if they can make our worst fears a reality by erasing every last bit of the data we depend on every day? What would they need to accomplish this? For one thing, they would require access to every computer in the world, as well as the means to affect the storage and delivery of every kind of information—financial, business, legal, medical, military, and so on. In other words, they would need a silk rope that stretches across the planet—a piece of software that everyone has and even thinks they need. That's what CompuLive is!"

Terror crept across the faces of the DRS members in Cole's lair. He would have been proud of this moment if the situation weren't so dire. He continued.

"If the Brotherhood has somehow hijacked CompuLive, they could conceivably reset everything, turn everything back to zero. Banks would be wiped out. Markets and governments would collapse. Records of any kind would be lost forever. Satellites, the internet, media, phones, even traffic lights—any tech that depends on computers could cease to function. It would be a disaster unlike anything we've ever seen."

Jimi said, "This is some scary stuff, Cole. But just because we don't own a piece of CompuLive doesn't make them suspect. We need evidence we can act on."

Cole nodded. "You're right. But the only way to test this theory was to fast-forward to the year 2000. So, I did the next-best thing: I pulled a computer off the network and reconfigured some code to make the unit believe it was 11:55 pm on December 31st. Then I took it offsite, powered it up, plugged into the internet, and waited. At 'midnight' it happened—the machine crashed, and every bit of data was lost. I then reconfigured it and began uninstalling each piece of software, one by one, resetting the timer, and starting the process again. In the end, I determined that only one application crashed the computer and caused a total meltdown: CompuLive."

Elvis smiled like a proud papa. "Good work, Cole. Now, that's real evidence! What else did you find?"

"From there I dissected the CompuLive code. High-level work. Wasn't as easy to crack as the government's stuff. I looked at everything and found something strange—a name that kept popping up in places that didn't make sense. He's not listed on the company website as a code developer. And yet his code is elegant. Even leaves his signature among the ones and zeros . . ."

"Albert U. Nedney!" Lennon said, barely able to contain his excitement.

"YES!" Cole exclaimed, matching John's enthusiasm. "However, I'm pretty sure 'Albert U. Nedney' is an alias. The name doesn't appear in any public records, but I found an email address for him. Surprise, surprise, it's a CompuLive address."

Jimi scratched his head. "Let me get this straight. Are you saying CompuLive is trying to make Y2K actually happen? That they killed Buddy and know about us? Are you telling us that CompuLive *is* the Brotherhood?"

Cole thought about this a moment.

"I don't have all those answers," he said. "But I know Albert U. Nedney is the key to finding them, and his trail starts at CompuLive HQ. But hey, this is the kind of stuff the Dead Rock Stars stop, right?"

Lennon asked, "Sure, but how do we fight something we can't see? Ones and zeros, Cole. What are we supposed to do with that?"

Janis said, "I don't care about ones and zeros. We've got a name and a place, and I can start with that. Cole, I want to know everything about CompuLive, inside and out. So, what do we do?"

This was the first time anyone had asked him what *he* thought they should do. They were beginning to see him differently now, as something more than a nerd in his secret lair. He was now a member of the team, accepted and approved.

Cole stood a little straighter and said, "We follow the data into the real world. Now's the time for some straight-up, on-site, real-time secret agentry."

Jimi laughed. "I feel you, Silky Cole."

"You aren't letting that go anytime soon, are you?"

"Absolutely not, Little Silk Rope," Lennon chimed in.

Cole nodded, "Looks like our next stop is the Silicon Valley."

Elvis laughed. "Whoa, Silky! Not just yet."

Cole's biggest fear was about to be realized.

"We've got to tell everyone else. Get the whole team on board. *Then* we go find this Nedney guy."

Cole wanted to bring up the mole but knew he shouldn't until he had absolute certainty. He would have to trust the King's judgment. After all, Elvis knew about the lair. Apparently, nothing happened around here without him knowing.

chapter

TWENTY-SIX

All the way back from the lair, Cole couldn't stop smiling. He said to Elvis, "Have you seen that show, *The West Wing*? I feel like we're in it right now. We're walking and talking and making plans while the fate of the world is at stake."

Elvis stopped dead in his tracks. "You kiddin' me right now?"

"Sorry, King. Seriously though, we've got to talk about this."

"Cole, I know what you want to talk about, and the answer is no. We are going to tell the team. The *whole* team."

"But don't you thi—"

"Son, we don't have time for this." Elvis turned to the others. "Jimi, make the call. Red alert. Everyone at the Bop in ten minutes. Janis, get Kennedy looped into the meeting; I want the big man in the know. John, knock on Jim's door; the only thing that guy will answer is his door."

For the next few minutes, as they continued walking alone, the King peppered Cole with questions about strategies for uncovering Nedney and how to shore up IT to keep the Brotherhood from watching their every keystroke. The one thing Elvis refused to talk about was keeping his findings secret from the rest of the team.

Cole sighed. "I bet Jed Bartlet would listen to me."

Elvis laughed. "Martin Sheen doesn't listen to anyone. Trust me."

★ ★ ★ ★

The theater room at the Bop didn't look the same as when Cole gave his presentation six weeks earlier. This time the room was configured in the round, with the "stage" at the center. Set up at the center was a table and some freshly printed maps and blueprints.

There was a definite buzz in the air. Cass Elliot had returned from the field and was hugging Janis Joplin. Jimi Hendrix and John Lennon were talking in a corner in hushed whispers with the occasional side glance. Karen Carpenter and Jerry Garcia were reminiscing and chuckling over a past mission. Jim Morrison was seated on the floor in the front, his legs crossed in the lotus position.

Cole dropped into a front-row seat next to Chris Wallace and asked, "This feel like a Death Star meeting to you?"

"New Hope or Jedi?"

"Both of them," Tupac said as he sat down behind them.

"Wait till Carrie Fisher walks in," Chris smirked.

"No way!" Cole blurted out with wide eyes.

"Nah, man, I'm playin'."

"Not cool, B.I.G. Not cool at all." Cole imagined trying to play it cool with Princess Leia in the room.

The lights dimmed, and everyone fell silent as Elvis walked to the middle of the room and set a duffle bag beside the table. Each of the Dead Rock Stars then produced a small, smooth rock from somewhere on their person, held it out, and recited together, "We have died to save lives."

Pac whispered in Cole's ear, "Don't sweat it, homie. You'll get your rock."

The King motioned to Cole. "Agent Denton and I will be leading this briefing. Cole, join me?"

Cole swallowed some air and stood up beside the leader of the most powerful secret agency on the planet.

Elvis didn't waste a moment. "Is the feed connected? Mr. President, can you hear us?"

Kennedy's voice crackled through the speakers, filling the room. "Yes, Elvis, loud and clear. Tell me some good news, please."

"Yes, sir." He began addressing the assembled team. "Now, y'all know the last few months have been challenging at best. We lost a beloved member of this team, even as we discovered a deadly new enemy. The Brotherhood has been wreaking havoc around the globe, and we really didn't understand their game or their objective. Until now. Cole, your stage."

Cole had thought about what he would or wouldn't say and ultimately decided to let it all hang out—except for the part about being convinced there was a mole in the room who smelled like teen spirit.

"Mr. President," he began, "Y2K is real. It's going to happen, and I believe the Brotherhood is at the center of it."

Cole downloaded what he knew about the threat they faced. He explained silk ropes, backdoors, the Y2K symbol, and the CompuLive connection. When he finished, he returned to his seat, confident he'd made a compelling case.

Before anyone could ask a question, Elvis reclaimed the floor. His tone was grave but determined. "In case you missed what's at stake, let me make it crystal clear. We are talking about an event of apocalyptic proportions. If Cole is right, the Brotherhood is dead set on destroying the world we have fought so hard to protect. These people are wrong, they are evil, and they killed Buddy because he found them out.

"The best we can tell right now, the Brotherhood's attack somehow involves CompuLive. At the stroke of midnight on New Year's Eve, every person, business, organization, and nation that depends on a computer could lose everything. Think about that for a second. Every bank account, every government secret, every nuclear launch code. Markets could fall, governments could crumble. Civilization as we know it could be lost in a matter of days."

Elvis paused to let the gravity of the situation sink in.

He then said, "We need a plan. Go."

The lights came up, and the room exploded with questions, comments, and discussion. The one question Cole heard again and again in varying forms was, "How do we fight something we don't fully understand? Something we can't see?"

Lennon stood up and said, "We go to Silicon Valley. Either the Brotherhood has infiltrated CompuLive, or CompuLive *is* the Brotherhood. So we infiltrate CompuLive and search for this name . . . what was it, Cole?"

"Albert U. Nedney."

John smiled. "Yes, thank you, sir. Mr. Nedney. We find evidence of this man and where to locate him. And then we hunt him down, youknowwhatImean?"

Most of the room nodded in agreement.

Cole could feel the intensity in the place. As he surveyed the room, he couldn't help but search for Cobain. He found him staring right back at him. Cobain glared at him and then walked over to talk with Jerry and Karen.

Within an hour, the team had devised a plan, and everyone was on board.

Elvis began to assign team roles. "Denton, Lennon, and Joplin—you'll run Electric lead team. Your mission is to infiltrate CompuLive HQ, locate intel on Nedney, and find evidence on the CompuLive servers linking the Brotherhood and Y2K. Rhythm team will be Cobain, Cass, and Morrison. You'll run covert security ops, eliminating problems before they arise. Lethal force is authorized. Roadies team will be led by Hendrix, Garcia, and Carpenter. You'll provide air support, transportation, and any additional equipment needed. Understood?"

Everyone nodded in agreement.

"As always, I'll be on lead vocals, running the show, but I won't be in the field as usual. I'll call the shots from comms with help from Shakur and Wallace and using Cole's new tech. It's where I need to be. I'll be watching everything and providing direction as needed."

The intercom system crackled, and again Kennedy spoke. "Elvis, as always, you have my full support. I'll notify EMS if need be, but this is your show. I recommend you utilize all resources at your disposal. Once again, the fate of the world is in the hands of dead men . . . and women. Good luck to you all."

"Uh, King," Cole said with hesitation, remembering the last time he interrupted Elvis. "Can I have Kurt on my team?"

"Why?" Elvis calmly asked.

"This man taught me to shoot," Cole said, loud enough for all to hear. "I'm kinda nervous about my first mission, and it would make me feel better if Kurt was at my side. No offense, Janis."

"None taken," she replied.

Elvis stared at Cole and processed his request for no more than two seconds, but it felt to Cole like a lifetime. They both knew why he wanted to keep Kurt close. "Okay, request granted. Janis, you're with Cass and Jim. Kurt, you'll be with Denton and Lennon. Cool?"

Cobain nodded approval.

"Okay, kids, only two more items to attend to. Cole, come back up here."

Cole tentatively went back to the front of the room and stood beside Elvis, who then leaned over to Janis. "You mind getting Cole his active mission key?"

"No problem, King. You mind if I recycle one?"

"I thought you might," he said, smiling.

Janis reached inside her tasseled satchel purse and unzipped a side compartment. She pulled out a smooth, round stone, then held it close to her face. With a warm smile, she then handed the rock to Cole.

She was looking at Cole in a way he had never seen before, as though she were at peace. Maybe not with everything. But at that moment, she was at peace with having Cole as a member of the team.

Janis smiled and said, "Cole, this is your key. Your token. Something you will always carry with you as a member of the DRS. I want you to know this belonged to Buddy. I hope it brings you luck. I know the two of you never met, but he would have really liked having you on the team. You remind me a lot of him."

Cole took the stone and held it in his hands. On one side were the initials "B.H." with a small cricket etched into the stone. He felt like he was holding a piece of history. On the other side was etched the shape of a skull, its mouth open and eyes in the shape of stars.

Before Cole could speak, Janis reached over and closed his hand over the stone. "It belongs to you now. This stone will grant you access to anywhere in the Netherworld, as well as to any vehicle, plane, or storage unit in the possession of the DRS. This rock might even save your life one day. Also, after this moment, you will no longer be under twenty-four-hour surveillance by the team. Congratulations!"

"Wait, what?"

Elvis slapped him on the back. "Trust and verify. What, did you think we were going to drop you off in the middle of a secret organization and not keep our eye on you? Besides, how else was I supposed to know about your underground lair? You think I have superpowers?" The King laughed and dropped into a karate-chop pose.

Elvis then turned to the rest of the room. "Next item. Everyone, gather 'round. It's sermon time."

They all formed a close circle around the King and began swaying in rhythm as though getting in synch for what would happen next. Cole followed their cue and joined the circle. His arms were crossed, however, and he realized he was the only one who didn't look completely at ease.

Most began humming a melody that didn't seem to conform to any song Cole knew. He thought it sounded like an orchestra warming up. Then a few agents started stomping the ground, as though marching into battle. The room swelled with emotion and expectation as Elvis began to pace the center stage.

"We've all been here before," he said. "It's not new . . . but it's different this time. Our enemy is prowling like a hungry lion. It sees us. It wants us. It wants to destroy everything we represent. Can you imagine what the world will be like if we don't stop them? We don't have a choice—we stand and fight. Each of us will risk his or her second life so that the world may never know about this threat. So that children can sleep at night in peace. So that the world spins on, getting better every year."

He looked around the circle in expectation. "Can you hear the music? Can you hear it calling your name? We have died to save lives."

Everyone repeated, "We have died to save lives."

"Can you hear the battle forming? Can you see the victory? I can! And I believe we will overcome!"

The stomping changed, and everyone joined in.

Stomp Stomp Clap.

Stomp Stomp Clap.

Stomp Stomp Clap.

Then Janis Joplin began howling the opening bars of Queen's "We Will Rock You," and the others joined in on the chorus.

Cole believed he knew the identity of the one who would soon have mud on his face. The big disgrace.

But for now, it was time to rock.

★ ★ ★ ★

As the room emptied, and the members of the DRS began heading to their various assignments, Elvis grabbed Cole and said, "Good work, kid."

"Thanks, King."

"I have one more thing for you."

"What is it?"

The King turned and started rifling through the bag he'd brought in with him. Then he produced something that looked like a child's onesie.

"Put this on before you leave for the mission," Elvis said.

"Is this a joke?" Cole stammered.

"Trust me, kid. And don't let anyone else know you're wearing them."

"Why?"

"You've got your secrets, and I've got mine."

"So . . . magic underwear?"

"Something like that. Trust me."

"I've got something for you to keep quiet, too," Cole said.

"What is it?"

Cole handed Elvis a burner cell. "In case this thing starts to go south, text me a message: '911.' You remember how to send a text, right?"

chapter
TWENTY-SEVEN

All Cole wanted to do was run, or make a joke about the whole thing, but neither was an option. He was strapped into his seat aboard a C-130 Hercules troop transport cargo plane being piloted by Jimi Hendrix. Cole's stomach was turning somersaults, and worse, he was unable to come up with anything funny to say to defuse his tension in the moment. His right leg restlessly bounced up and down like a jackhammer as the plane rumbled through the air.

Cass Elliott and Jim Morrison were seated to his left. Both were wearing khaki coveralls with a DRS logo affixed to the left breast pocket; the words "Dimension Restoration Services" were stitched on the back in black. Cass was wearing mirrored aviator-style sunglasses. Morrison's hair was pulled back in a neat ponytail, and he was sporting a fake mustache that Cole couldn't stop staring at. It was the kind of fake that was so bad it could only be real. After all, who in his right mind would subject his face to such an unsightly thing?

Janis Joplin sat across from Cole, wearing a modest full-length, lavender-colored denim dress and a heavy tan overcoat. She was reading *Harry Potter and the Prisoner of Azkaban*. Janis's graying hair was pulled into a tight bun atop her head, and she wore reader-style eyeglasses on the tip of her nose, the glasses secured with a strap around her neck. She looked more like a strict elementary schoolteacher than a rock star.

Cole thought of a joke and raised a hand. "Ms. Joplin, can I have a hall pass to go to the bathroom?"

Janis looked up from her book and sternly said, "That is quite enough from you, Mr. Denton." Then she smiled at him warmly.

Cole couldn't help but look over at Kurt Cobain, who sat apart from the others in the seat farthest from the cockpit. Cobain was wearing blue jeans, a plain white T-shirt, and a black tactical vest. He was packing pistols at his sides, with a half dozen ammo clips stashed in pockets all over the vest and a pair of knives concealed in padded sheaths in the small of his back. A black leather jacket was draped across his lap. He wasn't doing anything but staring at the floor.

John Lennon sat next to Cole, looking cool as a cucumber. He was wearing rose-tinted sunglasses, a scarecrow-style black-and-red flannel shirt, a brown leather vest, and faded blue jeans. He was cleaning a .45-caliber automatic pistol.

"Relax, man!" Lennon said to Cole, patting him on his knee. "This is going to be a cakewalk. We're only breaking into a secure corporate office on Christmas Eve, ya know? Besides, you're ready for this."

This failed to comfort Cole. He'd hacked many servers remotely but never on site. He had never broken into anyplace on any day, much less a corporate office on Christmas Eve with a bunch of dead musicians turned secret agents. He had also never hacked a server under extreme time constraints while looking for a clue as to how to save the world from impending doom.

"It's okay to be nervous, though," Lennon said. "I used to get nervous before missions. You want to know what I did to calm meself down when I first started?"

Cole nodded eagerly, afraid to open his mouth lest he throw up on a Beatle.

"I would, like, go back over my assignment again and again. Where was I supposed to be? What was my task? Who else would be doing what? I would walk through it all in my mind beforehand. You know, visualizing it."

Cole closed his eyes and tried seeing the task ahead of him.

"Imagine each step of the plan," Lennon said, "but don't worry about the result. We dunno what's going to happen. If something unexpected comes up, trust your training. Trust *me*. I'll be right there with you, so relax. Besides, would Elvis really send you into a hornet's nest your first time out?"

He had to admit, it did feel good knowing the DRS's best field agent would be at his side. If Cobain tried to pull anything, Lennon would be there to handle it.

As the plane began to descend into Northern California, Cole's comms earpiece crackled to life with Elvis's voice. "Showtime in five minutes. Costume up. Everyone, take your positions."

The King then called roll.

"Electric Team?"

"Electric is go, King!" Lennon replied.

"Rhythm Team?"

"Rhythm is good to go, E!" Janis said.

"Roadies?"

"Roadies are rolling, my man!" Jimi said from the cockpit.

"Live from the Netherworld, Lead is a go! Team, we died to save lives!"

★ ★ ★ ★

Janis Joplin shuffled through the front door of CompuLive's corporate headquarters, hunched over like a woman thirty years older, leaning on a metal cane and carrying a bulky handbag.

CompuLive HQ was a freestanding ten-story building nestled in a corporate park with other similar-looking buildings housing similar high-tech firms. Because it was Christmas Eve, the building was virtually empty. Inside the front entrance was a sprawling lobby with live plants and glass elevators. Everything was festooned for the holidays. The decorations included a colorfully lit thirty-foot tree adorned with silver garland, glass icicles, and what appeared to be ornaments in the shape of computer monitors. The front wall of the building was entirely glass, letting in copious amounts of natural light. The lobby's atrium extended up all ten floors, so that from the first floor one could see the vestibule of every other floor. Each landing had its own Christmas tree and red bow hanging from the railing.

Janis scanned the room, taking in her surroundings while looking like an awestruck tourist. She then shuffled over to the security desk situated under a giant CompuLive logo. There sat a young blonde woman in a white blouse with a CompuLive pin affixed to her collar and a name tag that read "Crystal." When the young lady stood to greet her, Janis could see that she was rather tall, athletic-looking, and wearing a grey pencil skirt. Next to her sat a rotund security guard in navy trousers and a short-sleeved mustard-colored shirt. He was casually watching a bank of security monitors.

200

"Hello, ma'am! What brings you to CompuLive on this lovely Christmas Eve morning?" the young lady asked.

"I sure hope you can help me . . . Crystal," Janis said, adjusting her eyeglasses to read Crystal's name tag. "I am lost as a goose in a snowstorm, and . . ."

Janis hesitated, biting her lip.

"Ma'am? Is everything okay?"

"Well, Crystal, I'm rather embarrassed . . ."

"It's okay. What do you need? We're here to serve."

"Well . . . I need a bathroom," Janis whispered in a barely audible voice.

"Ma'am?"

"A bathroom," she said, barely louder.

"A what?"

"A BATHROOM," Janis said emphatically in a shrill, high-pitched whisper.

"Ohhhhhhh." Crystal smiled reassuringly. "We're not supposed to let non-employees use our restrooms, but I'm pretty sure we can make an exception." Crystal looked at the security guard.

"Bag," he said, pointing at Janis's large handbag.

Crystal said to her, "Would you be so kind as to leave your bag here with Dave, the security officer, while I escort you to our facilities?"

"Oh, well, I guess so. David, you're not going to riffle through it, are you?" Janis said, pointing her cane at the portly man.

"No," Crystal replied, "he'll just watch it here for safekeeping. We have to make sure nothing dangerous gets into the building."

"Do I look dangerous to you, young lady?" Janis snapped crossly.

"No, of course not. We just have to follow protocol."

"Well, you're going to have to follow clean-up protocol if you don't allow me to use your facilities rather quickly."

"Right this way," the young lady said, motioning for Janis to follow her. The nearest restrooms were situated directly on the other side of the wall behind the security desk. Crystal pushed open the door for Janis and said, quite chipper, "Here you are, ma'am. I'll be right out here if you need anything."

"Thank you, young lady."

Janis went inside, and the door closed behind her. She paused for a moment to make sure the girl didn't follow her in, and then entered the first stall. She pressed a hidden button on the cane, and like a gumball from a vending machine, a small

201

ball came rolling out of the tip of the cane. Janis thought it looked like one of those new fizzy balls that made your bathwater smell like lavender or orange blossoms. She dropped the ball in the toilet, and it was immediately sucked down the drain without being flushed. Janis repeated this process in each stall, then did the same in the sinks.

"Bath bombs in place," she said quietly, touching her tiny flesh-colored earpiece.

Janis hunched over and shuffled out of the bathroom. Crystal was waiting for her outside the door.

"Thank you, young lady," Janis said. "You saved this old woman's vacation."

"You are certainly welcome. So, what brought you to CompuLive on Christmas Eve?" Crystal asked as they made their way back to the front desk.

"My son told me that the Silicon Valley was beautiful, especially around Christmas time. So I came all the way from Port Arthur, Texas, to see it for myself. So far, I'm very disappointed. It's just buildings and streets. I haven't seen one vineyard yet. Where do they make the wine?"

Crystal laughed very hard at this, maybe too hard.

Janis looked at her sharply. "What's so funny?"

"I think you're looking for the Napa Valley, ma'am."

"Ohhhh. What's the Silicon Valley then?"

"It's the technology hub of our country. All the most innovative products are being built right here in this little corner of California." They had arrived back at the front desk.

"So, there are no vineyards here?"

"Not that I'm aware of."

"May I use your phone?" Janis asked. "I need to call my son to come get me at the airport sooner rather than later. If I wanted technology, I'd just visit the Texas Instruments back home. I came for the booze!" She winked and swished her hips at the security guard.

"Of course," Crystal said politely, handing her the phone.

Janice dialed a number and turned away from Crystal and Officer Dave, feigning like she needed privacy. "Hello? John?" she said, speaking at high volume.

"Hullo, mum," John Lennon said from a van parked a few blocks away.

"I'm at . . . Where am I, dear?" Janis asked, turning back to Crystal.

"CompuLive Headquarters," Crystal said, speaking softly to encourage Janis to lower her voice.

"Commu-Life Headquarters," Janis repeated loudly.

Crystal didn't even try to correct her.

"Where?" John said loudly, playing along.

"The Commu-Life Headquarters. There's no wine anywhere! I'm going to fly back tonight, and I need you to pick me up at the airport." During this charade, Janis planted a bug that allowed Chris Wallace back at the Netherworld to hear everything happening at the front desk.

"Janis, we in," Chris said in her earpiece once the bug began picking up sound.

Janis handed Crystal the phone, and Officer Dave returned her bulky handbag.

"You didn't riffle through it, did you, David?"

"No, ma'am."

"Good," Janis said with a wink. "You might have found my stash."

She pulled a bottle of wine from her bag and handed it to the young lady. "Thank you for helping me today."

"You're so welcome, but we're not allowed to take gifts."

Crystal tried to hand it back

"Keep it!" Janis said sternly.

"Um, yes, ma'am." Crystal smiled awkwardly. "Thank you for the lovely gift!"

Janis gave her a stiff, small bow and a curt wave and then shuffled to the door. As soon as she was outside, she reached into her bag and found a tube of lipstick. She opened it and then pressed down on the lipstick like it was a button. Then she put the cap back on and dropped the lipstick into her bag.

"Bath bombs activated and bug in place," she said, touching her earpiece again. "Operation Restoration will commence in ten minutes."

"Good job, lil lady!" Elvis said from the Netherworld.

"Thanks, lil man in my ear!" Janis replied.

She then shuffled down the street until she was out of sight of Crystal and Officer Dave. At first, she continued hobbling. Then, like Verbal Kint transforming into Keyser Söze, she gradually stood upright, folded up her cane, and strode confidently into a parking garage a few blocks from CompuLive HQ. Parked on the second floor was a white paneled van with the words "Dimension Restoration Services" painted on the side. Janis disappeared into the van and then waited for what would come next.

★ ★ ★ ★

"It's everywhere! I mean *everywhere*. Please send someone quickly!" Crystal yelled into the phone.

"Yes, ma'am, we're on our way," Elvis replied. "Thank you for calling Dimension Restoration Services, where we restore your mishap to how it was before."

"Fine, just get here quickly. It's starting to pour into the lobby. This is an important place of business . . . I'm so fired!"

"Relax, ma'am. We'll be there in a jiffy to clean up your mess. Some other buildings near you have had the same problem today. Our crew will be there shortly."

A few minutes later, the DRS van came screaming down the street and screeched to a stop outside the front entrance of the CompuLive building. Cole, Cass, Lennon, Morrison, and Cobain all poured out of the van, wearing DRS coveralls and rolling in large boxes marked as containing various pieces of cleaning equipment.

As the team approached the front desk, Lennon asked in an American accent, "Where's the problem, ma'am?"

"I'm not sure," Crystal replied. "Water is pouring out of every toilet and sink on this floor."

"Okay, we'll need access to turn off the water mains and find the source of your problem. Ringo and Paul, you're with me," Lennon said, pointing at Cole and Cobain. "George, you and Pattie set up shop and start cleaning up the mess on this floor," he said to Morrison and Cass.

"Laying it on a little thick, aren't we?" Elvis said on the comms.

★ ★ ★ ★

Cass scanned the front desk as though looking for something, then asked Crystal, "Do you have a floor plan we can use to determine which areas might be affected?"

"Uh, I'm pretty sure there's one on our internal web page."

"That would be perfect," Cass said with a smile.

Crystal borrowed Officer Dave's desktop computer, entered her password, and opened up the internal web page. Cass took off her sunglasses and set them on the desk, then started navigating the computer.

"Thank you, ma'am. You just made our job a thousand times easier."

"Just fix this," Crystal said. "I can't get fired from this job."

"Uh . . . George," Cass said to Morrison, "I'll look for the floor plan while you get started vacuuming up the water on this floor."

Morrison nodded and wheeled a large box around the corner.

Cass scanned the menu, which had headings for "CompuNews," "Application Login," "Employee Info," "IT," "Human Resources," "Corporate Services," and "Legal." She clicked on "Employee Info" and brought up a new, rather extensive menu. She scrolled through the many options until she found "Building and Grounds." She clicked the link, revealing the building's floor plan. She pressed her finger to her ear and gave one long click.

"Okay, team," Elvis said from his comms chair in the Netherworld, "Cass is in. Everybody, look sharp and listen for her instructions. Jim, you're a go."

★ ★ ★ ★

At the first-floor bathrooms, Morrison came upon a quartet of maintenance workers trying to mop up the water spilling into the hallway. He opened the box, pulled out a wet/dry vacuum, and used it to begin sucking up water from the floor. He then looked at the guy nearest to him, patted him on the shoulder, and handed him the vacuum. The maintenance worker took the wet/dry vacuum without question and continued sucking up water. Jim then walked away and vanished into a stairwell.

"Who was that?" one of the maintenance workers asked.

"No clue," another answered. "Kinda looked like Jim Morrison. Just with a 'stache."

"I bet he gets that all the time."

In the stairwell, Jim clicked his earpiece twice.

At the front desk, Cass took a walkie-talkie from her belt and spoke into it. "Two, southwest."

"I'm sorry, what was that?" Crystal asked.

"I was just radioing to my co-worker where more leaks might be . . . if I'm reading this map right."

"Now there are leaks on the second floor? Oh, I'm sooooo fired!"

Morrison exited the stairs on the second floor and made his way to the southwest corner of the building and the main security office. He pulled a small disk from his coveralls, clicked a button on it, then slid the disk under the door. He looked at his watch. Ten seconds later, he heard a series of thuds from inside the office. He held his breath, opened the door, and found three security officers collapsed on the floor. He stepped on the disk, looked at his watch for ten more seconds, and then exhaled. He picked up the disk and put it back in his pocket. Then he gave one long click on his earpiece.

Tupac replied from comms back in the Netherworld. "I gotcha, Jim. Now log in to the website Cole created."

Morrison sat down at a computer terminal and opened the CompuLive web browser. He typed in the address Cole gave him: www.eyezontheprize.com. The website opened and prompted him to enter a password. Jim typed "wediedtosavelives." A new page opened with a circle in the center of the screen. It was labeled, "Click Here." Jim clicked the circle, and the screen went to black.

"Yeah, we got it! These silk ropes are banging!" Tupac replied. He could see everything CompuLive's security could see. The DRS now had eyes throughout the building.

★ ★ ★ ★

Officer Dave escorted Lennon, Cobain, Cole, and another large box to the elevator. He used his security key to give them access and pressed the button for the basement floor, where the water mains were located. As the four men rode the elevator down, a Muzak version of the Beatles' "All You Need Is Love" filled the elevator with sound.

"I love this song," Lennon said to Officer Dave in his regular Scouse accent.

The security officer smiled at him, then did a double take. Lennon shrugged, put a taser to his neck, and pulled the trigger. Officer Dave fell into a heap on the elevator floor.

"Jan," Lennon said, touching his earpiece, "we're in the elevator. You say the water flow should begin to recede in ten minutes?"

"That is correct," Janis replied from the van outside.

The "bath bombs" had created a chemical reaction that forced the water out of the pipes but did no lasting damage to the building's plumbing. Once the balls had completely dissolved, the water would return to its normal flow.

★ ★ ★ ★

Elvis said, "Jim has taken out the security guards and given Tupac access to the building's cameras. Cole should be free and clear to do his thing. Cass, what floor is the server on?"

"Ten," Cass replied from the front desk.

"What? It's on ten now?" Crystal cried. "That's the Executive Suite and server room. I'm going to faint. I need to sit down. Maybe AOL is hiring."

"Relax, Crystal," Cass said in a soothing tone. "Why don't you have a drink?" She pointed to the bottle of wine Janis had left behind.

"Oh, I can't. I'm at work."

"Maybe not for much longer." Cass shrugged. "Pour me a glass too, and this can be your going-away party."

Crystal eyed the wine with new interest.

★ ★ ★ ★

The elevator descended to the basement. Once the doors opened, Lennon dragged Officer Dave from the elevator and gave his teammates a playful salute. "I'll meet you on ten."

This was the part of the plan that scared Cole. John would tie up the security guard while he and Cobain continued to the server room. They had to get to the server, download all information on Albert U. Nedney, and get out in ten minutes, before "cleanup" was completed in the lobby.

Having Cobain stare over his shoulder would make his task more intimidating; not having Lennon there to look after him made it downright terrifying.

As the elevator started ascending, Cole glanced at Cobain, who gave him a slight nod. Unsure what this meant, Cole tried to play it cool.

"So, yeah. Seems like everything is going to plan."

"Shut up," Cobain said.

"Why?" Cole asked, louder than he intended.

Cobain glared at him for what seemed like hours, but it was only the time it took to travel between the sixth and seventh floors. "We're on a mission, that's why. Keep your focus. There's no time for your rambling. What's wrong with you?"

"What's wrong with *you*, man?" Cole spat. "You're a piece of work. Look, I get that I wasn't a musician, that I didn't *earn* anything. But you helped train me. You know I'm all right—"

"I want more than 'all right.' I expect excellence. Now shut up and do your job!"

The elevator doors opened. They had arrived on the tenth floor.

It was showtime for Cole. He shook off his anger, took a deep breath, and stepped out of the elevator. He clicked his earpiece twice.

"Southeast," Cass replied.

Cole could hear poor Crystal's voice in the background. "I've got to find a glass. Or I could just drink from the bottle. Who even cares at this point?"

Cole and Cobain made their way to the southeast corner of the tenth floor and found the server room. Cobain knelt and picked the lock with masterful speed, gaining them access.

The room was stark white with a row of cabinets housing hardware and wires. Cole had been in many server rooms before, and something about this one felt off. For one thing, it wasn't nearly large enough for a company this size.

"Kurt, this isn't right."

Cobain grunted. "Get busy and get what you need."

"Something's wrong. For one thing, every server room I've ever seen was in the basement. For another, CompuLive should have multiple buildings full of servers. This feels wrong."

Cobain shrugged. "Just stick to the mission."

Cole unscrewed the rear panel of the nearest server. He then pulled a laptop computer from the box they had been wheeling around. He plugged it in to the server and went to work, furiously typing.

Lennon was due to arrive any second now after disposing of Officer Dave; Cole tried not to think about the fact he had not reported in with comms.

Cole searched every directory and file he could find. Albert U. Nedney wasn't hard to find. Nedney, whoever he was, had written all the code himself.

"This is all wrong," he said. "It's empty!"

"What do you mean, 'empty'?"

"I mean, there are files here but . . . nothing important."

"So, what does that mean? Do you need more time?"

"No, I'm telling you there's nothing here to find."

"What about Nedney?"

"He's here in the code, but it doesn't mean anything. It's just his name, over and over again. It's meaningless."

"I'm confused," Cobain said. "He's in the files, but there's nothing linking him to the Brotherhood?"

"I'm telling you it's like *The Shining*—just page after page of 'All work and no play makes Jack a dull boy.'"

Cole looked up and studied Cobain's reaction. If he really was behind the Brotherhood, he might give off some hint of satisfaction that his plans were still safe and undiscovered. Something. But Cole detected no emotional response outside of rising concern.

★ ★ ★ ★

Back at the Netherworld, Tupac suddenly lost the CompuLive feed. All the video screens he had been monitoring went black. He reported to the team, "I've lost eyes on everything. I'm totally blind. Chris, can you hear anything?"

"Nothing. Just static. Cass, is everything straight?"

Cass Elliott did not respond.

"Cass, come in," Wallace said. "Jim, give me a long click if you copy."

No response from Morrison.

"What's going on? Can anyone hear me?" Chris looked to Elvis. "King?"

Elvis bit his lip. Then he asked, "John, do you copy?"

Silence.

"Kurt, do you copy?"

Nothing.

"Cole?"

Elvis swallowed hard and opened the phone Cole had given him earlier.

★ ★ ★ ★

"Kurt, this is not right. John should have been back by now." He pressed his earpiece. "Has anyone heard from John?"

There was no reply.

"What's going on?" Cole said, looking at Cobain, who appeared to be just as confused as he felt.

"I don't know."

Like a two-by-four to the face, it hit Cole. "Sally Fields! I know her!"

"The actress?"

"The girl at the desk! She's the one I interviewed with a few months back. She was a CompuLive executive. Why would she be working the front desk on Christmas Eve?"

"What are you talking about?"

Icy fingers ran down Cole's spine. The blond assassin. The song in the elevator. Albert U. Nedney. It had all been right there in front of him, and he'd missed it.

He had the wrong guy.

He felt a buzz at his side. He reached into the pocket of his coveralls and pulled out his cell phone. The text was from Elvis. It read, "911."

"Kurt," Cole said, panic rising. "I'm so sorry, man . . ."

"Why?" Cobain asked tersely.

"I'll tell you later. Just draw your weapon."

"Wha—?"

The door to the server room flew open like it was fired from a cannon.

Lennon burst through the doorway, pistol drawn, and fired three shots into Cole's chest, throwing him back against the wall.

As Cole was losing consciousness, he saw John Lennon aim his weapon at Kurt Cobain.

✯ ✯ ✯ ✯

Morrison slipped back downstairs after taking out the guards in the security office and found the four maintenance workers still dealing with the water in the lobby. As he approached, one of them said, "Hey, anyone ever tell you that you look like Jim Morrison?"

Morrison shrugged.

Without warning, one of the workers grabbed him from behind, catching him off guard. The other three spread out to attack from the front and sides.

✯ ✯ ✯ ✯

Cass was staring at her watch, counting down the seconds to when the water would begin receding back into the drains. She felt the room grow quiet. She could no longer hear Crystal's dramatic sighs.

Behind her, Crystal had grabbed the bottle of wine at the neck and was preparing to bring it down on Cass's head. Cass saw the movement in the reflection of her aviator sunglasses sitting on the desk, and she dodged the blow. The bottle shattered on the desk's marble counter.

"Crystal?" Cass said, with a note of disappointment.

Crystal dropped into a fighting stance and smiled. "Bring it, dead lady," she said.

The two women began brawling across the wet floor of the lobby of CompuLive HQ. Cass landed a punch in Crystal's armpit, grabbed her arm, and in one swift motion threw her into the Christmas tree. Crystal recovered quickly and came up holding a mock gift-wrapped present from under the tree and bashed Cass with it. Cass pulled a glass icicle from the tree and began wielding it like a knife, but Crystal deftly kicked it from her hand.

As the two women circled each other, Crystal sneered. "A sorry lot of secret agents you are. You didn't even know I existed. Langston worked for *me*. I ran the training center in Cleveland. I was the driver who carried out the Ammon assassination. I almost killed you and your partner at the hospital."

"That was you?" Cass laughed, catching her breath. "We thought you were a dude!"

"It doesn't matter what I am. *We* are the Brotherhood. No possessions. No greed. No hunger. No countries. No religion. Nothing to kill or die for. It's all going back to zero, and you can't stop it!"

At that moment, the white DRS van, driven by Jimi Hendrix, smashed through the entrance of CompuLive in a rain of glass, striking Crystal and flinging her across the room. She landed in a lifeless heap.

Cass jumped into the van. "What's happening?"

Jimi said, "We saw you fighting and thought you might need help."

Janis said gravely, "Cass, we've lost all communication from home."

From behind the front desk, one of the maintenance workers came crashing through the drywall and flew onto the countertop. Through the hole in the wall, the agents in the van could now see Jim Morrison fighting three other men. Cass and Janis pulled out their weapons and fired, eliminating two of his assailants.

Seeing the other two fall, Morrison leapt into the air, wrapped his legs around the head of his remaining opponent, and flung him to the ground, snapping his neck in the process.

"Jim, get in the van!" Jimi yelled as he threw it in reverse. Morrison dove through the open rear doors.

Moments later, Kurt Cobain came bounding out of the stairwell, a pistol in his left hand, firing wildly behind him. He was carrying Cole over his right shoulder like a sack of potatoes.

Officer Dave and the three other security guards Morrison thought he had immobilized were just steps behind Cobain.

Cass and Morrison jumped back out of the van and began firing at the men chasing Cobain and Cole. Morrison winged Officer Dave, sending him sprawling on the floor. The other three dove behind the front desk for cover. Cobain reached the van and, with Morrison's help, gingerly placed Cole on the floor of the vehicle.

"Where's John?" Janis screamed as everyone piled in.

"Go!" Cobain yelled.

Jimi mashed the pedal to the floor, and the van peeled out of the lobby and tore off down the street.

"It was John," Cobain said, between heaves, straining to catch his breath. "He shot Cole. It was John."

chapter

TWENTY-EIGHT

"**W**hy?"

It was the first word Jim Morrison had spoken in six years. He sat on the green shag carpet by the waterfall of the Jungle Room, holding his head in his hands as though the weight of the question were unbearable.

Kurt Cobain, seated at a small upright piano, answered him by playing the melody to John Lennon's "Imagine."

"NO!" Janis Joplin screamed. "That is *not possible*. John is our friend. John is family. This is all wrong." She buried her face in Jerry Garcia's shoulder, and he wrapped his arms around her, as if to shield her from the painful truth.

Cole Denton wanted to remind everyone this was Christmas morning, but the atmosphere at Graceland II was more like that of a funeral visitation. Certainly, it seemed nothing like a strategic meeting of elite secret agents, despite the fact the world was scheduled to end in less than a week.

Seated on the couch, Cole's every breath felt labored thanks to the bruised ribs that served as moment-by-moment reminders of Lennon's betrayal. The King's "magical onesie" had saved his life. But the experimental super-lightweight Kevlar body armor had not made him invulnerable, and Cole could feel each of the three distinct bruises every time he exhaled.

Jimi Hendrix rose from his seat on the lower staircase and said, "Jim's question needs to be answered before I believe any of this."

Cobain pounded the keyboard with his fists, sounding a chaotic crash of notes. After a moment, he said, "He asked me to join him."

Elvis Presley was hunched over in a small chair in the corner, inspecting the woodgrain of an acoustic guitar. He now looked up and fixed his eyes on Cole.

"Join you for *what?*" Tupac Shakur spat, incredulous.

"To actually *do* what we claim to be doing around here."

Pac just shook his head.

"Think about it," Cobain said. "Are we actually making a difference? Seems like there's a new threat every week. Feels lately like all we're doing is playing catch-up. The more lives we save, the more greed and corruption spreads. The old way isn't working anymore. You think this new kid is going to solve all our problems, King? We're too late . . . he's too late. John has always been a believer in the cause—maybe more than any of us. Janis, you know him better than anyone. Does it really surprise you?"

"That he killed the man I loved?"

Elvis took a deep breath. "The worst part is that Cole knew."

All eyes turned to Cole.

Elvis nodded at Cole. "He didn't know it was John, but he knew we had a mole. How else would anyone know about us if it didn't come from within? We are the most secret of secrets. All the clues, all the hints, all the data suggested this was an inside job. I just wouldn't believe it. I was wrong."

Cass Elliott spoke up. "It doesn't matter now. We are running out of time. It doesn't matter *why* John did it or *if* he did it. Someone is trying to end the world. We've got six days to stop the Brotherhood, CompuLive, and Y2K. That is exactly what Buddy would want—for us to stop moping around and start working the problem."

Chris Wallace walked over to Elvis and placed a hand on his shoulder. "Six days is cake. We got this, E. We Dead Rock Stars. We died to save lives, you feel me? I didn't miss my family growing up just to let the bad dudes win now. I don't know what John's thinking but making the world a better place can't mean losing your soul in the process. No sane person wants to end the world. That's some Dr. Evil-level crazy right there."

The others murmured agreement—all except Morrison, who simply nodded.

But Elvis had stopped listening. He was looking past Chris at something that had just caught his attention. He stood up, pointing to the lantern-style chandelier hanging from the ceiling. "How long has that light been like this?"

Cole asked, "What do you mean?"

"It looks different, like it's glowing in a different hue while we're talking."

Cole looked over to Pac and Jimi. "Guys, I need tools and a ladder."

Moments later, Cole was on a ladder, pulling apart the light fixture.

"That's odd," he said. "Is this an ethernet wire?"

Just then, the corded phone in the Jungle Room rang loudly.

Elvis glared at the phone. "Everyone out. Now. In one hour, I need all of you at the Bop." He looked around at the team. "We are going to save the world. Again."

Cole cut the ethernet cord.

★ ★ ★ ★

On the front steps of Graceland II, Cole stared at the back of Kurt Cobain, who was taking a drag from a cigarette while leaning against one of the lion statues.

"So, what's it going to be, Kurt?"

Cobain didn't look up. After a long exhale, he sighed, "What do you want, Denton?"

"Are you going to join him?"

Cobain stared at the ground. He tossed his cigarette down, mashed it out with the sole of his shoe, and shouted an expletive that echoed down the street. He sighed and turned around. "Who's the good guy in this story, Cole? He's not wrong. Neither are we. But . . . are we really making a difference? Are we really saving the world?"

chapter
TWENTY-NINE

ing. Ring. Ring.

Elvis ignored the phone, grabbed a CD off the shelf, and jammed it into the player. He searched until he found the track he was looking for and cranked up the volume. Harry Nilsson's "Without You" began playing. Elvis let the music sweep over him, soaking in the melancholy of the moment.

Ring. Ring. Ring.

He took a deep breath and picked up the receiver but said nothing.

The voice of John Lennon said, "I know you're mourning, King, and I know you grieve with music. But Harry Nilsson? That's low, King. Really low. You know how much I love that song."

"How long have you been spying on us, John?"

"It's what we do, King. We're spies."

Elvis's eyes welled up, and he could barely get the next words out. "How could you do this . . . to *us*?" Then the dam burst, and tears streamed down his face. "We're *family*."

"Family?" Lennon spat the word like one who had been holding his tongue for years. "*Family*, King?"

"Yes, family! I carried our brother's body out of that hotel," Elvis raged through the tears. "I saw what your people did to him!"

Lennon's demeanor shifted, and he cleared his throat. "Yes, well. Buddy wasn't supposed to die, King. That's why I killed Langston in Tennessee—he botched the Vegas operation. He was only there to plant seeds to keep you busy, to throw you off the scent. Like with that stupid symbol."

"But Buddy . . ." Elvis choked on the words. "He was the best of us."

"I know, King. I know." There was genuine sorrow in his voice. "It wasn't supposed to go down that way."

"So how *was* it *supposed* to go down?" The anger started to rise again in his voice. "What was that nonsense with the Elvis Presley Suite? And the stuff about the Colonel's accounts? Was I supposed to be next on your list of *accidents*? Why? Because I was in your way?"

Lennon laughed derisively. "*You?* You want to know why I set this whole thing up to look like the Brotherhood was coming after you? Because I know you're arrogant enough to think it *is* all about you! You, Elvis Presley, are many things. But smart enough to wreck this plan? No, sir."

"And so you shot Cole."

"That's on you, King. I've read Buddy's notes. I know it was *his* idea to bring a tech genius onto the team, that he'd identified Denton as the best fit. He shared that information with you. After Buddy died, that should have been the end of it. But no, you had to bring in someone who could wreck—" Lennon paused. "'We're a band, John. No solo acts.' Remember saying that? But you went out and got Denton and forced him on the rest of us. That's when I knew for certain there was no turning back. So, yes, I tried to take your boy off the board. But somehow, he was ready for it."

"If you read the notes, John, then you know I wasn't acting on a whim. Yes, it was Buddy's idea. And if everyone had known Buddy wanted him there, Cole would have been accepted by the team without question. You know what Buddy's opinion meant to everyone. But I kept it a secret because Cole needed to earn his *own* stripes—both for his sake and for the sake of the team."

Lennon let this go. Even he had liked the kid despite the threat he posed.

"Time's running out, King. Don't you think it's time to ask what you really want to know?"

"Why are you doing this, John?"

"Because I've known for years the DRS wasn't working. If you were honest with yourself, you'd see it too. What we're doing wasn't saving the world. We were just keeping it turning, satiating the powers that be and maintaining the status quo, youknowwhatImean? When you recruited me, King, you said we were going to change the world. 'Instant karma,' you said. But the world's the same, Elvis! Crooked as ever. Selfish as ever. Guilty as ever—just like you."

"I believe in what we do. *You* believed t—

But Lennon kept going. "Keeping peace, unearthing terrorist plots, quelling rebellions—all for what? Just to keep the current kings on their thrones and keep the little people little, then turn around and do it again tomorrow. It's time for us to step up and take real action. Something that make a lasting difference. We need to erase everything and start over. No kings. No countries. No religion. Nothing for people to kill or die for. Imagine, Elvis. Imagine a world where everyone is equal. A world at peace."

"So that's it then? You based all of this on a song?"

"Cheeky, no?"

"You know, you've ruined that song for me. Why couldn't you have based your plan on a different song? I don't know . . . how about 'GIVE PEACE A CHANCE'?"

"Nice try, King. But we're already on our way. The toppermost to the poppermost."

"But how, John? How would you even go about making this messed-up idea happen?"

"By turning everything back to zero. That's my plan. And it's going to happen in six days. At midnight, I will drain every bank account in the world to zero. I will shut down every power grid. I will make everyone equal—the great and small, the high and low. Even you, 'King.'" The word was dripping with sarcasm. "Even me."

"Stripping everyone of everything won't make everyone equal, John. It'll only throw the world into chaos."

"Maybe we need a little chaos right now! We'll soon see. But it's happening, and you can't stop it. In one week, the world will be born again, Elvis."

"You know we can't let you do this. We will stop you."

"Try as you will, King. But the die is cast. Even if you could stop me, you can't stop the Brotherhood. You may say I'm a dreamer, King . . . but I'm not the only one."

chapter

THIRTY

ole climbed the stairs to Janis's beautiful Victorian-style home, exhaling pain with every step. He started to knock, and the door cracked open at his touch. He pushed the door wide and found the house in shambles.

As he stepped into the foyer, he felt the broken shards of what appeared to have been a tea set. He could hear objects being tossed a few rooms over.

"Janis?" he called.

"Don't say a word!" she bellowed from the kitchen.

As he ventured in, Cole could see that every ceiling light fixture had been ripped from its socket. In Holly's study, he found the shelves empty and books and mementos strewn about the floor. Computer, monitors, and hard drives had all been unplugged with extreme prejudice. Massive rips gouged the once-ornate canvas of horn-rimmed glasses that filled the wall.

Cole knew what Joplin was doing, and it pained him greatly. An image of three flashes of fire, the smell of smoke, and the silhouette of John Lennon standing over him had repeatedly screamed across his mind, haunting him for the past twenty-four hours; searching for listening devices planted by your closest friend had to be devastating. Cole tried to imagine Lennon having tea with Buddy and Janis and wondered what the three of them had talked about on a random evening. The thought made him sick.

Janis barreled into the room. "Okay, I think we're clear. Let's talk." She had deconstructed her home in under ten minutes.

"Janis, I'm so sorry."

"Focus, Denton. We've got forty-five minutes till the meeting; let's make the most of it. John, Buddy, CompuLive, Y2K, the bugs—all of it. How does it fit together, and how can we stop him?"

"I've been thinking about Y2K and CompuLive and the connection with Vegas, Buddy, and the Brotherhood. I suspect some of the pieces were meant to send us on a wild goose chase. I think we might need to *Control-Alt-Delete* a few things and reboot."

Janis shrugged. "Let's get random. Shoot."

"Okay. If the threat is real, it's a zero-sum scenario. John's wiping everything out, so he doesn't gain anything from it in theory. Meanwhile, the Brotherhood has been on a destabilization tear that hasn't made sense. Add these together, and it appears Lennon wants to destabilize the entire planet."

"I'm tracking. Keep going."

"As I've said before, the Y2K everyone's worried about was an easy fix. Bill Gates and company have been on it for a while. Updates have been rolling out . . . unless . . ."

"Yeah?"

"If John has sabotaged one of the world's biggest software companies and is using it to actually carry out Y2K on a global scale . . . with that type of access and the current Y2K paranoia covering his tracks, no one would ever see it coming. They wouldn't know what to look for."

"So, what can *we* do about it?"

"Well . . . basically, we're talking about a Trojan horse of a different color. In theory, it wouldn't be that hard to stop it. We'd just have to pull it . . ." Cole's eyes went wide. "HOLY HORSE MANURE, that's it!"

Cole beamed at Janis. "Call the others. We need to change the location of the meeting. I think I might have a plan."

Then he noticed her expression had changed to something he'd never seen before. Beneath Janis Joplin's determined eyebrows there was a glimmer of hope.

★ ★ ★ ★

It was the strangest place Cole could imagine for a meeting, but it was probably the safest spot in all the Netherworld.

"This is a first," Chris said. "We've never had a strategic meeting at the fishing pond before. But at least we won't have to deal with the wrong kinds of beetles and bugs here."

"And we still have Wi-Fi," Janis said, holding up a device that looked like a personal digital assistant but was, in fact, an advanced prototype of something Microsoft was calling a Pocket PC. The device ran a form of Windows and was equipped with phone and internet capabilities.

Elvis called the meeting to order, then turned it over to Cole.

Cole flashed back to his presentation several weeks earlier when everyone was still skeptical of his presence; he had never felt more alone. Now, with all eyes trained on him and the fate of the world on the line, he'd never felt more alive.

"What is on every computer in the world?" he asked.

"Solitaire," Jerry said, and everyone chuckled.

"Besides Solitaire. I'm talking about CompuLive, the number one software addition in the world. It's used corporately, privately, even in chat rooms for Kurt Cobain lookalikes."

Cobain shot him a look. "What is your point?"

"The CompuLive mission was a setup. Nothing more than a trap. The Brotherhood was ready and waiting for us, and some of us have the bruises to prove it." Cole rubbed his sore ribs. "But I did manage to download something useful from those dummy servers. Al U. Nedney's digital print was all over the code I found there. Man, I should have seen it earlier. Al U. Ned. 'All you need' . . . is love. We all know John likes his little jokes."

Elvis interjected. "After speaking with John less than an hour ago, I can confirm: He is the one we're after. He left no room for doubt."

"So why CompuLive?" Jimi asked.

"CompuLive is everywhere," Cole replied. "Everyone uses it. *Everyone*. On the way over, I asked Janis to confirm that the U.S. government uses it for encrypted messaging."

Janis said, "I should have heard back from my sources by now." She tapped the screen of the Pocket PC a few times with a stylus, then said, "Confirmed. And it's not just our government. CompuLive is believed to have contracted with every first- and second-world country on the planet to provide them with a highly encrypted, non-commercial version for government use only. My sources at the CIA, GRU, and MI-6 all agree."

"BOOYAH." Cole pumped his fist.

Jimi looked confused. "That's *good* news?"

"So, what's the plan, CD?" Tupac asked.

"Well, if time weren't a factor, I could build a patch to stop the CompuLive Trojan horse from carrying out John's programming. That's the bad news: We can't force the stop. The good news is, I'm not sure we have to. We don't really have to *fix* it. We just have to convince every person in the world to uninstall the CompuLive software. Or at least enough of them to prevent a global cascade failure."

Chris asked, "How we s'pose to convince every government, business, and individual to uninstall the world's most popular software in the next six days?"

For a moment, no one said a word.

Somewhere nearby, a cricket was singing.

Jimi said, "We go to war. Not the kind of war we're used to lately, but the kind we fought when we were still 'alive' and singin' for our supper. I'm talking about changing the narrative. Bending public perception. I'm talking about making people believe something they already want to believe."

Janis said, "You're talking about destroying the reputation of an entire corporation. Maybe an innocent one."

"Listen, I don't know just how deep John's got his hooks into CompuLive, but we all seen enough to know they ain't *that* innocent."

"So how do we 'change the narrative,' as you say?" Chris asked.

"We put on a show—somethin' we're all pretty good at. Even my man, Cole." Jimi grinned and threw an arm around the shoulders of a self-conscious Cole.

At that moment, Elvis spoke up and took charge. "Okay, everyone, listen up. We go with three teams. Think more Lollapalooza, less Woodstock. Three stages, three shows, and we've got to slay on every single one.

"On the Headliner stage we've got Janis and Tupac. You're going to call everyone we know at the highest levels. The U.N., heads of state. Use every official and unofficial channel. Tell them that every nation's government must purge CompuLive from their systems immediately. Cole will build a safer system for them to replace it within a week or two, but for now we've got to stop the attack before it happens. After governments, contact major corporations and banks. Call in whatever favors you need to. Not only do they need to drop CompuLive, but they also need to reach out to their customers and competitors and spread the word.

"Jerry, Cass, Karen, and Chris, you're on the Tastemaker stage. This is the court of public opinion. Your job is to launch a media storm that will dominate the airwaves. We have a major advantage in that the time between Christmas and New Year's Day is traditionally the slowest news week of the year, so media outlets will be starving for content.

"You figure out a story that will terrify and motivate the most people and turn the volume up to eleven. Start with *Hard Copy*, *A Current Affair*, and *Inside Edition*. Feed them some story about hackers stealing people's personal information and accessing their bank accounts through CompuLive. Make it juicy and urgent. Then hit the twenty-four-hour-news channels—CNN, MSNBC, Fox News. Get them talking around the clock about a connection between Y2K and CompuLive.

"Don't stop there. Contact the wire services, newspapers, and tabloids. Call the *National Enquirer*. They run pictures of me every week. If you have to, tell them *I* started CompuLive myself and hired aliens to run it.

"One more thing: Mobilize the celebrities. Get 'em wearing 'They Are Watching' T-shirts and 'CompuDead' clothing. This is a full-frontal assault, people."

"CompuLive won't survive the week!" Cass said.

"Last but not least, the Brotherhood. Jimi, Kurt, Morrison—you're on Main stage. Hunt these guys down. Give no quarter."

Cole handed a folder to Cobain. "Langston was accessing a CompuLive chat room to receive orders. 'Equal=Equal.' You might start there."

"Thanks, man," Cobain said and gave him a nod. "Good work."

Cole didn't know what to say, so he didn't.

Elvis said, "The encore will be John Lennon. He'll come out of hiding once we do this. I'll be waiting for him when he does. And it won't be pretty."

The King looked around at his team. "Sometimes we fight with weapons. Sometimes we fight things we can't see. But make no mistake: This enemy is real, and he is deadly. John knows our moves. He knows how we think. He's been six steps ahead of us so far. It's time for us to do the unexpected. It's time we go public. We're about to create mass hysteria for the sake of the world."

D R S

chapter

THIRTY-ONE

Cole had been writing code for four days. Working in Elvis's guest house, he'd stopped only twice for a few hours' sleep before returning to his task of creating a viable CompuLive replacement.

He was feverishly typing when his email notification dinged twice, breaking his concentration. No one but the team had this email, so he stopped to check it out. There were two emails from the same address: tw1standsh0ut@CompuLive.com.

The first was nothing but an image, which took a moment to download. Cole eventually recognized something he'd seen in what felt like a previous life: a weather-worn number *4* barely holding onto the side of an airplane hangar.

The next email was another photo. Pixel by pixel the image formed on the screen from top to bottom. Cole soon realized he was looking at Savannah, bound with duct tape and lying on a sofa. Behind her he could make out Dr. Self and Taylor, too. All three looked weak and malnourished.

Another email appeared immediately. No pictures, just words:

```
You should have died, Cole.
For real this time.
We could have avoided all of this.
```

Save Savannah and your friends or save the
world.
Your choice.
You know I won't hesitate.
Imagine,
Al

Cole slammed his fists on the table, grabbed the 9mm semi-automatic sitting next to his laptop, and ran out the door.

★ ★ ★ ★

"I know where she is!" Cole shouted as he burst into the Jungle Room. He had to scream to be heard over the music Elvis was blaring to nullify any as-yet-undiscovered bug.

"Who?" Elvis replied calmly, seated in his leopard print chair.

"Savannah. He's got her, King. Taylor and Dr. Self, too."

Elvis furrowed his brow.

"I'm going to Boston to save her," Cole said, "and you can't stop me."

Elvis leaped from his chair like a tiger and pounced on Cole, twisting his right arm behind his back and taking him to the floor.

"I most certainly *can* stop you, son. You need to be writing code."

Cole twisted out of Elvis's grip and then sprang to his feet from his back.

"Impressive," Elvis said, lying on his side. He then spun like a top, attempting to sweep Cole's legs out from under him. Cole felt like Neo fighting Morpheus—he could see the leg sweep coming in slow motion. He jumped and laughed simultaneously.

"You're going to have to do better than that, old man."

Cole coiled his fists and crouched his stance, ready to fight.

Elvis came out of his spin and rolled to his desk, where he kept a .45 automatic strapped underneath. In one motion he grabbed the gun, cocked it, and aimed it at Cole.

"Jim has trained you well," he said. "But John's not going to play patty-cake with you. He will kill you. And he'll use any means necessary."

Cole relaxed his stance. Elvis could see the young man had come a long way, but Cole had to know he couldn't take Lennon, especially not by walking alone into his trap.

"So, what do I do? I can't let them die."

225

"We do it together, Cole. As a team. You're not alone; you have me." Elvis smiled. "You have all of us—your family." The King stood up and set the gun on the desk. He grabbed a comb from his back pocket and ran it through his jet-black hair. "But we can't lose sight of the big picture. We have to deliver the thing that is going to replace CompuLive on every computer. Where are you with the code?"

"It's getting there. It's not perfect, but it's a good start."

"Good. The sooner we can deliver the replacement, the better."

Cole nodded. "So, what's the plan for rescuing Savannah?"

"First, we assemble a team."

"But everyone's already on assignment. They're busy either taking down Compu-Live or tracking down the Brotherhood."

"We can't be certain, but I believe if we take down Lennon, we take down the Brotherhood. Sure, he has followers, but knowing John, I doubt he'd let anyone in deep enough to take over if we eliminate him. I suspect Jimi, Kurt, and Jim will agree that their mission and ours are one and the same."

"Okay, but John knows us, too. He knows our methods and capabilities. How can we beat him?"

"Yes, John knows us." Elvis paused. "He was one of us." He took a beat to feel it. Deep in his bones he felt the pain of the betrayal. The next moment, he shook himself from his mourning and refocused. "So we have to think outside the box. He doesn't know *you*. What would you do?"

A huge grin came over Cole's face. "Now you're talking, King!"

chapter

THIRTY-TWO

Friday, December 31, 1999

For Cole, the flight from the Netherworld to Boston was different from the Christmas Eve mission. That day he could barely sit still, he was so nervous. Ironically, it was Lennon who'd calmed him down and convinced him he was ready. Now, a week later, he was the one doing the reassuring.

"I know it's not what you're used to," Cole said to Elvis, Morrison, and Cobain. "But I think it will throw him off enough for us to get the hostages out alive and take down Lennon."

Morrison and Cobain looked at the King.

"You need to trust him. I do," Elvis said.

They nodded in agreement just as Jimi announced they were beginning their descent into Logan International.

"Surely Lennon's monitoring the flights, so he knows we're here," Cole said. "Time is still our ally but only if we move fast. We don't know how many of his people he has in there, but it really doesn't matter. It won't affect the plan. Stick to it."

Everyone nodded.

The local time was 2:40 a.m. when they landed. As the C-130 Hercules taxied toward the hangars, Cole could barely make out hangar four through the darkness.

The transport rolled to a stop several hangars away. Then Jimi joined the others in the back as they readied themselves.

"Vaya con Dios, gentlemen," Cole said earnestly.

They all looked at him for a moment, then laughed.

"Yeah, I don't know why I said that. It just felt right."

Each acknowledged Cole with a nod or glance, and phase one of the plan began. The cargo gate of the Hercules opened, and Cole watched the four rock legends peel out on motorcycles, screaming toward hangar four.

✮ ✮ ✮ ✮

"They're here," Lennon said, speaking to his hostages. "I figured they'd come, but I didn't expect they'd bring the Hercules. They may have brought the whole team. You must feel special."

Savannah was exhausted. She looked over at Taylor, who was passed out. Dr. Self might have been crying, but it was hard to tell. She didn't really know what Lennon meant by "the whole team," but it somehow inspired a glimmer of hope.

They had been trapped inside this giant hangar for the past few weeks. She wondered what the world thought had happened to them.

The first week, they were free to roam about, but there was nothing to do, so they got to know each other very well. Taylor hated clowns. Dr. Self loved comic books. Savannah had been renting entire seasons of the original *Star Trek* series from Blockbuster because the show made her think of Cole. She had some thoughts about Tribbles.

They were not allowed to explore the two planes sharing the space. One was an older six-seater Cessna Citation jet, its black exterior dulled by age and use; the other was a larger Learjet, jet black and sleek as a cat. Both had a faint DRS symbol on the fuselage near the rudder. None of them knew what the letters stood for, but it had been a topic of much speculation and discussion.

They had been shocked when they first got into the car weeks ago and saw that the driver was John Lennon. He looked older than the man everyone thought was killed in 1980, but there was no mistaking it was him. The recent popularity of Beatles memorabilia in stores and malls made it impossible not to recognize the man with the thick Liverpool accent who had imprisoned them.

Lennon came and went. When he was gone, he would leave some nondescript goons behind to watch over them. These rotated quite frequently. Savannah had only seen a few of them more than once. They weren't unfriendly, but they didn't say or do much of anything. Still, they were intimidating enough thanks to the Uzis they all carried. She'd thought several times about trying to fight her way out, but she didn't think Taylor or Dr. Self would be much help in a brawl. She imagined the heaviest thing they'd lifted in years was a video game controller.

Lennon wasn't unfriendly either. From time to time, he would pull up a chair and chat with the three of them about all manner and variety of topics. And when they started talking about music, they couldn't get him to shut up. That is, until the time when Dr. Self asked if he would sing them one of his songs. From that moment on his demeanor changed.

"No!" Lennon had snapped. "I am not your song-and-dance puppet. I am your captor. You'd best remember that!"

Since then, they had been bound and confined to the sofa and chairs in the center of the space and were only allowed to move from there to use the restroom. They were fed, but the portions were slight and the food barely edible. They had lost all their strength and, to some degree, their hope.

Savannah didn't know why they were there or what John Lennon wanted with them. She knew only that it had something to do with Cole's alleged death.

Lennon was communicating with his men on a walkie-talkie when he suddenly bellowed, "Motorcycles? What are they doing on bloody motorcycles?!?"

"We see only four of them," one of the goons reported from his post. "It looks like Presley, Hendrix, Morrison, and Cobain."

"Well, well, they sent the big guns," Lennon said, turning to Savannah. "But lover boy didn't come for you." Then he climbed some mobile stairs to watch their approach from the hangar's forward window.

Savannah's head was spinning. *Lennon, Presley, Hendrix, Morrison, and Cobain? Is this what happened to Cole? He joined a strange circus of dead rock stars? Are they at war with each other? Is Freddy Mercury going to jump out at any moment?*

"Sorry, love, but they don't know what they're about to walk into."

★ ★ ★ ★

The four DRS agents screeched to a stop outside the giant metal door to the hangar. Elvis pulled a megaphone out from behind his back and began speaking.

"We know you're in there, John. We know you've got Cole's friends. We've called the cops and told them the whereabouts of the three people missing from Boston. They'll be here at any minute."

Lennon took a step back from the window, looking perplexed. He hadn't expected this move. He then grabbed a crowbar off the platform and bashed out the window in front of him. He shouted back, "Involving the local authorities, King? Doesn't seem like your style."

"Well, John," Elvis replied. "Yesterday, all of my troubles were so far away . . ."

"What do you expect to happen when the police arrive?" He was genuinely confused. He was ready for a shootout or some type of complicated, *Mission: Impossible*–style rescue attempt, but he hadn't expected Elvis to risk public exposure. "How are you going to explain all this to them?"

"I'm hoping I don't have to," Elvis said. "I'm hoping you'll send out Savannah, Mr. Wainscott, and Dr. Self and let us take them home. Then you and I can discuss how you're going to explain your actions to the team."

"That's not gonna happen, King!" John said, his words dripping with disdain. "You can't stop what's coming. I know you've got Cole holed up somewhere trying to figure it out, but it's too late."

"You haven't watched much news lately, have you?" Elvis said smugly. "Compu-Live is finished. And Cole's probably going to drop by right about . . ."

★ ★ ★ ★

BOOM!

The rear quarter of hangar four exploded into a fiery wreck of metal and sheet-rock. The half-dozen Brotherhood goons closest to the blast were killed instantly. Savannah, Taylor, and Dr. Self were unharmed. The explosion rocked the platform where John was standing, and he was momentarily stunned.

Meanwhile, Cobain produced a grenade launcher from behind his back and fired, blasting a large hole through the front of the hangar.

Elvis shouted, "It's showtime!"

The four agents pulled their weapons and burned rubber through the new "door" Cobain had created.

Jimi led the way through the opening, then immediately peeled off to the left toward the controls to open the big hangar door. Morrison shot through the opening next, machine guns blazing as he rode with no hands. Cobain came third, making straight for Savannah, Taylor, and Dr. Self, under the protection of cover fire from Morrison. Elvis rode close on his heels, scouring the hangar for Lennon.

Meanwhile, Cole had come in through the back wall and found a safe spot near a pile of hangar debris. When the coast was clear, he made a beeline to the control room, found the stereo system, loaded a CD, and ratcheted up the volume. Ted Nugent's eight-and-a-half-minute cut of "Stranglehold" started echoing throughout the hangar.

Cole left the control room in haste and made his way through the rubble and chaos to the six-seater Cessna jet. The smoke gave him much-needed cover, but he knew once he cranked the engines he would be exposed. He climbed into the cockpit and found among the instruments a hollow compartment marked with a skull. He fished around in his pocket and pulled out the smooth stone that until four months ago belonged to Buddy Holly. He kissed the stone and said, "Come on, Buddy, give me some of your magic." He shoved the stone into the opening, and on cue the plane's twin engines roared to life.

★ ★ ★ ★

A dozen Brotherhood fighters were crawling about the room shooting wildly. Lennon started shouting orders as he made his way down the steps while firing at anyone he saw on a motorcycle. "Don't let them get away!" he screamed.

Jimi Hendrix had made it to the controls for the giant hangar door, and it began opening slowly. He then overturned a metal table and took careful aim at the Brotherhood men running around. He sniped a couple before his position was discovered, then he hunkered down and waited for the right moment to make a break for the Learjet. The smoke was burning his eyes, so he reached into his jacket for his gas mask and put it on.

Jim Morrison had drawn the fire of half the bad guys in the room and was leading them as far from the hostages as he could. Then he skillfully laid down his bike and tumbled into a somersault near the area damaged by the initial explosion. He took cover behind some debris and began targeting Brotherhood men from that vantage point. Fire had begun enveloping the hangar and was spreading along the walls and ceiling. The air was growing heavier with smoke, making it difficult to see what he was shooting at. Seizing an opportunity, Morrison put on his gas mask, and when the smoke was heavy enough to cover his movements, he jumped back on his bike and returned to the fray.

Kurt Cobain had made his way to the sofa where Savannah, Taylor, and Dr. Self were bound. John Lennon tried to thwart his efforts, but Elvis spotted him and began firing a .45 in his direction while riding with one hand. Lennon dove behind the couch, knowing Elvis wouldn't endanger the hostages. The King then veered away from the action toward the back of the hangar, disappearing into the smoke.

✷ ✷ ✷ ✷

Lennon could now hear sirens over the loud music, flames, and gunfire. The tide of this battle was clearly not turning in his favor. He needed to make a call—stay and fight or run and live?

He holstered his pistol, grabbed the walkie-talkie from his other hip, and began barking out orders. "Withdraw. Go to Shangri La. If I don't make it, carry on as planned. Go in peace, my brothers!"

On his orders, any surviving Brotherhood followers would make their way to any exit they could find and leave the battle behind them.

Cobain had arrived. He jumped off his bike and screamed, "John!"

Lennon wasn't afraid to exchange blows with Cobain, but he also knew he needed to move quickly if he was going to escape. He chose to run.

✷ ✷ ✷ ✷

Cobain resisted the urge to chase Lennon and turned his attention back to the three hostages, as per the plan. He slashed their duct-tape bindings and helped them up. The heat and smoke were starting to overtake the entire hangar now.

Just then the Cessna appeared through the smoke with Cole behind the yoke. He shouted out the window, "Help them into the plane, Kurt. Then get out of here!"

Cobain helped Savannah up the two-step boarding ladder and into the cabin, followed by Dr. Self.

✷ ✷ ✷ ✷

As Lennon reached an exit, he turned to see his hostages boarding the Cessna. When he saw Cole piloting the small jet, his rage exploded. He grabbed his pistol and fired wildly at the aircraft. The shot missed Cole but glanced off Cobain's shoulder as he was helping Taylor into the plane.

Lennon took aim to fire again, but just then Elvis emerged from the smoke and skidded his bike right into John's legs, taking both men to the ground.

★ ★ ★ ★

Under the cover of the smoke and flames, Jimi had left his secure position and sprinted to the Learjet. Morrison joined him after setting his motorcycle aflame and sending it careening into the makeshift hiding place of three Brotherhood operatives.

From the Cessna cockpit, Cole hollered, "Kurt, are you okay?"

Cobain waved his good arm. "He just clipped me. I'm fine!"

"Get to your plane!"

By now, Jimi had fired up the Learjet and was right behind the Cessna, ready for departure. Morrison had the stairs down and was holding out a hand, ready to help his wounded comrade into the jet.

The hangar let out a low moan. Its structural integrity had been compromised. They all understood that the hangar would collapse any minute.

"What about Elvis?" Cobain called, scanning for any sign of him.

Cole groaned and yelled, "He knows the plan, Kurt, and this wasn't our plan. I think he's going solo."

Cobain grimaced, nodded, then bolted toward the Learjet, clutching his shoulder and coughing as he ran. He took Morrison's hand and climbed the steps.

Both planes began rolling out the giant hangar door toward the runway.

"Cole, you're alive!" Savannah exclaimed, throwing her arms around him from behind. "And you can fly?"

"Fly? Yes," Cole said, wiping sweat from his brow. "Land? We'll see." He gave Savannah a desperate smile and shrug.

As the plane lifted into the air, Cole could see police cars and fire trucks pouring into the airport.

"Uh . . . guys . . ." Taylor said weakly as the plane was gaining altitude.

Savannah saw that he was covered in blood and pale as a ghost. "Taylor?!?" she screamed.

In their haste to escape, no one had noticed that Lennon's errant bullet had glanced off Cobain's shoulder and buried itself in Taylor's chest. Savannah tore open his shirt, revealing his blood-smeared torso.

It was too late. The bullet had done its worst.

Taylor gasped a labored breath or two and then was gone.

Cole could hear Savannah crying over him but couldn't bring himself to look back. He had to get the others to safety first. He had to stay focused on the mission.

★ ★ ★ ★

Jimi taxied the jet down the runway and took to the air immediately after the Cessna.

"We just gonna leave Elvis?" Cobain asked him, grasping his nicked shoulder.

"I think this might have been *his* plan all along," Jimi replied.

Cobain and Morrison just nodded as the jet took to the skies.

Jimi looked down and saw the hangar engulfed in flames as emergency vehicles began to encircle the building. Suddenly, several hangars away, the C-130 Hercules exploded violently, leaving no trace that the team of dead rock stars had ever even been there.

"Goodbye, old friend," Jimi said as they flew away.

★ ★ ★ ★

Elvis picked himself up off the ground. He could barely see, and his lungs were filled with smoke. Fortunately for both men, Elvis just clipped Lennon with the front wheel of his motorcycle to take his feet out from under him. But Lennon hadn't moved since; he was out cold.

The speakers finally gave up the ghost from the heat of the flames, and the final notes of "Stranglehold" groaned to a conclusion.

Then Elvis picked up Lennon and threw him over his shoulder, much as he had with Buddy four short months ago. He hobbled to the door that led to the same hallway Cole used when he first came to the hangar to hear his recruiting pitch. All these memories and more flooded Elvis's mind as he staggered down the hall. He knew the police would be out front, but he didn't think they'd have surrounded the building yet.

This hadn't been part of Cole's plan, but it was part of the King's.

He had business to attend to.

chapter
THIRTY-THREE

C ole picked up the radio. "Come in, Netherworld."

"I got you, CD. Don't change this course," Tupac Shakur responded. "Listen, I got news. Cobain just radioed. They are heading to phase two. You head home."

"Um, yeah, about that . . . I've got to make a stop first. We've lost a friend."

Cole tried his best to maintain composure.

Tupac said, "Sending coordinates now. There is a friend who can help. Adjust your heading for Montgomery, Alabama. Dude, I'm sorry for your loss."

"Montgomery. Got it. We'll head to base shortly after. Denton, out."

"Solid copy, Cole."

Never had a six-seater plane felt smaller than in that moment.

Self sat in the front seat in a state of shock, unable to control his body from shaking. Tears were falling from his eyes, but he was making no sound. In the second row, Savannah was covered in Taylor's blood. She had done her best to revive him but to no avail. Blood soaked the seats and floorboards, and there was nowhere to escape the tragic reality, especially with Taylor's lifeless body slumped over in the seat beside her.

Finally, after several minutes of silence, a trembling arm reached over and rested on Cole's shoulder. Cole reached back and grabbed Savannah's blood-soaked hand, and they all wept together.

Cole had imagined many nights what it might be like to touch her one more time. None of them involved a situation like this. He needed to get them on the ground in Montgomery as quickly as possible.

★ ★ ★ ★

When Lennon came to, he found his hands had been cuffed, his mouth gagged, and a hood placed over his head. His feet were free, but he was in no condition to make a run for it. He didn't move but remained awake and listening. He knew they hadn't gone too far; he could still smell smoke. He also heard sirens in the distance punctuated by bursts of gunfire. The gunshots caused him to flinch.

Elvis patted him on the arm, which made him flinch yet again.

"It's okay, John. I've got you. That's the sound of your so-called Brotherhood making its last stand with the local authorities. You and me, we've got other plans."

★ ★ ★ ★

Thirty minutes later, a nondescript Ford Bronco with darkly tinted windows pulled up to where the King was standing over Lennon, behind an abandoned storage facility a half mile from the hubbub at hangar four. Richie Valens climbed out of the SUV, nodded at Elvis, and together they scooped up Lennon and tossed him into the back seat with little care taken for his well-being.

Elvis checked the back of the vehicle and took a quick inventory. There were several rolls of industrial plastic draping, duct tape, several gallons of water, a few car batteries, jumper cables, a metal folding chair, a small kiddie pool, pliers, and some shovels.

He closed the rear doors, climbed into the front passenger seat, and said, "I see you were able to find everything I asked for. You know where we're going?"

"Where no one can hear him?"

"Exactly. Now, step on it. We don't have much time."

Elvis turned to the back seat and said, "John, I want you to *imagine* all the things I'm about to do to you. I wish I could say I'm not going to take any pleasure in it, but . . ."

Lennon lunged toward the door in a futile attempt to escape. Elvis rammed his right elbow into the hood he was wearing, and Lennon folded onto the floorboard.

236

Richie leaned forward and pressed play on the cassette deck. Lennon's recording of "Whatever Gets You Through the Night" began playing. Presley turned up the volume for the part about not needing a sword to cut through flowers.

"Oh no, oh no," Elvis sang as the Bronco sped off.

☆ ☆ ☆ ☆

The sun had risen by the time the small Cessna jet touched down outside Montgomery at an unregistered airfield. Waiting on the runway was a Chevy Silverado pickup truck, with a slender gentleman standing next to it in a cowboy hat holding down his silver windblown hair. Hank Williams Sr. walked to the back of the truck and let down the tailgate as the Cessna rolled to a stop alongside.

"I'm sorry to hear about your friend, Cole. Welcome to Alabama."

"Thank you, Mr. Williams." It was all Cole could muster.

As carefully as they could, Cole and Self moved Taylor's body to the back of the pickup. Williams had the proper gear in the back to protect the body and at the same time disguise what they were carrying as they traveled through town. He also had a change of clothes for everyone. None of them fit well, but they weren't soaked through with blood or smelled of smoke.

"I figured in this difficult situation I might lend a hand. 'Two Pack' let me know your ETA. I have the site all ready. Some of my local contacts will clean the plane before you head home."

Cole stuffed all the feelings as far down as he could. "Thank you, sir."

Williams didn't ask questions about where they had been. He just talked and said kind and gentle things. "This is my territory of sorts. I get to wear my hat and blend right in. No one thinks twice about a senior citizen in a wide brim and a pickup. Besides, it's been forty years! The world moves on. Hey, at least Alan Jackson wrote a nice song about me."

Cole couldn't pretend to know anything about country music, but Savannah expressed their appreciation for the kindness Williams was showing them.

"Family is family," he replied with a grandfatherly smile.

Twenty minutes later, they pulled into to a ranch with rolling hills. At the foot of one of the hills was a small cemetery with a few chairs and a beautiful oak tree. A hole had already been dug. The location was so beautiful that no one thought to ask too many questions.

Taylor was laid to rest in a handmade wooden casket and lowered into the earth. Then Hank Williams tipped the brim of his hat and left them to say their goodbyes in private.

"I'm sorry, guys," Cole said. "We don't have much time. I can't believe I'm about to say this out loud, but we're still trying to save the world from John Lennon and Y2K before midnight."

Savannah sighed. "I'm pretty sure I just saw Elvis Presley and a Beatle in a gun-fight, so I'm ready to believe you. I'm just thrilled you're alive." She grabbed Cole's hand, and they stood as close to each other as they could.

Cole asked, "Dr. Self, would you mind saying a few words about Taylor?"

"Yeah." Self cleared his throat. "I, uh, didn't know Taylor too well . . . at least, not until recently. He was in my advanced coding seminar last semester. Um . . . before it got super weird at the hangar, he told me something about what he wanted to do with his life. He wanted to move to a place like . . . well, like this place. A nice place he could call his own. A quiet place. He wanted to meet a nice girl and start a family. He was good with computers and had some ambition, but mostly he just wanted to find someplace where he could live a quiet life. He was a good friend. A good kid. I know he'll be missed by the people who loved him. It's a shame he had to go this way."

Guilt coursed through Cole's body. He couldn't escape the fact that Taylor had died because of him. It didn't matter that John Lennon had pulled the trigger. This was something Cole would carry with him forever.

"Anyway, that's all I got. Rest in peace, kid. See you on the flip side."

Cole shook his head and took a step forward. "I want to say something. He was my best friend. Loyal. Never doubted me. I wish I were more like him." Then he grabbed a shovel and tossed some dirt on the casket. He handed the shovel to Dr. Self, who did the same.

Savannah looked like she wanted to say something but didn't. She knelt and scooped the loose soil with her hands and gently let it flow from her fingers onto the wooden box. After the last of it fell, she raised a hand, parted her fingers, and whispered, "It wasn't long or prosperous enough."

★ ★ ★ ★

"Richie, this is far enough," Elvis said.

They had driven north along the coast for close to an hour and were well into Maine. Valens pulled the car over, and Elvis got out.

"Thanks, old friend. Sorry to have to pull you back in like this."

"It felt good to be back in the game, even if it was for just one drive."

"When you see Kennedy, tell him I've got to get away for a while. But, uh . . . I'll be back when the time is right."

"Sure thing, King."

Elvis grabbed the items he'd requested from the back of the SUV and casually tossed them on the ground. Then he hoisted Lennon from the back seat of the Bronco and tossed him on the ground, too.

Richie reached out his open window, patted the side of the car, gave Elvis a nod, and drove off.

"It's just you and me now, friend," Elvis said with a touch of venom.

chapter
THIRTY-FOUR

Lennon was not unconscious, but he wasn't fully awake either. His injuries from the hangar and Elvis's elbow weren't major, but the cumulative damage made him a little fuzzy. He felt like he probably had also torn some ligaments in his knee, but he wasn't certain.

Lennon listened carefully and realized they were near the ocean, probably on a pier. He could hear birds—seagulls to be exact. He could also make out the sound of waves crashing and a ship's horn bellowing in the distance. The smell of salt and seawater was in the air, and he felt a wooden surface beneath him.

Elvis removed Lennon's hood but left his hands cuffed.

"Ya gonna feed me to the sharks, man?"

"Something like that," Elvis said. "Actually, I think I might do to you what you did to your own man in Tennessee. Thus, my tools." Elvis waved his hands over the implements of torture like one of Bob Barker's beauties on *The Price is Right*.

Lennon looked about him. The tiny pier seemed remote enough that Elvis just might pull this off without anyone noticing. In the distance, there were boats passing, but the closest was at least a mile from shore.

"One thing I gotta know before we get started," Elvis said with genuine interest. "How did you do it?"

Lennon laughed from his belly. "You have completely underestimated me, man." He laughed again. "Well, if you really want to know, it was all me. I did it all."

"What do you mean, you did it *all?*"

"I mean, I began studying computers right after I joined the DRS. I knew they were the future, long before you or even Buddy saw it. I took correspondence courses. No one ever knew. In the early nineties, I started CompuLive. I put everyone in place and funneled my own resources into its growth and expansion. I built it from the ground up, all from the Netherworld. Denton was right, King—our backdoor was wide open for a long time. You were lucky no one ever found it."

Elvis appeared astounded. "Why would you do that, John? Did you *ever* believe in our cause?"

"EVER? I *still* believe! That's why I did all of this. I figured out early on that what we were doing would never truly change the world. If we were going to make it happen, we had to try something radical. A *revolution*, youknowwhatImean? But I knew you would never agree to it. YOU NEVER LISTEN TO ME. So, I did it all on my own."

"How? You didn't think up Y2K. That programming error happened a long time ago."

"Yes, but it planted a seed, didn't it? Inspiration, man. When I learned the Y2K bug was in fact a humbug, I conceived a plan to make it a reality—my reality. That's when Al U. Nedney was born. I started writing the code to implant a virus on every computer in the world. At the same time, I started recruiting the Brotherhood. When Buddy caught wind of the organization's existence and the work we were doing around the globe, I had to conjure up some misleading evidence and use a bit of sleight-of-hand to throw him off the scent. His death was a terrible accident, but I thought at the very least my dream had cleared the final obstacle. Then, after his funeral when you told me of your plan—Buddy's plan—to bring in Denton, it was as if Buddy were reaching out from the grave to snatch it all away. So, I sent my right-hand bird to Boston to hire the kid for CompuLive first. But instead, the brilliant little twit fell for your empty talk of family and changing the world together. And he ruined everything!"

Lennon's face was starting to turn red.

"It would have worked . . . *but he . . . ruined . . . it all!*" His rage spent, he quickly regained his composure. "It's a shame, really. It was beautiful code."

"Why the girl? And Cole's friends?"

"I had been keeping tabs on her in case I needed an incentive to help Denton see things my way. As it happened, I needed her to draw him out after he thoughtlessly failed to die in California."

Elvis sniffed. "That's a whale of a story, John." Then his voice took on a strange sadness. "But you've got to pay for Buddy. And now, since you're about to meet your end, do you want to sing one more song before you go?"

Lennon glared at him—and then broke down and fell to his knees.

"I can't sing anymore, King," he moaned. "When I had those three locked in the hangar, the old one asked me to sing for him. But I couldn't. It was like my soul wouldn't let me."

"It's because to sing you've got to be human, John. What you tried to do—what you've done—it's not human. It's twisted and evil. I'm not saying you're evil, man. At least you weren't . . ." There was a pleading tone in his voice.

Elvis then picked up a pair of bolt cutters and approached Lennon. He trembled as he held them over his former friend. He slowly moved them toward Lennon's hands. But instead of a finger, Elvis cut the links between his cuffed wrists.

Lennon slowly looked up at Presley, not quite sure what to make of the situation. "You've changed your tune rather quickly."

"Aw, man, I wasn't going to do any of this," Elvis said, pointing to the torture devices. "You know that's not me. It's not my way. I was just tryin' to spook you."

Lennon stayed on his knees. Elvis backed away, and the two just stared at each other for several minutes, sea spray making them both damp. This was New Year's Eve in Maine; neither the air nor water were warm.

Elvis finally broke the silence. "Come home, John. Richie's not too far. He can come back and pick us up. I don't know how, but we can make this right."

His offer took Lennon by surprise. But John couldn't see how he could go back. Especially with Janis still there. Still, returning to the Netherworld, even if it meant rotting in a cell, was not his least attractive option at that moment. He stared at the ground. Then he slowly nodded and extended a hand toward Elvis. The King approached him cautiously and took his hand to help him up.

Lennon lunged and drove his shoulder into Elvis's stomach, knocking the wind out of him and taking both men to the ground. Elvis hadn't let go of his hand, though. Lennon then elbowed the King's face, stunning him enough for him to let loose his grip. Lennon got to his feet, stumbled, and limped as fast as he could down the pier toward the water.

He wasn't fast enough. Elvis recovered quickly, dove, and caught him a few feet from the edge. The two men struggled and scrapped on the slick, wooden planks of the pier, neither able to gain a solid advantage over the other.

As exhaustion set in for both men, Elvis was able to maneuver into position behind Lennon. He then flung an arm around Lennon's throat and put him in a choke hold.

"Come on, John," Elvis pleaded. "Go to sleep."

Lennon felt the air slowly escape from his lungs. His eyes were getting heavy, and his mind started to go blank. Then his hand brushed by his side, where he kept a one-and-a-half-inch blade hidden in his belt. He mustered his last bit of strength to pull the blade and jab it toward Elvis's face. He missed the King's eye but cut him deeply near his left cheekbone. Elvis loosened his grip, and the oxygen came rushing back, giving Lennon what he needed to wriggle free from the King's grasp. He then jumped up and kicked Elvis's left leg in the perfect spot to pop his kneecap out of place.

Then Lennon stumbled to the edge of the pier and fell into the freezing water. The cold sent a surge of adrenaline through him, though Lennon knew it wouldn't last long before his systems began to shut down from hypothermia. He knew he had to use his last ounce of strength to get to one of those boats in the distance, or he was going to freeze to death in that water.

He started to swim.

★ ★ ★ ★

Blood gushed from Elvis's face, but his knee felt worse. He grabbed the bolt cutters he'd used minutes earlier and wrenched off one of the rubber hand grips. He bit down hard on the rubber grip, took a deep breath, and popped his kneecap back into place. Elvis howled with pain.

He clambered to his feet as quickly as he could but took only a single step in pursuit before crumbling to the pier in a heap. He had no chance of catching Lennon in his present condition. Elvis shouted in anger, "Run, you coward!"

Lennon, seeing that his former colleague could not give chase, flipped over into a backstroke, and called out, "I'm not the only one, Elvis!" Then he turned and resumed giving everything he had to reach one of the distant boats.

His knee throbbing, Elvis applied pressure to his cheek as he watched Lennon swim away. He could tell this cut needed stitches and would leave a scar. He wondered which scar would run deeper, the one on his face or the one John Lennon had left on the team.

He eventually lost sight of Lennon. He had no idea whether he'd made it to safety or not, but he couldn't stop looking for him among the waves. Eventually, the cold got to be too much, and he needed to stitch up his wound. So, he turned away and limped back toward the coastal highway.

He didn't know where he was going or how he would get there.

But he knew he couldn't go home.

chapter
THIRTY-FIVE

avannah and Cole shared a look that said both would give anything not to be confined in the small plane with Dr. Self right now as he peppered Cole with question after question. Savannah, too, was interested in what had happened to Cole and what would happen in the days to come. But most of all she knew she couldn't say goodbye again.

After Cole gave a brief and vague explanation of the DRS and its mission, Self let out a mischievous giggle and shouted, "I knew it!"

"I'm sure you had it all figured out." Cole exhaled. "Prepare for landing, everyone."

"Um, what does that mean?" Savannah asked.

"I honestly don't know. I just wanted to change the subject. We are here. Welcome to the Netherworld."

The first time Cole had seen this place he didn't know what to think. This time it felt like home.

Janis Joplin met them on the runway. "We did it, Cole! The news is reporting that every major government in the world has deleted CompuLive. Also, Kurt and the Jims are moving to phase two. We'll know more in a few hours. "

Dr. Self looked at Janis and blurted, "I saw you at Shea Stadium in 1970. I LOVE YOU!"

"Thank you, Dr. Self. I'm sure we'll have time to talk, but for now I need to get Agent Denton up to speed."

"Oh yes, of course. I love you. I can't help it. I've always loved you. You've taken several little pieces of my—"

"You can stop there, Dr. Self. You are too . . . kind." Janis looked at Cole and away from Self and rolled her eyes.

Cole muffled his chuckle and squeezed Savannah's hand a bit tighter than normal. They hadn't stopped holding hands.

"Janis, this is Savannah. Savannah, this is my friend, Janis."

"Savannah, I've heard a lot about you. I know this is all a bit much. Don't worry about trying to make sense of—"

Janis wasn't able to complete her thought before Savannah said, "Thank you, Janis. I'm okay. Really. This makes more sense than my last few months, for sure." She squeezed Cole's hand this time.

Cole needed to hear more. "Janis, details, please. What has been happening around the world?"

"The media are destroying CompuLive in the court of public opinion as we speak. Many countries have experienced their midnight. We are getting reports of some issues, but nothing crisis-level. Power grids, infrastructures, and financial markets are holding steady. In fact, because Y2K was a no-show, analysts are predicting the stock market will open to record highs on Monday!"

"I love CompuLive," Self interjected. "I chat with everyone. Even started a few groups myself." He beamed with pride.

"Lennon was trying to use CompuLive to destroy the world," Janis said in a pitch-perfect deadpan.

Self's smile faded. "Wow . . . okay. Wow."

Joplin continued briefing Cole. "Kennedy has access to the Oval Office. He convinced the VP to get your patch out on the internet. Since he claims to have invented it anyway, he was quick to offer his help and support. CompuLive has lost forty million subscribers and counting, and its stock is now worthless. Nobody will even take those free trial CDs at Circuit City anymore. You were right. So was Buddy. Cole, you helped save the world today."

Cole looked down at his hands. Some of Taylor's blood was still under his fingernails.

Jerry Garcia pulled up in a small golf cart with a tie-dye paint job. "Hey, guys! Welcome to the Netherworld! Dr. Self, I'm sure you're hungry. How 'bout you and Janis join me for dinner? Maybe even some ice cream. I'm sure you've got loads of questions."

Self shuddered. "The Grateful Dead?"

"Oh, forgive me. I'm Jerry. Nice to meet you. You a Deadhead?"

Dr. Self nodded and eagerly climbed into the golf cart. He looked at Janis and then at Jerry and back at Cole in utter amazement.

"Cole, we'll see you later?" Jerry asked with a glimmer in his eye.

Cole looked at Savannah and sheepishly shrugged.

Savannah said, "We'll see you later!"

Alone together for the first time in months, Cole and Savannah watched as the sun began to set and twilight descended over the Netherworld.

★ ★ ★ ★

"Go!" Cobain said.

Morrison shinnied up a drainpipe to the top of the Brotherhood training facility in Cleveland. Once at the top, he unhooked a rope from his belt, wrapped one end around his forearm, and threw the other end of the rope to Cobain and Jimi below. He then braced himself so he could support the weight of the two men as they scaled the side of the building. Under the cover of darkness, the trio might as well have been ghosts.

"I still don't know about this," Jimi said, once at the top. "John is the one who told us about this place. How can we trust him?"

"We made our sweep," Cobain said. "Thermals and infrared scans were negative. We cut the power to the building, and no one has come out. This place is quiet as a graveyard."

Jimi looked at Morrison to get his take, but Morrison was busy feeding a worm he'd found on the ground to a pigeon and seemed oblivious to their discussion.

"We've got to get inside and confirm for ourselves," Cobain said. "We know what to look for. We know how John thinks. Our orders are to either burn this place to the ground or eliminate anyone inside. Either way, we have to go in."

Jimi reluctantly nodded in agreement.

They located the same exhaust vent Lennon had used to enter the building weeks earlier and removed the covering. From his backpack, Cobain produced a camera mounted on a small remote-control vehicle, as well as a handheld monitor and controller. He switched on both devices and sent the vehicle down the shaft. They watched on the small monitor as the vehicle explored every inch of the ductwork.

"Everything looks clear so far," Jimi observed.

The vehicle eventually came to a vent where the camera could see the floor below. No one was there.

"It's empty," Jimi said.

"Let's go," Cobain said as he climbed in through the vent and began working his way through the ductwork. Morrison followed close behind, the pigeon sitting on his shoulder. Jimi brought up the rear.

The three men reached the ceiling vent and retrieved the remote-control vehicle. Cobain removed the vent, then pulled from his bag a plastic jar filled with dozens of marble-sized rubber balls. He unscrewed the lid, overturned the jar, and dropped the balls to the floor below. As they hit the floor, they scattered in every direction.

Nothing happened. No sensors were sprung. No tripwires were set off. No motion detectors were triggered.

Cobain looked at the others and nodded. Morrison lowered Cobain first. As he dropped to the floor, he turned on a flashlight and quickly scanned the room. There was no movement, save a few of his trigger balls still rolling about the warehouse floor. The room was almost entirely empty. Clean. Nevertheless, Cobain pulled his sidepiece—just in case.

Jimi joined him on the floor and drew his weapon as well. The two men positioned themselves back to back and began moving across the open floor. There was absolutely no trace of the training equipment, targets, tables, and weapons they had seen in Lennon's video.

Jimi spotted something on the floor a few feet in front of him. "Kurt," he whispered. "I found something."

It was an envelope marked with the Y2K symbol Buddy had discovered months earlier. It was too flat to be an explosive but might contain a dangerous substance. They weren't taking any chances. Both put on gas masks and gloves.

Cobain then used a set of surgical tongs to pick up the envelope.

It wasn't sealed.

He opened it and pulled out a folded piece of paper. Both men recognized John Lennon's handwriting. The note read:

It's too late.
I've won.
We get to begin again now . . .

It was fated
since time began.
I'd save the world somehow.
But if not—if you prevailed—
as surely as the moon and sun,
this dreamer's dream will never die.
I'm not the only one.
John

Cobain folded the letter and carefully placed it back in the envelope. Jimi produced a Ziplock bag, and Cobain placed the letter inside. Jimi sealed the bag and stowed it. Both men removed their gas masks.

"We need a team to analyze this building," Cobain said. "But as for us, I think it's time we go home."

★ ★ ★ ★

On the well-lit back lawn of Graceland II, Cole and Savannah sat together on the same lounge chair by the swimming pool and impeccably manicured garden. The night air had turned cooler, and Savannah shivered.

Cole pulled her closer. "Do you want to go inside?" he asked, trying not to sound creepy.

Savannah looked deeply into his eyes and said, "I don't want to go anywhere."

He chuckled. "Good, because we'd have to wipe your mind if you did." He made a fire in the firepit and turned on a pair of strategically placed heat lamps to keep them warm.

Hours went by. They talked about everything and nothing all at once.

Cole talked about his parents, his training, and what this new life meant to him. He talked about how he'd taken baby steps toward trusting people and feeling like this new team was the family he'd always wanted.

Savannah talked about school, her students, and wondered what everyone thought about her being gone. She also wasn't about to let his "new look" slide; she said the beard looked good on him.

He told her the DSR had plans ready whether she chose to stay or return to her life in Boston. The cover-up was already in motion. All that remained was to decide how many of them survived the fire at hangar four. The Brotherhood had been labeled a human trafficking ring, and the evidence was being delivered to local authorities. Commendations were already in the works for the police and rescue squads tasked to clean up the tragic mess. Although Taylor had been given a proper burial at Hank's ranch, his DNA would be found at the scene with enough details to confirm the worst for Taylor's family. Cole wished they could know the truth.

Without warning, Savannah grabbed him and kissed him.

"Happy New Year, Cole."

What was to happen at midnight on January 1, 2000 had been his primary focus for so long. But after the loss of Taylor, and now with Savannah in his arms, he had lost all track of time. "Savannah . . . Y2K. I gotta go."

Cole bolted into and through the house only to be stopped dead in his tracks by Chris Wallace standing between the lions on the front steps.

"Whoa, young playa."

"Chris . . . you scared me. What's happening?"

Biggie shook his head no and pointed back to the door.

"But what about—"

Wallace shook his head again and then folded his arms.

"Okay, I get it. You guys got this?"

Biggie said, "Man, the DRS been saving the world for over a hundred years and then some. We got you, CD."

Cole sighed. This story was just another notch in the belt of the King and his team of certified rock star secret agents.

This was Cole's first notch.

"Cool . . . I guess. Cool, cool, cool. I'm gonna go back and be with . . ."

Wallace waved him away with the slyest of grins.

chapter

THIRTY-SIX

"Is this going to be a problem?" Cobain asked as they emerged from the room Savannah hadn't been allowed to enter.

"No, man, I get it," Cole replied. "I don't like it, but I get it."

"After the mind wipe, come see me."

"Have you heard from Elvis?"

"No one has. That's why we are where we are."

Cole looked like he wanted to know more but was hesitant to speak.

"Don't worry," Cobain said. "When E returns, I'll be happy to step back."

"Okay. What about her?" Cole asked, nodding toward Savannah, who was standing a few feet away, waiting for his meeting to end.

"She can stay if she wants to. There's plenty to do around here."

Cobain made eye contact with Savannah, nodded to her, and walked away down the hall.

Cole grabbed Savannah's hand, and they walked in the other direction.

"What did that mean, Cole?"

"It means the Netherworld can be your home . . . if you want." While Cole didn't want to presume anything, he felt pretty good about the possibilities.

Savannah smirked as they strolled down the hall in the building called the Cleveland Compound. "Do you know how long I looked for my last condo? Months. I had to find just the right mix of mold coverage and rodent infestation to match my teacher's salary. I'm not sure I can just give up that place."

"We can have an exact replica of your apartment here at the Netherworld by next week if that's what you want. The team can even match your existing mold-to-rodent ratio. Your call." They came to another nondescript building, and Cole grabbed the door and held it for her while looking for a reaction to Cobain's offer. "You do want to stay, right?"

Savannah smiled warmly. "I guess I need to delete my Connextion.com profile before the 'mind wipe.' What was all that about, anyway? And that Cobain guy—a little scary. Have you ever asked him why the naked kid on the album cover? Creeper."

"Surprisingly, no. He's not much on sharing."

"Am I allowed to ask what your secret meeting was about? I'm not really sure how this works, to be honest."

"Um, me neither. If something like this has happened before, no one has told me about it." Cole paused for a moment, then decided to spill what he knew. "Elvis and Lennon are off the map. No one knows what happened or where they've gone or even if they're alive. Richie Valens apparently saw them both after they escaped from hangar four, but he won't say what he knows. And President Kennedy recommended Kurt to lead the team on an interim basis."

"Did you just say Richie Valens and President Kennedy? Anyone else you've failed to mention?" Savannah laughed in disbelief. "Well, from what you've told me about Elvis, I'm sure he knows what he's doing."

"Lovebirds!"

"Dr. Self," they simultaneously muttered, then turned to greet the professor.

"Ms. Joplin and Mr. Garcia have been so kind, feeding me and showing me around," Self said. "Looks like they've arranged for us to return home, but they sent me here first for some kind of procedure. I've been so caught up in this amazing place that I didn't really think to ask what kind of procedure."

At that moment a nearby door opened, and Tupac Shakur politely asked Dr. Self to step inside. He then motioned Cole and Savannah into the room right next to it. Inside, they found the room empty except for a two-way mirror and a wall-mounted speaker. They'd both seen enough television to know that the two rooms were for interviews and interrogations. On the other side of the glass, Dr. Self was seated at a table and facing their direction. Chris Wallace and Tupac were seated across the table with their backs to Savannah and Cole.

"What is this?" Savannah asked, both shocked and amused.

"The mind wipe, I guess," Cole whispered. "I've never seen one either. I'm just as nervous and excited as you are."

Through the speaker they could hear Dr. Self make several outrageously inappropriate attempts to appear relevant and hip. The two agents then began describing the procedure he was about to experience.

Tupac said, "Dr. Self, we are sending you back to Boston and your former life. The story you will memorize will line up with police reports and supporting evidence. Taylor and Savannah gave up their lives to save yours. You have been recovering from temporary amnesia in a hospital a few counties over from Logan International and hangar four."

"Wait, Savannah didn't die . . ."

"Dude, she did." Biggie sighed.

"I just saw her a few moments a—"

"Yeah, man. She dead," Chris said, trying to be patient. "As far as the world is concerned, she dead."

"But you? Not so much," Tupac said. "We're going to fly you to a location far away from here. We'll give you a car to drive back home in. Something nice, for all your troubles. You pick. You're going to take a few days and drive the long way round. We'll give you directions and all the information you need right after we wipe your mind."

Self shifted in his seat as sweat started beading on his forehead. "My mind? Guys, my mind is my money maker. We can't mess with that. Isn't there another way? What if I sign a waiver or something?"

Cole put one arm around Savannah, and his other hand found the smooth rock in his pocket. Savannah had given up her old life, her job, and everything to stay with him. He wanted to say something that he didn't know how to say. The next thing he knew, he was reciting the opening lines of the Bryan Adams song from Kevin Costner's *Robin Hood* movie.

Savannah shushed him. "I want to see them wipe his mind. And really? Bryan Adams? A little corny, don't you think?"

Cole had never loved her more.

Chris set a large metallic cylinder on the table and clicked a switch on the back. Several hundred lumens shined into Self's face. "I'm sorry, Dr. Self. It is time to wipe your mind."

With his forefingers, Tupac started a drumroll on the table. Then Chis clicked the light on and off repeatedly, while saying, "Bleep bloop bleep bloop."

Both men started laughing uncontrollably.

Self shook with a mixture of confusion and worry. "What is this?" he demanded.

"This is your mind wipe, man," Tupac said as his laughter faded. Then he leaned into Self, taking a somewhat more serious tone. "If you tell anyone about this place— anyone at all—everyone will think you gone crazy. No one will believe you. And then that fancy school of yours will fire you. On top of that, you should know that our resources have resources. So, if you even think about ever talking about this again . . . well, good luck with that. We know where you live."

Chris said, "Your mind has now officially been wiped. A plane is waiting for you on the runway. If we need you, we'll call."

Self wiped his forehead and started laughing. "I'm not sure what to say, fellas. I— It's like I can't remember anything!"

★ ★ ★ ★

A few awkward hugs were exchanged with some more small talk, because Self was having trouble tearing himself away from what he called Rock Star Heaven. Finally, he leaned in and whispered to Cole. "Love Shack, have fun saving the world. Call me if you need me. I'll be there."

As Self climbed the stairs of the midnight-colored Learjet, Cole could hear him asking someone, "Does this flight have drinks?"

Then the plane took to the sky and vanished into the eastern horizon.

The January chill caused Cole and Savannah to hastily retreat from the runway. Cole said through chattering teeth, "Let's go to the garage and get a ride back home. You have to see this fleet of cars."

Savannah asked, "Does any of this ever get to feel normal?"

"Nope. Never."

They heard a familiar rumble from some distance, and Cole knew he was about to be paid a visit by Jimi Hendrix in a blue Corvette. The roar of the engine mixed with the bouncing bass line of the Red Hot Chili Peppers' "Otherside" gave him away.

Jimi pulled up with a wink and a smile.

Cole asked, "Jimi, when do I get my own ride?"

"Man, I'm not Santa. You are a grown man. Order one. I've seen your lair—you know how to order."

"Cool. I'm still deciding between the vintage Batmobile and Harry Dunn's Shaggin' Wagon."

"We can open a pet store." Savannah giggled.

Simultaneously, Cole and Savannah shouted, "We got worms!"

Jimi shook his head. "Y'all got problems." He then remembered what he had come for. "Hey man, we got a situation. Might need more help from outside. Have you checked into that guy you mentioned? You know, the 'musty' dude."

Cole laughed. "Jimi, we've been over this. He's not *musty*. His name is Musk."

ACKNOWLEDGMENTS

There are many people we'd like to thank.

Kevin Thompson, thank you for introducing us to David Webb. David, as our editor, you have championed us and improved our writing. You have connected dots all while condensing and synthesizing our thoughts. It felt like we had a secret weapon. We love that you love this world, and we have enjoyed working with you very much. Please stop texting us after midnight. Thank you to Dave Swann for your excellent work in completing the manuscript.

Steve Brickhouse, thank you for helping our '90s tech and lingo to make sense enough that no one would ask too many questions. Also, thanks for being a part of the DRS reading crew along with Russell Hilton, Wrex, John Carroll, John Greedack, Chad Farneth, and Clayton Sanderson. Clayton, you were so much help you got a character name! For all of you among the Copperhead Den and nWp's, thanks for your friendship and support.

Thanks to John Paul Basham for introducing us to David Hancock and the fine folks at Morgan James. To all the many people at Morgan James who have helped us make this book a reality, we are so grateful.

From Jay

I met Kyle in 1996 and decided we would be friends. I'm glad he went along with it. Kyle is thoughtful, kind, and ever rock steady. Kyle, thank you for introducing me to

U2 and for watching the *Highlander* movies with me. Looking forward to book two and, hopefully, many more.

Several friends have been nothing but supportive throughout this process. Megan Phillips, Ethan Milner, and Kevin Johnson, thank you for always going along with my crazy requests. You all make me cooler.

Best Buds and the D.A. crew, thanks for being my friends.

I'd like to thank my mom and dad for having me first. Pops and KayKay, you are the best. I love you both. I am ever thankful for all the sacrifices you have made. Rachel and I are blessed to have you as an example.

To the Rutherfords, Cains, and Hurleys, it's wonderful to have family that accepts and loves so well. I hope I honor you.

Shantel, I love you with all my heart. Thank you for allowing me to do crazy things like this. Thank you for loving me and cheering me on. We may not be rich, but it hasn't been boring.

Finally, Hannah Chayse and Hope: I pray that you will dream big and work hard. Never let anyone tell you that you can't. We are Watsons. We don't quit. You both are, and forever will be, the greatest thing I ever did. I'm so glad you look like your mother. Go for it!

G&P.

From Kyle

In the fall of 1996, I heard a knock at my dorm room door. I was watching *Rocky III*. It was Jay Watson. I have a feeling if he hadn't come to my room that day, I might still be sitting there watching movies.

I had the idea for the *Dead Rock Stars* years ago, and I shared it with Jay. He said, "Kyle, let's do this!" I said, "Okay" but didn't mean it; I was just looking to change the subject. But Jay insisted, and he even wrote the first two chapters. They were so good that I thought, *Let's just see where this goes.* A few years later, here we are. Thank you, Jay, for knocking on my door, forcing me out of my comfort zone, and for being such an awesome friend. Thanks for writing two killer chapters that fired my imagination and inspired us to actually go for it. Oh, and thanks for introducing me to my wife.

Thank you to the constant, Jeff McKenzie, for reading an early draft of this book. I'm hoping never to take you out of the story.

To Brandon Palmore and Jason Rowell, thanks for your encouragement and always asking how the book is going. Let's play some tennis.

To George and Babs, thank you for your love, support, and amazing daughter.

Thanks to Mom and Dad, who encouraged me to chase this dream and even made it possible. Thanks for the faith you passed on to Wendy, Gena, and me. Thanks for the loving home you provided for us. Thanks for loving my family so well!

To Noah, Micah, and Lilly, thank you for allowing me to sit in my brown chair and write this book. Thanks for your love, support, and kind words, and thanks for making me a dad. I love you all!

To Joni, I am so amazed by your selflessness and love. Thank you for encouraging me and supporting me in this crazy idea. I can't wait for the Originals Book Club to read it. I love you!

ABOUT THE AUTHORS

Jay Watson and Kyle Wiltshire met in college and have been the closest of friends ever since. They've watched every single Highlander movie together on VHS, they participated in each other's weddings, and they still talk every day. They have committed their adult lives to cultivating stories and caring for people.

Jay deeply loves his wife and twin daughters and won't shut up about them. He works with people and is passionate about speaking and writing. He has built a disc golf course, saw Garth Brooks in 1993, and takes pictures with fish. His hair started going gray at twenty, and he still loves Will Smith.

Kyle is a husband, father, and writer who has seen U2 in concert eleven times. He tries to paint like Bob Ross and enjoys talking about the Star Wars universe on a very deep level. He loves pop culture and prides himself on being able to name the year any movie from the 1980s or '90s was released.

A free ebook edition is available with the purchase of this book.

To claim your free ebook edition:

1. Visit MorganJamesBOGO.com
2. Sign your name CLEARLY in the space
3. Complete the form and submit a photo of the entire copyright page
4. You or your friend can download the ebook to your preferred device

A **FREE** ebook edition is available for you or a friend with the purchase of this print book.

CLEARLY SIGN YOUR NAME ABOVE

Instructions to claim your free ebook edition:
1. Visit MorganJamesBOGO.com
2. Sign your name CLEARLY in the space above
3. Complete the form and submit a photo of this entire page
4. You or your friend can download the ebook to your preferred device

Print & Digital Together Forever.

Snap a photo   Free ebook   Read anywhere

Printed in the USA
CPSIA information can be obtained
at www.ICGtesting.com
JSHW081829061123
51547JS00003B/132

9 781636 981642